THE
PERFECT
NANNY

BOOKS BY SHARI J. RYAN

The Bookseller of Dachau

The Doctor's Daughter

The Lieutenant's Girl

The Maid's Secret

The Stolen Twins

The Homemaker

The Glovemaker's Daughter

LAST WORDS

The Girl with the Diary

The Prison Child

The Soldier's Letters

THE
PERFECT
NANNY

SHARI J. RYAN

bookouture

Published by Bookouture in 2024

An imprint of Storyfire Ltd.
Carmelite House
50 Victoria Embankment
London EC4Y oDZ

www.bookouture.com

ISBN: 978-1-83525-192-8
eBook ISBN: 978-1-83525-191-1

To those who spark a flame in my life...

ONE

FRIDAY, JUNE 9TH 10:00 PM

Tonight

"Place your hands behind your back and turn around. You're under arrest for the kidnapping of a minor," an officer commands, his voice husky and raw.

I've only heard these rights spoken on TV, usually after a high-speed car chase, or drug-bust. Nothing like this.

The last few minutes of my life are a complete blur, and my brain is struggling to catch up. "I—you don't understand. I didn't—I would never take any of their children—anyone's child." No matter how many times I keep saying it, it's as if I'm not speaking at all. No one is listening.

"I said, turn around," the officer demands. He grabs my arm and jerks me around. I stare at the lush arrangement of pale pink peonies on the decorative table in the middle of the foyer. A whirlwind of voices swirls around my head as a cold sweat climbs up my limbs. My knees threaten to give out, but I can't give this officer another reason to believe I'm resisting arrest.

Cold steel rings clang together as the officer's handcuffs

engulf my two wrists. The handcuffs tighten one at a time, pinching my skin so I can't twist my hands in any direction. My chest aches from how hard my heart is pounding. This is beyond anything I could think up in a nightmare. This must be a misunderstanding—an awful one.

"...Anything you say can and will be held against you in a court of law..."

Desperation writhes through me as the shrill of words bark up my throat. "I didn't do this! Please, I'm begging you! You're making a mistake. You have to—you need to believe me. Why would anyone think I'd take a child?"

"You have the right to an attorney. If you cannot afford an attorney, one will be appointed to you."

The officer circles around me, stopping when we're face to face. He's unaffected by the tears forming in my eyes. "Please," I whimper, along with a ragged breath. "Please, just let me speak."

"Ma'am, we've stated these rights for your protection. We don't place citizens under arrest without the presence of probable cause, which we have."

Mr. Smith, the stiff-necked affluent father of the two little girls I was watching tonight, paces through each room like an animal searching for its prey, his blonde hair fringed in every direction and his tuxedo unbuttoned and ragged. "And she tried to flee the scene," he snaps, following the officer's reminder for me to keep quiet. Mr. Smith swings doors open one after another, bellowing a name that I've only just heard for the first time. *Fallon.* His voice echoes through the house like thunder against a rolling hill. "Fallon, sweetheart, it's daddy. Where are you, baby girl?" Hysteria grows heavier through each word.

"I didn't try to run," I cry out under my breath.

Another officer is holding Mrs. Smith upright as she stumbles in her skintight sequined dress toward her white leather couch in the sitting room. She's gasping between each loud wail. Inky black mascara tears streak down her cheeks as she combs her manicured nails along her plunging neckline.

"She was here—our baby, Fallon," she croaks. "She was here when we left."

TWO

Nausea sloshes through me as pedestrians stare at the passing cruiser. I've always been the one watching from the outside, wondering what the person inside had done. How many times had I assumed wrong about someone like me?

"Please, can you hear me? I didn't take their child," I shout, my voice bouncing against the thick glass shield between us.

The ride isn't long enough to suffocate my burning thoughts and fears. When the back passenger door opens, I'm pulled from the seat and guided toward a steel door on the side of the police station.

Inside the interview room, the walls close in on me. Panic jolts through my blood, making me hot and cold at the same time. Sweat beads across the back of my neck. I'm desperate for air, but this enclosed space with glossy gray painted brick, white speckled linoleum floor, a faux wood cafeteria table and two folding metal chairs has no windows.

The other chair is on the opposite side of the table. I'm still in handcuffs, re-secured after they took digital scans of my fingerprints and a mugshot to keep on file.

In my twenty-seven years of life, I have never been in trouble. I was never even sent to the head office in grade school. The one time I almost got in trouble was for standing up from my desk in my seventh-grade English class before the bell rang. The teacher pointed at me and with a sharp tongue, said, "See me after class, Ms. Vaughn." The kids around me made the "ooooh" sound, highlighting the trouble I was in. I had never cried in school before, but I instantly burst into tears and couldn't catch my breath. The teacher rushed to my side to calm me down. She seemed remorseful and even apologized. The punishment had ended with a whispering statement that we all make mistakes, and she was sure I wouldn't let it happen again. She didn't make me stay after class that day. But the memory still sticks with me. I never look for trouble.

I wish tears would help me right now. I want to cry and beg for them to let me go.

A female officer makes her way through the heavy metal door, letting it close with a nerve striking metallic clang. *There's no use in intimidating someone already intimidated,* and I've cooperated despite my cries of innocence. I'm shaking so hard all my muscles ache.

The officer has shoulder-length coffee-brown hair tied back into a low ponytail. Her uniform is decorated with a badge, patches, and the embroidered name *Mead.* Her muddy-tan shirt and pants look snug, making her seem uncomfortable as she eases down into the seat across from me. She tightens her grip around a yellow-lined notepad full of scribbles then drops it onto the table and pulls her chair in closer. I wish her presence gave me relief, but there is a look in her eyes that says she's already made up her mind.

"Ms. Vaughn, do you know why we've detained you tonight?" Officer Mead pulls a pen from her breast pocket and clicks the top. Her cold stare sends a chill down my spine. She's ready to jot down what she hopes will be my confession. Her scrutinizing inflection demolishes the last bit of hope I had of defending myself.

I shake my head as my chin trembles, and I try to think of words that will mean something more than what I've already tried to convey. "No, ma'am. The Smiths accused me of kidnapping their baby, but I swear to you, I never knew that this baby existed," I reply, my voice broken and breathless. A shuddering inhale warns me I might fall apart at any second. I can't swallow against my dry throat. My bravery is wearing off.

"When did you first meet the Smith family?" Her sharp question slices through me, threatening to reveal whatever truth she's seeking.

"Today." It's taking all my willpower to stay calm. I would much rather blurt out my answers, so they'd know how big of a mistake it was to have me, of all people, sitting here.

"When is the first time you spoke to the Smith family?" Officer Mead continues, her words dangling from every syllable.

With another staggering breath, I stare up toward the blinding hanging lamp and think back to the day I spoke to Lara Smith over the phone—our one and only call. "It was late last week. Sunday, I think. The records are on my phone." They took my phone. They can see the interactions Lara and I had.

Officer Mead narrows her sharp tawny glare at me. It's a look my father would have given me as a child when questioning my honesty. "How many times have you spoken with someone in the Smith family?"

I wish it was clear to me before tonight that the one time I had spoken to Lara was one time too many. I knew the risks involved when posting an ad looking for a job. It's hard to trust that people are who they say they are, but I took a chance out of desperation. "Once last week when I returned Mrs. Smith's phone call after she left me a voicemail inquiring about the ad I'd posted. I was seeking a nanny position for the summer."

THREE

SUNDAY, JUNE 4TH 11:45 AM

Last week

The purr of a zipper punctuates the end of another school year. I never thought I'd still be in school at twenty-seven. Yet knowing I'm just a year away from earning my degree in psychology gives me the motivation to forge ahead. I'm ready for a career, and to start building a life for myself.

I watch my roommate, Willa, yank her suitcase off the beige slipcover that sloppily covers the sofa. In true Willa style, she straightens the throw pillow and leaves the gathered fabric in waves. "I can help you with you that," I offer. "How many bags are you bringing home?"

"I'm fine. It's just this one bag," she says with a pout. "Hales, I hate leaving you here, in a town that's days away from being one of the most crowded tourist spots in New England. Are you sure you don't want to come home with me? We have a guest room. My parents won't care." She grips the handle of her suitcase with one hand, the other on her chest. I hate that she's leaving, too. She's always stayed throughout the summers, but her parents asked her to come home and spend some time with them this time. They still pay her portion of the rent, so it's hard for her to say no, which I understand. I'd go home too.

I would love to go with her, but she lives in a tiny town an hour outside of a city with one small grocery store and a two-pump gas station. The odds of finding a summer job there are even worse than if I were to stay here. Plus, we still have to pay the rent on this place. Even so, if I were to leave Newport, it would seem a bit odd staying with Willa when my parents live fifteen minutes away. Dad has reminded me several times of how much money I could save if I lived at home. He isn't wrong, but to me, the university experience is about the social aspect and the sense of independence. Moving out was something I needed to do.

But Willa's big, doll-like eyes could make the most decisive person break.

I shift my attention to the scattered magazines on the coffee table and straighten them one at a time. "I wish I could go with you, I do, but I can't leave Newport right now. Plus, I'll be working through the summer," I remind her. I still need to pay my portion of the rent and I can't ask Mom and Dad for help when this apartment was my plea for independence.

"Well yeah, but only if you find a new job. It's slim pickings out there." She's right, and I've been losing sleep over this. I just didn't want to lay that stress on her with her getting ready to go home for the summer. "How many applications have you sent out?"

Newport is the go-to for anyone who wants to get away for the summer and work a seasonal job by the beach. It doesn't matter how early in the year we set out to find jobs. The chances of getting anything are slim because everyone seems to know someone here, even the tourists.

I had a job assisting at a children's rehabilitation center, but the division I worked in merged with another outside of Newport. The younger Newport staff members who hadn't yet earned their medical licenses were let go. It all happened fast, and it was out of the blue, so I've been desperately trying to find a new job.

Willa did offer me her waitressing hours for the summer, but it's important I find another position in my field since I'm working on a childhood psychology case study for my dissertation—a requirement to graduate. It must be complete by the end of the summer to stay on track.

I plop down onto the messy couch and look for a distraction, so I don't have to notice the wrinkled fabric again. My phone blinks from the used and dented thrift-shop purchased coffee table Willa and I adopted last year, and I grab it to see if the notification is anything more than spam. It's not.

"Aside from the ad I submitted to the community newsletter offering myself up as a nanny, I've sent out a lot of applications—I lost track."

"You posted that ad? I thought you were still debating if that was a good idea?"

"I did a few days ago, and someone's already called me to discuss a position. I'm talking with her at noon."

"To work as a nanny?" Willa asks, choking on her breath. "I thought that was a last resort?" Her auburn curls bounce along with the emphasis of her exasperation.

I glance down at my watch, noting the date that's creeping into mid-June. "I think this is my last resort. No one has responded to any of my applications."

"But what about..."

"I know, I know," I say with a sigh. "I'll be careful. You don't have to worry."

Willa clenches her eyes and scrunches her nose. "Hales... they haven't found this person yet. I thought that's why you were leaning toward not posting the ad?"

"It was my only backup plan. The woman left me a voicemail asking to talk. That's all I'm doing. I have a good head on my shoulders." At least, I think I do. Maybe Willa thinks otherwise.

Willa drops the sliding handle of her suitcase and it slaps back into the hard-shell case. "I can't leave you here like this."

I laugh because I think she might be joking. "What do you mean?"

"I'm not leaving you here alone this summer. Someone needs to make sure you don't end up as the *Nanny Killer*'s next victim."

The same thought about the infamous *Nanny Killer* had obviously crossed my mind. There has been a series of local killings, all nannies, in the Newport area over the last five months. I've read through the incidents. All the cases are connected by some weird online forum and details sent via an email prior to the nanny showing up at an address. I stand up from the couch and walk over to Willa, placing my hands on her shoulders. "I appreciate you worrying about me, but I think the versions of the *Nanny Killer* stories you read might be a bit distorted. Those magazines," I say, pointing at the stack on the coffee table, "contain exaggerated news so they can make sales."

Willa slips out from beneath my hands and leans in toward the coffee table, reaching between the stack of magazines. She pulls out a *Newport Daily* newspaper. "Hales, this story isn't exaggerated. It's been on the news, too."

"Look," I say, walking over toward the door where my purse is hung up. I pull out my can of pepper spray. "I will be okay. I promise you. Trust the fact that I'm not the type of woman to run up the stairs if a killer were chasing me. I know I'm not the most aggressive or forward person you've ever met, and wouldn't have that *Nanny Killer* screaming for mercy like you would, but I can sniff out a bad situation." I'm sure the *Nanny Killer* has been more than convincing to these other young women, but I can't let these incidents keep me from working with children, which I will be doing full time after I graduate with my degree.

"Haley, Haley, Haley, why are you so sweet and innocent? Why?" Willa groans, playfully stomping her leopard-print slip-on sneakers. "You are a whiz with psychoanalyzing everyone you meet within the first thirty seconds of speaking to them. But not everyone falls into the perfect personality categories like they're supposed to. We live in a sick world. You, of all people, know this." I wish I didn't have to know this truth and I wish she didn't either, but we can't hide from reality.

Before I can get another word out, Willa is dragging her suitcase back down our short hallway, catching the wheels on the plush runner.

"You're not really staying because of a job I might not get?" I argue, shouting after her.

She cackles and disappears into her bedroom. "Yes, my bestie, I am."

"You were just looking for an excuse not to go home," I holler to bicker. She was. She would much rather be here and closer to Jerry, her boyfriend, than a state away with her parents.

"Girl, you do not have to act like you've known me for seven years. It's an annoying quality," she jests. Some days, it feels like we've known each other for much longer than that. We've been through a lot together since meeting at freshman orientation.

Willa is a *Virtuoso* according to the psychology behind personality traits...always observing, planning, and thinking, has her hands in a dozen different projects at once and can't sit still. I see myself fitting into the *Defender* category, which is described as empathetic, loving, devoted and often a perfectionist to a fault. According to science, Willa and I make the best kind of friends and roommates. So far, science has proven to be true for us.

I straighten the slipcover, firming the edges, and smooth out the slight wrinkles. It's just about noon and my stomach is churning with nerves. I need this job to work out.

"Well, girl, we better get started on a grand plan for our summer of fun," Willa hoots, shuffling back into the living room.

"Are you going to be working at all?" I ask, knowing she doesn't have to work with how loaded her parents are, but Willa likes to keep busy. I want to enjoy the summer too, but I know jobs can get in the way of *grand plans*. I wish I could take a season off and just lay out on the beach without a worry in the world.

"I sure am. I just texted the boss. I explained my situation and told him it would mean a lot to me if I could keep my job. I pleaded just a bit, and in the end he caved."

"Even though you quit yesterday?" I ask, raising a brow at her. She's making it sound as if she had to jump through hoops of fire to regain employment. We both know that wasn't the case.

Willa shrugs. "I don't know. I guess my boss didn't want me to leave," she says with a hum. "He must have known I'd be back sooner rather than later."

"You mean, your boss who is madly in love with you and didn't want you to go home for the summer?" I tease her. "You and Jerry can't bear to be apart for more than a day."

They're so cute together, it's almost hard to watch, but only because I'm a little jealous I can't find anyone like him for myself.

"See, I've got this whole adulting thing down to a cake-walk," she says, tapping on the side of her head.

Willa took the last semester of school off to give herself a break, but before that she had doubled down on classes and earned more credits faster than I did. Her break led her to her waitressing job at the Cove where she met Jerry. After all's said and done, we'll both still graduate on time. I could have used a break too, but I know it's best that I focus on finishing up school before starting a relationship with anyone. I'm more linear than she is and like to follow order. She would rather watch life fall into place. Sometimes I wonder if the grass might be greener on her side.

"Thank goodness for that," I agree with laughter. "I need to go give that woman with the nanny job a call. Wish me luck."

Willa gives me an unsure smile and wishes me, "Good luck," as if it's a question.

"I'll be fine," I reassure her. The *Nanny Killer*...my God. Criminals must be running out of creative ways to get themselves locked up.

FOUR

I close myself in my bedroom, feeling the warm breeze skate through the open window, carrying a sweet aroma from the lilac bushes in the small garden beneath us. I twist my hair behind my ear, pull my phone out of my back pocket and plop down on the edge of my bed. With a deep breath and crossed fingers, I tap on the voicemail and hit the redial button.

I don't want to sound too desperate, I tell myself. *I just really need this job and a paycheck.*

Two rings and a click suck the wind out of my lungs. Willa's warning and my general nerves about securing a job hit me as soon as the woman answers my call.

"Lara Smith speaking..." She sounds busy, in the middle of several things at once. The rapid tapping against a keyboard follows her pause and all I can wonder is what she's typing while picking up a call.

I muffle my hand over the receiver to block the sound of me clearing my throat—a nervous habit I have before speaking to someone new. "Hi, Lara, this is Haley Vaughn returning your call about the nanny position."

The clickity-clack of her keyboard halts. "Oh my goodness,

Haley, I am so, so glad you called back. Your job post in the *Newport* newsletter stood out to me. And well, I'm in dire need of help with my daughters. School is letting out in less than a week. I'm not always this disorganized, but you know how crazy life can get sometimes. Anyway, thank you for returning my call."

The fluttering words give me a sense that she's likely always this disorganized, but I won't judge, not yet. "Life can get a bit wild sometimes. I completely understand what you mean. I'm glad we got to connect, too. I'd love to hear more about the position."

The typing restarts and she's mumbling under her breath. "I'm sorry. I was just replying to the school committee since we're trying to arrange this event—I'm getting off topic again. I'm sure you're a busy woman."

"Oh, please, take your time," I say, eager to just hear about the job.

"Well, I have twin nine-year-old girls, Madden and Blakely, and—my gosh, pick up the phone if you have so much to say," she grumbles in a cartoonish voice. "As soon as I think my inbox is empty, another is waiting. Sorry, again. Where was I? Oh yes, we're looking for someone to spend weekdays with the children. They need to be outdoors and off their devices. I'll need you to take them to their piano, swim, tennis lessons and—" Mrs. Smith huffs with a sigh. "There's a list. I'll make a list, but to sum it all up, I need another set of hands around here. I do a lot of charity work for my husband's business and my phone rings nonstop. I just can't give the girls my full attention sometimes, and it breaks my heart to see them bored."

"Yes, of course. I can't imagine how challenging it must be to have so much going on while taking care of your daughters." I use a summary of her own words to avoid being offensive. I'm aware it's hard for a mother to ask anyone for help with her children. I learned that in my first of the psych classes.

"Exactly," she says. "I thought it might be a good idea if you started by doing just a few hours before jumping into the full swing of things with them. Perhaps, if you're free Friday night, my husband and I have a gala to attend and don't have anyone to watch the girls..."

A commitment for the summer would be ideal, but I don't blame her for wanting to make sure everything works out between the girls and me first. "Of course. That sounds like a wonderful idea. I'd be happy to watch them next Friday night."

"Ah, music to my ears. In your job posting, I also noticed that you're a child psychology student. I'm impressed, I'm sure that major must be quite challenging."

"Yes, I'm focusing on Childhood Behavioral Health Counseling. I'm very passionate about my studies and love working with children."

"How wonderful! I'm sure you're terrific with children and that's what's most important to me, of course. I assume you must have your first-aid certification too?" I'm not sure why she thinks one thing has something to do with the other. I've spent a lot of time with children over the years, and no one has ever asked me for a certification. I close my eyes, wishing I could fib and somehow find a class before next Friday, but I'm not sure where I would even find one so soon.

"I'm so sorry if I've been wasting your time, Mrs. Smith. Unfortunately, I don't have my first-aid certification, but I would be happy to acquire one as soon as possible."

"Oh my gosh, I shouldn't have assumed. I'm just neurotic with my kids. I forget not everyone is like me," she says with laughter that resembles the sound of embarrassment. The typing begins again, along with a thread of silence that should fill with words I can't think of. I'm sure most moms are neurotic about their kids. There are different variations of neuroticism, but I wouldn't place a first-aid certification on either end of a scale.

"I'm sure I would be the same."

"I was just searching to see if—yes, oh good! There is a first-aid class on Wednesday night from five to seven at City Hall. If I pay for the class and certification, would you be willing to attend?"

"I could do that, yes, of course."

"I'll pay you for your time as well. If you could text me your email address and last name so I could send over the payment, I'll get that over to you. I can also sign you up while I'm on the screen. Should I just use this phone number you called me from?"

"Yes, that's fine." My heart is racing from the speed of her questions and the agreements I'm giving without thinking them through, but it's just a first-aid class.

"Once I receive your text message, I'll reply with our address, so you'll know where to find us on Friday night. Will six thirty work for you? The hourly pay is forty an hour—I try to be competitive since so many college students in the area go home for the summer. You're a rare find." I'm glad this conversation is over the phone, so she doesn't see my eyes bulging. I'm not sure I've heard a family paying a nanny or babysitter forty an hour, but I won't complain.

"That's very generous of you and yes, six thirty works fine."

She sighs with a sound of relief. "This is perfect. If you have any issues with the first-aid class, please let me know. Just don't forget to text me your email address. And..." She draws out her final thought. "Yeah, I will see you Friday night at six thirty! Thank you so much for calling me back, Haley. I look forward to meeting you. The girls will be thrilled, as well."

"Same here. Thank you so much, Mrs. Smith. Have a great day."

I fumble with my phone to send her a text message with my email address, wondering why I'm still feeling so frazzled. The moment my message goes through and a "delivered" receipt appears, I take a breath and fall back onto my bed. A certification will be great to have, and on top of that, I'm grateful it won't cost me anything.

My phone buzzes with a thank you. Mrs. Smith's address, and a second message with a Venmo payment for a hundred dollars follows. I didn't expect this much for a two-hour class if she's paying forty an hour. This might just be the best summer job I could get my hands on.

I tap the link to her address. Her house pops up on my phone and chills zing up my spine. There's no way...

FIVE

WEDNESDAY, JUNE 7TH 5:00 PM

I'm curious to see if this class includes CPR. I've been meaning to learn it but have yet to. It's one of those things I shouldn't have put off. I don't always know what to do in an emergency. I'm useless during those moments, but everyone should learn the basics.

I step inside City Hall, the only sound the humid stickiness of my soles against the marble floors. Flyers line the bulletin boards along the walls. A neon yellow paper stands out from the rest. Large black block letters warn about the dangers of not knowing CPR. Ironic.

The front desk is flanked by two ropes. A makeshift paper sign is taped to the edge of the counter and captures my attention: an illustration of a bandage covering a heart paired with instructions to find the first-aid class on the lower level.

I make my way downstairs, being careful not to trip within the dimly lit corridor. I peek through each windowed door until I spot a group of others filling up the college-style desks inside.

The class seems sparse considering I'm only a few minutes early. The half dozen others occupying the scattered desks show a similar lack of enthusiasm. I prefer the front and take a seat in the second row toward the middle—just close enough to be noticed.

"Welcome," a twenty-something-year-old man from behind the podium says. "What's your name?"

"Haley Vaughn," I say, draping my bag on the back of my chair.

"Perfect. Could you fill out one of these nametags?" He strides over, scuffing his dress shoes against the cement floor and sets a sticker and marker down. He takes the next minute to scribble his name on the whiteboard, "Ron," beside his podium, then begins to bullet out a list of discussion topics. I avoid looking up at the clock, knowing I've only been sitting here for a few minutes and I'm ready to leave. The crowd isn't vivacious except for sniffling and a few dry coughs.

"What are you here for?" the woman behind me asks. She asks the question like we're in prison, which probably doesn't feel too different from a musty windowless basement standpoint.

I twist in my seat to give her a quick smile. "Oh, just a requirement for a job I'm taking. How about you?"

She squints at my nametag. "Haley, what a pretty name." She sweeps her long dark hair off her shoulders, exposing her nametag. "I'm Roberta, and same. I'm an elderly caregiver. I can't believe it's already been two years since I took this course last." I didn't realize a certification only lasted that long.

"Oh really? That's good to know. I had no idea. This is the first time I've taken the course."

"I would just drop it in your calendar now so you don't have to think about it until it's time again," she says, tapping her fingernail against her temple.

"Great idea. Thank you," I say with a smile.

"What about you over there?" she continues, asking a younger man two seats away. "Jack, is that what your nametag says?" I turn back toward the front of the class, watching the instructor try to organize his papers.

"Yeah, Jack. I'm an assistant coach for youth sports," I hear from behind me.

"Oh, how exciting," the woman says.

Another person jogs into the room as if trying to make it in time before a school bell rings. "Traffic, sorry about that," he says to the instructor.

"You must be Liam Gellar, hopefully? Last one on my list for the night," the instructor says.

"Present," the man says, taking the seat beside me.

Ron tosses a sticker onto Liam's desk, and I offer the marker I still needed to return. "Thanks," Liam whispers.

I can't stop myself from trying to figuring out everyone's stories and reasons for being where they are. So naturally, I silently speculate that Liam is fulfilling an obligation like I am for work. Although he doesn't look like he just came from work judging by his worn jeans, a navy-blue Red Sox T-shirt over a long sleeve white tee, and complementary Converse chucks. Despite the wild mess of dark curls on his head, he still looks well put-together—typical for this town.

At five o'clock on the dot, the instructor dives right into the first topic of resuscitation. I pull my notebook out of my purse and unclip my pen from the binding coil. Only some people are taking notes, but I know I won't be able to retain everything without writing it down.

"I heard there's a manual," Liam whispers as the instructor turns his back to us to notate the differences between adult CPR and pediatric CPR. I glance at him, finding a cute smirk as he points to the table along the side of the room with stacks of manuals. "Excuse me, Ron, would it be possible to access the manuals before we go too far? I find underlining important facts is most helpful."

Ron spins around on his heels and tosses his head back.

"Thank you," he says, leaning in Liam's direction to read his name. It's been less than two minutes since he asked him for his name, but I won't judge with how many new students he must encounter regularly. "Liam. I can't believe I forgot to hand those out. Let's pass these down the rows and we'll pick up where we left off."

"I'll second that thank you," I utter, closing my notebook. "I've already taken down a half dozen pages of notes at school earlier today and my hand is sore."

"Oh yeah, what for? Are you a student?"

"I am," I say, slipping my notebook back into my bag. "I'm in the doctorates program at East Sail. What about you?"

"Ah, my alma mater's archrival. I graduated from Skybrook three years ago with my teaching degree, thus my reason for being here tonight."

I shake my head and smile. I never thought about the certifications teachers must need to maintain their positions. "What grade do you teach?"

"Ninth grade English."

"No way, really? That was one of my favorite years of English class. *Romeo and Juliet?*" I sigh and press my hand to my chest. "Is that still part of the curriculum?"

Liam chuckles. "You've got a good memory. It sure is. We finished the riveting world of literary devices among Shakespeare's most tragic love stories."

"I bet that's why you've chosen to teach ninth grade," I tease as the instructor returns to the whiteboard.

"Absolutely," he says, his eyes dancing with a smile.

I glance up at the clock, finding the one-hour mark approaching. Almost halfway through. I can do this—if only my eyelids didn't feel so heavy after a long day. I'm about to grab my soda from my bag, desperate for the caffeine.

"I'm going to stop here for a short ten-minute break. There's a vending machine down the hall toward the stairwell, restrooms to the right just outside the door and a water fountain to the left," Ron says, his hands pointing in various directions while keeping his eyes on the clock.

Just as we're all standing from our seats, a heavy crash bellows from the hallway, making the overhead lights and whiteboard vibrate. The shock holds me frozen, ironically the opposite of what we've been learning tonight.

"What was—" I utter.

A deflated sigh echoes from the front of the classroom. "Okay, change of plans," Ron says, holding on to the last syllable of his word while moving toward the door. "Everyone, stay here for a moment."

The lights flicker with static buzzing above our heads before going completely dark for fifteen long, quiet seconds.

"Um. I swear if the power goes out...I'll be out of this building faster than anyone can blink. No thank you. Not sitting in the dark beneath this ancient building," Roberta says.

In a silent response to Roberta, my pulse quickens at the thought of sitting here in the basement.

"The building is old. It probably blew a fuse," Liam speaks up. That was too loud to be a blown fuse. If it was, Ron has likely heard the noise before.

The longer we wait, the clammier my hands become. The classroom full of adults is startlingly quiet, considering the sudden commotion, and they don't seem as frazzled as I feel. I should sit down and breathe. Everything is fine. It's six o'clock on a Wednesday night.

Where did this guy go? Liam checks his watch and refocuses on the door. There's nothing to see. We don't even hear any activity in the hallway. Liam makes his way to the door and peeks out of the narrow rectangle window.

"Nothing is going on out there, but I'm not sure where the instructor went," Liam says, returning to his desk.

So much for our break... By the time Ron returns, the ten minutes will be up and I'm sure none of us want to stay later than we need to tonight.

"Are you okay? You're looking a little pale," Liam says, sliding his desk closer to mine. "There's nothing to worry about."

This is why I don't read or watch the news, or at least I try to avoid doing so. Rather than accept reality, I try to debunk stories like the one Willa was rehashing about the nanny murderer. Not to prove her wrong, but to settle my nerves. Each day seems like we're scooting toward the disaster that will have our state and our town in the headlines. I question how often I can assure myself that the rampant violence escalating across the country isn't close to home and that I'm safe. I still see plenty of clips on the news. I feel the pain of people telling their stories to reporters. They weren't expecting the unexpected. They were all taken by surprise like we are right now. What if it isn't nothing?

"I know."

"I'm sorry. I guess I'm numb to these types of alarms and drills. We practice them so much in the classroom that it's beginning to feel normal. The generation I'm teaching is being raised differently from how we were. They're tougher and more durable. It's both disturbing and beneficial for them. Everything must be treated with seriousness. Although I'm not sure that explains why the instructor hasn't returned yet." As Liam tries to ease my nerves, I can't help but notice a hint of apprehension as he bounces his knee.

"Sorry about that, everyone," Ron says, hustling back toward the front of the room. "A storm passed through and hit a transformer outside of the building. We lost power but the generator kicked in, so we're all fine. I apologize for that... If anyone needs to use the restroom, please feel free."

I didn't know we were supposed to get a storm tonight. There wasn't a cloud in the sky when I arrived.

From the corner of my eye, I notice Liam casually thumbing through the manual. I'm not sure I could be calm and alert like he is every day in a classroom full of kids. Yet, here I am, learning how to save someone if they're hurt. This world has weakened us all.

Ron speeds up the lesson as we're creeping toward seven o'clock, and it looks like we have one last topic to cover.

Burns and scalds—just as bad as blood. God, I hope these kiddos don't get hurt on my watch.

When the longest two hours ends, Ron calls each person up alphabetically to receive their certification before leaving. As usual, I'm one of the last, with a name beginning with the letter V.

I walk out of the classroom and pull out my phone to text Willa, wondering if the electricity is still intact at our apartment. Right as I hit send on the message, I spot Liam standing against the wall in front of a set of metal doors. Our height difference seems much more significant now that we're standing face to face. He must be close to six feet while I'm closer to five. "Well, at least we got what we came for, right?" he asks, holding up his certification.

"Yes, now I can pursue the job I'm after for this summer, watching two little girls who hopefully chew twenty times before swallowing a bite of food and don't like dangerous physical activity." We both share a laugh.

"Good luck with that one. My ninth graders get themselves hurt at a desk, sitting still. Kids, I tell ya."

"Well, I will keep my fingers crossed then. It was nice to

meet you tonight. Thanks for keeping me calm during the ruckus."

"It was nice to meet you, too. Normally, I wouldn't be so forward when meeting someone new, but I highly doubt we'll see each other again unless it's on purpose... Would you want to have lunch or dinner with me this week?"

If my cheeks are as red as they feel, he's probably safely assuming I've been living in a cave for years, not as someone in my mid-twenties living in a beach town. I don't get out much unless Willa drags me somewhere. "Uh—yeah, I think I'd like that." I fidget with my firefly charm necklace, trying to ease my nerves.

"You sure?" he asks, his dimples deepening at the corners of his lips.

"Yes, of course." I try to shake off the nerves.

"Awesome. Thankfully, I didn't rip the corner off my first-aid manual for nothing. That would have been a waste." He smiles and hands me the small piece of paper with his name and number scribbled down. "Send me your number so we can make plans, unless you change your mind."

He must sense my uncertainty, a result of all my bad luck with men over the years.

SIX

There's a mess of traffic weaving between City Hall and my apartment. All the brake lights are giving the streets a red glow. The summer rush is sweeping through early this year. Aside from some branches in the street and scattered puddles there's no sign of a storm tearing across the island, which reminds me that Willa never responded to my text, checking to see if the power went out. The parking lot lights are on, so that's a good sign.

I pull into the spot next to Willa's lime green hybrid SUV and sigh, already dreaming about planting my butt on the beach before my new job consumes the summer. I drag my bag out of the back seat and take a moment to sweep off the excess sand that's accumulated over the last couple of weeks.

After my hike up the three flights of stairs along the outside of the apartment complex, I'm greeted with a familiar Dave Matthews song pouring out from the doorway. Willa's love for music always brings a little extra life to this place, but I can't help wondering if we ever bother the neighbors. No one has ever said anything, but maybe it's because they know Willa—

loud, vibrant, and unapologetically herself. She attracts happiness and shares it with everyone around her.

As I push open the unlocked door, the aroma of tomato sauce and roasted garlic carries me into the galley kitchen where Willa is in all her glory, cooking up a storm. The glass slider to the balcony is wide open and the sheer curtains are fluttering like flags in the wind.

"I'm making dinner for my favorite person," she sings out, holding the dripping mixing spoon up to her mouth. While working at the restaurant, she's picked up some amazing cooking skills. My stomach grumbles like a mini thunderstorm. She already knew I would be hungry. We've been friends so long, she knows exactly what I'm thinking without me having to say a word.

"This wasn't necessary," I say. "You didn't have to do all this." I always worry my contributions aren't enough or as much as hers, but I do try my best to keep the place clean and organized.

"What?" she shouts over the music as her thick hair bobs around in a messy bun on top of her head. Willa rolls the sleeves of her way-too-large chef's coat up to her elbows. She'll say she needs to look the part if it's going to come out perfect.

"Echo, turn down the music," I say, but louder, hoping the speaker device can hear me over itself. The volume cuts down a few decibels. "You didn't have to go through all this trouble, but you sure do know the way to my heart." I stretch my arm out to loop around her neck, trying not to get too close to the splattering sauce.

"It'll be ready in about five minutes. How was your course? Did they have those CPR dummy dolls that you have to suck face with?"

I laugh while sliding open the coat closet and placing my bag on the floor against the side wall. "There was no sucking face, but it was informative—gory at points, but if anyone needs CPR, I know what to do."

"Aw, man...well then, I guess I know who to call if I'm ever choking," she says with a silly cackle. I wonder if I could save someone now after taking that class. I could use some more hands-on experience to call myself experienced, but I'd remember the instructed steps if need be.

I lean against the framed opening to the kitchen and rest my head on the wall. "Soo...there was a guy there."

"A guy?" Willa echoes. "What kind of guy?"

A smile pokes at my cheeks. "The kind who gave me his number."

Willa drops the wooden spoon into the pot and leans it against the side. "No, no, no. Not until I social stalk him. Give me the number and his name."

"He's a ninth grade English teacher," I tell her. "I met him at a first-aid course."

"Hand it over, lady," she says, shoving her palm toward me, wiggling her fingers.

She turns the burner down to low but keeps her hand outstretched, waiting for the little piece of the first-aid manual with Liam's phone number.

"Fine. I'm positive you won't find anything wrong with him." I pull the scrap out of my jean shorts pocket and slap it into her hand.

"Liam Gellar," she says with a "hmm" to follow.

"Watch the sauce while I grab my laptop."

"Did it storm here while I was gone?" I ask as she returns from her bedroom with the laptop in hand.

"We had some rain I think but it only lasted five minutes maybe."

"The power went out at City Hall."

"I guess the wind's kind of strong. The boats were all knocking into each other out at the wharf," she says, pointing toward the slider. Depending on the direction the wind is blowing, we either get slammed or skipped because of the inlet we're nestled in between two hills.

While Willa is typing away on her keyboard, I take a couple of plates out from the cabinet to dish out the food.

"Oh boy," she says. "You might want to see this." I guess I should have figured she'd find something. Not even a ninth grade English teacher can have a scratch-proof online history these days. I lean forward over the sink to the ledge of the open framed window connecting the living room and kitchen. She flips the laptop around to show me a picture that popped up. "Is that him?"

I press the back of my hand up to my mouth and lean in further. "It is," I confirm.

"Okay then. We check off the first box on my list," she says, her eyebrows dancing around. "Extremely good looking." Her chirp makes my cheeks burn.

"Where did you find this?" I stare at the picture of Liam dressed for the beach. The sight is not disappointing.

"A dating site. Don't worry, it's eighteen plus so no students would be on here. That gets another check on my list," she says with a cluck of her tongue.

I tug at her messy bun. "You and your crazy list."

"It worked for me, didn't it?" she asks, pointing out a valid occurrence.

"Yeah, yeah. Okay, I'm dishing the food out because I'm starving."

"I'd be hungry too if I got the number of this body...I mean, guy," Willa mutters.

"Hey, hey! What would Chef Jerry say if he heard you talking like this?"

"That he wants his number too," she says with laughter.

I dish out the food, knowing that for every minute of silence that passes while I do so is a step closer to checking off all the boxes of Willa's non-existent list.

I set the table, a beer for each of us, and plenty of napkins for my favorite tomato sauce. "All set," I tell her. She's still scrolling through a web browser sat on the stool at the window ledge but closes the laptop and joins me at the table.

"He has a clear record. He has minimal posts on his social media accounts, and most are about baseball and charities he contributes to. He has a typical teacher online presence. He's twenty-eight, has an August birthday, likes baseball—yadda, yadda... Okay, I think I have all the information necessary to give you the green light. Well done, lady."

I guess I'm glad I went to that class tonight for more reasons than one. I'm a believer in meeting someone when you least expect it. But who knows, he may not respond if I message him. Maybe he came to his senses on the way home. He could have been having a moment of desperation and saw one person in the class who didn't look like they were trying to plan out their escape.

"I want to meet him," Willa says, mouth full.

"No. No way, not yet. Not until I know he can handle your —your eccentric sunshine vibes."

"What? Why?" Willa drops her fork and huffs. "Haley. It's in your best interest..."

We both laugh, knowing this is less to do with my best interest and more to do with her curiosity. "Hmm...I can think of a few reasons, and you couldn't argue with one of them."

"Hales, come on." She frowns. "Leave Kyle out of this. No one could have known how that would end up."

SEVEN

FRIDAY, JUNE 9TH 6:00 PM

Mr. and Mrs. Smith's house gives me a far better understanding of the high-end hourly rate they can afford. It's easily worth over two-and-a-half million dollars with ocean-front access and has one of the best views of Newport's main bridge. The lifestyle of the rich isn't uncommon in this part of Rhode Island, but students like me rarely mingle with people like the Smiths. I'm intrigued, and excited to get to know the twin girls. I haven't done much research or studying about the financial influence on the psyche of young children. I'm hoping to gain some insight from watching and interacting with them. It will also help me with the research and case study I have to complete over the summer.

As I navigate the pebbled driveway, wrapping around a cluster of oak trees, I can't help but feel a twinge of anxiety about where to park. Their cars must be stowed away in the adjacent garage, but I don't want to park behind the wrong bay, assuming they'll be needing a car to go to this gala tonight. The rocks ping and pang against the undercarriage of my car as my tires crunch and my brakes squeal. There's no discreet way of arriving anywhere with my old clunker, especially against the surreal backdrop of their historic three-story manor. The gray and white brick façade speaks of high-class, but it's not a life I can imagine myself living. I've been an apartment dweller most of my life, finding comfort in smaller spaces that offer warmth and containment—not that I really have much choice, anyway.

The moment I close my car door, I notice the front entrance of the house open. Mrs. Smith appears to be clutching an earring between her fingertips as she watches me approach. She's even more gorgeous than the house. With long golden hair curled over her right shoulder and skin that glows in the sun's rays. Her eyes glisten like fresh pearls.

I'm suddenly very conscious of my torn jeans, black tank top, and old Birkenstock sandals. I wonder what she makes of me as I approach.

"You must be Haley," she says, her red-painted lips widening into a warm smile against her snow-white veneers. Maybe she's a celebrity—an actress of some sort. She fits the bill.

"Yes, um, I mean, ma'am—I hope you don't mind that I've come a bit earlier than you requested. I wanted to make sure there was time to get acquainted with the girls and to take in any guidelines you might have."

"Oh my God, please don't call me ma'am," she laughs, sliding her mouth to the side. "That makes me feel ancient. Just call me Lara."

I cover my mouth, worried I've offended her before stepping foot inside the house. "I'm so sorry. You don't look old, not at all. You're gorgeous." I sound as nervous as I feel. "In fact, you're striking—that emerald-green color complements you so beautifully."

Lara places her hand on her tan, freckled chest. "You are so sweet. Thank you," she says, taking the compliment. Although by the look of her faint dimpled smile, she seems more embarrassed than flattered.

"Your house is beautiful," I add, knowing that it will have to be the last of my compliments for a few minutes. I don't want her to think I'm trying to butter her up to be in good standing for the job.

"It is something else, isn't it?" she says, gesturing for me to follow her inside.

The foyer greets us with a harmony of light and modern décor. There's an overwhelming sense of space with a large round table centered beneath a dazzling chandelier. Two living areas are set off to each side, a grand stairwell to the right and a path that leads to another area of the house beyond the short hallway across the room. The walls are bright, flat white with matching intricately decorated trim. The artwork along the walls is large and abstract and it makes me think she hired someone to decorate. As large as this house is, I can't say I blame her.

"The girls are patiently waiting for you in the back of the great room. Follow me," she says, taking an envelope off the foyer table and leading me down the short hallway into another open space. The kitchen and dining room veer off to one side and we take two shallow steps down to another room. This must be the great room as I spot the two adorable young girls sitting quietly on the sofa. With a wall of floor to ceiling windows behind them, the space feels wide open and endless as the view stares out over the cliff toward the ocean.

"I am so excited to meet you, girls," I tell them, leaning down to bring myself to their eye-level. "I'm Haley. What are your names?"

The girls stare at me with wide eyes and don't answer right away. Their legs dangle from the couch, swishing from side to side almost in unison. "Girls, don't be shy. Madden is on the left and that's Blakely on the right," Lara introduces them.

It appears they're identical, but Madden's duckling blonde hair is chin-length while Blakely's is in waves draped over her shoulders. They have beautiful hazel eyes and are dressed like little dolls in matching paisley blue rompers.

"I love your names. They're very pretty," I tell them, crouching to my knees so I'm not hovering over them. "I got here a bit early so your mom could show me around before she and your dad leave. Maybe you could help!"

"That's a wonderful idea," Lara agrees. "Why don't we show Haley your bedrooms and the bathrooms." She nudges her head to the side and grits her teeth to get them to move. I wonder how many nannies and babysitters they've been around. They seem so shy. "My husband should be down to meet you soon. He was just finishing up when you arrived. You know men—they think they need five minutes to get ready, but they end up needing twice as much time as we do."

I laugh to be polite, but I don't have much experience sharing space and time with a man, except the year I was in a relationship.

The girls walk ahead of me, giving each other inquisitive glances every few steps as if they're sharing a silent language only the two of them know. I've read a lot about twins and know it's a common trait they share. They're often so close that they exchange thoughts with just a look.

"So, what are your favorite hobbies?" I ask them while we head up the stairwell.

"Madden likes mermaids and I like to draw and color," Blakely says.

"She's right. I do like mermaids," Madden follows but with less fervor in her response compared to Blakely's.

"Like Ariel?" I question.

"No, like the real mermaids that live in the ocean," Madden replies with a hint of haste.

Lara peers over her shoulder and widens her eyes in suit with a smirk.

"Well, we have that in common then because I also love mermaids," I say. "Do you like to swim?"

"No," Madden says. "I can't swim."

"But we're learning," Lara interrupts with a sarcastic chuckle.

"Oh my gosh. I was the worst swimmer at that age. I think I had arm floaties until I was twelve," I add with laughter.

"Same. That's so funny," Lara follows.

We reach the first bedroom and Blakely steps ahead. "This is my room." I would have guessed by the color on the walls.

"Bubblegum pink is one of my favorite colors, too," I say. *Or it was when I was their age.* "It's such a happy color." I stop to take in the color coordinated polka dots along the stark white comforter and matching drapes. It looks like a little girl's dream room.

A second door in the bedroom leads to their shared bathroom, and then into Madden's bedroom. "This is Madden's room, the third door on the right if you're in the hallway," Lara says.

Madden's room is light-blue, and the tapestries are a mixture of tropical colors. Pictures of mermaids line the walls and I see a mermaid tail blanket draped over the end of her bed. "It feels like you live in the middle of the ocean," I tell Madden.

She smiles and leads us out of her bedroom and back into the hallway. "That's Mom and Dad's room." She points diagonally to the right. "And—"

"You must be Haley," a tall slender man in a tuxedo says, walking out of the bedroom Madden was just pointing toward. "I'm Corbin. It's a pleasure to meet you. Lara has been raving about you for days, telling me you're the perfect fit for the job with our girls."

I guess I have high expectations to live up to. She took a lot out of our brief conversation and my college credentials.

"You left your phone on the dresser," Corbin tells his wife.

"You missed a call." Lara takes the phone and studies the display for a second.

"Oh shoot. I am so sorry. I will be right back. I just need to return this call before we leave." She has the phone up to her ear and a finger pointed upright as she pivots around and returns downstairs.

"I assume the girls have shown you around?" Corbin asks, taking Lara's lead in returning to the stairwell.

"The bathroom. We didn't show her where the bathrooms are yet," Blakely says.

"Ah, well, there's one to your right," he says, pointing to the darkened room, "and our master bathroom, which they know not to go into. There is a guest bathroom downstairs outside the great room. You probably passed it on your way up here."

"I'm sure I can find it. Are there any rules for the girls while you're gone?" I'm sure neither of the girls appreciates me asking this question, but I should be familiar with the household rules.

"They know the rules," Corbin says, his voice deepening as he gives each girl a lingering fatherly look. "No sweets after eight, no scary movies, and no hide-and-seek. Someone likes to hide, and someone forgets to seek. It never ends well," Corbin says with a chuckle as he ruffles his hand through Blakely's hair.

Madden and Blakely stare up at Corbin as if they're confused about his rules. "Dad, you said—"

"No, no hide-and-seek. That's the end of the discussion."

EIGHT

FRIDAY, JUNE 9TH 6:30 PM

I'm not sure if I'll have kids of my own someday, much to my parents' dismay. I'm sure I'll have a clearer view of my future once I graduate. But if I do have children, I'm not sure I'll be the type to trust anyone as quickly as the Smiths have done with me tonight. My willingness to sit through the first-aid course must have satisfied Lara and they left with seemingly little worry. Other than telling me the girls had already eaten dinner and showing me where to find the first-aid kit, there was little else to discuss.

The twins are quiet as they rummage through two bins of what looks to be forgotten toys that they've pulled out of the closet. A sigh and a pair of slouching shoulders tells me neither are interested in playing with anything in front of them. The air is heavy with the weight of their silence.

"So, what do the two of you like to do at night? Do you like board games or doing crafts? Blakely, I know you said you like to draw, right?"

"We don't do much at night," Blakely responds, her voice shrouded with a weariness as her gaze probes the depths of the toy bin, searching for answers within.

"You must be worn out from a long day at school most nights I bet," I respond, trying to be subtle with my inquisition.

"The long days at school are nothing compared to the long nights...here," she says. Her response is the one that will lead to many other thoughts and questions but none that I can vocalize after only meeting them a half hour ago.

Madden stands from her spot between the coffee table and sofa and meanders toward the wall of windows, stopping in the center to stare outside.

"It must be nice to live so close to the ocean. You have such a pretty view from these windows."

"Sometimes," Madden says. "Other times, it can cause trouble."

"Trouble?" I question, finding the mysterious inflection within her words a bit concerning.

"She just means we aren't allowed to go down there by ourselves," Blakely follows.

I twist the hem of my shirt behind my back as I watch Madden roll her eyes in response to Blakely. I have more questions to follow the last but know better than to ask them too quickly.

"Hmm, let's see... Do you girls have any favorite movies?"

Madden turns away from the window and stares at me as if my face is hypnotizing. "We like to play hide-and-seek," she says.

Blakely glances up at me, curious to see whether I'll go against their dad's wishes. That's a big no. "I don't think your dad wants you playing that game. Maybe we can come up with something else to play," I offer.

Madden huffs and crosses her arms over her chest. "It isn't the game he has a problem with. He doesn't want us hiding in their bedroom," she says, turning back toward the landscape outside the window. "There's nowhere to hide in there anyway. It's a dumb rule."

It's not uncommon for parents to request that their children stay out of their bedroom, especially when someone else cares for them. I've had plenty of babysitting jobs where the parents have kept their doors closed, which was enough of an indication that it should remain that way.

"That's okay. Everyone needs to have a private space, right?"

"That's not why," Madden says.

I spot Blakely picking at a hangnail while gritting her teeth. "Madden got in trouble for going through some important papers Dad had on his nightstand and she spilled some water—"

"Blakely!" Madden shouts, stomping her foot. "Why do you always have to be the perfect princess?" Madden sneers.

"Don't call me a perfect princess," Blakely snaps back. "It's not like *I* went through Dad's papers. It's your fault!"

"Okay, okay," I say stepping in between them. "There's no need to go into your parents' room tonight, so I don't think it's anything we need to worry about, right?" That answers my question about how well the two girls get along. I assume this event must have been a recent occurrence which is probably why Madden seems bitter about their father's new rule. Redirection is always a good move. "How about we watch a movie?"

Of course, they must agree on one, which may be challenging. "We've seen them all," Blakely responds, dropping a handful of blocks from her hand into the toy bin. She slugs over to the couch and sinks into the deep cushions, taking the remote into her hand.

"We haven't watched the new mermaid movie," Madden says. A spark of excitement flits through her shoulders and she skips to the sofa, plops down and tears the remote out of Blakely's hand.

"Hey!" Blakely whines.

"I know where the movie is," Madden tells her. "Don't worry."

Blakely huffs and crosses her arms in frustration. "Fine but can we have popcorn, too? We always have popcorn when we watch a movie."

"Do you have popcorn?"

"Yes, I can show you where it is," Blakely answers. "Follow me."

Madden is flipping through channels with what seems like tunnel vision, so I follow Blakely into the kitchen. She reaches for the pantry door and yanks it open. The hinges moan in the face of a black hole before Blakely flips on a light and illuminates the large walk-in storeroom. It's no surprise to find the space larger than all the closets in my apartment. I've seen pantries like this on Pinterest, but never before in real life. Baking ingredients, grains, and pasta are all organized in clear containers with fancy labels adhered to the outside and on the shelf below are wicker baskets, adorned with dangling labels marking each with a different type of snack. Another shelf holds canned goods, and the bottom shelf is empty, covered in a thin layer of dust displaying only a void for whatever was there before but never replaced. How much food does one family need before the expiration dates pop up?

Blakely's fingers pull the wicker basket with the microwavable popcorn label toward her. She retrieves two packages. "This should be enough for the three of us." She hands them to me and strides out of the pantry like she's on a mission. "There's a popcorn button on the microwave. The last babysitter could never figure out how to use it, but I'm sure you can."

"Well, let's see here," I say, spinning around until I spot the microwave camouflaged as one of the white cabinet doors.

"You're off to a good start, since you at least found the microwave." Blakely giggles, covering her little hands over her mouth.

"Was your last babysitter nice?" I inquire, curious about why the last sitter no longer works here.

"Well—" Blakely sings.

"Did you hear that?" Madden asks, storming into the kitchen as I remove the plastic wrapper from the popcorn bag.

"Hear what?"

"How could you not have heard that?" Madden continues, grabbing Blakely by the arm before dragging her toward the front of the house. When I have the popcorn in the microwave and find the mysterious "popcorn" button, I hear their feet stomping up the stairs.

They're nine, the age of newfound independence, so I'll let them have a minute in case Madden wants to talk to her in private.

Since I'm alone in the kitchen, I pull my phone out of my back pocket and check for any missed messages.

My heart blips when I see Liam's name pop up. I sent him a text yesterday, but he hadn't responded. I figured he'd changed his mind, but by his message, I don't think that's the case.

Liam: *So sorry I didn't reply to you yesterday. I wasn't trying to play hard to get. There was an end-of-year field trip with the ninth graders, followed by an annual school art show I had to attend. By the time the teachers finished cleaning up, it was almost ten. Anyway, I'm rambling... Would you like to have dinner tomorrow night?*

Me: *You don't have to explain. I completely understand how busy your schedule must be. I'm watching the two little girls I was telling you about. It's my first night on the job. So far, so good (fingers crossed). Tomorrow for dinner sounds great. Send me the time and place!*

I slide my phone back into my pocket. I don't want to get

lost in a text conversation with Liam and have the girls catch me using my phone when I'm supposed to be with them.

"Girls, the popcorn is just about—" The microwave beeps over my last word.

They either didn't hear me or are choosing not to return. I switch out the bag of cooked popcorn for the popped package and hit the start button once more.

"Madden, Blakely!"

A faint hum of whispers from upstairs sends a shiver down my spine. I head towards the stairs much slower than I should be moving, given my concern about where the girls have disappeared to. The floors creak beneath each step and the hint of quiet laughter, or possibly a cry draws me into Blakely's dark bedroom. "Girls?" I should sound more confident in case they can hear my nerves.

With no response, I continue through the dark bathroom and then into Madden's room. I feel around the wall for the light switch, but when the light finally floods the room, I find nothing. I hope they aren't in their parents' room. Another shiver ripples through me.

I peek out into the hallway and venture down toward their parents' room, hesitant to open the door unless necessary. There's another door at the end of the hallway, so I move to check there first. "Blakely, Madden, I don't think this is funny. We aren't playing hide-and-seek. You already know this." Something metal falls to the ground and I can't tell which direction it came from. My palms feel clammy as I reach for the door at the end of the hall. "Girls, please..."

Just as I wrap my hand around the doorknob and draw a deep breath in, the two of them bolt out of Blakely's bedroom with their hands behind their backs.

"Were you hiding from me?" I ask, squinting through one eye while also forcing a small smile so I don't come off too accusatory.

"We thought we heard something, but it was just someone walking their dog outside."

"Ah, okay..." I'm suspicious of their behavior, but I don't want to cause any tension with them after just meeting. "Well, the popcorn is just about ready. Let's find some bowls and get comfortable on the sofa."

They both leap ahead of me, grabbing one side of the railing to make their way downstairs. I was sure they were hiding something behind their backs, but I guess not. "Wait, I have to use the bathroom first," Madden says, returning upstairs. "I'll be down in one second."

I watch as she makes her way to the second door on the right side of the hallway and closes the door behind her.

"Are you sure everything is okay?" I ask Blakely, who's lost the hop in her step. "Yeah, of course. Next door's dog is one of those sad-eyed hounds and makes a loud whining sound when he doesn't want to go home. He likes the grass under our trees, but Dad doesn't want him on our grass because he said we have dog poison there and it's dangerous for him. He even put a little sign in the grass, but the dog doesn't understand."

"Aww, the poor pup. Who can blame him for wanting a patch of nice cool grass?"

"That's why he doesn't want to go home. We wish he didn't have to leave," Blakely says with a chuckle. "We love him. We want a dog, but Mom and Dad say we don't have time for more responsibilities."

I can't tell if there is more meaning behind her words or if she is mirroring a form of sarcasm she hears around the house.

"Well, dogs *can* be a lot of work," I add, understanding why Mr. and Mrs. Smith might not want to add more to their plate.

"Not as much work as Madden and I are," she mutters while making her way over to the bottom cabinet in the kitchen where she finds a stack of mixing bowls. She pulls two out, places them on the counter, then pauses as if something's shocked her. She twists her head over her shoulder and cranes her neck to look beyond the curve of the hallway. "Madden, is that you?"

"I think she's still in the bathroom. Did you hear something?"

"Oh, um, I guess not," Blakely says. "Madden likes to sneak up on me. I don't like it when she does that."

There isn't much to see except for the view into the empty living room.

My mind rests with ease when I hear the bathroom door open upstairs, followed by Madden's bare feet barreling down the stairs.

NINE

FRIDAY, JUNE 9TH 8:30 PM

The girls haven't said much to each other since Madden returned from the bathroom, but they peer over at one another once every few minutes, almost as if they're checking to see if the other is still where they should be. They seem nervous, but it's hard to tell if it's because I'm new to them or if there's something else.

At least the movie has distracted them for the most part. Though I can't figure out why they are so hooked on this copycat version of *The Little Mermaid*.

The grandfather clock gongs from the living room as it has done every half hour and I glance at my watch, realizing Mr. and Mrs. Smith didn't mention a bedtime, and I forgot to ask. With Blakely restlessly sprawling out and resting her head on the arm of the couch, I assume it's close to that time. As she shifts, Blakely's dress crumples up, revealing a few large bruises on the side of her leg. I force myself to look away before she notices. They don't look like playtime bumps. But it's always tough to decipher why a child could have bruises, especially when it's so common, depending on how active they are.

I spot the remote on the coffee table and tap the pause button.

"Hey," Madden whines. "It's not over yet."

"You can still watch more, but I'm curious about your bedtime. What time do you get ready for bed?"

They're both silent, but Blakely twists her lips from side to side as if she's debating whether to tell the truth. I can sense the tension growing between them. "Nine, but sometimes Mom and Dad let us stay up until nine thirty on the weekends."

"What time do you wake up in the mornings?" Many parents stick to the pediatrician's guidelines regarding how many hours of sleep children need.

"Six thirty or seven," Blakely says without thinking this answer through.

"You wake up at six thirty. I don't wake up until seven," Madden corrects her sister.

"How about we compromise on a nine fifteen bedtime?" That will at least be close to the ten hours children their age need. "But you need to put your pajamas on, wash up and brush your teeth now, and then we'll watch the movie until bedtime."

Madden shrugs and slugs off the couch. I take her willingness to move as a silent gesture that she's okay with the deal. She spins around and takes Blakely's hand and pulls her up. As she's doing so, I notice an odd-shaped bruise on the bottom of her wrist. I could be mistaken, but it looks like the shape of three fingers.

Maybe they fight with each other. They seem close, but they don't agree on everything, just like most siblings.

The two of them thud through the great room and into the kitchen, making their whereabouts clear up the stairwell. I don't want to invade their privacy while changing, but I'll stand in the hallway in case they need something.

I take my time hiking up the stairs, glancing at each framed portrait on the wall. The photos grow in age toward the top of the landing, starting when the girls were babies. They still look like they did when they were toddlers—adorable children. Mr. Smith has dark hair and Lara is blonde, but I might not have assumed her hair color was natural upon meeting her at first tonight. I suppose one of them must have natural blonde roots with how light the girls' hair color is.

Drawers open and close and I can hear the fabric of their clothes hitting the hardwood floors. At the sound of a door flinging open and bouncing off a rubber door stop, I peek into Blakely's room, finding their shared bathroom door open, the fluorescent light illuminating the connecting space between their rooms. I step in past Blakely's bed and move toward the bathroom, finding her in pajamas and ready to wash up.

The Smiths have installed double sinks, probably to prevent sibling bathroom fights. I turn the faucet on for Blakely since she is squeezing the life out of the tube of toothpaste. "Want some help?" I offer.

"Nope, I got it," she says with a small grunt. As I expected, the toothpaste piles onto the bristles and into the basin of the porcelain sink, but the running stream of water washes the excess away. I take a step back toward the door to give her some space and observe the matching white wooden footstools and the white fluffy bathmat. I then notice that Blakely's knee-length pink-and-purple striped nightgown reveals more bruises on her other leg, too.

A paranoid parent would call attention to the bruises if they didn't want me to suspect anything, which would signify that they just play hard. Of course, not everyone falls into a neat psychological category either. If I say something about the bruises, they will likely repeat the comment to Mr. and Mrs. Smith, which could appear like I'm questioning more than just the bruising. I'm sure that would result in never hearing from them again, but maybe only if they're hiding something.

Madden bursts out of her room and into the bathroom,

joining Blakely at the second sink in the bathroom. I'm not surprised to see her in a mermaid nightgown or her toothbrush handle being in the shape of a mermaid tail.

"How many minutes has it been?" Madden asks with a mouthful of toothpaste.

I glance down at my watch. "Only five minutes. You are both super speedy. I bet you'll have time to finish the movie at this rate." The movie can't be more than another thirty minutes. It's already been playing for an hour and a half.

"It's probably almost over," Blakely says after spitting her toothpaste into the sink.

"While you're finishing up with your teeth, Madden, I'm going to use the guest bathroom downstairs. Do you need help with anything else in the bathroom first?"

"Nope, we'll be down in a second," Blakely confirms.

The guest bathroom is so large, I can't hear anything outside. The silence urges me to hurry, so I'm not leaving them unattended for more than a minute or two, especially after the scare they gave me before the movie. Once I get to know them better, I'll have more of an idea of the boundaries they need and want.

As I venture into the great room, assuming they'd be ready and waiting on the couch, I see I was wrong to assume. "Girls?" I call out. "Are you still upstairs in the bathroom?" I shout up the stairwell, loud enough to ensure my voice carries.

They don't respond, yet again, so I make my way back up the stairs. I walk in through Blakely's well-lit—but empty—bedroom and check the closet, finding nothing but organized clothes and shoes, then head into the bathroom. The glass doors on their bathtub are open, exposing the empty basin, so I move on to Madden's room, checking under the bed and in her closet too. They aren't in here either. I'm beginning to think of the real reason their last sitter is no longer here. Did they hide from her all the time?

"Blakely, Madden, where are you two?" I sound less than pleased, which won't urge them out of whatever spot they're hiding in, but we've already been through this once and I can't let them break their father's rules. I'm sure there's a good reason for his rule—one I might not want to know at this point.

After making my way back into the hallway, I spot their parents' door again. It's still closed. "Girls, this isn't okay. You're disobeying your father's rules and I don't think he would be very—" Before I finish my statement, I think about the bruises I've seen on both of their bodies. What if he was responsible for those? What if he has a lot of unnecessary rules? Am I being too hard on them?

The silence is deafening, and I can't let this go on any longer. "I hope you aren't in your parents' room. I would feel very disrespectful walking in there to look for you if you're hiding somewhere else. I was hoping to be your nanny for the summer, but if they find out I went into their bedroom, I'm not sure they will still want me here." I'm blabbing to the walls. They don't respond. There isn't even a whisper of noise this time.

The Smiths' bedroom door taunts me and I know there's no way around it unless I'm going to start going through every nook and cranny of this gigantic house. I twist the knob and poke my head inside. There's still a bit of light left in the room from the sun setting behind the house, but there's no sign of the girls, just a basic master bedroom and each corner of the room visible from the doorway. The en suite bathroom is just off and it's the only space I can't see into. Their room smells like a combination of expensive cologne and even more expensive perfume. I'll probably be coated in the scent when I leave the room. They'll know I was in here. I move quickly toward the attached bathroom and flip on the light just long enough to search the space. The glass shower makes it easier for me to cross this room off the list.

As I make it back out into the hallway and resecure the Smith's bedroom door, I call out to them again, my heart starting to pound. "Blakely, Madden? Girls, please. We're running out of time to finish the movie. Where are you?"

Maybe they're downstairs somewhere. I spin around, ready to head back down the stairs, but realize I forgot about the door at the end of the hallway. I'm sure it's just a closet, but I wouldn't put it past them to hide in there. I open the door, finding it to be an entrance to another level of the house—an attic, maybe. The lights are off and I'm not a fan of dark spaces, especially ones hidden from the rest of the house's floor plan. They wouldn't be up there. *Please don't be up there.* "Girls?"

A slight breeze from up the stairs wooshes around me; the air is filled with a faint scent of paint. I run my hand across the wall in search of a light switch, not finding one as I take the first couple of steps up toward the next floor.

A fit of giggles grows from behind me. *Thank God.*

With a firm grip on the railing, I jog back down the steps and listen for another giggle. One of them cracks under pressure within thirty seconds of me standing between their bedroom doors in the hallway. I find them huddled in Madden's closet beneath her hanging dresses and behind a shoe rack.

"Boo!" they both shout.

My heart quakes and my stomach muscles unfurl from the knot it was in. I want to tell them how rude their behavior is, but they aren't my children to scold. "That wasn't very nice. You worried me and I thought we agreed not to play hide-and-seek tonight?"

Blakely crawls out of the closet from behind the shoe rack and groans. "Yup, she's just like all the others," she says.

I cross my arms and let out a sigh to warn them that I'm not pleased. "I think it's time for bed," I tell them, looking down at my watch again.

"No, you said we could watch the rest of the movie!" Madden whines.

"I'm sorry, but you broke the rules, and it just took me too long to find you. I'm afraid you'll have to finish the movie tomorrow."

"Well, that's not going to happen," Madden mutters.

"Why not?" I ask.

"Never mind," she says, crawling out of the closet before trudging to her bed.

TEN

I'm surprised the twins went to bed without putting up more of a fight. I'm sure they don't like me very much since I didn't let them finish the movie. Still, if I'm about to spend my summer taking care of them, I can't let them take advantage and ignore the rules.

I still have about an hour before Mr. and Mrs. Smith return as they said something about being home before eleven. With time to fill, I meander around the first floor, admiring the professional décor. There are a couple of rooms that make me wonder if they're ever used, like the library of sorts with its strangely bare shelves. Then there's the room in the far corner, opposite the great room. I flip the light switch, finding a built-in desk framing a widescreen monitor and matching filing drawers on each side. The two sets of French windows have upholstered benches over more drawers. I bet this room gets a lot of sun during the day, especially looking out over the ocean. The neutral and pastel colors between the walls, throw rug, and furniture have a feminine feel. I wonder if this is Lara's office. She did mention that she does a lot of charity work for her husband's business.

My mind is spinning with assumptions about this family and yet I can't pinpoint any one answer to my questions. I'm still trying to figure out what Mr. Smith does for a living. I should have followed Willa's style and done a couple of online searches about them. These are things I should know before taking a long-term position. Walking into situations with blinders on can lead to a poor ending. I know that better than anyone.

I pull my phone out of my back pocket before pulling out the tufted cream-colored desk chair. My display flashes with a time and restaurant name from Liam. I chuckle, finding the irony that it would be the restaurant where Willa works. She has never missed the Saturday night rush so I'm sure she's on the schedule. Since Newport isn't a large town and only a handful of popular restaurants are typical dinner date spots, the chances of him choosing this one isn't too surprising. Now Willa can meet him before I even consider bringing him back to the apartment. She'll be thrilled.

Disregarding what would be normal behavior—sitting in someone's living room and keeping my hands to myself while I wait for the parents to return home from their night out—I take the opportunity to wake up their sleeping computer. It's surprising they don't have this password protected, but I'm guilty of removing mine since it's a pain when I'm trying to log-in quickly. I open a browser and wait for the search bar to appear.

Who are you, Corbin and Lara Smith?

I click inside the search bar and watch the list of recent searches populate in the dropdown. A person can learn a lot from someone's search history.

- *Child psychologists, specialty with twins, Newport, RI...*
- *Child psychologists, Newport, RI...*

- *Child therapists, Newport, RI...*
- *Why would the department of children's services be called on a family...*
- *How to entertain bored children during the summer...*
- *Children haircuts, Newport, RI...*
- *Classifieds with nanny listings in Newport, RI...*
- *Nanny services, Newport, RI...*
- *Newport Newsletter...*
- *What's the difference between a nanny and a babysitter...*
- *Best makeup foundation to cover bruises...*
- *Divorce attorneys, Newport, RI*
- *Marital Counselors, Newport, RI*
- *Mediators for marriages, Newport, RI*
- *Party supplies...*
- *Lawn services in Newport, RI...*
- *Recipe for chicken piccata with low sodium ...*

Some things are just hard to unsee. I clap the mouse on the desk to move the pointer, close the browser window, and click the sleep mode button on the top left menu. This is what I get for snooping. I can only imagine what's in those filing drawers.

I tuck the chair back in and hit the light switch, before making my way back to the main living room full of uncomfort-able-looking furniture. There is no give in the leather couch cushion when I sit. I might as well be sitting on concrete.

With my phone clenched between my hands, I open a new incognito window in my internet browser and search Lara and Corbin Smith of Newport, RI.

- ***Unmatched Generosity:*** *Corbin and Lara Smith Fund Groundbreaking...*

- ***Leader of Innovation Spearheads Startup:*** *Corbin Smith, Newport Rhode Island...*
- ***The Extraordinary Hosts:*** *Corbin and Lara Smith throw extravagant soiree to benefit...*
- ***Beyond the Boardroom:*** *Corbin Smith promotes work-life balance to enrich family bonding...*
- ***Humanitarian Heroes:*** *Corbin and Lara Smith receive recognition for...*

My God. They must want people to think they're going for sainthood but based on their internet searches and the odd bruises on the girls, I have a suspicion they might be trying to hide whatever truths exist, or might exist, within these walls.

After a dozen searches and pages, nothing but glorified articles pop up. I didn't realize how long I had been searching for evidence that they aren't as perfect as they appear, and get a fright when the motor of the garage door hums against the house.

A moment later, Mr. and Mrs. Smith walk in through a door on the other side of the stairwell—I assume the door adjacent to the garage bays. They look just as perfect as when they left.

"Hi, Haley. How was everything?" Lara asks, keeping her voice quiet so it doesn't travel up the stairwell I assume. She places her emerald-green sequin clutch with golden fixtures down on the foyer table and makes her way over to me while plucking her earrings out.

"Great. The girls were well-behaved. We watched a movie and had some popcorn." I'm going to leave the hide-and-seek unless she asks because—

"They didn't trick you into playing hide-and-seek, did they?"

I stand up from the uncomfortable couch and slip my phone

into my back pocket. "They were just being silly girls. It was no big deal." It was no big deal to me, but Lara's anger shows within the sharp arch of her brow.

"Unbelievable. We give them so few rules and they still can't follow them. I am so sorry. I'll pay extra for whatever trouble they caused."

Extra? It's part of the job. Kids will be kids. "Oh no, you don't have to pay any extra. They were no trouble at all."

"Everything okay?" Mr. Smith asks as he enters from a different side door that seems to be connected to their garage.

"They did just what you thought they would do," Mrs. Smith says.

Mr. Smith scrapes his palm down the side of his face and stretches his neck to the side. "I'll handle it."

"They were just playing. It wasn't a big deal," I say, feeling like I just threw the poor girls into a world of trouble.

"I know, but we have rules," he says, trudging up the stairwell in his patent leather shoes.

His footsteps seem to carry on for days. I stand and watch the back of Mrs. Smith's head as she studies the path her husband just took.

"Well, I'm going to let you be. I hope I didn't get the girls in any trouble. I enjoyed my time with them tonight."

Mrs. Smith spins around. "You are an honest woman and I appreciate that. For that reason alone, I would like to offer you this position for the summer if you're still interested."

Should I be? Part of me would like to walk out of this house and forget everything I might or might not have seen tonight. The other part of me would be doing a disservice to those two beautiful little girls. And my bank account...

"I would like that," I say, forcing a smile.

"A week from Monday is their first day of summer break. How does that sound? Nine to five?"

"That sounds grea—"

"Lara? Do you have—" Mr. Smith calls out from upstairs, but the end of his question is lost.

"Corbin, what are you shouting about?" Lara replies. "You're going to wake the girls. Come downstairs."

Corbin trudges halfway down the stairwell. "Haley, where is Fallon? Did she fall asleep in the great room?"

"Fallon?" I question. "Who—is that a nickname for one of the twins?"

Corbin huffs a stalky laugh. "No, our baby. Fallon. Where is she?"

"There's no baby," I reply, looking between the two of them, waiting for one to start laughing about a prank they're playing on me.

He returns down the stairs, his feet heavy with each step as he returns to his wife's side. "Are you being serious?" he asks.

"I was here to watch your twins. I don't—you have a baby?"

Mrs. Smith whips around toward me, her eyes bulging with panic. "Haley, where's Fallon?"

My stomach drops as I try to piece together what they're talking about. I clutch my hands over my chest, unable to see anything but the red veins in her eyes growing larger. "I'm sorry, I'm confused. I don't understand what you're asking."

"Did you check the twins' bedrooms, bathroom, and closet?" Lara asks Corbin, who's now whipping through the main floor like a maniac.

"Yes, yes, of course I did. She's-she's not upstairs," he calls back.

Lara pushes past me to head toward the stairs. "Fallon?" she shouts. She stops halfway up the stairs, grabbing the banister to turn around and face me. Her face reddens and turmoil fills her eyes. Her neck pulsates with panic as she screams, "We hired you to watch all three of our daughters. Where is she?"

"You didn't mention a third child," I say, clasping my hands over my chest. "You-you didn't...I don't know what you're—"

"Fallon. My God. Where is she?" Lara digs her fingernails into her neck as she darts up the rest of the stairs. Her ragged breaths become quieter the farther away she goes.

Corbin continues running circles around me, trekking through the living room and into the kitchen, his dress shoes thudding like a hammer.

Lara returns downstairs within seconds, strands of her hair wisping over her dewy face as she gasps for a breath. "Where is she? Just tell me, please," she cries out.

My lungs fall flat as I try to digest what's happening. "I—I would if-if I knew but—I never knew about Fallon," I say. My stomach curdles as confusion and panic sweep through me.

Lara's hands fly up to cover her mouth, her blood red nails contrasting against the whites of her eyes as she stares deep into my soul, waiting for an answer I don't have for her. "She wasn't with you while watching the movie? She would have fallen asleep there."

My heart stops as her questions register the truth of her accusations. I know what I agreed to when she hired me. There was no mention of a baby. I'm sure of it. Her words continue to burn through me as I take a step backward in defense.

"Why won't you just tell us where she is? What kind of person does something like this? Is this some kind of sick practical joke?" Mr. Smith bellows, his hot breath burning my skin as he steals the only space left between the three of us. His fists clenching by his sides as his eyes bore into mine.

"I—I didn't do anything. I swear to you, I—" I stutter as a surge of anxiety electrifies my nerves. "Y-you ne-never mentioned—" I'm verging on hyperventilation, my mind at a loss and not knowing what to think or do.

"I'm calling the police. She's not here," Mr. Smith shouts,

his voice bouncing off the surrounding walls. He pulls his phone out of his pocket and charges back up the stairs.

"Where would she have been?" I ask, my words grasping for sound from my dry throat.

"What in the world are you asking? She would be in plain sight," Mrs. Smith shouts before charging back up the stairs. I follow her, desperate to see where she's going to look for this unmentioned child. She reaches the door at the end of the hallway that's now open and lit up with a glow illuminating the set of steps that go into another space.

Lara is shoving furniture around as I approach the top step, finding myself engulfed by lavender walls. She tears sheets from the mattress in the crib, screaming, "Fallon!"

I'm in a nursery with gabled windows. A white rocking chair is draped in a purple fleece blanket in the corner and a white dresser and changing table line the farthest wall. In large block letters hanging from the wall is the name Fallon. My blood runs cold, my skin becomes numb as my knees threaten to give out.

I spin around and scramble back down the stairs past Madden and Blakely, standing in their doorways, their eyes wide with horror.

This must be a misunderstanding, but how? No one forgets to mention a baby.

Mr. Smith steps away from the front door as I descend the last few stairs and I'm overcome with the urge to flee. I need to get out of here.

The moment my foot touches the main floor, he bolts in my direction, stopping just in front of me. "You're not going anywhere, Haley, not until you tell us where our baby girl is..."

A bone-shattering crackle tears across the sky, releasing a heavy downpour. Thick raindrops batter against the door and windows as it feels like I'm decomposing beneath Mr. Smith's condemning stare. He might as well pin me against the maple round table in the foyer. As if the house is judging me, the empire chandelier with its many tiers of crystal droplets hovers like a spotlight pinpointing my every move.

Blaring sirens erupt outside, and my heart races faster than the pelting rain drops hitting the windows. I lunge for the door but am held back when Mr. Smith's grip flings me backward.

Blinding red and blue lights probe my eyes through the entryway windows. Mr. Smith's earlier words weren't just an empty threat. He had called the police.

"Haley. Please. We don't want any trouble. We just want our daughter back," Mr. Smith pleads. His loose bow tie swings with each word. His neck is red and blotchy above the top button of his white dress shirt, making his distress more apparent now that he's removed the black tuxedo jacket.

I take a short-winded staggered breath. I gasp for air and shake my head. "But I don't— wh-who are you ta-talking about?" I cry out. Shock has a chokehold around my neck, making my words hoarse as I try to answer the same questions over and over.

"My baby..." Mrs. Smith shrieks, slapping her arms over her chest, digging her fingernails into her bare shoulders where her strapless emerald gown clings to every curve of her body from her chest to her knees then fans out behind her and spills onto the floor like wet paint into a short trail behind her feet. "My God...where could she be?"

I stare into her pain-ridden eyes, a hint of copper swirling around her brown irises. "Yo-your t-two daughters are upstairs." I do everything I can to remain calm, despite feeling like I'm losing my mind.

"Fallon?" Lara moans, stepping closer toward me, her heels clacking against the hardwood floors.

Thuds against the door make my heart shudder as I decipher between the thunder and a fist pounding against the wood. "Newport Police," a man announces.

Mr. Smith brushes by me and opens the door as if safety is on the other side. "Oh, thank God you're here," he says, breathlessly. "Please, please, please help us. We're just—we're horrified and don't know what to do. We just want our baby back." Mr. Smith rests his hands on the officer's shoulders as he pleads for his help. Several other officers stand behind him for backup. I'm forced to back up to allow more space for all the officers to step inside the foyer. Each of them gives me a look as if I'm a wild animal on the loose, one who might attack them if they come too close.

"She was taking care of our children. Now, our baby is gone," Lara cries out, pointing her finger at me.

I shake my head. "No, no, I knew nothing about a third child. She wasn't here when I arrived. There were just the two little girls."

"Okay, okay. Let's take it easy," the main officer says. He looks to be around my father's age: gray hair, tired facial lines, and a potbelly. "Ma'am, did you leave the house with the children this evening?"

"No-no, sir. I-I-I had no reason to leave the house tonight." I'm seeking an empathetic look in any of their eyes, finding nothing but blame.

"Miss, is that your vehicle out front?" He doesn't have to point to the one he's asking about. My car is the one worth less than Mrs. Smith's dress.

"Yes, sir. But—"

He holds up his hand. "Thank you."

Two of the five police step out of the house and head for my car. "I-I haven't d-done anything they are accusing me of," I state, wrapping my arms around my waist to quell the nerve-ridden pain.

"Fallon, our daughter—she *was* here when we left this evening, but now she isn't. How is she even defending herself?" Mrs. Smith squawks.

The officer leading the questions takes a moment to scan the foyer as if there would be a hint of a missing child somewhere around us in this hollow room. "Mr. and Mrs. Smith, have you checked *every* area of the house?"

"Yes, yes, of course," Mr. Smith shouts while wringing his hands together in despair.

"Please, check again."

Static zings through the radio clipped to his chest. "We believe we have something. Does the family have a hairbrush for the child?"

Evidence? From where?

"Stay here," the officer says, pointing at me as he walks around two guard-like officers at the door to meet the others outside. "Do you have a hairbrush for your daughter? One only she uses?" The officer directs his question to Mr. Smith who can't keep himself still even after going through each room and closet of the house again.

"Yes, yes, of course." Mr. Smith runs up the stairs and returns within a brief minute, reaching a white baby hairbrush with soft bristles out between the two officers standing in the doorway. One leaves the house with the brush pinched between his gloved fingertips.

The lead officer returns within a few moments, just long enough for my pulse to quicken to the point of making me dizzy. Upon his return, he steps toward me with a narrow glare. "We found a blanket and baby bottle in the back seat of your car. Do those belong to you?"

"A nursery blanket and baby bottle? I don't know what you're talking about. Those aren't in my car."

"Yes, they were. We found them there just now," he says, pointing over his shoulder toward the front door.

"But—no. No, I didn't put them there," I argue, my breath running ragged.

"Okay, okay. Let's not make this any harder than it needs be."

"I'm not," I shout through hysteria. "I'm telling the truth!"

The officer shakes his head at me as if he isn't listening to a word I'm saying. "Place your hands behind your back and turn around. You're under arrest for the kidnapping of a minor."

ELEVEN

My hands are shaking as I dial Willa's phone number. I have stored very few numbers in my memory these days with our cell phones never being more than an arm's length away. She's probably asleep, and she's a heavy sleeper. God, I hope she answers.

The call connects, and the sharp ring of a landline I haven't heard in ages rattles in my ear. My stomach twists and tightens like a sponge, one someone is wringing the water from.

"He-llo?" Willa answers, her voice croaking.

"Willa, it's me. I need your help. I was detained and brought down to the police station for questioning—"

"What? Wait...wait, slow down. I—you've been—what?" she stammers. None of this makes sense to me and I'm not sure there is any way to make it much clearer to her.

"The Smith family accused me of kidnapping one of their children. I don't know what's going on, but I didn't do anything. The police questioned me for hours but they're letting me leave now."

"Okay. I—I'll be right there. Are you at the Newport police department?"

"Yes," I say, my voice losing its sound. "Hurry. Please."

"I'm on my way."

As I hang up the phone, tears burn the backs of my eyes. I stare up at the fluorescent lights, trying to keep them from falling down my cheeks. "This way," the female officer who has been escorting me says, leading me down the hallway toward the front entrance.

I pass a couple of holding cells. Only one of them is occupied, but I've only ever seen a jail cell on TV and never imagined being this close to one.

"Your car was impounded following the search. Someone will have to bring you down there to retrieve it. They charge by the night. The clerk will give you a card with an address and phone number so you know where to go."

"Okay," I say, sound barely scratching through my throat.

The officer scans her badge against an ID reader and the metal door before us screeches open and remains open just long enough for us to walk through. The door closes with a metal clanging that echoes between my ears. "You can retrieve your personal belongings at the station clerk's window then take a seat in the lobby and wait here for whoever is picking you up."

"Thank you," I utter, shuffling toward the clerk's window.

"Haley Vaughn is released from the initial questioning but has been told to be accessible for any further questioning that might arise. Mark her down as a person of interest for now."

"Just give me a minute, ma'am," the woman behind the Plexiglas window says before closing the opening seal to continue the conversation with the officer in private.

My verbal acknowledgment goes unheard. Person of interest? I don't know what that means other than they can call me back to do this all over again. I can't think of any other questions they would have for me.

I take a seat in one of the blue plastic bucket chairs, inhaling the musty stench of body odor and mildew with a hint of lemon-cleaner that's doing little to mask the foul stench.

I lean my head back against the wall and shut my eyes, trying to convince myself I'm anywhere but here.

The memory of the conversation with Mrs. Smith last Sunday reels through my head as I try to recall key moments that stood out. I want to confidently remember that she said I would be watching her twin daughters. I know she said they were nine. That would have been the time she told me about another child of a different age.

No one mentioned the baby when I arrived tonight. I wasn't brought up to the third floor where the baby's nursery was. I wonder if Mr. Smith assumed Mrs. Smith had already taken me up there, but a baby would have woken up and cried. I would have heard something during the five hours I was there. A baby requires much more than the mere mention of a bedtime they forgot to tell me about. They eat at certain times and need diapers changed. Neither Blakely nor Madden mentioned a word about a sister.

None of this makes sense. I don't understand anything that's happening.

TWELVE

SATURDAY, JUNE 10TH 5:00 AM

The double glass doors across the lobby squeal, jolting me out of a half-sleep. Willa storms inside, looking more like she's coming to visit me in a hospital bed rather than picking me up at the police station. Her hair is a mess, curls everywhere, half up, half down. She's in flannel pajama pants and a tank top. It's obvious she literally ran out of the apartment after I called.

The moment I stand from my seat she throws her arms around me, holding me as tightly as I need to feel safe.

"Your belongings are here when you're ready," the clerk says, placing a plastic bag outside the window.

I don't know what time it is or how long I was trying to block out my surroundings while rehashing everything that's happened over and over. All I know is I'm in a fog as I take my bag of personal belongings and sign papers agreeing to attend court on the given day of any hearing. I scuff my feet out of the high-security locked doors that have been released temporarily for me to walk through.

We don't say a word until we are deep into the parking lot. "My God, Hales, what happened?"

"I'm so sorry," I say, a sob bucking up my throat.

"Sorry about what? Just tell me what the hell happened?"

I shrug, struggling to lift my shoulders with her arm around me. All I can do is shake my head, because there is no answer. There is no logic. I'm as logical as someone can get. I analyze everyone, including myself and every situation. I'm always confident I know what's going on around me and I have everything under control. Losing control is the worst thing that can happen to a person, and I refuse to let that happen to me again. I won't.

But I have.

"They came home and went looking for a baby that I never saw, never knew about, never heard of..."

"Do you think it's some kind of misunderstanding?" Willa asks, scratching the back of her head with a look of confusion that matches how I feel.

Misunderstanding. How is that even possible? "I—I just don't see how."

"You said you were watching two nine-year-old girls," Willa says, giving me just a tiny sense of sanity.

"That's what Mrs. Smith said to me when I called her last Sunday. I had no reason to think there were any more than two children at their sprawling mansion."

"Okay, okay. Get in the car," she says, unlocking the doors with her key fob. The cheep-cheep is like music to my ears after listening to metal doors rattling around all night. I slide into her coconut-infused car and bury my head back into the seat, relishing the cushion and the soft fabric.

"I'm at a loss for words," Willa says, closing herself into the driver's seat. I still don't know what time it is, but the sun is just starting to rise over the horizon, so maybe around five in the morning. "Wait, where is your car?"

I'm squeezing the plastic bag containing my purse, phone, and receipts that were in my pockets and feel a small card stapled to the top. It must have the information about the car pound. "They impounded it after the search. I'll have to get it tomorrow—I mean, later today."

The engine roars and the dashboard lights glow in a matching lime green to the exterior paint. It's ten past five. I was in that hellhole for over five hours. The thought of ever going back makes me want to vomit. Being called a person of interest gives me little hope that this is over.

"Oh okay, we'll go later in the morning to pick it up," Willa says, pulling out of the parking lot.

"There's still a missing baby. I can't imagine what could have happened to her but knowing that they think I had something to do with it...I feel sick."

"You might have just been at the wrong place at the wrong time," Willa says, shaking her head.

"That doesn't happen in real life. People don't just find themselves in situations like this." What I'm saying is completely inaccurate. Victims are chosen at random all the time. Robbery, kidnappings, worse... How could a baby be taken from her crib without anyone noticing?

"Girl, we both know anything could have happened. Look, we aren't going to come up with an answer without any other facts or evidence, so after we get your car back, we need to start calling around to find you a good attorney."

A good attorney means an unaffordable one that only wealthy people can employ. If I could afford a good attorney, I wouldn't be desperate to spend my free time during the summer as a nanny. I would be researching for my dissertation.

Willa, on the other hand, is a trust fund baby. College tuition and room, board, and food, has been paid for by her parents since she started school here. Though we've gone through the program together since freshman year, we're finishing with two different degree types. Mine within the Behavioral Health program requires extra courses, so Willa decided to take the last semester off for a "mental health break," which the school of psychology couldn't argue with, before returning in the fall to complete her practicum hours and dissertation. We should both still earn our degrees around the same time if all goes according to plan, but she will have no debt and can be carefree while socking away the money she earns at work —the job she loves because of the boss she loves. I'm not so lucky. I'll be paying off student loans until *my* kids go to college. I try not to think about the cost of the career I want. Until something I need and can't afford comes up, that is.

"I won't be able to get a good attorney. I can't afford an attorney. I have enough to pay the pound to get my car back, and that's about it right now. I'm on my own."

"No way. If they come back after you for more questioning, you need someone to defend you. Not having an attorney is like a death sentence—I mean, that's not a possibility here. You need...you absolutely need someone. I'll pay. It will be fine."

"No, you're not paying for an attorney. I'll figure something out. Please—the last thing I want to do is ask for financial help. I'm mortified, stupid, and I obviously should have been smarter about taking this job. I should have known it was too good to be true."

Willa growls, her way of showing frustration loud and clear. "I will help you however you will allow me to help. Even if that means stalking the hell out of these sewer rats to dig up trash on them, then that's what I'll do."

"You won't find anything online."

"How do you know?" she asks, jolting her focus from the road to me and back to the road.

"I tried doing a search on them just before they got home."

"You did?" she gasps. "Did you find anything?"

"Yeah...my gut told me something wasn't right. Their browser history confirmed it."

THIRTEEN

SATURDAY, JUNE 10TH 9:00 AM

I've spent the last hour lying semi-awake wondering how long someone can go without sleep. I didn't sleep for even a minute from when we got home until now, but I might have fallen into a trance while staring at my ceiling fan. My mind won't slow down. No matter how many times I replay everything in my head, there's no more sense to be made.

"I'm not going to let you sit in your room all day again," Willa says, knocking on my door as she opens it.

"What else am I supposed to do aside from walking around town wondering how long I have before I'll be pinned for a crime I didn't commit, then potentially get locked up in prison."

My phone buzzes on my nightstand and I lean over to check who's calling. The name on the display forces a rush of heat through my face as I grab the device and press the answer button. "Hello?"

"Haley?" Lara's shaky voice says. She gasps a few times, sounding as if she's been crying heavily ever since I last saw her, which I don't doubt. "Please, help us and the police find her."

"I have never seen her. And how can I help you when you told the police I did something to her?"

She takes a stuttering inhale. "She was there when I left. She was in her crib," she utters. "Please, I'm begging you to help us find her. Is it money you want?"

I pull the phone away from my ear and stare at the display screen as if it just scalded me. "Money?" I reply. "I didn't take your baby. I'm sorry that she's missing, but I didn't touch her. I didn't know there was a baby in the house. You didn't mention—"

"How can you say this to me?" she cries out. "I'm dying from heartache and you're telling me I never mentioned my own daughter?"

She didn't. She never said a word. How does she not know this? Why is she lying?

"We shouldn't be talking, Lara. You filed a person of interest report against me. I can't do anything to help you, but despite the blame you inflicted on me, I am so sorry for what you are going through. I can't imagine having a missing child." I press my hand to my chest, feeling wrong but right saying what I am to her. I wouldn't wish something like this on my worst enemy, but I don't have any information that will help her. Any exchange between us will only cause more issues for me, I'm sure.

"Please," she cries out. "I didn't even tell the police about the bruises I found all over Madden and Blakely this morning. They said you hurt them last night."

"What? No way. I didn't lay a hand on them. I noticed those bruises too. Those weren't from me. I would never hurt a child. Never."

"Haley, I'm trying so hard to keep myself together...if you would just help me—please. We can work this all out."

"What is she saying?" I hear her husband's voice in the background.

I pull the phone down to my lap, my hand shaking as I press the end-call button. My throat tightens and tears fill my eyes as

I lose focus on my phone. I hope they find their baby and I hope the other two girls are safe. But there is nothing I can do right now.

"Was that her?" Willa asks, her eyes wide and full of questions.

I nod. "She still thinks I know where her daughter is, and she thinks I hurt the twins last night. If she reports me for that too—" I cover my mouth, wishing it would stop the sobs from belting up my throat.

"She obviously knows you were released from the police station so why would she keep insisting you know something or had something to do with this?"

I stare toward my pair of fuzzy slippers off the side of my bed, watching the fuzz blur into the back of my mind. "Maybe there's no one else to blame," I say, realizing that all these arrows are wrongfully pointing in my direction because there is no other direction.

Willa sits down on the edge of the bed, breaking my gaze on the slippers. "This is seriously messed up, Hales. Have you called your parents? Do you want me to call them?"

I swallow the lump in my throat, feeling it create a wave of nausea in my stomach. "No, no. I don't want to worry them. Once I have more information, it'll be easier to explain. I hope."

"True, but they might be able to help you find an attorney." She thinks I do everything on my own as a form of defying dependencies. My parents are by no means wealthy.

"They can't help with this." They could tell me they'd help, and they would, but it wouldn't be by hiring an attorney.

"Even if it's to protect you? You're their only daughter. I can't imagine your dad denying you whatever you might need. You have the most loving parents, Haley. Don't be above asking them, please."

Willa only knows the front my parents put on for others. I don't know anyone who wouldn't call them the kindest people they've ever met, but things aren't always as they seem. I wish I could explain all that she doesn't know about my parents, but now isn't the time. It's never the right time to open that can of worms.

"I'll think about it," I say, hoping to move away from the topic.

My phone rings again. Willa takes it from my hand and flips it over to see who's calling. "It's her again. My God," she grumbles.

"No, I can't—" I say, breathing heavily.

Willa ends the call and places the phone down on my night-stand. "Let her calls go to voicemail. You don't owe her anything, okay?"

I stare at the phone as if it's going to jump up and hit me in the face. "Yeah."

"Okay, try to relax or—actually, let's go get your car so we can cross that off the list of concerns. Then we'll come home so you can take a shower and unravel a bit. This is all just too much at once."

I nod. "Okay, yeah," I say, trying to swallow against the growing lump in my throat.

Willa grabs her keys and purse, then my keys and purse and hands them to me. I follow her, feeling like a zombie walking in a daze. The only thing to startle me into blinking is another buzz from my phone, vibrating in my back pocket. *Go away, please just go away.*

With my car back in possession, and two-hundred dollars poorer, I stand in the hot shower for almost an hour, waiting for my thoughts to evaporate into the steam. But despite my phone being in my bedroom, I can't help feeling like it's attached to my skin, threatening to buzz again.

I'm afraid of what will happen when the Smiths get mad that I'm not answering their relentless calls. I'm not even sure if Lara has already told the police I hurt Madden and Blakely. She can't truly think I caused those marks... She must have seen them before I arrived.

She must know where they're really from. When the expected buzz rattles my bones again after a two-hour break, I hold my breath and clench my eyes, praying it's neither Lara nor the police. Relief filters through me when I peek through one eye, finding Liam's name on display.

Liam: Hey...just confirming our plans for tonight. Are we still on?

I toss my head back against my headboard, wondering if he already knows what happened last night. Regardless, there's no way I can go out tonight. I'm not exactly in the right headspace for a date.

Me: Hi Liam, I'm so sorry but I'm going to have postpone tonight. My first night on the job didn't go as well as I thought it was going and... Some things happened that you most likely wouldn't believe, even if we had known each other for years. I'm probably not the person you want to be around.

"Crap," Willa scoffs from the living room. "Hales, come here quick." Willa's shout forces me to stop rereading the message I just sent Liam.

"What is it?" I ask, making my way over to her as I drop my phone to my side.

The volume on the TV grows louder and I enter the room just in time to hear:

"Breaking News, local child missing. Authorities believe she has been taken from her home and the parents think their new babysitter could have played a part in the disappearance of their child. Haley Vaughn, a twenty-seven-year-old Newport resident was detained late last night for questioning. There has yet to be an update pertaining to Ms. Vaughn."

An old photo of me flashes across the TV screen. Stomach acid rises to the back of my throat, forcing me to keel forward.

"The local police are conducting a thorough search and investigation to find the child. Stay tuned for developing information."

As the camera cuts back to the news station, I feel the last of my hope deplete.

"They don't seem to have any details still," Willa says. "I think that's a good thing."

Not for the poor baby who's missing from her family, and not for me, whose photo just flashed across the news as a potential suspect.

"I don't know." I drop down onto the couch next to Willa and plop my head on her shoulder. "Do you think the police are going to call me back to the station for more questioning?"

Willa sighs. "I don't know, girl. Regardless of whether they do or don't, you didn't do anything and they can't just make proof appear out of thin air. We must have a little faith in the system, right?"

"There was proof," I say, my voice becoming hoarse. "There was a blanket and a bottle found in my car." That so-called evidence must be the reason the police were so quick to believe the Smiths last night.

"But you didn't put it there..." Willa says. I appreciate the statement rather than her questioning me, but it's too easy to think I was responsible.

"No. I didn't leave their house between the time they left and came home."

The lines in Willa's forehead deepen and she shakes her head. "Maybe one of the girls was playing outside while you were—"

I only used the bathroom once. I would like to think I would have known if they'd left the house, but then again, they were hiding from me too.

My phone buzzes again. This device is beginning to burn a hole in my hand today. My heart flutters as I flip it over to check the message.

> Liam: What happened? So long as you're all right, you don't need to worry about cancelling tonight.

I take my phone again and debate how to respond. He probably saw the news. That's probably the only reason he's messaging me back.

> Me: I'm not entirely all right. The family I was working for had me detained by the police last night. They accused me of taking their child, a third child I knew nothing about. I'm not sure what's going on, but I would never do such a thing. I'm pretty shaken up.

That's more than I've ever confessed to someone I've met for less than a few hours. With the breaking news reports, it's better just to be forward with the information since there's no telling whether he's already seen my photo flash across the news report.

Liam types a response but doesn't send whatever he is about to say. The little dots flicker for a few seconds then disappear again. I wouldn't know what to say to me either. I deserve his silence after what I did last night. He should know that's an option for him.

Liam: I'm confused but if I understand correctly, this is obviously some kind of misunderstanding. There must be a way to prove that, right?

Me: It's more than a misunderstanding. I'm not sure how to prove anything when all I have is my word.

Liam: Is there something I can do to help?

Me: Don't take it personally that I'm cancelling our dinner plans. Would you take a rain check?

Liam: I can do that. Or, if you're even in the mood for just coffee or ice cream, we can always meet at Skippers since it's at the far end of the wharf behind the lobster shack. It's fairly secluded.

Ice cream has the potential of being a good remedy for a prison hangover. Although I'm not sure there's enough ice cream in the world to undo what I went through last night.

Me: Ice cream is almost always the best answer to everything.

Liam: And ice cream can cause brain freeze, which technically...can make your thoughts temporarily go away.

For the simple fact that he made my mouth almost twitch into a hint of a smile, I'm beginning to regret cancelling tonight.

Me: I could use a distraction...

Liam: Name the day and time and I'll be there.

Me: How about mid-afternoon?

It's clear I got no sleep last night. I'm never this forward or decisive when it comes to making plans, but I'm desperate to focus on something else for a minute.

Liam: Today?

Maybe that was a little too forward after cancelling our plans for tonight. Shoot.

Me: Unless you'd rather wait...

I probably would if I was him. There's no way to make this situation sound much better.

Liam: No, of course not. Today is perfect. I'll meet you there at twelve :)

FOURTEEN

Even though I know it's just in my head, I feel like everyone I walk past is staring at me. I even dug out my baseball cap and accessorized with large-frame sunglasses. Two days ago, I left my apartment hoping to have a decent summer with some spare cash. Now I'm afraid of what news awaits me each hour of the day. The evidence the officers found came up inconclusive since my fingerprints weren't on the baby bottle they found in my car, but I wonder how long it will be before they think they've found something else that can be considered evidence. I was so frazzled when the police took me away that I forgot to mention the search history on their computer, and now I wonder if it would be suspicious to bring it up now as an afterthought. I would hope they would take a look for themselves if they're searching all possible sources for evidence. All I know is, I was in the house with the two girls alone that night regardless of what else is said. The public will believe whatever they hear.

The warm breeze hits me like a sheet of ice. I'm cold to the bone and nothing can warm me up from this nightmare. Even the sight of Liam makes me think about smiling but instead, my stomach churns and my heart races for the wrong reasons. What if he asked me to meet him here so he could tell me I'm crazy and question how I could do something to an innocent child?

"I'm not sure if your disguise is working," Liam says, tilting his head to the side. He teases or tests a smile as he walks toward me. His hands are resting in his pockets and he's slow to approach, likely getting a sense of how skittish I am.

The sun reflects off his cobalt eyes and paints a slight gingery hue along his dark messy waves. He's in board shorts, beach sandals, and a surf brand T-shirt. He seems far more relaxed and comfortable than I am. I'm jealous.

"Please tell me you didn't watch the news earlier today," I utter when we're close enough for only him to hear my words.

His chest puffs out as he takes a long inhale. "I did see it, but like the reporter said, it's a developing story. It seems like the media just needs to hear what you have to say, right?"

"Liam, it's sweet that you offered to get ice cream with me, but I truly don't want to pull you into this. You're a teacher. You shouldn't be seen with me."

He grins as if what I said is funny or cute. "What's your favorite flavor?" He is purposely overlooking my legitimate concern for his wellbeing.

"Strawberry."

"Cone or a cup?"

"Cone," I answer, reaching into my purse for a few dollars.

He walks away before I can remove my hand from my purse and proceeds to the ice-cream shop window to order. "I got it."

As if the sun is a spotlight, hovering only over me, I can't stop myself from peering in every direction, wondering who's around. A news truck with a reporter is at the outer edge of the wharf, where the village street of shops meets the inlet. While I know they're down here often to report on various activities in the area, I can't help but wonder if anything they are about to report on has something to do with the Smith family.

I can't even tell myself I'm just paranoid. I'm beyond that.

I hurry to the corner of the ice-cream shop to stay out of sight from the news crew. "You know," Liam says, handing me my cone of strawberry ice cream. "You could just go down to the reporter, introduce yourself and tell the truth about what really happened last night. You could flip the coin."

My mouth falls open just considering the idea. "No, there's no way. I shouldn't—I can't. I don't know what the right thing is anymore, but I don't want to make any public statements."

Although I was the one who thought watching two children would be a *good* idea.

Liam's idea to approach the news crew makes me want to jump off the pier, but the more I think about it, the more I feel there might be some value to the idea. Someone guilty of a crime wouldn't approach a news crew and be so upfront and direct. They would be in hiding.

My ice cream is beginning to melt as I stare at the crowd watching the reporter prepare for the camera.

"I'm sorry. I didn't mean to cause more stress," Liam says. He hands me a napkin to wrap around my cone.

"No—it's not—did you receive an Amber Alert?"

Liam lowers his ice-cream cone and tips his head to the side, his forehead wrinkling with a look of contemplation. "The thought didn't even cross my mind. No, I didn't receive an alert."

"I would have thought that would be the first thing the police had done last night."

"Something is off about this situation. Not for nothing, but the police let you go after questioning you. If there was clear evidence that you had done something with the child while the Smiths were gone, I'm not sure they would have released you from custody."

There was evidence. In my car of all places. The police said the evidence wasn't conclusive enough to use in the case and my fingerprints weren't on the baby bottle.

"That's true, but their investigation isn't complete, and I'm worried about what else they might question about me being there last night. The police could still show up at my door with an arrest warrant. I just feel like this is far from over."

"I don't think that'll happen," he says, "honestly."

"I've never met up with a man for an ice-cream date and discussed the probability of my impending criminal record," I say, while taking a painfully cold bite of the melting scoop of ice cream. "I can only imagine what you must be thinking of me. I still can't understand why you're here. I think most would have run by now. I probably would have."

Liam spots something behind me and gestures for me to turn around. A free bench awaits us against the wooden grates lining the wharf. "Do you want to sit over there?" he asks, pointing toward the bench.

"Sure," I say, and we walk over side by side, before rigidly taking a seat. All I can wonder is what he's truly thinking about me.

"You know...something I've learned as a teacher is how to read a person by their eyes. It's funny because I never would have picked up on this hint before working with so many four-teen- and fifteen-year-old kids. I call it the doe-eyed effect." He leans back into the bench and stretches his legs out as I try to find a more comfortable position on the flat, unforgiving wooden bench.

"Doe-eyed? Meaning innocent and naive?"

Liam smirks and pulls one foot in, scraping his heel against the sand-covered wooden pier. "No, the ones with the big, endearing stares are the ones I find guilty. There's panic and frenzy in the eyes of the innocent because they didn't pre-plan the moment of being questioned for something they didn't do."

I'm not sure I believe that. Willa gives me that doe-eyed look all the time. I know she never lies to me. "Hmm. Are you sure?"

"There's a science behind it." If there's a science behind it, it should be something I know about from my psychology degree. "It has something to do with cognitive demand."

"The attempt to form truth and logic increases cognitive demand," I say as if I'm reading from one of my textbooks. I never paired that trait up with lying. I should have—I've covered the topic in my courses. "I can't argue that theory."

"In any case, you aren't telling me a story with a doe-eyed look, so you're innocent—and also dripping ice cream on the ground."

As I peer down between my feet to where the ice cream is landing, the top scoop falls to the ground. "Oh my God. How about now? Haven't you realized yet that I'm not great company?" I ask, trying to laugh through my embarrassment.

"You failed to notice I sat on the bench to rest my arm over my shorts where I also dripped ice cream." He lifts his arm to show me the stain. "I think we're in perfect company."

"Fair enough." I stare at my sad cone and feel more motivated than ever to do something other than sit here feeling as if the world is staring at me. "Maybe I will give the reporters a statement so they have their so-called-update to me being a suspect in questioning."

"Wait, before you do that—" Liam reaches over with a napkin and dabs the corner of my mouth. "You don't need strawberry ice cream on your face while being brave. You can't be blushing either. You might give the cameraman the wrong idea."

"Maybe I won't give a statement," I say with a chuckle. Liam's laughter is endearing and unexpectedly calming. "Thank you for taking a chance on this mayhem I'm embracing."

"Well, some like me compare certain types of mayhem to a summer's day. I think Shakespeare might even agree."

"I think Shakespeare meant 'thee,' not mayhem," I argue.

"And I would agree with him on that too," he says with a quick wink.

He has successfully distracted me. I can give him that. The news crew is still down the wharf and I'm still debating my action plan.

"Are you buzzing?" Liam asks.

My phone has been going off in my purse for the last couple of minutes, but I don't want to be rude. "Yeah, it's fine. Whoever it is can wait." What if it's the police? Hopefully it's just Willa.

"You sure?" His expression morphs into concern. I don't want him to think I'm avoiding calls either.

I take my phone out of my purse, finding that the buzzing sounds weren't calls, but a string of texts from an unknown number. While I stumble my fingers across the keypad to unlock my phone, I try to release my held breath, assuring myself the police wouldn't be sending me text messages. Only Willa, but she wouldn't be coming up as an unknown contact.

The display finally opens in full view so I can focus on the messages.

Unknown Number: You committed a felony.

A felony? My pulse quickens and a flash of heat steals my breath. What is this?

Unknown Number: What were you thinking?

Unknown Number: Obviously, you weren't.

Unknown Number: How could you walk out of the police station as if you're innocent?

Unknown Number: Where is the child, Haley?

Unknown Number: This isn't something you can run away from.

My vision focuses and blurs between each short message. The messages don't stop. They keep coming, one after another as if preprogrammed. I stumble through the settings on the text, suddenly forgetting where to find the block-number option. Every button I click resets me back to the text screen where they continue popping up and scrolling upward. Sweat beads over my forehead and the sun feels like it's gotten hotter over the last minute.

Unknown Number: I see you looking at the news reporter.

Unknown Number: Don't do anything stupid.

I hold my finger down on the power button with force as if the harder I push the faster the phone will turn off, the phone doesn't shut down and I don't know why so I shove my phone back into my purse. "Everything okay?" Liam asks.

"No, but I should get going. I'm—I'm so sorry. This isn't you, or it has nothing to do with you. I shouldn't be out and about right now. Plus, it's not a good idea for you to be seen with me. The last thing I want is for this mess to affect anyone else." I can't sit still after seeing those text messages. I'm not sure what to do but it seems like I'm being watched.

"I totally understand," he says, taking my hand as I stand up. "I wish there was something I could do to help."

"I know, and I appreciate that more than I can explain. I

wish we were here under different circumstances and could have gone out tonight like we planned."

"Yeah, it's a bummer, but if I've learned anything in life... nothing will ever be perfect for any circumstance," he says. "However, I can't even begin to imagine what you must be feeling right now either. Just know, if you want to talk or text, I'm around."

He seems like such a good guy. Of course, this would all happen like some crazy circus where I can't have it all or even just one good thing at a time. I toss what's left of my soggy cone into the trash and wipe my hands off on the napkin he handed me. "When I get out of this mess, I want a redo. Would that be okay with you?"

"I'll be here," he says. "Literally, right here because...I love ice cream, so yes, it would." Liam wraps his arm around my neck and gives me a quick hug. "Take care of yourself. Be strong. I told you, you're innocent and soon everyone else will see it too."

He smells like coconut, beach salt, and spice and I know I will regret walking away.

Even if I stayed, I'd still receive the next message on my phone when I took it out of my purse.

Unknown Number: Newport is such a safe town, isn't it? The police will find more evidence to prove you're guilty. I promise you.

FIFTEEN

As I head back down the pier toward the main area of the wharf, paranoia spikes my pulse. I don't know if I'm taking steps away from or closer to whoever is deranged enough to be watching me while sending me text messages. My imagination is getting the best of me as I convince myself people are glancing at me as I walk by them. I whip my head over my shoulder every few seconds, sensing someone walking in my footsteps. The wharf is a popular location and it's a beautiful day. It's normal for there to be so many people here.

The news crew at the edge of the wharf is packing up as I come closer to where they were filming.

My phone buzzes again and this time it feels like an electric zapper clenched in my hand. I squeeze my fingers tighter around the edges of the phone, wishing I was strong enough to crush the device.

Another buzz.

Another change of heart. I need to do something. I can't just run from whatever might or might not be following me.

"Excuse me!" I call out toward the news crew. I'm just close enough that they'd hear me, so I hold my hand up, drawing more attention to myself than I wanted.

A camera-ready woman with long black hair, fire-engine red lips and lashes that curl up toward her eyebrows, pivots on her four-inch stilettos, her skintight pencil dress making her look robotic as she twists toward me.

I slap my hand against my chest, trying to catch the breath I shouldn't have lost from walking at a normal pace. "I know something about the missing baby," I say, trying to keep my voice low but loud enough for her to hear from the car length's difference between us.

"The missing baby," she says, her brows furrowing, stress lines that no viewer is intended to see tug along the sides of her eyes.

"Yes," I say, peering to each side, wondering who's watching and listening. Also wondering why she's repeating my words as if she doesn't know what I'm talking about.

"The Smith baby?" She takes a few steps closer to me, her mic still clenched in her fist.

I tug on my necklace and twist the chain around my finger. "Yes. I was the person watching the two other children last night and the one the Smith family accused when they never mentioned a single word about the baby."

"Will you answer some additional questions?" the woman asks me, waving her hand around behind her to get the attention of her crew. "And what's your name?"

"Haley Vaughn, and yes, I will." If I had a lawyer, they might advise against this decision, but I don't and I need the public to see whatever it is Liam claims to see in me —innocence.

As the reporter is gearing up, my phone buzzes several more times. Each time the vibration sounds louder than the last.

"Ready?" she asks, repositioning herself to stand by my side.

From the corner of my eye, I see her nod her head as a gesture to the cameraman.

"Three, two—" he points his finger toward us.

"This is Annalise Baratto, reporting live for Channel 4 at Bowen's Wharf. We've just had a breaking discovery regarding the case of missing baby girl, Fallon Smith. The fifteen-month-old was abducted by an unknown source yesterday and this young woman beside me, Haley Vaughn, was the hired nanny initially accused of kidnapping the Smiths' youngest child while watching over the other two Smith children. Haley was detained as a suspect shortly after Mr. and Mrs. Smith returned home to find one of their three daughters missing. Haley Vaughn claims to have no knowledge of Fallon Smith's existence." Annalise Baratto holds the microphone up in front of my chin. "Haley, in your words can you describe the situation from where you found yourself caring for two young girls to then being accused of abducting a third child you knew nothing about?"

I can't stop myself from staring into the camera as words purge on their own. "I was hired to watch twin girls last night. The Smiths never mentioned their third child to me, but now she's missing, and they blamed me when they got home. I was in as much shock as they were, and very confused about their accusation. I don't know anything about this child, and I had nothing to do with her disappearance."

"Wow," Annalise says. "How did you meet the Smith family?"

"I was looking for a summer job and posted my caregiving experience in a classified ad. They called me."

They called me. Why? Why me, of all people?

As if my phone is trying to answer my silent questions, it buzzes again.

"I can't imagine what you must be going through, blamed for such a heinous crime."

"They keep calling me, and I think one of them might be following me too." I imagine the unknown number must be Corbin, following up on Lara's calls, but I don't really know.

"Cut," Annalise says, allowing the microphone to dangle from her hand. "Are you being serious?"

"Yeah." Sound barely forms as I try to answer.

"Okay, I think we're going to wrap up here. Thank you for answering those questions."

"Oh, did I say something—"

"We just—we need to collect some more information before reporting anything more, but we truly appreciate your time." She hands the microphone to one of the men handling the camera equipment, and spins around before stopping to face me once more. "Uh, take care of yourself. Maybe take an Uber home."

Then the person watching me would know where I live.

I shove my phone into my back pocket and check my surroundings, as if I was about to jet out into traffic. There isn't an alternate route back to my apartment building, no side road I can escape into, out of sight. No matter what I do, I'm leading this person right where they want to be and there isn't anything I can do about it.

"Hey!" I close my eyes and continue walking, moving quicker without appearing to be in a panic. "Haley, hold up." The muffled shoutout makes me stop walking. I take a long pause before deciding to turn around. The scuffing footsteps grow louder, and I turn before I run out of time to get out of reach if need be.

I blink a few times as I focus on Liam, holding the side of his lip. His hand is covered in blood. "Oh my God. What happened?" I run to him and pull his hand away, finding his lip split. I shove my shaking hand into my purse and pull out my small travel pack of tissues and pull them all out. "Here." I press a ball of tissues to his lip. "My apartment is just a couple blocks that way. Come with me so I can clean you up. Who did this to you?"

"Some guy on a skateboard. I don't know if he was aiming for me or if I just got in the way, but his fist flew into my mouth on the way by."

"Where did he go?"

"I don't know. It took me a second to regain my bearings and by the time I looked around I didn't see him anywhere. There were a few of them on boards. I was heading away from the wharf when the crowd gathered around you as you were talking to the reporter. I stopped to see if I could hear what the woman was asking you but then I was blindsided."

This could be unrelated to the text messages. Or they could have seen me talking to him and took him as a target. What if this happened because of me?

"I'm so sorry."

"It's not your fault and I'll be okay. I didn't hear any part of what you two talked about but, I saw it ended quickly, and you ran off after the cameras moved away. You looked flustered so I wanted to check on you."

"Will you please let me help you? I should be well-versed in first aid at least," I say.

Liam chuckles at what would have been funny in any other circumstance. "I appreciate the offer, but I'm just going to head home and get cleaned up. You can always check on me later," he says with a smirk.

The only relief I have now is seeing the street ahead of me clear of other pedestrians and finding no one lurking behind. Liam jolts across the street, taking off in another direction and I pick up my pace to get home, hoping I get there in one piece.

Just as I enter the cement walkway to my complex, my phone rings rather than buzzes. Out of habit rather than avoidance, I check the display, finding Willa's face, her contact photo smiling back at me.

"Hey," I answer, breathlessly, relieved it's her and not the unknown.

"Where are you?" Panic rattles in her voice.

"Just outside, why?"

"I found something," she says.

SIXTEEN

SATURDAY, JUNE 10TH 3:30 PM

I close the door to my apartment and twist the deadbolt. Sweat drips down my back and I can barely catch my breath from just walking up three flights of stairs.

"Thank God, you're home," Willa says, slapping her laptop shut in the living room. "You won't believe what I found."

"You found something?" I sputter with a huff.

"Oh my God, Hales, are you okay? You look like you've been running."

I shake my head, and set my sights on the refrigerator, needing a bottle of water to unstick my tongue from the roof of my mouth.

The seconds feel like minutes by the time I pour water into my mouth. Heat radiates through every limb as my temples pulsate.

"Haley?"

With one last gulp before screwing the cap back on the bottle, I collect my thoughts of all that's happened in a mere hour. "Someone is—someone is following me. I think. I don't know. I'm getting text messages from an unknown number. Whoever it is, they're watching me."

Willa takes me by the elbow and pulls me over to our crumpled slip-covered couch and scoots in beside me. "First, take a deep breath. You're going to hyperventilate." Willa practices yoga daily and preaches every trick in the book to help someone relax. Most of the time it works, but now, I'm not sure if anything will be able to calm me down. "Good, now one more." She breathes along with me, guiding me to try and hold the air in my lungs a bit longer than I would and to release it slowly. "I thought you were just going to meet Liam for ice cream. When did all of this come about?"

I inhale through my nose once more before answering. "While I was there, my phone was buzzing like crazy. This person just kept sending message after message. I left the wharf feeling freaked out. Then with a split-second decision, I told a news crew on site that I had information about the missing baby. I thought—"

"What? Haley...why would you do that?"

"To clear my name? The monster they are accusing me of being wouldn't go in front of a reporter and give their side of the story, right?"

Willa's face contorts with a combination of concern and confusion. "Yeah, a monster probably would." She waves her hands in front of her face. "We're getting off topic and you still need to calm down. I'm sorry if I'm upsetting you more. I'm just worried about you. You shouldn't take part in any interviews without an attorney by your side."

Shame weighs heavily on my head and I rest my elbows on my thighs to lean forward.

"I found some information on the Smiths," Willa utters.

I swallow hard like I'm forcing a marble down my throat.

"What did you find?"

Willa runs her hand in circles along my back, between my shoulder blades, which is making me more nervous for whatever she's about to say. "Lara came into her fortune before marrying

Corbin, but as money typically goes, it caused some kind of big feud between her and her family that erupted at a fundraiser. She was arrested for disorderly conduct. The article isn't too detailed but it's clear Lara has had a troubled past."

I contemplate her words, unease gnawing at me. "But I don't know if her fortune has anything to do with a missing child," I say, my voice reflecting my uncertainty. "Do you?"

Willa's downcast expression tells me she's as puzzled as I am. "No, I guess not, but this just makes me feel like an attorney is crucial. We need someone to defend your innocence."

With the Smiths continuing to blame me, it's becoming clearer by the minute that unless I fall into a pile of money soon, I'm going to be taken down without a chance to protect myself.

My shoulders slouch forward, the heaviness of our discussion anchors me to the sofa as I lose sight of hope. "Did you find any other information?"

Willa inhales sharply and her eyebrows lift with a hint of hope. "I did. There's a public deposition summary on file with the Newport County Court. It's about thirty pages and it's going to take a bit to get through. Maybe we can find something in there." Willa takes her laptop from the side arm of the couch and lifts the screen, and the glow illuminates her slight expression of optimism. "I'll download it and we can print it at the library."

I forgot to remove my phone from my back pocket when I sat down, but the incessant buzzing commences, reminding me I'm sitting on top of it. *Too bad I didn't just break the thing.* I lean to the side and tear it out before tossing it onto the coffee table where it continues to buzz.

Willa freezes, her fingertips still pinching the laptop screen. "Is that whoever—"

"No one else texts me this much," I grumble.

Willa places her laptop down beside her and leans forward to take my phone. "Hales, you have thirty unread messages."

"I don't know what to say or if I should say anything. I shouldn't, right?"

A look of concern flickers across Willa's face as her eyebrows furrow. "Uh—okay. Here, I'm going to download an app onto your phone that will help us trace the unknown number." Willa never fails to think on her feet unlike me who succumbs to the paralysis of fear.

"Okay." If we find a name associated with the contact, I can report it to the police, but it's hard to think the police will help me when I'm still a person of interest.

"I'm reading through the messages too," she says, leaning back into the couch. She props her foot up on the coffee table and swipes her finger up and down the display on my phone.

Her silence is much louder than she must intend, and my anxiety is riveting through me like I've been injected with caffeine.

"Liam wants to make sure you made it home safely," she says, her words calming me for a moment as I think of the distraction he offered, the one I wish I could have back now. "That's sweet of him."

Liam is sweet and thoughtful, and I should check on *him* after what happened at the wharf, the poor guy.

Willa places my phone down. "Oh..."

"What?" I question, eager to know what's popped into her head.

"Did you say there was something in Lara's list of online searches that mentioned a marital mediator or something?"

"Yeah, but they seemed like any other couple while leaving their house for the gala last night."

Willa's gaze is fixed on her laptop screen. I lean over to see what she's looking at but she's tapping her pointer finger gently against the keys as the cursor blinks on an empty search bar.

"Does anyone ever really know when a couple is having

issues?" Willa asks. "Even on social media, we see what people want us to see, not the truth."

"I guess not, but what are you thinking?"

"I'm not sure. I'm trying to piece this all together." She seems a bit defeated, matching the way I feel.

I like to think I usually know what to do in most situations. Yet, I can't see clearly through any of what's happening.

Two piercing alarms erupt from either side of us, making me jump from my seat. My heart lodges in my throat as I fleetingly search for the cause of panic. "What the—"

My phone flashes on the table as the alarm repeats. I notice Willa's phone also lighting up on the table next to the kitchen. She grabs my phone before I lunge for it then tosses her head back. "There's the Amber Alert," she says. "I was wondering why there hadn't been one if a child had already been missing for almost twenty-four hours. I would have thought they'd send this out right away."

I'm clutching my chest, all my muscles tighten and ache. I take the phone from her hand and focus on the Emergency Alert stating:

EMERGENCY ALERT
Active Amber ALERT - Abducted child
FALLON SMITH
1 year old, white, female, blonde hair, brown eyes
Unknown mode of transportation. Unknown suspects.
Last seen at: 1113 Ocean High Road, Newport, RI
Call 9-1-1 with information.

"The word 'suspects' is plural," I point out to Willa.

"I saw... That's good. That's really good," she says, pinching her lip while staring at me with an emotionless flat expression.

After hearing about Liam's defining doe-eyed look earlier, there's no other way to describe Willa's expression... She knows her words aren't true, but she's looking right at me while she says them. I need honesty, not false hope.

As if she can read my thoughts, her eyes widen, and she pokes her finger into the air. "You know what...we need to get the deposition printed. Then there's something else I think we should do."

SEVENTEEN

Police sirens ring across the county now that there's an active Amber Alert. Everyone on the streets looks like they don't know what to do except check the perimeter. If someone abducted a baby, they've had plenty of time to travel across the bridge and leave the state, but the efforts in town are apparent.

"Has a picture of the baby been posted anywhere? Do people know who they are looking for?" Willa asks as we slink through the crowds on the curb.

"Just the family portrait Corbin showed me. She was just an infant in that one," I say. "There weren't any portraits of her on display in the house but there were photos of the twins. You would think their third child would be in the same bunch."

A new thought has crossed my mind. I've learned about women who have experienced losses with babies, and some find unique methods of therapy to heal their broken heart. Maybe Lara lost a baby in utero and kept the news private, but now wishes she had support. What other way to do this than to make a public scene? Though her friends and family would know if she had been pregnant or be questioning her story of having a fifteen-month-old child no one knew about. My scattered thoughts bring me back to looking to displace blame for something that has gone very wrong, or right depending on her frame of mind.

The library is quiet, and the computers are all free of use. "It'll just take me a minute to pull the file off my thumb drive and print," Willa says, plopping down at the first computer in the row of singular tables with matching devices.

I take the seat beside her and pull up the web browser to do another search on Lara and Corbin Smith, but the same results come up each time. "Did you find the deposition in the courthouse files?" I ask her.

"Yes, and there wasn't anything else listed with their names." Willa stands from her seat and hurries over to the front desk.

"That will be six dollars," the librarian says, her narrow glasses perched at the tip of her nose as she stares down at what I assume to be a screen beneath the countertop.

I reach into my purse to pull out the twenty I know I have in my wallet. "Willa, here," I call over as I see her reaching into her purse too.

"I got it," she says, shooing me off.

My parents were like Willa, always giving, helping, and covering everyone's checks at restaurants. They had the money and were never frugal with it. It seems ironic now, thinking back to their mantra of "a selfless person with riches will gain more from every penny given." I wanted to believe it was true and I did. Until it wasn't.

I stare out the library window through the tops of pink azalea bushes. Every person walking by seems preoccupied with their phones. Phones have become a source of comfort over the years—a way to hide from reality. I felt the same until today. My comfort has been stripped away with the messages I've received. Although the messages stopped right after Willa downloaded the call tracer app, I'm not going to assume I've seen the last of them.

The ground beneath me vibrates when Willa jumps back into her chair and slaps the stack of papers from Lara's court deposition down onto the edge of my small desk.

I've only just skimmed the cover page when something stands out like a neon flashing light in the dark. I take the paper, bringing it closer to make sure I'm seeing what I think I'm seeing.

"What is it?" she asks.

I point to the subject line that reads: Larissa Hoyt Smith vs. City of Newport.

"Larissa?" Willa asks.

"Lara is Larissa?" I question out loud.

Willa flips through the few pages and scans her finger from line to line until she stops where the court transcript begins. "Well, I saw this:"

By Ms. Lemur

Q. Good afternoon

A. Good afternoon

Q. Could you please identify yourself and state any additional names you use or have gone by in the past?

A. Of course. My name is Larissa Smith, but I go by Lara for short.

Q. Smith is your married name, correct?

A. Yes, it is.

Q. And what is your maiden name?

A. My maiden name is Hoyt.

"Oh my God," I utter, placing the paper down and grabbing the mouse to pull up a browser.

"What? What's wrong?" Willa asks.

I type the name "Larissa Hoyt" into the search bar, watching as a list of articles and images appear on the screen.

My face burns as if I'm standing next to ignited flames. I click "Images" on the search function, needing to match Larissa Hoyt's face with Lara Smith.

"Is that Lara?" Willa asks. "Is she a celebrity or something?"

I scroll down a bit more, finding more photos including one from almost a decade ago. "This is the Larissa Hoyt I remember. She's married to Corbin Smith, going by Lara Smith, and I didn't recognize her." It's clear why I didn't with such a drastic change in appearance between then and now, but how did I not know it was her?

"That can't be her in that old picture. That woman in the picture on top and this one—they're two different people," Willa says.

"No. She must have had a lot of work done. A lot. She's unrecognizable, except for that heart-shaped beauty mark beneath her eye." Her makeup was covering it yesterday, but it isn't covered in some of these more recent photos.

"Haley..."

"Trust me. I know they are the same person."

"You knew her thirteen years ago?" She pauses for a minute and taps each finger into the air, mouthing the count of consecutive numbers. "So, when you were fourteen?"

"Have a great day, sweetheart. Don't forget, come right home after school," Mom says, giving me a tight hug and a kiss on the cheek. I'm thirteen. I should be able to do what I want after school like all the other kids.

"I will. Love you, Mom." I readjust my backpack over my shoulder and scoot out the front door, jogging down the steps before the school bus peeks over the hill.

"Freak," a voice hollers. I glance over my shoulder, finding Larissa Hoyt sitting on a white plastic picnic chair smoking a cigarette beneath the upper deck of the duplex. Her thick, mascara-coated lashes squint over her heart-shaped beauty mark. She's surrounded by her usual group of friends, girls who pencil matching beauty marks onto their faces so they can look like she does. I knew them before they had beauty marks, but Larissa has always had hers. When we make eye contact, she and the other girls laugh.

Ignore her. She's just a jerk, I tell myself.

Larissa is eighteen and gets a ride to the high school every morning. Sometimes her ride shows up before the middle school bus but she's often still here after I leave.

I always try my best to ignore her. Mom said it's the only way to not give her the satisfaction she's looking for.

I turn back toward the basketball court where the bus stops and take in a deep breath to keep moving. "I love the time of day when my mommy lets me out of my freak cage too."

"Yeah, me too," another girl says.

"Oh wait...we don't live in cages. That's just Haley Vaughn-Trapped." Larissa laughs again. "Don't worry. There's only seven more hours before you're locked back inside with the other trolls."

Her words and voice fade into the background as I cross the

street, but everything replays in my head while I try to push it away.

Dad is their landlord and has to beg them to pay their rent every month. He's given eviction warnings, but he doesn't have the heart to ever kick anyone out. Because of that, Mom and Dad said Mr. and Mrs. Hoyt might feel comfortable saying rude things behind our backs, but it's most likely due to embarrassment about the rent, and them not wanting their children to know about their financial troubles.

By the time I get to the bus stop, tears fill my eyes. I sniffle and wipe them away as quickly as I can with the sound of the bus's engine rumbling up the hill. I know better than to listen to Larissa but with how popular she seems to be, I'm always wondering how many others must think I'm a freak too.

"Yes, I knew her when I was thirteen. And I'm sure her family still hates mine just as much as they did back then, or whoever is left of them, that is."

"For what? What could any of you do to make anyone dislike you?" Willa laughs thinking this is a joke. I wish it was.

I look around the library, finding it still empty, but I don't want to be here anymore. My stomach hurts, coming to realize whose house I was in last night. If I knew...I never would have taken the job. "I don't want to talk about it here." I clear the browsing history and log out of the guest dashboard before standing up with the stack of papers.

"Haley, I've known you for...forever and you're kind of freaking me out right now."

"I'll explain everything, just not here."

Willa follows me out of the library, the wind blowing hard against us as we head toward our apartment. I hug the stack of papers to my chest, making sure I don't lose any.

"Do you think she remembers you too?" Willa asks as we step out of the library.

"I would think so."

"Then why would she hire you if her family hates yours?" Willa continues. Her questions are the same questions I have, and there are no answers percolating yet.

"I don't know," I answer, picking up my pace as the pit in my stomach grows larger by the minute.

"Slow down, Haley. I can't keep up with you," Willa says, grabbing my shoulder.

"I just want to get home." I might be better off leaving the state, but I'm not allowed to do so until after the hearing—whenever that might be.

The only sounds between Willa and me are huffs as we trudge up the stairs and make our way into the apartment. "Why did her family dislike yours?" she asks again, placing her hands down on my shoulders. "Let me help you."

"She and her family lived in the duplex my parents owned when I was thirteen."

"So?" Willa questions, pushing for an explanation.

She's dredging up memories I have buried, ones I've kept locked away in the back of my mind. I stare at her for so long, silently pleading with her not to make me tell her the story. My parents still talk about that day. They say talking about it is a form of therapy and I can't argue, because if anyone knows that therapy comes in different forms for everyone, it's me.

"Oh my God," she says, her voice croaking. "Just tell me. What happened?"

"There was a fire in our town house complex. Lara's twin sister, Libby, didn't make it out of the building."

Willa claps her hand over mine. "Hales... Were you in this fire too?"

"I got out in time, but yes I was." I still remember the screams, trying to listen for where they were coming from, but the smoke was rising, and flames were crawling up the walls like vines and I couldn't help anyone but myself. I was thirteen."

"Did anyone else—"

"I'm not sure how many people were injured. I just know there was one person who didn't make it out alive. After that, I spent the next several years trying to forget about the fire to avoid the memories from resurfacing. That's why I don't go home very often."

"But I don't understand. Why would Lara's family hate yours?"

I shrug. "I don't know. They blamed my dad because he was the landlord. But he wasn't even home when it happened. I think blaming someone else made their grief easier to live with. It's the only reason I can think of."

Except, it isn't...

EIGHTEEN

SATURDAY, JUNE 10TH 6:30 PM

The white noise of the bathroom vent doesn't have the same effect it typically does. The purpose is to keep the room from fogging up when there's steam. I thought it might also help with the fog I seem to be stuck in.

My back is against the inside of the door, and I have my case study notebook open on the floor in front of my pretzel crossed legs. I might not be able to write anything legible with how hard my hand is shaking but I need to get my notes of observation from Friday night. Maybe it'll help me piece more information together too.

- Bruises on children
- Madden's obsession with mermaids
- The sound of a whining dog
- Girls aren't allowed to play hide-and-seek... Why?
- Unhinged internet search history... Lara or Corbin?
- Marital issues between Lara and Corbin
- Girls speak as if they aren't allowed to have anything when they seem to have everything

- A nursery on a separate floor from the other bedrooms
- Lack of photographs of third child
- No mention of a third child
- Lara lost her sister in a fire. Effect?
- Inherited wealth from lawsuit on Lara's side
- Lara claimed to support Corbin's business. With her wealth
- Me...a member of the family who was sued for Lara's family's loss.

I'm not sure I can add more information for most of these observed points from just one night in their house. This list could span a hundred different directions, but I think it should all connect somehow. The only thing I know for sure is that I am not a coincidence in their story.

Bruises are common among active children. Mermaids are a common fantasy among children. A whining dog might have no relevance to Friday night. They may not want the girls playing hide-and-seek because they live on a cliff over the ocean, and I didn't see any sort of fence.

Lara's family, the Hoyt family, were not wealthy thirteen years ago. Then Lara's parents took my family for everything we were worth, blaming us for the fire and the death of one of their children. Dad thought he had the proper insurance to protect us if anything ever happened to any of the housing units, but he said the Hoyt family found a loophole, so Dad lost all his assets paying the lawsuit. Lara's family has already taken everything from my family, and after that financial gain, it's clear she lives the life of luxury.

My head bounces against the door as Willa knocks for the third time in an hour. "Haley, you can't stay locked in there all night. Why won't you come out?"

We only have one bathroom and I have a suitable bedroom

to lock myself in, but I needed a more confined space and white noise. I close my notebook and pinch it under my arm before standing up and unlocking the door. "I'm sorry," I tell her, avoiding eye contact.

"What can I do to help you?" she offers.

"I wish there was something. I appreciate you asking me," I say.

"So, is Lara holding you accountable for the loss of her sister or her child? Because her child is missing—no one has declared she's dead, right? The entire county is searching for her child as we speak."

The more Willa talks, the more sense I lose in what I thought I was drawing a conclusion to. I have nothing to do with their missing daughter and I'm not responsible for the death of her sister. I was thirteen. Just thirteen.

"I wish I had answers that would help me understand why any of this is happening, but the only thing I know is that Lara's family has a history of taking everything from me."

"What does that mean?" Willa asks, tossing her hands into the air as she follows me into my bedroom. This is why I closed myself in the bathroom. I need to process all of this and it's hard enough to do with just my own thoughts.

"My parents were the landlords of the building, and the court held them responsible for an oversight on an electrical license, which voided the insurance policy and left them open for a personal lawsuit."

My statement forces Willa to stop in my doorway. I assume she's trying to place all the pieces of this puzzle together, but it doesn't take much effort. "Her family took everything from your family because of their loss?"

"That's what happened, yes."

"None of this sounds fishy to you?"

"It all does, but it doesn't matter what I think, obviously.

They have the power to take people down so that's what they're trying to do, again."

Willa continues to ramble, but I stopped listening after she asked me if this sounds fishy. My phone, that I left on my bed before closing myself into the bathroom, didn't experience the same break. "The messages are back."

Unknown Number: You should have left this state while you had the chance.

Unknown Number: You think you're finding answers quicker than the police.

Unknown Number: You're wrong.

Unknown Number: It won't be long before you can convince yourself you're innocent.

Unknown Number: This won't stop until you do.

Unknown Number: It's a warning, Haley.

Unknown Number: Because I can make you stop.

Unknown Number: I can make you go away. Forever.

Willa reaches over me and grabs the phone. "Let me check the app to see if it can trace the contact."

My heart pounds as I sit on the edge of my bed, pressing my fingernails into the mattress. I try to take a deep breath, but I can't.

The name could be random. It could be fake. It could lead to someone, or it could take me nowhere.

"Uh," she says, exasperating with a huff.

"What? Who is it? My stomach is in knots right now," I complain.

Deep lines stretch across Willa's forehead and her brows knit together. "Haley, this—"

I take the phone from her hand to see what she's looking at and it takes less than a blink to feel sick to my stomach. "What is this?"

"I didn't—"

"Is this a joke?"

On the screen, listed as the source of the messages, is Willa's full name: Willa Woodrow, Newport, Rhode Island.

"Why would I put the app on your phone if I was playing games with you?" she asks, the doe-eyed look at full tilt.

"I don't know. Why would you?"

Someone is using Willa's name as a cover-up, or Willa is using her name as a cover-up. We have less than a handful of friends in common, most of which we haven't talked to since we moved off campus a couple of years ago. Jerry, her boyfriend and boss, and Willa are the only people I see on a regular basis. He works crazy hours and does not have enough time in his normal day to toy with either of us like this.

"I'm taking my phone to the police station. Maybe they can give me a better answer."

"You were just released, thank God. Do you really want to go back there right now?" Willa wraps her arms around her stomach, hugging herself for comfort. "This is making me sound like I have something to hide but, Haley, come on, we've been best friends for years. You know I would never do something like this to you. I stayed here in Newport for the summer because I was worried about you staying alone."

"I didn't do anything to anyone so I shouldn't be concerned about going to the police station, should I?" I reply, ignoring her plea of innocence.

"I'll come with you. Okay?"

"No, I—I need to go by myself. I have to sort this out, and if someone is weaponizing your name, I'll put a stop to it."

"Which is why I should go with you. It's my name."

If my world is going to continue caving in on me until I'm buried alive, I feel like I should move forward on my own, but I guess this isn't just about me anymore—not with her name mixed into the mess.

NINETEEN

SATURDAY, JUNE 10TH 8:30 PM

I wasn't expecting there to be a wait at the police station, but I suppose tracing a phone number might not be top of their priority list. I should have mentioned that the person sending me messages could have something to do with the Smith case when we arrived, but I was so flustered I only mentioned the need to trace some threatening messages I'd received. I would like to give more details now, but the desk where the station clerk sits is still vacant. The woman hasn't returned from wherever she went almost a half hour ago.

"You should just go home," I tell Willa, resting my head back against the wall behind my chair. "There's no sense in us both sitting here."

Willa pulls her thick curls behind her neck and twists them tightly around her finger before releasing them into bouncing springs. She fans herself with a brochure about the effects of drunk driving she found on the seat beside her. I thought it was just me who was sweating, but I guess not. It's hot in here, which isn't helping my patience. "I'm not leaving. I've been sitting here with you this whole time for a reason, one I'm not sure you're understanding."

"I know this isn't your fault," I tell her. "I'm just at a complete loss and have no control over what's happening to me." I need answers. I want to feel safe. I want to know if all of this would still have happened if I hadn't taken the job with the Smith family. I just feel like I couldn't be further from the answers or explanations.

"Ladies, you can follow me," a female officer says, rising from one of the desks in front of us. We stand and follow her around the bullpen until we reach the wall of office doors. She gestures for us to walk into the second room on the right. "Detective Straton will assist you."

There are two black metal chairs with leather padding facing Detective Straton's tidy desk, with only a yellow lined notebook set down in the center. I don't recognize him from the other night, but he's as clean cut and rigid as most of the other uniformed men walking around the station. And though he seems young to be a detective, I'm hoping it means he's good at what he does. "Have a seat please," he says, waving his hand toward the two chairs while he studies his notepad for a long moment before glancing up again. "Ms. Vaughn, you were just here last night in conjunction with the missing Smith baby, is that correct?"

I'm not surprised to be greeted this way, not when the case is still hot. "Yes, sir. They brought me in for questioning then I was released."

"Yes, I see that here in the notes."

"I was in the wrong place—" He lifts his hand and nods his head. It might be a gesture to show his understanding, but I don't know what anyone thinks about me after last night.

"And you are?" he says, shifting his hard stare over to Willa.

"Willa Woodrow, sir. I'm Haley's roommate."

"Why don't you tell me what's been going on," he says, leaning back into his chair and intertwining his fingers over his midsection.

I wonder what these detectives and officers are like when they're off duty. There's no personality behind his eyes, no emotions to trace along his face, and no urgency to move us along so he can move on to his next task.

"Following the events last night, I began receiving disturbing messages from an unknown number. Someone is following me, watching everything I do. The last ones I received were threats, telling me to stop, but I don't know what that means. I haven't responded to any of them. Willa downloaded a tracing app onto my phone to see if we could capture a name, but when we did, the information showed her name with a different phone number."

"I'm not responsible for any of the messages, sir," Willa chimes in with a nervous inflection as she squeezes her palms together on top of her lap.

"I assume whoever this person is must know the two of us, but neither of us knows anyone who would do something like this."

Detective Straton is scribbling down notes on his pad and nodding his head. "And you said this all began following the events last night, correct?"

"Yes, sir," I say.

"Do you think the messages have something to do with the missing child?"

"Yes, I do. The person sending the messages also warned me not to approach the news reporters on the wharf earlier today. They were clearly watching me and knew what I would say if I did answer any questions."

Detective Straton places his pen down on the notepad and straightens his posture. "Will you consent to a search of your phone records?"

"Yes, of course."

"Wait here. I have a paper I'll need you to sign to give us your consent and then I can extract the data to investigate."

I was hoping he'd have information for me right away, but they send us on our way with a promise to update me soon. Aside from telling me not to respond to any of the messages that may or may not continue, I still feel like raw bait out in the open.

Tourists still fill the streets even on a Saturday night at sunset. Most have changed out of their beach apparel to something more appropriate for dinner by the water. Despite how anyone is dressed, whoever is watching me could be wearing anything and still blend in with the crowd.

Willa's phone rings and I watch as she reaches to pull it out of her purse, her hands still trembling. I feel responsible for her being dragged into this—whatever this is. "One second, it's Jerry. He's been worried. I just need to let him know what's going on," she says, connecting the call and moving a few steps ahead of me.

Her voice trails off after she says, "Hey, baby..." I'm not sure if she's speaking quietly so I can't hear her or if there's just too much chatter around us.

The hill toward our apartment glows in orange hues as the horizon lines divide the sun in half, but as I think about getting a few hours of sleep, I realize tomorrow is just another Monday. I still have another final to get through, and I'm not sure how I'll be able to focus on studying.

I'll get through this. I have no choice.

A scuffle behind me steals my thoughts—and my breath—as a gloved hand claws around my mouth and nose with so much pressure the air locks into my lungs. I can't make a sound. An arm wrenches around my stomach and I'm pushed into a narrow alley between two blocks of souvenir shops.

My heart is in my throat, my stomach churning. I'm trapped in a feral struggle, feet grazing the ground. I fight against their hold, but I'm weaker than they are. Shock overwhelms me. I can't even twist my head and a cold sweat steals my strength.

Whilst panicking, I try to focus on my senses: a dumpster, a metal fence, musty fabric from the glove over my face, and my feet scraping against the uneven pavement.

The person shoves my back up against the brick edifice and pins me at the neck. They're wearing a ski mask and a black sweatshirt with their hood pulled halfway down their face. "I warned you," a raspy voice seethes. Their other hand moves to grip my neck, and they squeeze so hard my tongue jolts out of my mouth. I can't even blink as I stare at the black-clad figure. My head is becoming heavier and harder to hold up. Air isn't moving through my lungs. I try to kick my feet to fight my way out of this hold, but my pulse is weak. A cough threatens to purge up my throat but lodges on the way. The cold sweat becomes icy, and I give in to the numbing blindness.

TWENTY
SATURDAY, JUNE 10TH 9:30 PM

"Haley!"

Darkness sloshes around me like ocean waves at night, the moon is hiding behind clouds. The water is neither warm nor cold—it's nothingness.

I've seen nothingness before but haven't felt its touch. Some things we never forget, even after thirteen years have passed. I had forgotten this indescribable feeling.

There's so much smoke, it seems impenetrable, but it isn't. I can't see where I'm half walking, half crawling, trying to move as quickly as I can with no sense of direction. I've lived here for years and know every nook and cranny of our home but can't find the front door. A radiating heat encircles me, and I try to stay in the center, hoping the flames aren't engulfing the door. In our six-unit townhouse, we live front and center. I wonder if everyone else has already found their door and if I'm the last. Shouts and screams come from every direction, but it could be the sound of the alarms I'm hearing too.

I remember learning about a scalding hot doorknob and what it means in a fire. It's the only door I can reach though, and I believe it should lead me out to the front porch. I'm coughing so hard; I'm gasping for air by the time I wrap the fabric of my T-shirt around the doorknob and shove it open. A gust of wind spirals through the smoke that was following me out the door where I fall to my knees. Everything in front of me is blurry but it isn't nothingness. I drag myself toward the few steps leading down to the front path and again struggle to take in air, gasping through what feels like a narrow straw.

I rest on the grass, feeling the cool blades tickle the side of my cheek. Just after I close my eyes, someone lifts me up, cradling me in their arms and carrying me away from the townhomes. Lights flash around me, red and blue, but it hurts to keep my eyes open for too long.

"Where are you parents?" a man shouts.

I try to speak but I can only choke on the air in my lungs. I shake my head, trying to tell whoever asked that they aren't with me, but I know my answer isn't clear.

"Were they inside with you?" He asks the right question this time, and again I shake my head to say no. They were out and have no clue what's happening to their home or me, at least not at that moment.

"Haley, can you hear me?" Hot hands grip my shoulders and fingernails dig into my flesh. "Open your eyes. Come on, girl, open your eyes!"

The screams of sirens grow in the distance. They sound just like they did that night thirteen years ago. I've heard them since of course, but it's different when you think they might be coming for you. I try to take in air, but it feels like I have something lodged in my throat, making it seem impossible to steal any oxygen from around the blockage.

"I don't know. I just found her this way. She was behind me. Then she wasn't. I searched up, down, and in between each of the blocks we were on and then I found her back here."

Willa. That's her voice.

"Haley. Her name is Haley—she's my roommate. I didn't see what happened because I was on the phone walking ahead of her."

Who is she talking to?

"Haley, can you open your eyes for me?" an unfamiliar female voice asks. My eyelids won't move, no matter how hard I try to lift my lashes. Light bleeds through them before someone pries my eyes open, momentarily blinding me.

Multiple hands are touching me, my neck, my wrist, my torso, head. I don't want to be touched. "Okay, Haley, I'm going to put a cervical collar around your neck to prevent further injury until we can get you checked over." The thought of something else touching my neck sends a chill up and down my limbs. I'd rather remain in the dark here where I can't see what's happening around me, so I try to ignore the plastic support tightening around me. Then another object tightens around my mouth and nose, but I feel movement of air going into my lungs. It just doesn't seem like enough.

"Could I please come too?"

I don't hear an answer to Willa's question, but I feel her hand embracing mine.

No one has told me I'll be okay. I don't know what I look like or what state they left my body in. Is it just my neck that feels injured? Or is it more?

"Haley, could you try to open your mouth for me? Air is passing in and out of your lungs, but it might feel like it's hard to breathe since you have some swelling. We're going to take good care of you."

My heart pounds against my chest as I try to open my eyes again. Blinking fluorescent lights attack my aching eyes but I can see two blurry faces. "There you are," the woman says.

Minutes must have gone by before the blur clears up, allowing me to see a paramedic and Willa. Tears stain Willa's red cheeks, but she squeezes my hand a little tighter. "I'm so sorry I stepped ahead of you. I shouldn't have left you," she cries.

"Okay, let's try to relax," the paramedic says, but I'm not sure if she's speaking to me or Willa.

The ride to the hospital doesn't take very long but while being rushed around on a stretcher, in and out of doors and down a hallway, I wish I hadn't opened my eyes. I don't like hospitals. The blood—there's always so much of it here.

"You're going to have to wait out here for now," someone tells Willa.

Her hand slips away from mine and I clench my eyes closed, feeling another round of panic overwhelm me.

The plastic collar has been removed and I'm able to breathe easier now, even without the oxygen mask. I still don't know what the damage is, and the wait is making me sick to my stomach while reclining in this hospital bed alone, staring at a closed curtain.

"Haley Vaughn," another woman calls out as she pulls the curtain out and around her, entering the small space I'm confined within. "I'm Dr. Darcy," she says, placing her tablet in between her arm and side. "I have good news for you. The CT scan, MRI, and blood work have all come back clean, which means the injury to your neck is superficial. You'll likely have bruising and soreness, but no permanent damage." The doctor seems to force a smile while staring at me and I'm not sure I understand the look on her face. I'm grateful to be okay but there's something else she's not saying and it's scaring me.

"Thank you," I say, my voice scratchy and broken as if I have laryngitis.

Dr. Darcy takes a hold of the rolling stool beneath the computer anchored to the back wall and glides it to my side before taking a seat. "Do you remember anything that happened tonight? It appears you were strangled. You have a few welts on your cheeks and forehead too, indicating a struggle."

"I think the person was a man—they were, uh—dressed in all black, had a mask, and pulled me off the main road."

"It was a man?" she replies.

"I'm not a hundred percent sure. They were taller and stronger than me. The person whispered something, but I can't remember what." I try to clear my throat, still feeling like something is stuck around my tonsils. "That's when they shoved me into the wall and choked me."

"I can't imagine how scary that must have been," she says, resting her hand on top of mine. "I'm going to have an officer come in to speak with you before we give you discharge papers. Medically, you are fit to leave the hospital, but we want to make sure to keep you safe too."

How many officers will I have to speak to today before something worse happens to me?

A knock on whatever is metal around me and outside of the curtain startles me. Dr. Darcy opens the curtain. "Come on in," she says.

"Haley, I'm—"

"Detective Straton," I say, finishing his second introduction of the second longest night of my life this week.

"I'm glad you remember me," he says, scratching at his eyebrow. It was only hours ago that we spoke.

"The call came in with your name, so I wanted to make sure I was the one who came down to talk to you." He takes his cap off and holds it between his hands in front of his waist. "Haley, do you think the messages from that unknown number and the incident tonight are related?"

"It's hard to think they weren't related."

"Do you remember anything this person said? If they said something."

I try to recall what happened before everything went dark. "I'm pretty sure he said something just before he strangled me but I'm not sure what. I just remember thinking he must have been the one sending the messages."

"Can you say whether he was taller than you? Was he thin, average build?"

I shrug. "Most people are taller than me." I'm five-foot-two. "He was tall enough to say an average height and build but I can't give many more details."

"I understand. Well, unfortunately, we haven't gotten any information back regarding that phone number yet as it seems to be coming from a burner phone. We have officers searching the area you were attacked in, but someone who took the time to disguise themselves likely won't still be walking around looking that way. What I need from you is to keep the doors locked at home and try to avoid going anywhere alone until we can gather more information. In the meantime, I'll take you and your friend home for the night to ensure you get there safely."

For all I know, this cop could be the one who's after me. I shouldn't get in his cruiser. I probably shouldn't even give him any more information than he already has.

TWENTY-TWO

SUNDAY, JUNE 11TH 6:00 AM

Detective Straton took us home and swept through the apartment to make sure he was leaving us in a safe place. He also said someone would remain on guard outside for the night.

If only I could sleep. Willa didn't get much sleep either. We're both curled up on the couch under a mess of blankets and pillows, staring at the longest thread of recycled news clips that has already played throughout the day.

Willa glances over at me for the fifth time in the past twenty minutes. "You need more ice. That pack can't still be cold." She groans while pulling herself up from the couch, snatching the melted ice pack and slugs through the living room on the way to the kitchen. I've yet to look in a mirror and I'm wondering how long I can go without doing so.

"Thankfully I don't have to go onto campus today. I can't imagine going in there looking like—" whatever it is I look like. I can't even imagine the stories people could conjure from speculation. "I guess I won't look much different tomorrow when I have to take my last final."

Willa doesn't respond to my statement right away. Instead, she returns from the kitchen and carefully presses a fresh ice pack against my sore neck. "I'm sure your professor will understand if you have to reschedule your final."

"I doubt that. They want to finish up for the summer just as much as the students."

Willa's focus skates toward the coffee table, and she takes my phone in her hands. She stares at the display for a few seconds then holds my phone up in front of my face so the facial recognition feature unlocks my phone. I should be thankful the phone still recognizes me. "What popped up?"

"Girl, Liam has been texting you like crazy. He's been super worried about you since you didn't respond when he checked to see if you got home safely yesterday after your ice-cream date."

"My response isn't going to make him worry less," I mutter.

Willa closes her eyes and takes in a sharp breath through her nose. "The guy had a bloody lip the last time you saw him. I responded on your behalf last night while you were still out of it and told him you were safe now, but you had been jumped and we were at the hospital. I felt he should know in case this person who attacked you was the same one who hurt him."

I slouch back into the couch cushion, defeated. "What else did you tell him?" I know I sound aggravated, but I walked away from him yesterday to spare him the trouble that's following me around like a leech.

"He wanted to come to the hospital, and I told him not to, and I'd let him know how you were doing in the morning. He wants to stop by. He offered to bring over some breakfast if you're up to it."

"No, I don't want him to see me like this."

"Okay, so normally I would understand where you're coming from but with him being injured yesterday too, I don't think we should close him out of the loop. He might have more clues about who could have hit him, and it might help the detective and his team gather more information on your attacker."

"The detectives aren't concerned with me. There's a child missing. I'm sure I'm the last concern on their list."

As if I needed a highlight reel to underline my statement, the silent video of Lara and Corbin holding each other outside of their home in the dark, still dressed in their evening attire on Friday night has been shown once every half hour on repeat.

"Police are still searching for fifteen-month-old Fallon Smith who disappeared from her home on Friday night," a news reporter's voice overlays the video. It was filmed in front of the police station during a press conference yesterday. Lara and Corbin are both in dark sweatshirts, with red eyes.

"What are your thoughts at the moment?" a reporter from behind the camera asks them.

Lara sniffles and takes in a shuddering breath. "If anyone knows anything about our sweet baby," she says with a gasp. "We know the first thirty-six hours are—" A sob erupts from her throat, stealing the remaining words she was going to speak. Her hand trembles as she covers her mouth, holding her stare squarely on the camera lens as if it was a person giving her unthinkable news. Corbin turns her away from the camera and buries his wife into his side.

"Please, no more questions," he says, holding his hand up.

The video cuts back to the news station and the two reporting anchors sitting at their curved table. "She *is* correct, Greg. The first thirty-six hours *are* the most crucial," the female anchor says.

"Our thoughts and prayers go out to the Smith family during this difficult time. If you know anything about this missing child, please call the Newport police immediately," Greg, the co-anchor echoes.

Willa curls her hands into fists by her side, her shoulders up by her ears. "My God."

"That poor baby," I say. "I can't imagine what condition she must be in right now, or if she is even with someone." I shudder at the thought, imagining a helpless child crying their heart out with no one around to take care of her.

"Haley. This is obviously bigger than a missing baby. Look at yourself?"

"I don't want to see," I tell her.

"I get it. I do. Hales, please, listen to me. I can't just sit back and watch this evolve. This is becoming more than even I can just help with. That's why I asked Liam to come by. The more people around you right now, the better off you'll be. It's bad enough you won't let me help you with an attorney."

"Okay, okay," I say, holding my hands up at her. "Please, stop." The headache I've been battling all night is throbbing again.

"This could happen again. You can't be alone right now, and I still have to work. I need you to be on the same page as me. I'm doing this because I love you, Haley."

"Doing what?" I ask, feeling like I missed part of whatever plan she's referring to.

"You need to let Liam help if he wants to help. Who else beside me can you depend on right now?"

"I literally just met him. I couldn't ask him to be my body-guard or whatever it is you're thinking."

"I will ask him," she says.

"No," I argue, "you won't."

"He's on his way over with breakfast," she says, holding my phone against her chest. "I'm hungry. So, deal with it."

I try to lunge forward to retrieve my phone from her grip but the muscles in my neck feel like they're shredding when I move too quickly, which keeps me hostage in the same position I've been reclining in all night. "You can't just—"

"Fine, what about your parents? I'm sure they will do what-ever they can to help."

"No," I snap. "Do not call or message them. They're— they're out of town right now and I don't want to worry them.

Promise me, you won't, Willa?" That's the very last thing I need right now.

"Okay, okay," Willa says, taking the hint as she holds her hands up in defense. "I'm going to see if there's still a police officer guarding the outside to let them know we're expecting company."

Willa drops my phone but at the other end of the couch, which feels more like a city block away. The only thing within my reach is the remote. I change the channel with hostility for torturing me with the same clips over and over.

Another news station pops up next and though my sour stomach is telling me to keep flipping through the channels, the sight of a new view of the Smiths' home holds my stare hostage.

> *"For almost thirty-six hours, fifteen-month-old Fallon Smith has been missing from her parents and two older sisters after being taken out of her crib. An investigation has been underway since Friday but without any trace of what could have happened to this little girl. Officials are asking residents to be vigilant and keep a lookout for a young child with short blonde hair and blue eyes."*

The house has been closed off with yellow caution tape and there are cruisers and reporters all around their property. Lara is far behind the reporter, close to the front steps where she has her arms wrapped around both twins.

The camera pans in toward Lara, past the reporter, catching a view of her, worse for wear than the prior clip. This time, she's without makeup, in a gray worn sweatshirt and loose jogging pants. The girls are now beside her but still in their pajamas, both squeezing a plush toy in their hands as Lara's hands rest on their shoulders. It's clear the girls don't want to be standing there in front of a camera. They're trying to move away from Lara, but she seems to have a good grip on them. I'm sure the struggle is insignificant as the world focuses on the mother in turmoil. However, I do wonder where Corbin is or why he isn't standing with them. Maybe he's out with the search party. I would be if it was my child. I wouldn't be able to sleep or stand still knowing she was out there somewhere without me.

The front door opens, my chest tightens like a vise squeezing my ribs. I hit the power button on the television, wanting to avoid a watch party. Willa walks in first, takes a couple of brown paper bags out of Liam's hands and brings them into the kitchen. He moves past her with a tray of coffees and sets them down on the table in front of me then kneels beside me. The expression on his face is a mirror of the sight I've been avoiding. He's not in the best shape either as more bruises have bloomed across the left side of his face overnight, but his lip looks better.

He hasn't said anything, and the silence is making me squirm. "I'm so sorry this happened," he says eventually, his voice tender and gentle—the way a therapist would speak to a troubled patient. "When's the last time you took something for the pain?"

"She needs to eat first," Willa shouts from the kitchen. She's taken on a nurse-mode since we got home. It's made me think about what it would be like to go home alone, to no one after what happened. I realize I spent so long dreaming of independence and freedom while growing up, but as of late, the thoughts of loneliness scare me. Willa has Jerry and as far as I can tell, she's eventually going to want to live with him, as she should.

I'll be alone. I don't want that.

Liam reaches toward my face, and I jolt, but he sweeps a strand of hair away from my cheek and curls it behind my ear. "It's okay. I know you said you needed some time to figure this all out yesterday, but this isn't about me looking for another date. Let me help a bit. I won't be overbearing or get in your way." It's as if he can hear my thoughts. Maybe I'm more transparent than I thought.

"What about work?" I ask. "Don't you have to be there?"

Liam smiles and releases a quiet sigh. "Shh," he whispers with a light chuckle. "It's Sunday—no school today."

The way he is gazing at me...it's like he sees something in me—maybe something I haven't discovered about myself yet.

Willa brings out a plate of muffins and a stack of napkins. "He got a few different flavors since he didn't know what you like. You're so thoughtful, Liam, and adorable," she coos.

Willa's compliments to Liam make my cheeks burn. She's been more direct with him in just a few minutes than I've been the two other times we were together. "You didn't have to go through all this trouble," I tell him, "But this is—you're very sweet."

"You know what I've learned about you in the very short amount of time I've known you?" he asks.

His question has a simple answer, the only answer I can come up with. "That I'm a magnet for trouble and bad luck?"

Liam tilts his head to the side and purses his lips. "Mmm, no. I've learned that you only give and never take even if you are desperate for a hand. It's noble, but not practical. If someone wants to help you, let them help. What if they want to be a giver too? You can't just hog the role of good person." A smile unfurls across his lips.

"Yup. You hit the nail on the head," Willa says. She cups her hand around her mouth to shield her face from where I'm sitting. "But if you're aggressively kinder, she buckles under pressure."

I poke the back of her leg with my sock-covered toe. "Hey! Don't give away my—"

Another knock on the door.

My breath catches in my throat as I stare at the door, wishing I could see through the wood.

"Detective Straton," he announces from the other side of the door.

"I'll let him in," Willa says.

He steps in and closes the door behind him, still dressed in the same white polo and khaki pants he was wearing last night. "Gellar? Long time no see, bud. How's it going?"

"Jackson," Liam replies. "I didn't know you were promoted to detective. Congratulations, man. That's great." Liam stands up to shake Detective Straton's hand.

They know each other. I shouldn't be surprised, what with how small the year-round community is here. If someone grows up in Newport, they know everyone else who did, too.

"Family or friend?" Detective Straton asks him.

"Friend. Just checking in on Haley to see how she's holding up."

"Ah," Detective Straton says. "Okay." He straightens his shoulders and loops his thumbs into his belt loops. The hint of tension between the two men piques my curiosity, making me want to know more about how they know each other.

TWENTY-THREE

SUNDAY, JUNE 11TH 8:00 AM

Just after Detective Straton leaves, a wave of relief sloshes through me. They have a suspect in custody for last night's attack. They haven't gotten to the bottom of the unknown number, masked with Willa's contact information, and he couldn't give us any information on whether this person was connected to the Smith case. I'm still very much in the dark.

"Small world, huh?" Willa asks me.

I've been so consumed with staring at the black screen of the television I forgot she was sitting next to me on the couch. "You mean Liam and Detective Straton?"

"Yeah. I know this isn't a big town, but I wonder how many people grew up here and stayed."

My conversations with Liam haven't flowed into our pasts or where we grew up, family life. Each time we've been together there have been more pressing topics to discuss unfortunately. "That's a good question," I reply.

"Do you know if Liam grew up here?" Willa curls her knees into her chest then drapes a blanket over her shoulders.

"I'm not sure. I guess I kind of assumed he did."

Liam returns to the apartment after walking Detective

Straton out ten or fifteen minutes ago. Maybe they were catching up. "Everything okay?" I ask him.

"Oh yeah. He used to patrol at the school I work at. I never knew why he left or why he was replaced, but his promotion makes sense. He's a good guy." I know I'm reading too far into everyone's words and inflections, but he doesn't sound overly convincing. I'm also running on little to no sleep and shouldn't fall into my bad habit of psychoanalyzing anything right now. "I'm glad they have a suspect in custody."

"Do you think there's any correlation between the guy from last night and the one who sideswiped you at the wharf?" I ask.

Liam shrugs. "I gave Jackson the best description I could of the skateboarder. He said there might be a connection, but he couldn't confirm. He's looking into it." I'd prefer these instances to be coincidences rather than entangled, but we were together when the unknown contact was messaging me. Nothing would surprise me.

What I really want to know is why Corbin wasn't in the picture with Lara on the news this morning. He's the one who was so strict about the girls not playing hide-and-seek. Then there were the bruises on both girls, and the internet search history showing someone looking for a marriage mediator. I'd love to know if they have Corbin in custody as a suspect.

"There's so much more to this than what anyone is noticing," I say, glancing over at Liam who seems glossed over while staring out the sliding doors.

"Like what?"

I consider telling him about the townhouse fire, but I'm not sure I can muster the story again. Willa is staring at me, likely curious if I will bring it back up but I think it's consumed me enough over the last day.

The messages, Lara's phone call, my past connection to her. All the pieces are scattered around me but none of them match up. "I don't know. I think that's the problem."

"Just before you got here, we saw Lara being interviewed on the news. The two little girls were by her side and looked like they hadn't slept in days. However, their father wasn't with them, which seems odd. I wonder if he could be the suspect they have in custody?" Willa questions.

Those unknown messages could easily have been from him.

"He wasn't with his wife and kids?" Liam asks Willa.

"No, but it could have been a coincidence too."

"He could be out looking for the baby," I add.

Liam rubs his hands around the back of his neck. "You know, maybe I can talk to someone at the elementary school and see if there's any information they could share with me. If one of the Smiths' children is missing, I would be hard pressed to think the other two aren't considered to be in danger. Maybe there's a history within the family that the public isn't aware of. Yet."

I wish it could be so easy to just ask someone. "Would there be privacy laws protecting the Smiths within the school system?" Liam releases his hands from the back of his neck, red marks left behind. A question to the wrong person could get him in trouble. "I don't want you to jeopardize your career for a question."

"Yes, but there are sometimes perks to living in a small community. Plus, I'm friendly with one of the admins there. Let me see if I can find out some information. I won't press, but anything more than what we know right now would be helpful."

"Hales," Willa says, shaking her head. "Just let him see if he can find anything out. Look at you. After last night, whether the person was Corbin, or whoever...laws have been broken. Now isn't the time to be worried about following all the rules in life."

I guess I can't argue her point. I've never gone looking for trouble, but that didn't stop trouble looking for me.

TWENTY-FOUR
SUNDAY, JUNE 11TH 7:00 PM

Liam left a few hours ago after Willa canceled her shift at the restaurant tonight. Neither of them want to leave me alone, which I appreciate, but I can't remain a hostage in this apartment either. I have to get to my class tomorrow and I need to study all night, which seems like an impossible feat after hardly sleeping the last two nights.

"How's the studying?" Willa asks, poking her head around the living room wall to check on me, as she has been doing on the hour every hour.

"Still brutal," I say, clicking off the web browser on my laptop and going back to my study guide.

"Do you think Liam would be able to come back for a few hours? Jerry just called me because one of the waiters didn't show up for their shift at five then called out sick an hour later. They're short staffed at the restaurant. He said he understood if I couldn't leave you, but—"

"Please go to work," I say, dropping my head back against the sofa. "I'm fine. I'm not going anywhere. The door will be locked."

Willa leans her head against the corner of the wall. "Could you at least ask if he's free to come over?"

I consider the thought but both she and Liam have already done so much for me today. I don't feel right asking for more. "I really can't. He already spent hours over here today. He has work tomorrow and might need to prepare lesson plans or something. I'm just going to be studying all night anyway."

Willa's quiet for a long minute then lets out a groan. "I'm going to be checking on you, so promise me you'll keep your phone next to you."

I slide my phone closer to my lap so she sees it's beside me. "I promise."

Willa rushes around the apartment for the next twenty minutes, trying to get herself ready to leave for her shift. It's like watching a swinging pendulum, the number of times she walks between the kitchen and her bedroom. She needs to look her best while at work. Even though she and Jerry have been together so long, she still feels the need to keep up with her appearances. If I worked at a restaurant, I would be disheveled, running around in those circles.

With a kiss on the cheek and a toss of her bag over her head to sling across her body, she takes one last look in the mirror next to the small coat closet and grabs hold of the front door-knob. "Secure the door chain when I leave. I won't be home past eleven thirty since it's a Monday tomorrow, but I'll call you when I'm able to cut out of there, so you'll know when to expect me home."

"Don't rush because of me." I shift my feet that are propped up on the coffee table and spot Willa's phone on top of the stack of magazines. "Don't forget your phone."

"Oh my gosh. Thank you," she says, turning back toward me. I lunge forward, forgetting about the pains in my neck and grab the phone, instantly regretting my decision to move so fast.

I wince and grit my teeth, trying not to let a whine escape as I stand up to hand her the phone.

"Hales! I can get it," Willa says, rushing toward me. "Please take it easy."

"I will. I promise."

With a look of hesitation pinching at the right side of her cheek, she lets out a sigh before stepping out and securing the door locks with her key from outside.

With sluggish steps, I make my way to the door so I can secure the chain lock like she instructed.

The moment I make it back to the couch and stare at the dark TV, I remember I should be studying for the final that I'll probably fail with my head in forty places at once.

With another groan, I grab my textbook and notebook off the side table next to where I'm sitting and stare at the four-hundred-page book that makes my brain hurt.

Taking notes helps me organize information in my head, and over the past hour or so I have managed to copy down the entire textbook unit on Psychology and Ethics. Every page has facts that will likely be on the final, but this last section isn't sitting correctly with me. Even after dissecting each line, I can't understand how ethics can be such a roadblock to helping someone. I read the topic header once more and shake my head.

Naturalistic Observation: Reactivity and the Ethics of Concealed Observation

I've read this section so many times in the last couple of weeks, trying to wrap my head around the pros and cons of the subject matter. The cons are that this topic is controversial to itself and can't be used as a form of practice on patients.

Except, I don't understand the purpose of observing anyone with their understanding and agreement of the observatory process. It's human nature to act differently when being watched, which can have varying outcomes depending on the person's feelings toward the study. Although unethical, I believe the only way to get a true understanding of someone's environment and behavior is to observe without warning. The ethics of psychology don't always work in a patient's favor but to practice and maintain a license, one must be always ethical.

At all times. No matter what.

Ethical.

If the Smiths continue to blame me for their missing daughter, I won't have the chance to obtain my license to practice. It seems like they hold that power in their hands, and until the search is over for their little girl, there's no way to know how this will end. I need some kind of evidence, proving that there is more to this story than anyone knows.

I glance down at my phone and tap the screen to see the time. It's almost eight thirty. I close my laptop, notebook, and textbook, and stack them on top of the coffee table.

My purse and keys are on the entryway table beneath the wide rectangular mirror. I shouldn't be venturing out right now, but time is not in anyone's favor. I slide open the closet door, grab my oversized sweatshirt and slip my feet into my running shoes. My baseball cap sitting on the top shelf of the closet catches my eye, and I take that too.

I'll be back before Willa's shift is over and since I'm taking the fire escape down to the ground level, avoiding the security guard, no one will have to worry about where I am.

TWENTY-FIVE
SUNDAY, JUNE 11TH 8:30 PM

I lock the doors as soon as I slide into the driver's seat of my car and check over my shoulder into the backseat. It's something I used to do out of habit when I first started driving around alone at night, but those fears had slipped away the older I became. They're back now.

While navigating the back roads along the coast, I find myself squeezing the steering wheel tighter and tighter the farther I go. There's a steep hill that leads up to the cliff's peak and the area is quiet compared to what I witnessed on the news this morning. I figured there would be flashing lights coming from every direction. I've always wondered if police stop searching for a missing person at a certain hour due to the darkness. Maybe they're searching somewhere else. The wooded area around the property is thick, but not dense.

I'm not sure what I was hoping to find here tonight but I needed another look at the area, and I was curious if their back window would still be uncovered where it stares out over the cliff. I can't see the back of the house from here though.

My palms are covered with sweat as I pry open the car door to slip outside. Even my breaths sound louder than usual. If I can just catch a glimpse of what they are like behind closed doors, it would be insightful. Just something, I guess.

The wooded area connects the hill up to their property line against the far end of the cliff overlooking the ocean. I move slowly, waiting for my eyes to adjust to the darkness so I can see where I'm going while weaving in and out of trees. The lit bridge off on the horizon offers enough of a glow to give me a hint of where I'm stepping as I try to avoid dry sticks and pinecones. The unmarked dirt path begins to decline as I reach an area closer to the edge of the cliff. The wooded land doesn't drop off like the ledge behind their house does, but the downward hill is steep while heading toward the water.

"She's not here!" a voice echoes against the rocky terrain that spills into the lapping water.

"Will you just give me a damn minute?"

What was that? I tiptoe a little further, closer to the edge of the woods, to get more visibility of the small shoreline. I take my phone out of my back pocket and open the camera to zoom in like a pair of binoculars and click record while I'm at it.

My heart thunders through my entire body and the urge to choke on the air I'm pulling in too fast is forcing me to grit my teeth and tighten my muscles. I can't make a sound.

Lara is holding a flashlight and Corbin is in a wetsuit, dripping wet.

"A minute?" Lara huffs back. "We've been out here searching every night. What are we expecting to find at this point?"

Corbin whips his head toward his wife and though I can't get a clear look of his face, his body language screams with tyranny. "A body, Lara. We're looking for a body so we can find it before they do."

They think the baby has drowned.

"Maybe she's lying," Lara says. "What if that's the case?"

Corbin throws his arms up in the air and drops his head

back. "Yes, Madden was lying to us when she said she took Fallon for a swim to meet the mermaids. And she must have been lying when she said she didn't understand why she didn't come back to the shore when she told her to, as well."

"Don't yell at me," Lara grits out. He isn't yelling necessarily but his frustration is clear as day. "This is your fault. You know that, don't you?"

"My fault?" he argues. "I've been telling you she needs psychiatric help for years, but you insisted she would grow out of this nonsense. If we had tended to her troubles, our baby would still be alive right now. So now, Lara, this is not my fault. It's time for you to take some responsibility for your lack of action."

My foot slips along a pile of pine needles, crackling over a couple twigs. I drop down to my stomach, praying they didn't hear anything from down there. If it was daylight, they would likely have seen me, but it's much darker where I am than where they are.

A bolt of light flashes over my head and I panic, knowing they've heard me. "We're done. Let the police continue to search the water with their equipment. It's been three days, Lara. This is just an inlet to the ocean. There have been six high and low tides since this happened, which means—you know what it means."

I don't want to miss anything they're saying but I need to move so there's a barrier between us. I scope out the area around me, finding the only place to go is to the side of the shed at the far edge of the cliff, close to the entrance of the woods. I move slowly, trying to snake my way up the hill and across the grass while I try to catch my breath without sounding like I'm hyperventilating.

My phone is buzzing in my back pocket, and I should have figured this would happen at the very worst moment. My hand trembles as I reach for the phone and push my back up against the side of the shed. I lower the brightness on my screen as far as it will go, so I can type out a response to Willa's message asking if everything is still okay. But before tapping out the second word, my body freezes as if I've been hit by an electrical current.

When fresh air splashes against my face after emerging from a darkness I couldn't have predicted to find here, I gasp for more air before I make a run for my car at the top of the hill. Lara and Corbin are still arguing down by the shore, giving me hope that I still get out of here without being seen. All the while, I'm trying desperately to sort out the abundance of scattered realizations. I should have known...

My eyes dart around in the dark as I look for the easiest path up the hill but a flash of light wavers over my head. *Crap*.

"Hey! Who's up there?" Corbin shouts. Heavy footsteps in the pebbles grow louder and grunts of exertion follow. He's coming this way.

Panic drives through my veins and I run as fast as I can up onto the street. I can't let him see my license plate and he has a flashlight. I may not make it out in time. I may have shot myself in the foot.

I can't swallow against the dry air, making my lungs feel like sandpaper as I reach my car. Never in my life have I pounded so hard on the gas pedal, and I've also never been so thankful for rubble flying up around my car as I take off rather than burning rubber against pavement, which could likely be traced back to my tires. My gaze is locked on the rearview mirror rather than the dark road in front of me, but I need to know he doesn't manage to catch up to a level where he can shine the light on the back of my car. I turn onto the first street on the left and continue going way too fast for a residential neighborhood. Four more turns down shorter streets and I'm nearing the main road.

I'm not sure when I took my last breath but I'm lightheaded and doing my best to keep myself in check. My hands slip up and down the steering wheel, the sweat acting like grease after crawling along the dirt and grass.

I need to slow down, or I'll get pulled over. I'll look guilty. I look guilty. I am guilty of spying. I have evidence on my phone that says I was trespassing on their property to unethically observe their behavior. Only, I assumed whatever I might learn would be from peering into their wide-open back window. I got far more than I could have imagined.

Madden is responsible for all of this, but they wanted to make this look like someone else was to blame. Madden is only a little girl. But hearing Corbin lash into Lara for failing to find her a therapist...it makes me wonder what Corbin was hoping to gain from shouting out such a detrimental confession? Unless he was hoping someone *would* overhear... The search party would then be looking for a body in the ocean, rather than an abducted child. It could take years to find a body in the ocean, if ever found at all. Maybe Corbin doesn't want Fallon to be found, but that doesn't mean she's dead.

Against my better judgment, I pull out my phone to send a text while I'm driving up the road. I need to talk to Liam. Willa won't be home for at least another two hours.

Me: Could you come over?

I swing my gaze between the screen of the phone and the

road, back and forth like a ping-pong ball, waiting for a response.

Liam: Are you okay?

Me: Yes, but I don't want to be alone.

Liam: I thought Willa was home with you?

Me: No.

Liam: I'll be there in twenty. Don't worry.

I check the rearview mirror again, hearing Liam's voice play in my head as I recite his text. "Don't worry." I don't think he would be texting so calmly if he knew what I know now.

I pass by my apartment and continue driving straight ahead. I can't go home yet.

TWENTY-SEVEN

SUNDAY, JUNE 11TH 10:30 PM

The adrenaline rush is beginning to feel like I've had more caffeine than anyone should consume in one day, but I need to be able to think straight before making any sudden moves.

Liam is waiting outside of my apartment door, his hands gripped around his phone and his eyes glued to the screen while he paces in a small circle. I can't seem to catch my breath after running up the stairs, which attracts his attention.

"Where have you been?" he asks, his words stumbling out with haste.

"I'm sorry. I was trying to clear my head. Driving usually helps, but it didn't work," I say, reaching into my pocket for my key.

"I thought you were home when you texted me?"

I shake my head and open the door to let us inside, then close it just as quickly and secure the locks and chain.

"You're supposed to be taking it easy, why would you be out alone at night right now? We wanted someone to be with you all day to make sure nothing happened." We. He and Willa are the "*we*" against me. If I sit around and wait for everything to unravel, I will be as useless as an untied ribbon.

"I know but...I've had this bad feeling, like I've been wrong about some of the details regarding the Smiths. I keep spinning over the question of why they would have blamed me for their missing daughter. I wanted to believe it was a response to their panic when they couldn't find her, but at the same time I know I can't overlook the fact that no one mentioned a word about Fallon before I was left alone with their twin girls. What if the police are looking in the wrong places? What if the Smiths know more about their daughter than they're letting on?" *If I know something, I should say something. It's the right thing to do.*

"I'm sure that's not the case," Liam says with what clearly sounds like a morally supportive assumption. "Is that what you were doing? Looking for evidence? What could you find that the police haven't at this point?"

"I know. I just feel so helpless right now," I explain, dropping my keys and purse onto the entryway side table.

"Well, I don't think you're going to find much just driving around town, but I understand it's hard to just sit here and wait for information too," Liam says, quirking his lip to the side.

With savage emotions running through every cell in my body, I step in closer to Liam and wrap my arms around his waist, desperate for an embrace—for someone to hold me tightly and tell me everything will be okay. It seems like we're still strangers in so many ways, and we are, but I'm drawn to him—the comfort he keeps offering without the pursuance of reciprocation.

He wraps his arms around me, and the warmth thaws the chill within my frozen muscles. Neither of us speak because I've probably gone from making things awkward to uncomfortable in a matter of seconds. I try to pull away, realizing I might have made a wrong assumption about the possible one-sided connection between us.

"Hey, it's okay. You don't have to be tough all the time." He gently presses my head against his chest, allowing me to hear how fast his heart is beating. A quickening pulse is caused by excitement or unease. "Tell me what's going on so I can help."

"I shouldn't have dragged you into all of this," I tell him, again, feeling the need to constantly apologize for disrupting his run-of-the-mill life.

"You didn't. When we met, none of this was a reality to you. Some might say we met each other at just the right time—a moment where you might need someone to tell you everything will be okay. It wouldn't be the worst thing in the world if I was that person, would it?"

Kyle—the man I spent one year with, thinking nothing could ever be better—always said "everything will be okay." A false statement only filled with a fake sense of security. Yet, I still desperately seek the words from whoever will share them with me. It's the dumbest line anyone can speak because no one knows what will happen five seconds from now. Yet, it's a pacifying mechanism; a mother's hush when her child is suffering with a broken heart, or a Band-Aid when someone is losing too much blood. Words that mean nothing and everything.

"How do you know?" I ask the question with no truthful answer then look up at him, still giving him the benefit of the doubt that he might try to come up with a logical response.

"My gut says so," he whispers while leaning down to touch the tip of his nose to mine. His breath feathers against my lips, sending a flicker of sparks through my cheeks. I close my eyes and press my hands against his chest, feeling his heart pound. Mine thunders in response. Liam's lips brush against mine and I surrender without another thought. His hands tighten around my lower back, and I reach up around his neck, slipping my fingers through his short, wavy strands of hair. I melt into the heat of his body as if it could offer me salvation, leaving me completely consumed.

Breathing becomes difficult the longer we are woven

together in this timeless moment, but I ignore the need for air. I could forget everything else if we could stay like this.

Liam struggles to pull away and I lean in closer, greedy for more. We close the gap between us several more times before either takes a breath. I press my hand against my cheek, feeling a shy smile grow across my tingling lips.

"That probably wasn't—wasn't what you were looking for when you said you didn't want to be alone?" he asks along with a hoarse chuckle.

He gently coils a strand of my hair around his finger then loops it behind my ear. His gaze holds mine hostage, captivating all my thoughts, and for a moment I forget I messaged him to come over or why I had even messaged him in the first place. "I'm not sure what I was looking for, but that felt like it was more than I could have hoped to find."

Liam strokes his thumb down the side of my face then loops his arm around my back. "Why were you out?" he asks, walking me over to the couch.

The momentary break between trouble and more trouble is slipping away.

I take a seat in my usual corner of the couch, and he sits beside me, leaving just a little space between us. "In psychology, we often focus on patient observation which can offer more insight than any spoken word. However, depending on the case and the patient, if the person knows they are being observed, they could put on a performance, which would give inaccurate results when notating behavior. The only way around this is—I drove to the cliff where the Smiths live."

Liam leans forward and rests his elbows on his knees, his forehead scrunching with thinking lines. "You were spying on them?" he asks.

"Yes and no. More yes than no. I'm desperate for answers. The night I watched the twins, the back wall, which is floor to ceiling windows, had no curtains or blinds and it was the room the family spends time in so I figured I could catch a glimpse of what no one else was seeing."

The more I say, the worse this sounds. I was spying on the Smith family and there's no way to sweeten the truth. "You could have been caught trespassing," Liam says. "That would toss you right back to where you were on Friday night." He's not wrong, and I appreciate the calm nature in which he's speaking because Willa won't respond the same way.

"I have evidence," I say, choking out the raspy words. I cup my hand around my throat, feeling a sudden ache from the bruising I have been trying to ignore all day.

"Did you take photos or something? I'm not sure who you'll be able to show those to if you were taking them from their property. That's why police require a search warrant. It's a person's right not to be—"

"I know. I know all of this. And you're right. But they weren't on their property, and I wasn't on their property when I garnered the evidence."

"What do you mean?" He scoots forward on the couch to straighten his shorts then fiddles with the salty white woven bracelet on his wrist.

"Mr. and Mrs. Smith were down by the shore. I was in the woods on the edge of their property line. They were arguing. He had just come out of the water, and she had a flashlight. They were looking for the baby and clearly said one of the twins was responsible for losing the baby in the water. I recorded the entire conversation."

Liam leans forward, pressing his elbows into his thighs and runs his hands down the sides of his face. "Wow. Uh..." he sighs and runs his fingers through his short messy hair. "We should bring the evidence to the station."

"Yeah."

"Is there any chance either of them might have seen you?" he asks.

"I don't think so." I'm confident I got out of there before Corbin was able to wave his flashlight in my direction.

"We should go now."

"We?" I respond, questioning the meaning. I keep asking this, but he's made it clear he isn't going anywhere and intends to stick by my side.

"Yes, I'm going with you to the police station. Let Willa know we're leaving while I use your bathroom quick."

She's going to freak out if I leave her a text that says we're going to the police station, especially without additional context but I also don't want anything in writing on my phone seeing as the police already needed to scrape the data from it to trace the unknown contact.

Rather than tell her where I'm going, I leave it simple with:

Me: Hey! I'm with Liam and going out for a bit. Nothing to worry about.

I stand up from the couch while scrolling through my photo album to separate the video from the rest of my personal pictures. I set it to a private album and slip my phone into my back pocket.

Everything for me could go back to normal after I turn in this video. I'll happily go back to being jobless, opposed to being an easy target for a sick family. Of course, I feel terrible that they did lose a child, and I wouldn't wish that on anyone. But this is not the way to handle death or grief and if Madden was responsible, she does need psychiatric help before she does something more to hurt the rest of them.

I'm essentially protecting all of them. That's what I need to believe.

TWENTY-EIGHT

SUNDAY, JUNE 11TH 11:30 PM

"It's weird that I didn't know what kind of car you had, isn't it? Or, pickup truck, I should say." I should know more than I do.

"Most of the area is walkable. I don't know," he says. "I drive around more in the off-season since there are less pedestrians but in the summer months it feels like it takes longer to get anywhere in a vehicle than it does by foot." He makes a good point. For me though, the inside of someone's car or truck is like a front row view into their persona. Is the person neat or messy, do they like the radio or a playlist, does the interior smell like a purposeful fragrance or just remnants of someone's shampoo and soap?

Within seconds, I confirm most of what I've already figured out about Liam. His interior is spotless, smells clean but also of a hint of sunscreen, and the radio is satellite on an Indie Alternative station. He's unquestionably a beloved teacher with a passion for the beach. "I shouldn't be keeping you out so late the night before a school day."

"You know what kind of game I would play with my fourteen-year-old students right now? They're awful at it."

"A game?" I ask, curious to what he'll suggest.

"Go the next five minutes without thinking of something negative and in five minutes, you will feel better. It's not easy when you're telling yourself to only think positive thoughts but if you can get through it, you'll see that I'm right."

"I wasn't being negative. I was being considerate," I argue.

"You're worrying too much. Worry less until there's something more to worry about. You'll be able to see farther into the murky distance. I promise."

He pulls out of the parking lot of my complex, and I force myself to take a deep breath to accept the challenge of his game. I'm not sure how to focus on anything but what's going on, especially if I think about where we're heading. Maybe I'm not supposed to be thinking. I rest my head back against the seat and peer out the window into the sepia scene of streetlamps beneath the starlit sky. Shops are closed for the night and there are only a few people still walking around.

What if Corbin is just blaming Madden and using her as a scapegoat? She's nine. She won't go to prison for making a mistake in thinking her baby sister could play hide-and-seek with the mermaids. Could Lara be that naive?

"I can hear your thoughts. You lose," Liam says.

"What?" I slap my hands down on my legs. "That's not fair. You have no clue what I'm thinking."

He chuckles and pulls the turn signal down to make a left at the next street. "You're thinking this could somehow work against you and what if...what if...and...what if. Can you tell me I'm wrong?"

I huff out a lungful of air because there is no way to sway my thoughts in any other direction. Every decision I make will have a consequence and if everything isn't thoroughly thought out, I could... "What will they do if they find out a nine-year-old girl is responsible for the death of her sister?"

"There are child correctional programs and psychiatric facilities that specialize in helping children who have conditions that need to be addressed. If one of the girls did do something to her sister, it does need to be handled. You can't spare her of what trouble lies ahead because you wouldn't be helping her in any way."

"What if it wasn't really her who took the baby into the ocean?"

"The evidence says otherwise," Liam argues valid points.

"Which is why I'm worried that she could be the dad's scapegoat maybe."

"Or the mother could be too. That's true. But that's not your trial and case. That will be theirs to determine. Right now, you need to clean your hands of this situation because you had nothing to do with it and you shouldn't be involved, regardless of how awful this all is."

"All I can ask is 'why' to everything. Why weren't there pictures of the baby? Was Fallon even their baby?" I've gone from questioning the existence of a baby to wondering if the poor thing was kidnapped and drowned by these rich gold diggers. Maybe it's another ploy to suck someone dry of their money just like Lara's family did to mine.

Our conversation carries us into the parking lot of the police station, and I can't believe I'm back here for the third time in three days.

I wonder what they're thinking when they see me walk through the front doors again. I still haven't gotten an answer on the unknown caller, and I know nothing about the suspect they have in custody.

"Back again?" the dispatcher at the front desk says as a greeting. She's middle aged with blonde hair tied up into a coiled bun with bangs that must be held firmly in place by a lot of hair spray since each strand sways together side to side as she speaks.

"Yes, ma'am. I—I have evidence, or what I believe to be

evidence regarding the Smith baby. Is Detective Straton in by any chance?"

Her brows arch as she glances down at her computer screen and types something out. "No, he's off for the night. Someone else can help you," she says before radioing an officer to come out to the front.

Another detective steps out from the double doors. He is older than Detective Straton, has salt and pepper dark hair, a golfer's tan, and age lines that tell me he's been here a while and is around the same age as my parents.

"Haley Vaughn?" he asks.

"Yes, sir."

"I'm Detective Ray. You were here the other night for questioning, correct?"

"Yes, sir."

"And you are?" he says, turning his attention to Liam.

"Liam Gellar, a friend of Haley's."

"Okay, why don't you come back into a room with me so we can discuss what you've found."

We follow the detective through the steel door frames and barren walls and the nerves in my stomach are already preparing for the unknown. I'm sure the question of why I was there in the first place is going to be forefront before we even get to the video, but I have no choice.

The room is identical to the one I was questioned in the other night, empty with a table and a few chairs. I wish I could be on the other side of the table, asking what I think might help get to the bottom of this case because then I might be calm and relaxed, sipping from a steaming hot Styrofoam cup of coffee.

"I have video footage of the Smiths confessing that one of their daughters was responsible for the baby drowning in the ocean. They were by the shore behind their house, she with a flashlight and he in diving gear." The words are hard to get out in just a couple of flowing sentences without running out of air.

My heart is racing like I just sprinted up a steep hill and I'm shaking. I don't know if I'm worried this will work against me or if this is the key to letting me be free of this nightmare.

Detective Ray places his coffee cup down and presses his elbows down against the table to lean in closer to my side of the table. "You have this on video?" he asks, disbelief flaring his nostrils.

I swallow hard and place my unlocked phone on the table with the video ready to play. "Yes, sir."

He runs his hand through his hair and leans back against his seat. "Wait a minute. Why were you on the Smith's property tonight?"

My face scorches with heat. "With all due respect, sir, I've been blamed by the family, stalked by an unknown contact, and attacked on the street. I know the police department is doing everything possible to get to the bottom of this but it's hard to sit in my apartment like a squatting duck, waiting to be targeted again. My gut told me something isn't right with that family, and I wanted to see if—"

"They happened to be outside, talking about the death of their child?" Detective Ray tilts his head to the side, questioning my actions, which I knew would happen.

"She's desperate for answers," Liam says. "I can't say I blame her for trying to find anything that could relieve her from being a part of this."

"Did you know she was planning to do this?" Detective Ray asks Liam. I'm not his responsibility. Why would he even ask something like that?

"No, he didn't. I went of my own accord and called him after," I speak before Liam has the chance.

"I wasn't on their property. I was in the woods, and yes, they were outside. In all honesty, I was hoping to see something through their wall of windows facing the cliff behind their house."

"Okay, okay, just hold on...do you have an attorney or anything?" He holds his hands up and huffs.

"No, I can't afford one. I'm a twenty-seven-year-old student who needed a summer job. Now I'm here. I'm telling you the truth. I could see through their window from the woods, but I didn't need to strain my vision since they were down at the shoreline."

Detective Ray inhales sharply and takes the phone from the table and hits the play button to watch the footage.

I squeeze my hands together on my lap, digging my fingernails into my opposite knuckles. My knees bounce furiously as I wait for his reaction at the end of the video.

I didn't realize I was filming for so long until I shift my gaze from my phone in his hands to the clock behind him on the wall. "Wow," he says. "Can you give me a minute?"

We don't have the opportunity to say okay before he's out the door. "I hope this is a good thing," Liam says.

I'm not sure I feel so optimistic.

A few quick minutes pass before Detective Ray returns with a clipboard and papers. "I will need you to sign this release form to give us access to the footage. You do have the right to a public defender at any time if you would like to consult with one first." He hands it to me, and I sign as fast as I can, wanting to do whatever possible to avoid prolonging this visit.

"Thank you. I don't have anything to hide on my phone," I say with a shrug. "I'm not sure a public defender is necessary at the moment."

"Understood. I'll just need another few minutes. I'm going to take your phone with me, and I'll be back with it after we pull the video."

"Oh okay," I say, nodding and shaking my head at the same time.

Liam places his hand on my bouncing knee. "It's okay. You didn't trespass." But I did when I was by their shed. They don't need to know that, but I'll pray there weren't cameras somewhere I didn't notice.

"I just want this to be over."

"I know. It isn't fair that you've been pulled into this mess."

Clearly Lara and Corbin don't agree.

Detective Ray returns with my phone. "We have everything we need from you now. If we have any other questions, we'll be in touch. Please continue to take precautions and do not return to their property or the borders of their property. Allow us to do our job, okay?"

I think that's my slap on the wrist. "Yes, sir."

Just as we make our way back toward the front lobby, we see and hear several cruisers fly out of the parking lot with their sirens blaring. "This is a good thing," Liam whispers.

"Is it?"

TWENTY-NINE
MONDAY, JUNE 12TH 8:00 AM

I hardly remember climbing into bed last night after Willa freaked out for a half hour while I explained everything that had unfolded through the night. My mind should be clear after handing over hard evidence, but I guess that was unrealistic hope on my part. I'm just grateful I slept for a few hours.

Today needs to carry on like a normal day. I have a final at ten and it's the only thing I should focus on.

I grab my phone from my oak nightstand and tap the screen, finding I've slept much later than I thought. It's already eight. I'm not sure if I should feel relieved or concerned that I don't have any notifications scrolling along my display like I usually do in the mornings. Not even my news app has updated since last night.

I click through my settings, checking the wi-fi connection and various modes the phone could be set on after the police had it in their possession last night.

Nothing seems out of order and the wi-fi looks to be connected.

Out of instinct I tap the text bubble icon, searching for a blue dot indicator that I've missed a message. Maybe I'm not remembering correctly but Liam said he'd let me know he got home okay. He's a grown man. I'm sure he can take care of himself, but I still feel responsible...or maybe I just care whether he got home safely. Last time I worried about someone getting home safely at night, they proved my concerns to be justified. I know I can't control every part of life, but I have a bad habit of taking too much of the blame for things that are out of my control. I didn't pour alcohol down the other driver's throat or tell them to drive twice the speed limit down a one-way without headlights in the middle of the night. But it still happened, and Kyle was just going home from my apartment on a school night. Everything *wasn't* okay, but maybe if he told me *it was* that night, it would have been. That childish irrational thinking won't help me much in my career, but as a human, we all over-think things sometimes.

I type out a quick message to Liam, doing what I promised myself I wouldn't do.

Me: Good morning! I'm just making sure you got home okay last night. Thanks again for helping me. It means a lot to know you care.

I stare at my sent message, waiting for the little "read" receipt to appear beneath the sent words. I wait several minutes until my eyes blur from staring at the same spot on my screen for too long.

He's fine. He's probably on his way to work or already there.

I leave my phone on my bed and head for the bathroom to shower and get ready for class. *Placing an object out of reach can defy the need for control.* That fact might be in the cognitive behavior section of my final today.

Without my phone, I'm forced to think of everything that has impacted my life this past week. Maybe phones are a good distraction for certain people—people who want to forget about the world around them.

"Haley!" Willa shouts, knocking on the door.

"Yeah?" I rub my eyes to wipe the soap away and poke my head out between the wall and shower curtain, finding the bathroom full of steam. I must have forgotten to turn on the vent again.

Willa opens the door a crack and I hear the vent rumble above my head. "It's like a sauna in here."

"Sorry, just trying to wake up."

Willa clears her throat and pauses a moment. "Speaking of waking up... I received a call from an unknown number this morning."

My soaking wet hair dribbles onto the floor tiles surrounding the bathmat. "Who was it?"

Willa's gaze drops to her bare feet then glances back up at me. "It was your parents, actually."

"Oh...really?" I ask, sounding dumbfounded. *I am.* A knot forms in the pit of my stomach and I close my eyes for a moment, pulling my head back into the shower and sliding the curtain back toward the wall. "I don't know why they would—"

"They've been trying to reach you..." Willa's voice trails off, leaving her statement dangling like a loose thread.

Questions spiral through my mind, wondering why they would reach out to Willa. "How did they even get your number?" I ask out loud but more for my confusion than hers.

Willa pauses for a moment before responding. Maybe she's trying to figure out the same thing. "I have no clue. When I answered, your dad told me who he was. I figured you had given them my number in case of emergency."

"Maybe," I utter, although I don't recall doing so. They've met Willa several times as we've been roommates since our first year of college. I'm sure the numbers could have been exchanged at any point, but they haven't used her number until now.

"Yeah, maybe..." Willa mirrors my response, but punctuates her words with a question. As I think through the possible reasons, adding silence to the foggy room, she interrupts the pause. "They called because they said they haven't been able to reach you. They thought your phone had been shut off and wanted to know if you were okay."

I toss my head back, getting a face full of cold water from the shower head. *Shit.* I reach for the faucet nozzle, silently pleading for more hot water even though I know I've already been in here long enough to use it all up. "That's so weird. What did you tell them?" The water runs dry from the shower-head while I wait for her answer. I shiver against the chill, left watching droplets dribble down the shower tiles one drop at a time.

"What should I have told them?" she asks, hesitation bearing weight on her question.

That this was their decision, not mine. "Nothing. They have no reason to be calling you."

"Hales...seriously?" Willa's voice echoes with disbelief as her feet clap against the bathroom floor.

"Could I have my towel?" I ask, sounding meager in avoidance of her question.

The flimsy towel rack thuds against the back of the bathroom door just before she shoves her arm into the shower, holding my purple towel. I wrap myself up, which does little to eliminate the icy sensation running through my nerves. "If you think they had no reason for calling me, why did they say they've been trying to reach you for almost two years? Two years, Haley. Any time you mention them, you talk as if you spoke to them yesterday. I've heard you on the phone with them..."

Willa's words slice through the steam-filled-air and pin me to the clammy shower wall.

When I gain the courage to step out of the shower, I avoid Willa's unblinking eyes, but I don't have many places to look since the mirror is covered with fog. "It's a long story," I say, wishing that would be enough to satiate her desire for an actual answer.

I'm not sure she will understand the decisions I've made when it comes to my parents. We all have our personal burdens to bear but mine—my parents are the reason I want to help people who suffer with mental illnesses.

"Why, Hales?"

I shake my head. "It's too much right now."

"What's too much? I'm completely lost. Why haven't you mentioned this? We talk about everything, but *this*, of all things, is off limits? I don't understand."

I finally turn to look at her, finding the disappointment and confusion written along her dewy skin. Her brows furrow and her shoulders shrug before leaving me alone with her lingering questions.

I understand why she would think she knows everything there is to know about me. That's how friends are, and roommates for that matter. She does know almost everything about me, but some stuff is better off left in the past.

After taking a moment to collect my thoughts, I step out of the bathroom, holding my towel tightly around my chest. She's standing in the hallway, leaning against the wall, hurt evident in her eyes. "I'm so sorry if you feel like I've been dishonest with you. That's not the case. I just—some things are easier to keep buried."

"I get it, Hales," she says, "but this was a pretty big surprise. I still can't wrap my head around the fact that you haven't spoken to them in so long." She presses her hands to her cheeks and stares through me like I'm a piece of glass. "It's like there are all these sudden mysteries about you and I'm questioning how I've known you for so long without actually knowing you for so long."

"I'm sorry they woke you up with their call."

"I don't care that I was woken up." She slides a hand over her eyes and shakes her head again. "You talk about them, often. I know I'm not imagining that. Why would you lie about them?"

I haven't lied. They both keep public profiles on social media, and I can see what they're up to all the time without having to talk to them. "I would never lie to you."

Willa's door cracks open and Jerry peeks through, squinting his tired eyes. "Everything okay out here?"

I didn't even know he was here. When he stays over, it's late at night after he closes the restaurant, so I don't usually find out until the morning.

I tighten my towel around my chest again, feeling more naked than I am. "Yes. I'm sorry if you were woken too," I say.

"No, no, I'm fine. Just making sure you ladies are okay." With Willa's room still blacked out from her darkening shades, I can only see Jerry's hands on the doorframe, his messy black hair formed into a mohawk, and wrinkled sheet lines imprinted on his stubbly face.

"We're good, baby. Go back to sleep," Willa says. "I'll be back in a minute."

Jerry runs his fingers through his messy locks and sighs. "Are you sure? You two sound hangry. I can whip up some breakfast if that'll help?"

"We're not hangry, babe. I'll be back in a minute," she says, turning toward him to give him a kiss and gently push him back into her room.

"Okay, okay," he says with a chuckle. The door closes and seconds later we hear his body thump against the mattress.

"I have a final in an hour and my head is still spinning from last night. Could we discuss this later? I'm not a bad person,

Willa. I just have a lot of things that I need to keep compart-mentalized for the sake of my health. Can you trust that answer?"

"Yeah, of course," she says, dropping her gaze to the floor. She forces a small smile to add to her lie.

"I'm sorry. I just—this truly has nothing to do with you and everything to do with me." I can't believe I just said that—those words always cause the other person to think it's more about them than they did in the first place. It isn't my intention with her, but I just can't think straight.

"I get it." She doesn't. She's been fortunate enough to escape most forms of trauma in her life and I would pay to be walking in her footsteps rather than mine. Regardless, my woes don't need to be her problem, which is why I have kept them to myself. "Don't worry, okay? I want you to do well on your final. We'll talk later when you get home."

I'm trying to show an expression of gratitude, but I probably look nauseous from knowing my parents have desperately and successfully tracked Willa down because they saw me on the news. If I had taken just a few more minutes to think through my decision the other day, I could have avoided this additional trouble.

I close myself into my room and give in to my growing obsession to check my phone—an obsession I just fed while finding that my message to Liam still hasn't been read. I'm not just a fool who can convince myself everything is fine.

THIRTY

I wish I could tell myself that the stares and whispers were a figment of my imagination but on this side of the campus, I see the same people day in, day out which means I'm familiar to them. I keep thinking if I didn't volunteer my interview, I might have stayed out of the limelight—I might not have been attacked on the street. The whole reason I did what I did was to keep my name clean and away from the Smiths' mouths. Now I'm not only covered in bruises, but they are probably still pointing a damning finger at me.

The old stone building is hot and muggy as it has been the last couple of warm weeks. The hallways are emptier than usual probably because some students have already finished their finals and left to go home for the summer. Half of the rooms are set up to be cleaned with seats shoved to one side and the shades closed.

My classroom is still full of life, a mixture of energy from the vast number of personalities that make up this major. Before branching off in this direction with my studies, I assumed any person who worked within the mental health field was of the same variety: calm, caring, a listener, and intelligent. Most are, but there are subsets beginning to show as we grow closer to the end of the curriculum next year.

I can tell who will likely practice from the book and who will venture off to find alternative methods of therapy. There's also a separation between those eager to work with children and those who prefer to focus on adults. Then there are specialists for addicts, grief, trauma, abuse, forensic, medical, education... The list goes on and on. My focus is on childhood psychological behavior, but this class, Affective Neuroscience, is a requirement of all psych grad students, which has been more of a debate and discussion class to cover varying opinions on trending practices.

I'm grateful the professor is already here, which eliminates the possibility of small talk with classmates.

"Hey, everything okay?" Sarah, the woman who has sat beside me all semester asks. "I saw on the news this morning that Corbin Smith was taken into custody for collusion in hiding facts pertinent to the missing child case. I can't even wrap my head around all of this. You must be spinning over it still too, huh?"

"Yeah, it's—uh—it's keeping me up at night. But I don't know anything more than you do so it's just one surprise after another right now," I say, smiling as I tap the eraser of my pencil against the desk.

"Do you think the parents had something to do with their missing kid?" she pries, like many of us here unintentionally do.

"I have no clue." I redirect my gaze toward the front of the classroom, knowing she will read my cue.

"Please place your phones on silent mode or turn them off and put them away," the professor drawls, reciting the same thing he says anytime he's passing out an exam.

I take my phone out of my bag to make sure the volume is silenced, finding that Liam still hasn't responded. I know he must be at work now and likely was when I first messaged, too.

We haven't exchanged messages during the school day before, so I should stop thinking something has happened until I have a reason to do so. With confirmation that my phone is on silent mode, I return it to my bag and rest my arms back on the shallow desktop in front of me.

My hand cramps from writing. This professor is the only one in the school who still avoids the use of laptops or any technologically advanced device for test taking. There were so many open-ended questions that I haven't the slightest idea how I did. I place the test down on his lectern and silently hope he isn't teaching any of the classes I need to take next semester.

The classroom became a dungeon as the clouds swept in midway through the test. It might have rained too. But the sun is peeking through the clouds and causing a strong glare against the windows of the exit doors. I can finally breathe now that my finals are over.

I press on the metal bar along the door, listening to the clunk as I step outside into the wet air. "Haley Vaughn, do you have a moment?"

"Haley Vaughn, would you mind answering a couple of questions for us?"

"Excuse me, Miss Vaughn, Channel Four here—we've just come to learn that Corbin Smith has been taken into custody for involvement with his missing daughter."

I hold my hand above my eyes to block out the sun, finding at least a dozen reporters encircling the cement path that leads to the student parking. Are they allowed on campus?

I wish I hadn't stopped for a moment to regain my bearings because they've taken the opportunity to move in closer like starving beasts staring at the only prey nearby.

"No, I—how did you find me here?"

"Your roommate said you weren't home when we knocked on your door. Can you—"

"Did my roommate tell you where I was?" I continue questioning them, ignoring their pursuit.

No one answers me. Willa wouldn't do that to me, would she?

"Miss Vaughn," another reporter shouts. "Corbin Smith appears to be quite troubled. Can you tell us if you felt threatened at all by him the night you were babysitting their children? Is that where all your bruising came from?"

I should have expected this would somehow be turned on me again. Even with the presented evidence, I'm still on the hook. Why just Corbin? Lara was clearly involved in their verbal exchange at the shore last night.

"No, I'm not sure when, why, or how for anything you're asking," I reply as I chug forward. I know they won't just give up. They'll follow me until I reach my car and then they'll know what I drive if they don't already know. I'm sure they do.

"Do you think their daughter, Fallon, is still alive?"

"I don't know anything more than you do," I say sharply.

They're like piranhas and won't stop until they suck me dry.

"Haley, is it true your townhome, the one your family owned, burnt down thirteen years ago, killing Lara Smith's sister?"

The question sucks the air out of my body and replaces any last bit of warmth with ice, freezing me to the core. This story isn't private. It was very public, and I've experienced this bombardment from the media before.

Just keep walking. I don't have to answer anything. There is so much I'd like to say.

"Did your family stay in contact with the Hoyt family after they lost one of their children in the fire?"

"Haley," a female voice shouts from behind, "could you tell

us a little bit about Kyle Williams. Were you two in a committed relationship when he passed away?"

My throat tightens and I can't swallow against the thick of my tongue. I don't understand how these reporters live with the guilt weighing down their shoulders. Kyle has nothing to do with my home that burnt down thirteen years ago, and I had nothing to do with his accident.

My tunnel vision is closing in around me as I cross the street to the parking lot. A blaring honk howls from my right side. It's like the scream of someone burning to death, a sound I wish I could forget. I gasp and clutch my chest as I trip over my feet, stumbling forward onto the road.

The tires squeal to a stop in front of the crosswalk I'm on and I look up at the luxury SUV, finding a brunette with long straight hair and large dark sunglasses staring at me with her hands in the air as if she has more rights than I do. She honks again as I'm trying to pick myself up from the middle of the road. "It's a crosswalk!" I shout, my voice hoarse and sticky with phlegm.

I scoop up my bag and hold it against my torso as I continue walking toward the lot. Not one of the reporters could be bothered to offer me a hand up.

When I reach the curb along the parking lot, I glance over my shoulder, finding the same dozen still following me but at a car-length's distance. Nothing I say will make them stop so I pick up the pace, reach into my pocket for my key fob and unlock the car door as soon as I'm within arm's reach. I lock the doors and toss my bag down onto the passenger seat. They look like zombies, slugging over here as if I'm going to roll down my window and start talking. Before they have the chance to block me in, I pull out of my spot and skim by them, thankful no one is in my way when I pull out onto the road.

I reach over to my bag and feel around for my phone, pulling it out as another wave of unease sloshes through my stomach. I touch the screen and peer over quickly to see if there are any missed calls or messages.

With a couple displayed, I take a turn down a side street filled with a row of on-campus apartments for upperclassmen and pull up against the curb. I glance in my rearview mirror to confirm the reporters aren't behind me, then bring the phone closer to see what I missed.

1 Missed Call from Lara Smith

1 New Voicemail

I've been sitting in the parking lot of my apartment complex listening to Lara's voicemail over and over, wishing I could hear the silent words in between the spoken ones. She's sobbing, pleading for my forgiveness and rash accusation, and she's terrified and doesn't know what to do.

What in the world would make her decide to call me of all people? Surely, she has friends and I know she has family. She's out of her mind if she thinks I'm going to call her back.

As if she knows I'm staring at the transcribed voicemail, she sends me a text message that makes me want to add her to my blocked caller list.

Lara: I know what you're probably thinking...

Lara: You have no reason to want to help me after accusing you...

Lara: And I'm sure you're wondering why I hired you.

Lara: I'm also sure you've figured out who my sister was and think that has something to do with this.

Lara: That's not the case. I remember how kind you were after the fire. I remember you brought us flowers all on your own and told us how sorry you were for our loss. For thirteen, you were far more mature than I was at eighteen.

Lara: It stuck with me, and I felt awful when my parents sued yours for damages and death. It didn't bring back my sister.

Lara: Then I saw your name in the classifieds and saw how well you were doing in life and...I figured maybe it was a sign that I could make things right with you after everything we had gone through.

Lara: Please, Haley. Can we talk?

A sign? She wanted to hire me to make things right... Until her finger was pointing directly at me as she blamed me for her missing child.

My phone stops buzzing, and I peer out the window toward Willa's car parked three spots down. She's waiting for an answer as to why I haven't spoken to my parents in two years. I'm sure she asked them why when they so kindly pulled her into our family issues—trying to make me sound like a horrible person for pushing them out of my life. I can only imagine what they filled her head with this morning or what she thinks she knows about my relationship with the two of them.

I tap the screen on my phone, glancing at the messages from Lara again. If only these texts were from Liam, I might not have a pit growing at the bottom of my stomach. I need to put that thought out of my head until the end of his school day though. My worrying thoughts are irrational, unlike Lara's.

She shouldn't want to talk to me after so obviously involving me in this situation. An attorney should be guiding her on how to handle this matter.

With the car ignition still running, I pull the gear into reverse and back out of my parking spot. I step on the gas and peel out of the lot, watching my apartment blur into the distance behind me.

In the very first psychology class I took, we studied the importance of perspective-taking, a method of attempting to see through another's eyes, embrace their thoughts, empathize with their emotions, and take on their story as if it were our own. When we can adjust our mindset to match those we are trying to help, we form a better connection, and the probability rate of successful treatment rises. The method sounded easy at the time. I grew up learning to put myself in someone else's shoes before assuming I knew everything there was to know about them. As a child this isn't particularly difficult, but as an adult there are multiple layers to work through before successfully understanding the inner workings of another adult's mind. A common adult can retain and access up to hundreds and thousands of memories and experiences at any given moment.

Lara's life was uprooted thirteen years ago when her sister died in the fire. The trauma likely caused a plethora of compound side effects, many of which could have gone undiagnosed and unrecognized even by herself.

A cry for help can't always be seen or heard but it can be a trap.

Everyone else would call me foolish, but I'm okay with that. I'm not. I'm intelligent and I fear for a nine-year-old child's wellbeing, maybe two.

I pull onto the pebbled driveway, listening to the now familiar crunch beneath my tires. The front door doesn't open upon expecting my arrival. Natural responses are best found when someone is unexpectedly confronted.

With a sharp finger, I press the doorbell and inhale sharply, ready to hold my breath until the door opens. It'll keep me from weakening and running off.

The wait feels like an eternity before the door opens. Lara stands in front of me, almost like a purposeful mess with her hair in a casual floppy bun on the top of her head. She's in sweatpants and a stained gray T-shirt. No makeup. Just Botox-filled skin, plump lips traced with age lines and aging sunspots scattered along her cheeks. She peers down at the phone locked in her grip. "What are you doing here?"

Her throat can't produce a smooth sound, each word crackles like radio static.

"I received your messages."

"You could have responded," she says.

"I can leave," I offer.

"No, no," she says with exasperation.

"What do you want from me?"

She flattens her free hand out in front of her, fixating on her fresh manicure—fresh as in, happened after her daughter went missing fresh. "Corbin is being detained. He took the blame—come inside. I can't afford to have anyone else spying on us."

I'm not supposed to know anyone was spying on them. "Spying?"

"Never mind," she says, closing the door as I follow her into the house that has been giving me nightmares for days. "Wh-what happened to you? It looks like you were beat up." She brushes her finger around in a circle on her neck, referring to the bruises on mine and lets out a loud hiccup.

"I was." Following the hiccup is a face full of booze-laced breath.

She narrows her eyes at me as if I'm lying. What would I have to gain out of lying about the handprints on my neck? "By who?"

"Honestly, I was hoping you would tell me since everything

that has happened to me in the past few days has been because of you."

Lara presses her hands to the sides of her face and scrapes them down to her neck. "I didn't know any of this was going to happen."

I don't believe her, and I don't need to see a special look in her eyes to think so. "Why would Corbin just take the blame? And what did he take it for?"

"I—I do need your help with Madden. Tha-that's why I hired you in the first place. She's an angry, angry little child with mean thoughts and we don't know why. We-we've treated her the same way we've treated Blakely, and now—and now," she says, holding onto the last syllables as if they're a tune, "I've had to send Blakely to stay with a friend to keep her safe while we work through everything."

I close my eyes and shake my head. "What did Madden do, Lara?" She needs to tell me before I can say much else and it's obvious she's drunk.

Lara swallows hard and clasps her hands around her opposite wrists, digging her nails into her skin. "We—we um, think she brought-t-t Fallon down to the ocean and, splash-sh-sh, she just drowned."

I don't see how this is Madden's fault. No one was watching her when she did this. She's nine. Maybe she thought her sister could swim. Although, I recall Lara saying something about working on the twins still learning to swim. "It could have been a horrific accident," I suggest. If that's the case, Madden is going to need a lot more therapy than she might be considering. "And if this was a possible accident, why would Corbin take the blame?"

"It was-sn't an accident," she whispers, cupping her hand around her mouth. "Madden has des-spised Fallon's existence since the day she was born. The warn-warning signs were there, and I was in denial." She throws her hands up in the air then lets them drop to her sides. This story matches up to what I heard them arguing about the other night. "Corbin wanted to spare Madden from being questioned or from whatever might happen if someone thinks this was anything but an accident."

"So, you tried to criminalize me?"

Her hands tremble. "I—I jus-s-t was-sn't in my right mind."

There are many things I can say to her, but none are as kind as she's being to herself. "Did Madden tell you she thought she would drown if she took her swimming?"

A dull series of thuds echoes through the foyer, and I turn in the direction I hear it coming from. "What is that?"

"Nothing," Lara says.

I hear the thuds again. "That's not nothing. Where's Madden right now?"

"In her-her room, where she belongs, Ha-ley. Where else would she be?" The thuds are fists pounding against a wall.

If they think Madden purposely drowned her sister, she should be speaking to a therapist, not locked in her room.

"I want to talk to her."

"No, no. Ab-absolute-ly not."

"What was the purpose of you trying to rope me back in then?" I ask, folding my arms over my chest. I'm doing every-thing possible to keep my poise so I don't appear as fearful as I am.

"I wanted you to help her, yes, but I didn't think you would just show up at my door." So, she didn't have time to prime her yet.

"You said you're running out of time. To me it sounds like the perfect time to act and for you to stop drinking."

I step to the side of Lara and make my way toward the stair-well as the thuds continue. Lara tries to keep up with me, her hand pulls at my shirt, but the fabric slips from her fingers. "I said no!"

I wrench my hand around the doorknob of Madden's door,

finding it twists easily but the door itself won't budge. I shove my shoulder into the wood and push to get the door to open. "Madden?" I call out.

"Let me out!" she shrills.

"Do not let her out. She's-s-s a murderer. Why do you think we're all bruised and battered? I try to cover it up, but I can't," Lara snaps, pulling herself up the stairs as if she has two broken legs.

Bruised and battered. "The kids are both covered in bruises. But you appear untouched. Madden's a child," I remind her. "Not a monster."

Lara shakes her head furiously. "No, she hurts us, and herself. She's dangerous."

"You're the only source of danger here that I see."

"She'll murder you too if you aren't careful," Lara says, tripping on one step.

THIRTY-TWO

It takes six solid shoulder shoves to the door before I'm able to move whatever is blocking it inside while Lara tries to tug me away with a weak grip on the back of my shirt. "Do-don't go in there," Lara bellows.

I twist my upper body with force to loosen her grip and squeeze in through the small opening of the door, then slam it closed behind me and replace the heavy dresser to be flush against the door.

Madden is sitting on her bed, her back against the wall with her legs crossed like a pretzel as she brushes her fingers through a Barbie doll's long hair. I spot the other door that leads into the bathroom then Blakely's room and rush to check if it's locked or accessible.

I jiggle the doorknob, finding it to be locked as I figured but with the lock being on the other side, Lara can still make her way into this room. I scan the tidy bedroom, looking for another piece of heavy furniture, finding a white wooden toy box. I push it across the floor and wedge it diagonally between the threshold and side wall. It's not as heavy as I was hoping but it should do enough to keep Lara out while I talk to Madden.

I kneel at the side of Madden's bed, watching as she continues to brush the Barbie doll's hair. "How long have you been locked in here?" I ask her.

Madden shrugs. "She won't let me out. She said it's my fault daddy is in jail."

"Why does she think that?" I ask.

"Because of Fallon."

There was silence in the hallway for just long enough to figure Lara had made her way through Blakely's bedroom. The lock pops open and she's trying to pry open the door.

"No, no! I don't want her to come in here!" Madden screams. She jumps off her bed and runs across the room to the toy box, sitting on top to add more weight. "I didn't do anything! I didn't do anything. I didn't know anything..." Madden continues to scream while pressing her fingers into her ears and clenching her eyes. Her cheeks become red, but her voice does not give out.

I follow her, trying to gently take her hands from her ears and close them into mine. "It's okay. Shh. It's okay. Just take a breath."

"No, no, you don't understand. Nothing will ever be okay again. They blame everything on me. Just me."

"Did you take Fallon to the ocean?" I ask, keeping my voice at a whisper as Lara continues to bang and push against the door.

"I don't know. I don't know. I don't know," she says, pulling her hands back to replace her fingers in her ears. "I don't want them to take me away."

"Who?" I ask. "Who will take you away?"

I'm leaning my weight against the toy box too, but I feel the strength of Lara's attempt to get into the bedroom. "I'll call the police. Don't think I won't!" she threatens.

"And tell them what? That you've barricaded your daughter and locked her up in her bedroom so she can't speak to anyone?" I shout back. I'd like to add the fact that she just referred to her as a murderer too. The only thing that's clear to me now is that Madden has been inflicted with psychological abuse.

"Who do you think they're going to blame then, Lara?"

To my surprise, she stops pushing against the door. She doesn't respond. Madden's screaming comes to a pause and there's silence within the room and outside the two doors. She's either calling the police or coming to her senses.

"She's a thief. She only loves Blakely. She never wanted me or Fallon. She doesn't even love Daddy. But no one likes my mom. No one."

"But why?" I ask, trying my best to remain calm so I can bring her energy level down too.

Madden shrugs. "She tells people I'm a handful. I think I make her life hard."

"No, no. I don't think that's the case and you shouldn't assume something like that," I tell her, placing my hand on her shin—her bruised shin.

"Do you feel unsafe here?" I hope Lara can't hear me. I'm speaking as quietly as possible, but God only knows, she probably has cameras and mics set up in each room of this house.

Madden nods her head, confirming my concern.

"Okay, I'm going to get you some help. Is that okay?" I don't care if it's okay but I'd rather she thinks she's in control of the decisions being made about her life.

She nods again.

Just as my pulse slows the slightest bit, another wave of force pushes against the dresser on the other door. "There's no way out," Madden whispers.

I pull my phone out of my back pocket, my hands shaking so fiercely, it'll be hard to type anything out.

A message from Liam is pinned to my display. He's apologizing for making me worry but everything is fine, and he'll call me after work. I wish that was the worst of my concerns right now.

I open a new message box and add 9-1-1 in the *To* field. During the first aid course, we learned about the ability to send text messages to 9-1-1. I never knew we could do this before. I'm sure Lara would be grateful to know her forced licensing came in handy for me.

> Me: *Emergency services needed. A nine-year-old child has been locked and barricaded in her bedroom. The mother is intoxicated and angry. The child claims she feels unsafe here.*
>
> Dispatcher: *This is 9-1-1. May we connect you to a dispatcher through a phone call?*
>
> Me: *No, I don't think that's safe.*
>
> Dispatcher: *Okay, understood. Could you please send your address to confirm your location...*

The police arrive much quicker than I thought they would and without the alarming sirens, which I appreciate. Lara doesn't need any additional warning that the police are about to be at her front door.

Within seconds they're banging tersely at the front, which I can easily hear through the window.

I don't hear any movement from within the house, making me wonder where Lara is and what she's doing. I consider moving the bureau and opening the door, but I think it's best if I wait here with Madden until the police make their way upstairs. I'm already going to have to explain why I'm locked in here with her, but I have the text messages on my phone to back up my story.

"Are they breaking the door?" Madden asks, sliding off her toy box and moving over to the window. It sounds like they are. Muffled shouts filter in through the door. Madden runs across the room and jumps back onto her bed. "Are they going to take me away now?"

"No. They're going to keep you safe."

"I don't want to be taken away. Will they put me in jail when they find out about Fallon?"

"Why would they put you in jail?" It's the last of the questions I'll be able to ask her with the sound of footsteps barreling up the stairs.

"Because Mom said I killed Fallon."

The police try to open the bedroom door and find resistance. "If anyone is in there, move away from whatever is blocking the door so no one gets hurt."

They make their way in rather quickly, finding Madden on her bed and me kneeling by her side. "Who is responsible for all this?" the police are asking me.

"She was trapped in here by her mother. I was able to shimmy inside but when Madden said she didn't feel safe here, I did what I could to keep us in the room."

"Is that true?" an officer asks Madden.

Madden nods with uncertainty in her eyes.

"How did you know she was in here?" the officer asks, looking at me.

"Her mother sent me several messages asking if we could talk, telling me she needed my help. I came over and heard Madden thumping to let her out."

"Where is the mother now?" the questions continue.

"She was trying to get into the room but then everything went silent. I don't know where she is now. I stayed with Madden."

The officer is jotting down notes as two other officers scout the room with flashlights. I'm not sure what they're looking for, but it could be anything from a missing baby to a clue as to why another one of the Smiths' children is holed up in her room while the father is being detained.

"Are you hurt?" the officer asks Madden.

She clutches her arms around her stomach. "No, but—" she says.

"Are you sick, sweetheart?" the officer changes his tone a bit to reflect Madden's words.

"Mom says I'm sick here," she says, lifting a hand and placing it on her head. "But I don't want to be."

THIRTY-THREE

MONDAY, JUNE 12TH 5:15 PM

The same questions are asked repeatedly, an interrogation technique to catch someone in a lie. There were only so many ways I could describe the minute-by-minute occurrences of what happened after arriving at the Smiths' house. I'm not sure where Lara disappeared to or where Madden was taken after we arrived at the police station, or if Blakely is truly safe somewhere. I don't know if Madden is responsible for all she's being blamed for or even confessing to, because kids can so easily be manipulated to do and say what someone convinces them to. The police offered to let me meet them at the station for questioning, but I didn't want to leave Madden until I knew she was here safely, so I sat with her in the back of the police car. Another ride I'll never forget.

It's sad knowing she likely won't be going home anytime soon, and for multiple reasons, not just because she needs therapy.

It's never ideal to separate a child from their family but the options aren't great due to the decisions they've made.

Once again, I've walked out of the police station with the problems still floating around me like a cloud of dust. I haven't received a call since the night I was detained, and I'm not sure if I'm still considered a person of interest, but I'm sure it's clear I'm not the person they should be focusing on now.

I needed someone to hold my hand after experiencing trauma at a young age. Therapy was the least of what was best for me, but nothing was an option as my family was being sued for every dime we had. At least that's what my parents told me. They tried to help me overcome the nightmares of surviving the fire but there was nothing they could say or do to fix what happened, or to bring back our belongings that were forever lost.

The day has come and gone as I stand outside of the police department, waiting for Willa to pick me up. I don't think she'll be thrilled to bring me back to the Smiths' house to pick up my car, probably even less so than she is to pick me up from the police station again, but I couldn't explain much when I called her for a ride.

An old slate-gray Durango pulls into the lot and my stomach tightens as I squint toward the vehicle. The car moves toward me faster than I can focus on the driver and by the time I confirm my concern, it's too late to run and hide.

I hear the brakes grinding into place and the rickety door squealing open on the driver's side. "My God, Haley," he shouts, shuffling over to me with eagerness.

I wrap my arms around my chest and hold myself tightly. "Dad, what are you doing here?"

"What are you doing here?" he asks, his head tilting to the side with frustration. He runs his hand over his bald head and growls before stepping up to me. He grips his hands around my arms and inspects the bruising along my neck. "What happened to you? It looks like you were in a fight. Are you okay?"

"There isn't a simple explanation," I reply, squeezing my arms even tighter. "I'm fine."

"You call that fine?" he replies, his voice becoming grittier.

"Please...just don't—"

He takes a step back, the small space I need to take in a lungful of air. "Look, your mother and I have tried to give you the space you've demanded from us, but it's been two years, Haley. Two years. Do you have any clue how long that is when you're a parent? Then to see your face on the news of all places...and now I find you and it looks like you were beaten to a pulp. My God."

"I'm twenty-seven, Dad," I remind him. "You shouldn't have had to try and give me space. I'm a grown woman and I had to enforce boundaries because you didn't respect them."

"Yeah, yeah. Whatever. I don't care if you're fifty. You're my daughter—my daughter who blocked our phone numbers after we agreed to give you this so-called-space you needed." He presses his hands to his hips and paces back and forth along the one large cement tile he's standing within.

I peer around the parking lot, searching for Willa, wishing she were here so I could jump into her car. "How did you even know I was here?" My heart flutters with anxiety, witnessing a storm of anger illuminate Dad's eyes.

"It doesn't matter."

It does matter, and I know that Willa spoke to him earlier. She's the only answer.

"Willa isn't coming to pick me up, is she?"

He shakes his head. "No, no she's not. You're coming home with me so we can talk everything out." Dad has never been one to reach out a gentle hand with the offer of help. Forceful love and unity are the only options between us, which is why I had to create distance.

"I don't want to go back home with you," I say, keeping my voice down since I'm just outside of the police department.

"Okay, well I'm not just going to get back in my car and drive off, leaving you here. We obviously have some issues that need to be discussed and worked out and I think you know me well enough to know I don't just give up. Your mother and I have given you your space and told ourselves you'd eventually come back, and everything would be okay again. Were we really that awful to you?"

His eyes are stained red, but it could be from stress, high blood pressure, or tears. I won't speculate. "Where is Mom?"

"At home."

"How did you get Willa's number?" I ask, keeping my eyes glued to the blurry tree-lined horizon.

"We found her parents' information online, called them and explained that we were trying to reach you and couldn't. They gave us Willa's phone number so I could hopefully get in touch with you. After talking with her this morning, I called back a bit ago to see where I could find you. She said you'd be here."

I can't believe Willa let me down. I may not have given all the details behind the reasons I have to keep a distance from my parents, but what I did say to her should have been enough to make her understand that my decision was important to me. Everyone I trust eventually lets me down, which is why I never completely trust anyone. It's a hard lesson to keep learning and re-learning, but it's become clear this is my life.

"Please get into the car, Haley," Dad says, waving his hand toward the passenger side door. He's wearing an old worn T-shirt displaying a silhouette of a man on a tractor riding in toward a rising sun. His shorts have holes and are frayed at the bottom, and his sneakers are almost worn through the sole. Whenever I ask him why he dresses this way, he says he prefers comfort over style. Even as a landlord and building manager, he didn't seem to care about his appearance, and I always wondered what tenants thought of him.

We're in front of the police department and if I argue with him about this, I'll attract the wrong kind of attention. I don't need that right now. I'll give Mom and Dad what they want by going to their house and rehashing everything that's happened between us. Then we'll have to go through this ordeal of me putting another wall between us again. People don't change. Nothing will ever be different or better between the three of us. They've proven this fact too many times.

"I can't stay long. Do you understand that?" I exhale heavily and step closer toward the passenger side door and lift the hot metal handle, feeling the door wobble as I open it. I don't know how this thing is still running in one piece. The car smells like grass clippings and sweat with a faint scent of coffee. I roll down the window as soon as I sit down and close the door. I almost forgot about picking up my car from the Smiths' house. I won't be asking Mom or Dad for a ride after we rehash the past while they act like I'm the one who has torn *their* heart out and stepped on it a million times.

"Yeah, sure. I understand. I'm always just supposed to understand, right?"

He knows why, but I'm sure he wishes he could forget the reason I had to push them away.

After fifteen minutes of tourist traffic exiting the hot spot destination, we cross the long metal bridge connecting Newport and the bordering island of Jamestown, where I grew up.

The short, narrow roads are all too familiar. The gray blue shingles, white door and four one-story windows with white shutters are crammed together to give the impression that the house is the size of any old house, except it's not. There are barely three rooms and a basement only a child could walk through and no attic. We had no secrets in this house because it was impossible to keep anything from each other.

Dad's one word question is still dangling between us as we step out of the car. Mom will think this is some desired reunion when I was merely cornered at the police station.

I follow Dad inside, finding everything in its place as usual, but something must be rotting in the kitchen, or maybe no one has taken out the trash in too long. There are flies circling around my head and the air is damp between the narrow walls. It doesn't have to be like this.

Mom is sitting on the couch, staring at the unusable fireplace and doesn't acknowledge either of us walking inside. "Honey, I found her," Dad says, as if I need an introduction while I'm just a few steps away.

Mom's tired eyes sway over to me. Her lips part as if she might say something. Her hair has turned completely white, a drastic change since she would always color her roots every four weeks, without fail. It's like she's aged ten years in the last two. Her raggedy clothes tell me she's stopped looking at her reflection and I wonder why, or maybe I don't. "Haley, you came back?" She stands from the couch and reaches toward me as if I'm a mirage that might disappear when she makes physical contact. "What happened to your neck? You're hurt. Did someone hurt you?"

"One of them probably attacked her after she spoke to a reporter," Dad says.

"One of who?" I recoil.

"Larissa Hoyt—whoever she is affiliated with. Who knows?"

"That menace of a woman," Mom grunts. "Was it her?"

"I don't know who did this to me," I say, rubbing my hand against the swollen bumps on my neck.

"We'll keep you safe, sweetheart." Mom must know I'm not here by choice. When it comes to the two of them, I've never had a say in what goes on around here. They are set in their ways and believe they raised me with proper care. But I was a prisoner of their control—their pet rather than daughter. No matter how many times I tried explaining my feelings to them or asking them to allow me space to grow and experience life on my own, they continued doing what was "best" for me.

Getting out of this house and living on campus has been life changing for me but even from a town away they still tried to impose their power of control regarding every decision I was making. Their calls were incessant, multiple times a day. The text messages would never stop. They needed to know where I was at all times of the day. They went as far as showing up on my doorstep several times a week.

I got to the point where I had to decide what was best for me, so I told them I needed a break from them. They fought me on the topic until I was forced to give them an ultimatum. I told them if they didn't respect my wishes, I would have no choice but to leave the state—leave them for good. I blocked their phone calls and moved off campus to an apartment. It was the answer to my issues with them, at least for the last two years.

"When we saw you on TV, we were hoping you would come back here to explain what was going on. We gave you the break you said you needed from us, but we can't ignore the trouble you're in." She gently places her arms around me for a hug and something inside of me tells me to lift my arms and hug her back, but I can't. I can't offer a form of affection I don't feel, and I can't forget everything that we've been through, no matter how much time has passed.

"This isn't my home anymore," I tell her. "And I don't need your help." Allowing them back into my life would reopen the door to manipulation and control. I can't go through that again.

"Haley, why in the world would you go near any member of that family? Larissa? Lara—whatever her name is now?" Dad scolds me. That's how it starts with him—the belittling comes first. "And how can you say you don't need our help? It's obvious you do."

I grit my teeth and press the heels of my palms into my pulsating temples. "Why won't you listen to me? I didn't know who I was dealing with when I showed up at their house. She fooled me," I say, looking back and forth between the two of them.

"We all make mistakes, sweetheart," Mom says, not picking

up on my sarcasm.

"We do all make mistakes," Dad follows.

"Mistakes?" I ask them, pulling away from Mom, needing more space. "Is that what you tell yourselves? We all get to come back from mistakes?"

"Well, no. I didn't say that. I think we all know that we can't always undo what we've done wrong," Mom says.

"Exactly. You two are the perfect example—your 'mistakes' caused me so much pain and discontent, and no matter how many times I tried to tell you this, you acted as if you never heard a word I said. I've stayed away from you both for so long because I am aware that you can't always undo what you've done wrong. Case in point," I say, waving at myself.

Mom and Dad share a look and shake their heads. "We didn't make a mistake with the way we raised you. We stand by our decisions," Dad says.

"Okay, enough with the blame," Mom shouts. "The Smith family is going to come for you, Haley. You need to stay here until this is all resolved. You must know it's the right thing to do considering the consequences you've already paid in the past few days." Mom shakes her head and peers down to the floor. "You know, no matter what happens...we will always do what we can to protect you. That's all we've ever promised, and we will stand true to our word." Mom holds her hands in prayer over her chest.

I glance over at Dad, hearing a groan rumble in his throat. He's holding his head in his hand. "Your mother is right, but this ordeal is out of control. You need to stay here until things are resolved with that baby."

Trying to reason with them has never gotten me anywhere but I keep thinking they'll hear me someday. "You want to protect me by holding me hostage in this house again? No. Not again. I can't go back to that life. You need to let me go." I back away from them, moving closer to the front door so I can run.

THIRTY-FOUR

When a person ignores a problem, the problem will eventually become indestructible.

My parents haven't learned this fact.

"Haley, don't do that—don't leave like this. You can't just walk away from us again. Your decisions affect those who love you. Don't you see that?" Mom cries out.

"What decisions? I don't even know what you're talking about. I was a good daughter, one who always complied with your desire to puppeteer my life. You left me no choice but to push you away. I needed to have my own life and I still do. I deserve to have that. I didn't invite you back in. I didn't ask for this."

Dad throws his arms up in the air as his face burns red with rage. "You actually think you didn't invite us back in?" he shouts. "What the hell are you talking about?"

I run out the door, knowing I need to get away before he decides to chase after me. My pulse is throbbing in my temples as I run down the corroded driveway, wondering what lengths Dad will go to follow me. The need to have control over me is like a drug addiction.

"Hi, Haley," our neighbor shouts from across the street. "Long time, no see. How the heck are you?"

"I'm doing great," I shout, waving as I run past their house. "I hope you're well too!"

I hear him laugh. "It looks like you're running from something. Remember that's what I used to tell you when you were younger." His words trail off and the echo of his laughter follows me down the street. *I remember it well.*

No one ever knows what happens behind closed doors. Little did he know I was trying to run from something.

While racing down the street, I order an Uber to meet me a couple of streets down so I don't have to stand around and wait. When I reach my destination, I stop and drop my hands to my knees, gasping for air. The pain in my neck pulsates along the bruises, reminding me that I shouldn't be doing anything strenuous, like sprinting.

A silver sedan turns onto the street. I walk forward, meeting the car in front of the bushes where the two street corners meet, and climb into the back seat. "Hi there," he says, glancing at me in the rearview mirror.

"Hi. I'm in a bit of a rush. I'm so sorry."

He seems to understand and steps on the gas, leaving quickly enough that even if Dad stepped out of the house and got into his car, he wouldn't have time to catch up and follow me.

My heart races for the duration of the ride to the Smiths' house, which appears quiet. For all I know, Lara could be hiding somewhere, but I'm sure the police searched thoroughly. Maybe they found her, and I just don't know. It seemed like they were still heavily searching when Madden and I left.

I pull my car keys out of my purse and grip them in my hand, ready to jump from the Uber into my car as quickly as I can. "Thank you for the ride," I tell the man.

"Good luck," he says in response. If only he knew.

I make it into my car and pull around the curved pebbled driveway, skidding a bit as I hit the flat pavement. I don't know who I'm running from or who I'm running toward but I don't want to be anywhere near this house either.

———

Back at my apartment complex, I race up the stairs toward my front door, telling myself I'll figure out what to say to Willa later. Right now, I want to be alone in my room with only my thoughts. Sweat covers every inch of my body and my breaths are completely ragged by the time I reach my apartment. I'm lightheaded, enraged and upset all at the same time.

Stress and panic levels start with a racing pulse and end in an unconscious state when a body can't handle any more. With my front door open and an unexpected person sitting on my couch, I'm not sure how long I have before I hit the floor.

Willa snatches me by the wrist and yanks me into the apartment and locks the door.

"Why is she in our apartment?" I utter, knowing no matter how quiet I am, she can hear me or read my lips, being just a few steps away.

I have so many questions for Willa right now, but this is not one I thought I'd have to ask.

"She wasn't given a choice," Lara says, standing up.

The locks on our door say otherwise. We have a peephole, intended for seeing whoever is out in the hallway.

"The police are looking for you," I say, steadying myself against the wall as adrenaline spikes through my blood. I reach my free hand down to my bag to retrieve my phone.

"Don't, please don't call the police. Not yet," Lara says, holding her hands out as if I have a weapon in my possession.

"You're kidding me right now... I will not be assisting in this coercion."

"This isn't a coercion, Haley. Do you have any clue what it's like to be afraid of most of your family?" Her timing is ironic, so much so that I can't help but snicker.

"You aren't the only person in the world with a screwed-up life, and to be fair, you assisted in screwing up mine."

"Me?" Lara asks, pressing her hand against her chest, her mouth agape with shock.

"What the hell is going on?" Willa shouts. "Haley, she threatened further injury to you if I didn't let her inside. That's why she's in here and not out there."

"No, I didn't," Lara squeals. "How dare you lie!"

What other purpose would Willa have to let Lara in unless it was by threat? On the other hand, Lara would be more worried about breaking a nail than causing a physical altercation. I only know it's not the time to question my ally here. Lara needs to go.

Willa moves behind Lara and holds up her phone while placing her finger in front of lips. She's texting someone.

Anger isn't going to solve anything right now and I need to reel my thoughts in so I can handle this carefully. I place my phone back in my bag and show her my empty hands. "Please sit down," I firmly suggest.

Lara shakes her head, her greasy hair flopping around. "No, I can't—no. I need your help."

"What is it that you think I can help you with, Lara?" I ask, calmly.

"I didn't do any of this," she replies. I'm sure she knows her answer isn't sufficient and won't help any of us.

"That's something you need to discuss with the police," I state.

"They won't believe me. They'll only believe you because you're the one who called to tell them I had Madden locked up. If she was your child, you would have locked her up too."

"I think that is how we ended up in this situation. I wouldn't lock a child in her room. Regardless of what you think or know Madden has done, you are not the person who can help her."

"She hates me," Lara grunts. "She wishes I was dead. She would do anything for a different mother. And the worst part is, I don't know what I've done so wrong for her to feel that way toward me. All I've done is give her love and it has never been enough." There must be more to this than she's admitting.

"She's nine," I reply. "And if you're so innocent, why did you flee from the police?"

"She lies. She lies better than I ever could."

"She's nine," Willa echoes my last response.

"Lara, when did Madden start showing signs of anger?" I ask, stepping in closer to her, causing her to take steps backward. "Not just childhood anger but threatening signs that you might be in danger?"

"Since she was old enough to show that emotion, I don't know," she says, wrapping her arms around her waist. She sounds unsure about her accusation. "She's psychotic."

With that diagnosis, it's clear she hasn't consulted a doctor yet.

"I—if anything, she might be presenting symptoms of conduct disorder. She's young to be categorized as psychotic." This is according to psychological studies. I know everyone is different, but Lara shouldn't be assuming a diagnosis. "While the condition can sometimes be categorized as a hereditary illness, the symptoms typically only present themselves when a vulnerable person encounters environmental influences that exacerbate the traits. And in your case with identical twins, Blakely would also show the same signs unless they have unique external influences."

"I don't even know what you're talking about," Lara shouts. "I've raised my girls the same way. Not one of them has been treated differently than the other."

She should watch her back with Blakely if that's the case, and if Lara's correct about her theories—Madden being responsible for purposely drowning Fallon, she'd be safer with the police.

"This could have been prevented had you gotten Madden the treatment she needed."

"They would take her away from me," Lara cries out. "Do you know what they would do to her?"

I do, but it's clear she doesn't understand how psychology works with young children. She sacrificed the rest of her family's wellbeing on an account of her selfish unfounded fears. "Instead, she took Fallon away from you—forever." My words are brutal but sometimes it's the only way to get through to someone who can't see past their own nose.

My statement creates a thread of silence between us, making it easy to hear the aggressive thuds coming from the outside of my door. "Newport Police, open up!" Thank God Willa sent for them.

Lara crouches next to the couch, wrapping her hands over her head as if she can hide herself in plain sight of the door. She needs help too. The whole family does, clearly.

Willa shimmies over to the door, pressing her hand to her chest as she releases the lock. I keep my stare glued on Lara, wondering if she's about to pull a weapon out of her loose sweater.

The breeze from the door rushes against my back and police swarm the apartment, detaining her with ease as if she's a doll. "Do you have any remorse for what you did to me and my family?" Lara whimpers. "I'm not responsible for everything you hold against me, but you're responsible for everything I hold against you." She isn't making any sense. "It was your fault my sister died. It was your fault my parents became money hungry vultures and made me marry Corbin. Your mistake is my demise, and yet, you still don't see it that way."

"Enough. Quiet down," an officer tells Lara, pulling her up to her feet.

The scene of watching the police take Lara out of my apartment strikes a nerve.

That night—the night of the fire when paramedics were tending to me, I saw the police taking Lara with them, but I was sure it was because she was shouting and screaming at the top of her lungs to rescue her sister. She was pleading with them to let her go back upstairs to help find her. The police held her back. They kept her contained, not allowing her back near the building that was crumbling to the ground. I felt sorry for Lara, almost like I do right this second. Mom and Dad said the girl's body wasn't found but the building had burnt down so quickly, it wasn't a surprise that no one could find her. If she had gotten out somehow, her disappearance wouldn't make much sense. I heard her screams, but maybe it was all a scheme to rob my parents in a lawsuit. I was too young to understand the lengths someone would go to get what they wanted. Their family had nothing. Dad couldn't collect rent from them for months sometimes, but he felt bad for their situation and let it slide. He saw the good in them when there may have been nothing but evil. For all anyone knows, Lara could have started the fire that night so her parents could claim the insurance payout. It could have all been a lie, just like she could be lying about Madden and Fallon now. Is she the one with hereditary psychosis?

Willa places her hand on my back and for a long minute I forgot why I was so angry with her. "Are you okay?"

I shrug her hand off my back. "No, I'm not okay. Why would you tell my dad where I was?"

I'll get to the part where she let Lara into our apartment next.

"What? I didn't talk to your dad. I went to pick you up at the police station, but you were gone, and your phone went right to voicemail when I called. Why would I call your dad when you made it clear you have some big issues with them? I was upset that I didn't know what was going on with you, but I would never hurt you like that. You're my best friend, Hales."

"How could I know what to believe? If that's true, I don't know how my dad knew where I was," I tell Willa, staring out toward the dark balcony doors, wondering who else knew where I was today.

THIRTY-SIX

THIRTEEN YEARS AGO

I'm not sure how old I was when I began to question the word "normal," but I was taught that the word means...*common, similar to something, and doesn't stand out from a crowd.* The word is tossed around my house like it's our last name and I wonder if Mom and Dad are confused about the meaning too, because they always refer to our little family as the most normal people anyone must know. Except, we aren't like anyone else who lives in this multi-family townhome, especially in comparison to the family next door.

There are so many days when I walk up our front steps after school and hear shouting from the neighbors. One of the kids will storm out and slam the door, or it's the wife who leaves. The family isn't happy, or at least that's what it sounds like to me. Maybe because I don't have any siblings, there's a lack of arguments in my home. My parents seem to love each other and get along, maybe more so than other parents. Or maybe it's because Dad isn't home most of the day. He travels around Rhode Island checking on the properties he owns and manages, including the one we currently live in.

I let myself into our townhome now, not finding Mom in her

usual spot in the kitchen. She loves to cook more than anyone I've ever met in my life and says the kitchen is the only place she ever wants to be. I don't really like to cook, even though she's taught me how to make every one of her favorite recipes. It always feels like work, just work.

"No, Gary. This will be the fourth month. This building costs a fortune. We can't just let tenants slide because you feel sorry for them."

I stop moving, afraid to make a noise. I want to hear what Mom is talking about. She must be on the phone with Dad since I can only hear half of the conversation. "They said that?" She continues to question him. "Which one of the kids is it then?" Mom makes some humming noise in the back of her throat. "We've never noticed anything, but things are that bad, huh?" She's never questioned Dad as much as she is now and I'm very curious as to who they're talking about. "Charity? Are you kidding me? We aren't a non-profit foundation." A loud exhale followed by a muffled groan breaks up the conversation. "I'm greedy. That's nice of you to say. We have needs too, Gary. Shall I remind you of those or should we pretend that it doesn't exist like we always do?" Needs? What needs do any of us have? They've always been very clear about the difference between needing and wanting something and we are fortunate enough never to need more than we can comfortably afford. "Well, fine. Do what you must. And yes," she grumbles, "I will have dinner waiting for you on the table at six p.m. sharp, as requested, dear." Mom throws something across the room, and I can only assume it must be her cell phone.

I step into the room without knocking. There usually isn't a need to knock since their door is always open, but my appearance causes her to gasp and clutch her chest. "What are you doing home so early?" Her eyes look like they might fall out of her head.

"It was an early release day. There's a teacher meeting. It's on the calendar." She never forgets anything that she's added to the calendar. "Are you okay?"

"Yes, yes," she scoffs. "Of course, I'm fine. Everything is fine. I dropped my phone while I was dusting the dresser."

I consider telling her I've been home longer than the time it took for her to "drop" her phone but seeing as I don't think she's being honest; it might be best if I don't tell her I overheard her conversation with Dad.

"You look like something is bothering you, sweetie. How was your algebra test?"

"Good. No, I'm not upset." I guess I can lie too since I'm pretty sure I failed my math test.

She makes her way around the bedroom and gives me a tight squeeze with a loving groan. "I love you. I always miss you so much when you're at school."

"I love you, too."

I leave her bedroom with my backpack still slung over my shoulder and close myself into my bedroom. One of the families in the six-unit townhouse isn't paying their rent and Dad is allowing them to get away with it because something is wrong with one of the kids. Those are the only broad facts I pulled from the conversation. There are only two other townhomes occupied with kids, the people next door and the quiet family with a toddler and a newborn who live behind us. A fighting family is a sign of distress. My bets are on the Hoyts. But I wonder what's wrong with which of the kids, something that would prevent Mr. and Mrs. Hoyt from paying their rent?

I return to the hallway, finding Mom and Dad's bedroom empty and the bathroom door open. She's either in the kitchen or in the family room upstairs. A stack of pots and pans clanging answers my question and I make my way into the kitchen. "Mom?"

She lifts her eyebrows and presses a smile into her dimpled

cheeks as she turns to face me with a pot clutched between her hands. "Yes, sweetheart?"

"Is something wrong with one of the Hoyt kids?"

Mom pulls the pot into her chest, clutching it firmly. "What do you mean?" she responds quickly.

"Is one of the Hoyt kids sick?" I ask again, rearranging the words.

"Why would you ask something like that?"

"Because I overheard you and Dad talking when I got home." There's half of my honesty for the day. I can wait on the truth of how I think my algebra test went.

"You were eavesdropping?"

I shake my head, furrowing my eyebrows. "No, I happened to hear what you were saying when I walked into the house."

She sighs and releases the pot to one hand and holds it by her side. "Haley, you have nothing to worry about. Everyone is fine and whatever you think you heard most likely isn't true."

"Is it Larissa?"

"Haley, I think we should do a better job at minding our business."

"If someone isn't doing well, I would like to offer to help. Isn't that the right thing to do?"

Mom shakes her head furiously as if I'm way far off with my assumption. "No. You don't know what you're talking about, honey. The situation you heard half of is not what you think and has nothing to do with who you think it does. Please, I'm going to ask you to drop it and not bring it back up again, okay?"

I stare at Mom, waiting for her to blink, but it's like she's frozen within her thoughts. "Do you want me to make dinner?" I offer. "I don't mind."

"No, no. I want you to focus on whatever homework you have."

A door outside slams and the storm door follows, making a racket. We both look toward our front door as if we can see clearly through the white sheer curtain covering the window. I walk past Mom and stand beside the window to peek out.

"Why are you so awful?" Larissa screams, her long hair flying in the wind behind her as she pounds her fists on the storm door. "Do you know what kind of damage you are causing us? Every single day, you and your issues are all that matter. What about the rest of us? Don't the rest of us matter? Huh? God!" She pounds her fists again and whips her head toward our door, seemingly catching my wandering eye. She squints and sneers before charging down the steps and out onto the wide driveway.

"That's who Dad is helping?" I ask. "They've only been living here five months. Does that mean they've never paid their rent?"

"Who?" Mom replies.

"The Hoyt family next door."

"Haley," Mom scolds me, gritting her teeth with a firm look of frustration. "Not another word about this. Do you understand? Your father does not need to know you overheard any of that conversation." She lowers her head but lifts her eyes, pinning her stare to my face. "Okay?"

"Yes," I answer.

"Promise me you won't mention any of this to your father when he gets home."

I hesitate but only because she's never asked me to keep anything from him before. Open communication is what keeps a family close. Maybe we aren't as close as I thought.

Maybe it's all just an act.

"Yes, yeah, I promise. I won't say anything."

"You should try to get some sleep," Willa says, startling me from the living room couch, the display of her phone glowing against her face in the dark. I was on my way to the kitchen for a glass of water.

"Why are you still awake?" I ask, whispering. I'm not sure if Jerry has come over at any point in the last couple of hours since I've been in my bedroom with earbuds in, or if Willa is the only one here. If he is here, I assume she'd be in her room with him, or he'd be out here too. In any case, she's usually asleep by now if it's not a work night.

"I'm worried about you, Hales," she says, her voice scratchy, likely from being overtired.

"That makes two of us," I reply.

"Every time you leave the apartment, you end up in some kind of trouble—more trouble than you've already found in the last few days. There must be something we can do to pause this ride or get you back on track with the focus on your life, and your life alone."

That's all I've been thinking about for hours, finding a way to extract myself from this tornado. Thankfully, my last final is over, so at least that won't be a reason to go anywhere, but there are still many other loose ends I have to tie up, one being the job I no longer have. "I've been looking through job postings for the last hour. I'm on the same page as you."

"Would you reconsider a waitstaff position at the restaurant?" she offers. "We could work together that way."

Willa has been trying to get me to apply for a position at the restaurant for the last couple of years but I'm uncoordinated and clumsy, which doesn't make for the best waiter. Plus, I need to be focused on a position that can add value to my psych degree. I still have a case study I need to write by the end of the summer and my research subjects are detained. "Maybe. I don't know right now." I continue into the kitchen and take a glass out of the cabinet next to the sink.

"How did things go with your parents?" Willa sounds hesitant to ask me the question after everything that has gone on today, and I wish she was more hesitant than she sounds so maybe she wouldn't have asked me at all.

"Not great."

"Oh yeah?"

"Yeah," I reply.

"You know, the couple of times I met them throughout the years, they seemed like very nice people. I can't imagine why—"

"Please, don't go there," I say, turning on the sink to fill my glass. "Everyone seems so pleasant and put together when they are outside of their homes, but no one knows what a person's like behind closed doors."

"I suppose," she says as I walk back into the living room. "Did you end up finding out who called your dad?"

"Nope. Another endless loop of questions for me to over analyze."

I find myself staring at her eyes, wishing I could decipher what's going on in her head right now. Either she or Dad are lying about who told him to come pick me up. Despite never believing a word that comes out of Dad's mouth, I don't see a logical reason for him to make up a story about calling Willa to find me. Willa, on the other hand, would have to confess to throwing me under the bus and calling my dad when she clearly stated she would never do something like that to me.

"Well, I'm going to try and get some sleep," I tell Willa, holding my glass up to her as I continue into my bedroom.

"Goodnight, Hales."

After locking myself in my bedroom, I place the glass down on my nightstand and grab my phone to view the untouched notifications that have stacked up on my display. I never called Liam back. He did call like he said he would. He's even left a couple of text messages to tell me he wants to make sure everything is okay.

It's late, but my midnights are becoming no different than noon with this lack of sleep. I thumb out a quick message to apologize for the delay.

Me: I'm so sorry I missed your call and messages. It's been another long day full of surprises. I hope you had a good day.

I toss my phone onto my bed because I doubt Liam will be responding at this hour. I think he said tomorrow is his last day of school, so I'm sure he's in bed by now. But after slipping into a pair of shorts and a tank top, a response pops up on my screen. I scoop the phone up with a rush of excitement.

Liam: I'm so glad you messaged. It's probably weird for me to tell you I was worried about you all day, but I was. I hope everything is okay... Are you able to meet for a late lunch tomorrow? I'm out of school at eleven.

A smile inches across my face as I reply.

Me: Yes, please. I'd love that. Let me know where.

I shouldn't be smiling. A baby is still missing, and two other children's lives were uprooted today. I feel awful for them, knowing what kind of trauma this will likely leave them with as they get older. It makes me wonder which poison is worse, being lied to for years or learning the truths that were buried beneath lies.

THIRTY-EIGHT

TUESDAY, JUNE 13TH 8:00 AM

The morning has come too quickly for my exhausted mind as a phone call jolts through me like an electric shock. It's too early for the call to be about anything good. I feel around for my phone connected to the charger on my nightstand and lift the device above my face, squinting through one eye to see the number. Newport Bridge Law Firm is listed as the company name beneath the number.

"Hi, this is Haley," I answer, trying to sound like I'm awake rather than climbing out of a grave.

"Haley Vaughn, hello, and good morning. I apologize for the early call, but I'm a public defender, Jared Keffner, for the town of Newport and we're gathering evidence to support Madden Smith's case. Timing is of the utmost importance, as I'm sure you can understand. Therefore, we're wondering if you would be able to meet with us this morning?"

"Us?" I question. "I—what are you hoping I can help with?"

"My apologies. As Madden's defender, it would be myself, Madden, a social worker, a psychologist, and you, if you are willing to lend us some of your time and knowledge pertaining to anything you might know about Madden, it could assist us with this case."

I run my hand down the side of my face and then over my eyes, trying to make sure I'm taking this all in properly. "Um, I'm not sure I have tangible evidence to assist—I only spent a short amount of time with her." As the words come out of my mouth, guilt coats my veins like tar. With how awful Lara was to me when I was thirteen, it makes me wonder how she's treated her children. There's cause and effect for everything. There could be an effect on Madden if I don't help her and there could be an effect on both me and her if I do. The last thing I want is any further involvement in this case, but I also don't want to ever feel like I'm the cause for another one of their children to go missing—or worse.

"Madden personally requested you as you have been very understanding of her. She thinks you might be able to help her. Those are her words," the man says, clearing his throat.

That poor little girl is breaking my heart. The words come out of my mouth before I've had a chance to think them through completely. "Sure. I can meet with you. Again, I'm not sure how helpful I'll be but if Madden has requested that I be there, I will." Even if it's just a familiar face, which is unfortunate considering how little I know her. She must be terrified, and I told her everything would be okay the other day. I sincerely hope I was telling her the truth.

"Perfect. We can meet you at the courthouse at nine if that time will work for you?"

I pull the phone away from my ear to squint at the time. It's eight. I can make it there in time.

"I'll be there."

"Check in with the court clerk and tell her you're meeting me, Jared Keffner," he says, repeating his name. "We'll see you soon, Haley. Bye now."

When the call disconnects, Corbin's words echo through my head.

"I've been telling you she needs psychiatric help for years, but you insisted that she will grow out of this nonsense. If we had tended to her troubles, our baby would still be alive right now..."

Whether Madden was involved with what happened to Fallon or not, Corbin's statement isn't false. If they thought Madden needed psychiatric help and they ignored this, they neglected her, ultimately putting her in this situation. Or...she's just the easiest target to blame.

It doesn't take long for me to wonder what Madden might have said about me or why she thinks I can be of much help. I might have been the only one to give her hope. I'm not sure if she's been allowed to see Lara or Corbin, or even Blakely.

I hope I didn't say anything I shouldn't have said to her yesterday. The moments in her bedroom were so stressful and upsetting. I was trying my best to console her in such an unthinkable situation. But if there's anything I can relate to and understand, it's the feeling of loneliness when the only thing she must need is a hand to hold. The world can turn against someone quickly in the shadow of a tragedy, and stories will be formulated and branch off into dozens of different directions. All eyes are on Madden as people continue to speculate the truth of what happened to Fallon, and the word of a child can only bear so much weight in the face of evidence, or worse, the lack thereof.

THIRTY-NINE

TUESDAY, JUNE 13TH 9:00 AM

A cool, foggy morning without a hint of sun makes for less congestion downtown and a quick ride to the courthouse. The drive was just long enough to make my stomach twist into knots like a fresh piece of taffy. The nerves won't be leaving anytime soon, not while I'm here.

I make my way up the two shallow sets of cement steps toward the dark double doors of the historical building. I've only been here once for jury duty, but it was a while ago and I don't remember much about the layout inside. I do remember the officers standing guard at metal detectors upon entering the building. I place my purse down on the conveyor belt and walk toward an officer with a metal detecting wand in his gloved hand. The detectors remain silent, and my bag is handed back to me, sparing me an extra pat-down.

A sign for the court clerk pulls me off to the side of the open foyer and up to an attended window. A few people are moving about inside the adjacent room shuffling paperwork and making photocopies.

A middle-aged woman in a dark fitted summer dress, a perfect tan, and her hair pulled back into a French twist takes a seat on the other side of the window and smiles. "How can I help you?"

I look disheveled in comparison, but I only had an hour to put myself together. "Hi, yes, I'm supposed to be meeting with Jared Keffner in just a few minutes."

She swivels to the right in her chair and takes a hold of a computer mouse, tapping it a couple of times before clicking. "Do you have ID on you?"

I reach into my purse and slide my license out of my wallet to hand to her. She scans it on a small machine next to her desk and watches her screen before removing my ID. "All set," she says, handing it back. "You'll want to go down to the public defender's office. It's around this corner." She points to my right where I see a conjoining hallway. "Then straight down the hall, two rooms from the end on the left. You can't miss it."

I take my ID and slip it back into my bag. "Thank you."

The hallway isn't lit as brightly as the foyer but isn't as long as I was expecting it to be. The public defender's office has plenty of windows outlining the door, allowing me to see Madden seated at a table inside among a few other unfamiliar faces.

I knock, watching a younger man look over in my direction and hustle for the door. "Yes," he says, "are you—"

"Haley Vaughn," I respond.

"Jared. Great to meet you," he says, holding his hand out to shake mine. "Come on in."

Madden doesn't say anything but perks up in her seat and waves at me with a small smile. Her cheeks are flushed, and her eyes are watery. She looks so small sitting at a table full of stiff adults in professional attire.

I'm not sure if I expected Corbin or Lara to be here too, but I know Jared mentioned a social worker, which I assume to be one of the two women sitting on either side of Madden.

"This is Ms. Jillian Mann, Madden's assigned social worker," he says, gesturing to the woman in the black polka-dot skirt suit who stands up to shake my hand. "And over here, we have Ms. Kandice Maxwell, a well-versed child psychologist." She stands up to shake my hand as well. Her emerald-green blouse and short coppery hair reflect the fluorescent lights as she moves around. Kandice holds her stare over me like an Arctic blast. The slight lift of her eyebrow suggests she doesn't like the fact that I'm here, which makes me wonder if she's truly here to assist Madden or drain her of information that could be held against her. I know everyone in this room is supposed to be here to protect Madden, but protection doesn't always mean setting someone free.

I feel out of place and I'm more confident now that I won't have much influential purpose here. Regardless, I take a seat across from Madden and make myself comfortable in the high-back chair as Jared paces around the table. "This is part of our pre-hearing preparation where we collect as many details as we can. Our goal is to build the best defense possible for Madden." I nod with understanding, assuming he's catching me up on what the others have already heard. "As you know, most details about the case came to fruition the night you were left to babysit Madden and her sister, Blakely. By having you here, we're hoping you can confirm occurrences that took place that night. Anything discussed here today will only be used for legal purposes."

"Of course," I say, feeling more comfortable knowing that I knew absolutely nothing about Fallon that night.

"Great. I'm going to have Ms. Kandice take over with the questions now," Jared says, taking a seat next to me in front of a notepad and pen. "But first, Madden, we all want you to know that we understand how challenging this situation is for you, especially at just nine years old. But it's so important that you are completely open and honest with all of us so we can help you, okay?"

Madden swallows what looks to be a lump in her throat and folds her hands together on top of the table, squeezing her fingers so tightly they lose circulation. "Okay," she says.

"Perfect," Jared replies.

Kandice twists her chair to face Madden and folds her hands on top of her lap. "Okay, Miss Madden, let's start by you telling us, in your own words, what happened when you were with Fallon last?" Her voice is higher pitched than the average adult but not like nails on a chalkboard. It's as if she wants to sound like a child to resonate with her. I'm not sure that always works the best when trying to have a mature conversation with a child though.

Madden peers at me and twists her lips. Her forehead crinkles, and she takes a deep breath.

I give her a nod, urging her to respond to Kandice. With another deep breath, Madden opens her mouth to speak. "Well..."

Nothing follows and I'm wondering if she's nervous or debating where to begin.

"Maybe we can start with something a bit easier. What kinds of things did you and Fallon like to do together?"

Madden shrugs and squints her eyes. Her jaw swivels back and forth and she twists her head to look at the hanging blinds along the window. "She just turned one at the beginning of spring, so she just learned to walk. I taught her because Mommy wasn't ready to have three kids running in different directions."

"Did Mommy say that or is that what you think?" Kandice follows.

"I heard Mommy say that when she was on the phone."

"Did you hear her say anything else?"

Madden sighs and peers down to the carpet. "No, but I know she never wanted Fallon. She said Fallon was a mistake."

"Hmm," Kandice says. "What does a mistake mean to you, Madden?"

Another shrug. "I don't know. I guess it's something people do by accident, but I don't know how Mommy could have kept Fallon in her tummy forever, so...I'm not sure what she meant."

"What about Daddy? Did he ever say anything like that?"

"He's always working, or tired, or hungry. Mommy said that's how most dads are."

Kandice allows a smile to form along her lips. "I think all families are a little bit different, but sometimes it's hard to know who does the most work, right?"

"Yeah, they fight about that a lot," Madden says.

"That must be so difficult for you to watch," Kandice says with a wide-eyed gaze. "Have you had a lot of babysitters or nannies?"

"No, Haley is the first babysitter we've had since Fallon was born. I don't really remember the others."

I could swear we had a different conversation. I was under the impression that I was replacing a nanny who didn't work out.

"Oh, okay. That must have been a fun treat," Kandice says with a real smile.

"Yeah, we had fun with Haley. We watched a new mermaid movie and had popcorn, but then Blakely and I got in trouble for playing hide-and-seek, so Haley made us go to bed."

I almost forgot about the hide-and-seek debacle. No one looks at me when she says this but I'm wondering what they're thinking about me and if I was the one who came up with the rule of not playing hide-and-seek. I can only take a guess at why Corbin had made that rule, but it certainly had nothing to do with me.

Kandice tilts her head to the side and exaggerates a pout. "Oh no, why is hide-and-seek not allowed?"

Madden stares at Kandice as if she should know the answer to her question. "Mommy and Daddy think I hid Fallon but then forgot to find her."

"Is that what happened?" Kandice responds, her eyebrows furrowing.

"I don't know."

"Was your sister, Blakely, playing with you when you and Fallon were playing hide-and-seek?"

"No," Madden says simply without a change in expression.

"Did you teach Fallon how to play hide-and-seek?" Kandice asks.

Madden straightens her shoulders and presses her hands into the chair next to her legs. "No."

"But your mommy and daddy think you did?"

"I don't understand," Madden replies.

There are so many different questions I would like to ask her right now because I don't think Kandice is getting very far or will get anywhere by the way she's tiptoeing around the subject. "What about the mermaids? Did Fallon like mermaids, too?" I ask, interrupting Kandice. If the intent is to garner information to protect Madden and they asked me to be here, there's no sense in keeping my mouth shut.

"Not as much as I do, but I told her the mermaids live in the ocean behind our house. I asked her if she wanted to play hide-and-seek with them like I do. But she's a baby so she didn't reply."

"Were you talking to Fallon about the mermaids when you were down by the water?"

Madden stares down at the table and furrows her thin blonde brows. "Yes...I mean—I'm not supposed to—" Madden looks up at me, clamps her teeth and her lips pull back into a look of guilt. "I'm sorry."

"What are you sorry for?" Kandice asks Madden, looking at her and then me.

I'm not sure why Madden is stumbling over her words, but Kandice must think I know.

"I—I don't know. This is all scary and confusing. I don't understand what happened or why I'm here."

I place my palm down on the table and stare at Madden. "It's okay," I tell her, hoping my calm tone will release some of her tension.

"Did you talk to Fallon about finding a mermaid in the ocean that day?" Kandice asks, continuing her questions before Madden can reset her thoughts.

"Yes, but I'm not sure if she ever saw one. I would be jealous if she did though."

Jared taps the cap of his pen on the table a few times and Jillian, the social worker, is scribbling notes down, her pen scratching along the paper. "My God. If this baby is not in the ocean, we're sitting on borrowed time. We need to get to the bottom of this," he mutters.

I'm going to take a wild guess in that Jared isn't used to representing children.

"I understand your frustration Mr. Keffner, but we need to have a bit of patience right now," Kandice says.

Jared leans his head back and folds his hands behind his neck. "Madden, where do you think Fallon is right now?" Jared asks, pushing aside the childlike exchange.

Madden twists in her chair to face my side of the table. "I don't know where she is." Madden grimaces and folds her arms over her chest.

"Do you think she's still alive?" That's a hard question to ask a nine-year-old regardless of the situation.

"Maybe," she says, with another shrug of her shoulders. "Maybe not. Mommy would be happy if she isn't, though."

The chairs around the table all scrape against the floor, signs of discomfort from everyone. My chest tightens, wondering what Madden might say next and I feel the urge to fidget in my seat the same way she is right now.

Kandice takes in a deep breath and presses her lips together into a tight smile before saying whatever is conjuring in her mind. "Madden, I'm sure your mommy loves Fallon very much, just as much as she loves you and your sister, Blakely," Kandice says.

"No. That's not true," Madden says, new confidence showing in her suddenly straight posture. "Just like she prefers Blakely over me. Blakely is smarter and more helpful than I am so she's Mommy's favorite. Still, Mommy doesn't hate me as much as Fallon, I guess. She hates Haley more because she said it's her fault that Fallon is missing."

Jared slices a look at me as if I knew Madden would say something along these lines. "I thought you didn't know the Smiths before the night you were hired to babysit them. Why am I just learning about this now?" Jared grumbles. "What else do I need to know?"

"Lara and I knew each other thirteen years ago," I say, my throat tightening beneath the remaining sore areas around my neck.

"That's when Mommy's sister died."

I close my eyes, wishing Madden would focus on what's currently happening rather than what can easily be misconstrued from the past. Though, it shouldn't go unknown that Lara knowingly hired me when I was in the dark to who she was through her changed names.

"Lara's sister died?" Jared questions.

Nausea laced memories fill my head as I try to pull myself together to speak. "Yeah, we—ah—we lived in the same town-home complex and there was a fire. Her sister didn't make it. My father was the landlord and their family sued ours for negligence with building maintenance. I was only thirteen at the time."

"So Lara is blaming Haley and Madden for Fallon's disappearance," Jared said. "Interesting." He presses his fingers through his sweat-glazed hair. "Madden, if there's a chance that

Fallon is somewhere besides in the ocean right now, we need to know so people can try to find her."

"Well," Madden says, looking up to Jared through her long white lashes. "What if Fallon was never born?" Madden asks.

"Was she?" Kandice blurts out.

Madden's chest moves up and down, showing erratic breaths, nerves...something. "I don't know," she says, a sob breaking through her throat.

"I noticed there weren't any pictures of Fallon at home," I say. "Have there ever been pictures of her hanging on the walls with yours and Blakely's?"

Jared hums with a sound of encouragement as if his interest is more piqued than it's been since I arrived.

"When Mommy and Daddy were asleep one night, I took them down and tore them up," Madden says. "I also deleted them from Mommy and Daddy's phones. They leave them on the kitchen counter a lot, especially when they're arguing over something."

"Oh my goodness. That must have made you so sad to do such a thing with those photos," Kandice says. "How come you felt it was important to do that?"

Madden plucks at a thread on her solid white T-shirt and pauses for a moment before answering. "To make Mommy like me more."

"Do you think that worked?" Kandice asks her.

Madden shakes her head. "No. She just cried and shouted at me, asking me what was wrong with my head. I told her she's the one who said she wishes Fallon was never born and I was trying to make her feel better."

There's a wave of subtle gasping breaths from the adults at the table and I'm wondering if the rest of them are just figuring out how deep the root of this issue truly is.

"Madden, do you have aunts, uncles, or grandparents that you see often?"

"No one likes my mom," she says, keeping her gaze set on her lap.

Jared clears his throat. "Okay, I think we're going to take a short break. Haley, we really appreciate you coming down here today. We're going to continue with some additional questions to Madden, but I don't want to hold you up here. You've been very helpful so far. I may be in touch again if we need any more of your assistance. Would that be okay with you?"

Just when they might get more information out of Madden, they're having me leave. I thought I was supposed to be her trustworthy support system.

FORTY

TUESDAY, JUNE 13TH 1:30 PM

I lucked out in finding a street parking spot outside of the wharf and have been sitting in my car for the last ninety minutes, making notes on everything that was said during the meeting. Not enough questions were asked, at least not while I was there. If their objective is to prove Madden is innocent, I'm not sure they have enough proof. It's hard to tell what the purpose of me being there really was. I hardly spoke. I wonder if they were interested in watching Madden's body language toward me, thinking it would help them unearth a significant answer that could help with the defense.

I would love to know if someone has pulled up a birth certificate for Fallon or found any other photographs of her aside from the one family portrait they have when she was a newborn. There are so many loose ends to all of this, but I know I'm not privy to that level of the investigation findings.

I close my notebook and slide it between the center console and the passenger seat before grabbing my purse and heading toward the sandwich shop where Liam and I have plans to meet.

With the weather a bit cooler today, it seems like a good

excuse to wear a hooded sweatshirt and oversized sunglasses to walk down the wharf. At least there aren't any news reporters here today, or not yet.

Until now, I haven't given much thought about how long a search party lasts before it dwindles, and people begin to come to terms with the unlikelihood of recovering a missing person. Maybe it's just the media that switches to another topic and the investigation continues far beyond what most people realize. If the family didn't despise me, I would be out looking too. Maybe I should just do so on my own. All I know is that I wouldn't be able to give up if it was my child and I wouldn't be at home while people were searching for her unless I knew for sure she was gone. If they think Fallon drowned, there is still a body somewhere. They need to find her.

A spine-twisting chill rattles through me with the thought of a baby's body washing up onto a shore.

While swallowing the tense knot in my throat, I spot Liam sitting at a wrought-iron table with an ocean blue umbrella opened overhead. He's in a tropical button-down shirt, jeans, and loafers—possibly his celebratory outfit for the first day of summer vacation. I remove my hood to make myself less inconspicuous, allowing him to notice me right away. "Hey, you," he says, his vibe chipper and uplifting as he stands to greet me with a hug and a kiss on the cheek.

He smells like spiced coconut again, and it might just be my new favorite scent. I remove my sunglasses and try to perk myself up a bit, so I don't look like I've been watching a little girl's life fall apart at the courthouse for the last couple of hours.

"Oh, I'm so glad we got to have lunch today. It's been a long couple of days, but you're done with school for the summer now, right?"

He holds his arms out to the side and spins around. "Does the outfit convince you?" He chuckles.

"If I had known that was a thing, I would have found some-

thing tropical to wear after I took my last final yesterday."
Instead, I could pass for being dressed for winter.

"Well, not to worry because we have all summer for tropical
things," he says, pulling out a chair for me.

I'd like to think so.

"So, did you pull the *old teacher move* and watch a lame
movie this morning for the final three hours?" I ask with a
snicker, teasing him as we both settle into our seats.

"Hey now!" He shuffles a napkin across the table toward
me. "I am not one of *those* teachers. We played music trivia."

I sigh to relinquish my insult. "Well, that's not the most
boring thing, I suppose."

"And you? I'm afraid to ask what you've been up to since I
saw you the other night." He folds his arms down on the
tabletop and leans in toward me as if whatever I might say
should be kept quiet.

I huff and take the stray napkin to fiddle with while I talk.
"A lot, but to make a long story short...let's just say Lara has
deeply incriminated herself. She and her husband are both
currently detained. Madden, one of the twins, is with a social
worker, and the other, Blakely, is at a friend's house. There are
still no discoveries on the baby, though."

Liam shakes his head and plucks at a loose laminated corner
of the menu. "That's ridiculous. I'm happy the spotlight is off
you obviously, but it's awful to think about what those poor kids
are going through."

I take the other menu, wanting nothing more than to focus
my attention on the list of sandwiches. "Let's talk about something else today. Like...tell me your life story. I need to know
more about you."

Liam releases the flap of the menu from between his
pinched fingers and glances up at me with a raised brow. "My
life's story?" He crosses his arms over his chest and leans back as

if to get comfortable. "Okay, but this might take a while." His smirk says otherwise, but I'll go with it.

"I have time," I reply, leaning back into my seat too.

"Okay, but..." he says, pointing at me, "for every bullet point of my life's story, you have to do the same in return, deal?"

I smile and set the menu down on the table. "Deal."

"Many moons ago..."

I tilt my head to the side and smile. "Come on, the real story..."

He readjusts his posture and straightens his T-shirt. "Okay, okay. I think I mentioned that I grew up in the area. I had a typical upbringing for the most part." He pauses for a moment and tilts his head to the side like something just made him uncomfortable. "My dad passed away when I was seventeen and my mom passed away five years ago. A heart attack and cancer."

"Oh my God, I'm so sorry. That's terrible. They must have been so young, too."

"Yeah, I guess good health wasn't in the stars for them, but they hated doctors so maybe there was a chance for early intervention. Guess we'll never know."

"Are you an only child, too?"

He sighs and leans back in his chair. "I wish," he says, laughing off the question. "Siblings are a pain in the butt."

I might prefer a pain-in-the-butt-sibling over being an only child to my parents. "I've heard they can be annoying," I say, avoiding the awkward response of telling him he's lucky.

"So, let's just cross families off the list for now. Ex-boyfriends...go," he says, grinning.

A waiter interrupts our conversation and I'd like to thank him for doing so when he introduces himself and holds out an order pad.

"Hi, I'll have the chicken salad wrap and water with lemon please," I request.

"I'll have the same," Liam says, slipping my menu from my hand to hand the waiter both.

"Sure thing, it'll just be a few minutes," he says.

"I didn't forget the question I left off on," Liam says with a snicker.

I grumble and toy with my necklace as I try to come up with a way to make my past sound less depressing than it is. "Well, I did have a boyfriend for a while. His name was Kyle, but there was a drunk driving accident. End of that story. Other than that, there was a kid named Billy when I was younger. We never dated or anything but that was the name I drew all over my school notebooks a million times with hearts, x's, and o's."

"Aw, a school-girl crush," he says, smirking at me. "Did you ever confess your feelings to him?"

"Definitely not."

The waiter swings by with our waters and a couple of straws and leaves just as quickly. I grab my straw, desperate for something to tear apart during this awkward twenty-questions game.

"Why not?" Liam continues.

"He was the most popular boy in school, and I was probably the least popular girl. I'm just glad I knew well enough that life doesn't mirror the fantasy of a romance book where opposites of variance still manage to attract each other."

"Never say never. That was my motto in high school." He plunges his straw into his cup without the same need to shred the straw wrapper first.

"You had a school-boy crush too?" I tease.

"I guess you could call it that. Unlike your story, I told this girl how I felt, and she went running for the hills. Even then, I said, someday she might change her mind," he says, laughing. "That's where my never say never mantra came in. At this age, it might be safe to say that will never happen though." He takes a sip of his water and shakes his head. "God, being a kid is ruth-less, isn't it?"

"I wouldn't go back to those days if someone paid me millions."

Liam glances toward the back of my chair. "I think you're buzzing."

I'm going to throw my phone in the ocean if the calls and messages don't stop. Every buzz gives me a mere panic attack now. I twist around and pull my phone out, finding Newport Bridge Law Firm calling again. I groan. "I'm so sorry. I need to take this call. I'll just be a second."

"No worries," Liam says, curiosity poking at his left arched brow.

"Hi, this is Haley," I answer the call.

"Haley, it's Jared Keffner again. Thanks for all your help this morning. Would it be possible for you to return to court tomorrow for the arraignment? It's not a typical request but Madden isn't agreeing to a particular plea, and we might need some reinforcement. She seems to have a good relationship with you. It might be helpful to have you in the courtroom if need be. Would you be available at nine tomorrow morning?"

I stall answering because I'm completely out of my element. I've never been a fan of court TV shows or understood the process of how trials work. I don't have an attorney of my own and I'm supposed to be supporting this little girl who I hardly know. Of course, if I say no, I'd be letting a possibly innocent child down, one whose parents might end up in jail for God knows how long. "Sure, yeah, I can be there."

"The team and I appreciate your cooperation and assistance. We all want the best for Madden and just want to make sure that's what comes out of the arraignment tomorrow."

"Understood," I say.

"Great. See you then. Bye now."

I disconnect the call and place my phone back in my bag. I

drop my head into my hands and try to calm myself down to stop the millions of thoughts swarming my mind. "Everything okay?" Liam asks, squinting as if he's nervous to hear what I'm about to say.

"The public defender thinks I can help Madden during the arraignment. I can't say no. She's just a little kid."

Liam adjusts his backward cap and leans back in his chair, stretching out his legs closer to my feet. "I get it. My life's work is with kids. They're hard to walk away from in a time of need. I admire you for doing what you can for her, especially with everything that family has already put you through." Liam takes my hand from the side of my face and squeezes it in his. "You're a good person. Good people are hard to come by these days."

I'm not sure there's such a thing as a good person.

The waiter brings our food to the table and asks if there's anything else he can get for us. I need a lot but nothing he can get for me.

"We're good, thank you," Liam says.

"Hey, Mr. Gellar!" We both twist around in our seats, looking toward the source of the shout. A young kid in board shorts and a surfer T-shirt with chin-length messy blonde hair holds his hand up toward Liam as he walks toward us. "The answer to that last question was Radiohead, 'Exit Music.'"

"You looked it up, didn't you?" Liam grips the arm rests of his chair with a look of shock.

"No, I knew the answer, but the bell rang."

"That's fair, but for extra credit, tell me which Shakespeare play the song was inspired by?" Liam asks him.

"*Romeo and Juliet.*"

"Yes! Yes! Way to go, buddy. This is why I teach, Mr. Henning. Right here." Liam waves at the kid with pride. "Those two extra points you needed on the final are yours. Enjoy your summer."

The boy lunges for Liam and gives him a quick hug. "Thanks Mr. Gellar. You, too! And you too, Mrs. Gellar!"

"Oh, no..."

He's gone before I can tell him he's mistaken and that I'm not Mr. Gellar's wife. But I guess that's not important with the cheesy grin plastered across Liam's face.

He's clearly passionate about what he does. It's rare to meet a person and feel like you just know them instantly, but he just has a way about him that draws people in—like he's carefree without a worry in the world. It's refreshing. He's drawn me in, even as a wrecking ball swings through my life.

Maybe he could give me some pointers on how to conceal the pain we all seem to walk around with.

FORTY-ONE

Just when I think I've reached the end of this ordeal, I get thrown back into the ring. I take a seat toward the back of the courtroom, feeling like I have no reason to be here if they are just requesting a plea from Madden. However, as I settle down and glance toward the front of the courtroom, I notice Lara and Corbin seated at one table with their attorney, and Madden at a table across the row sitting beside Jared Keffner. Then there's Blakely with an older woman sitting in the second row.

Lara and Corbin are both silent, staring down at the table-top. Madden scans the room, eventually spotting me. She smiles and gives me a quick wave, which attracts Lara and Corbin's attention. They do not smile or wave in my direction because I'm obviously part of their deranged plan that worked against them.

As inconspicuously as I can, I give Madden a small wave in return with a quick smile.

I'm curious if Lara and Corbin will have their own arraignment or if this is all grouped into one session. Lara made herself look guilty when she ran from the police the other day. I can't imagine her hands are completely clean here today. Though fleeing the police is a different crime than what they are accusing Madden of.

"All rise for Judge Evans," the court bailiff announces as she stands next to the door behind the bench. I straighten my black skirt and dry my clammy hands off on the sides of my legs.

The judge, an elderly man without a speck of hair on his head and a bull-dog grimace makes his way to his seat, adjusts his black robe, and sits. "Be seated," he says.

The courtroom is silent except for heavy breaths, and bodies squirming in their seats. The room isn't full, but there are press with notepads, the psychologist, social worker, and a handful of people on the other side behind Lara and Corbin too.

I take my notebook and pen out of my bag, planning to take down notes for whatever reason there might be, but also, the case study I will be writing.

"Good morning," Judge Evans says, holding his focus on the pile of papers pinched between his fingers. "We are here for the arraignment of Madden Smith." He glances over his podium and down to the table where Madden is seated. "Miss Smith, you are present today because you have been accused of a crime pertaining to your missing sister. Do you understand this?"

Jared leans toward Madden and whispers something.

"Yes, Your Honor."

"I'm aware this is a tragic matter, and that Madden is a minor. Since this is a family court session, we will move forward with tolerance and sensitivity for all involved."

Lara bursts into sobs, holding her hands over her mouth. Corbin loops his arm around her shoulders and pulls her in closer.

"Miss Smith, it's very important that you understand the reason for this proceeding—this meeting. I will be reading the charges against you, then you will have a chance to reply with what we call a plea. This means you will say whether you agree with the charges or disagree. If you disagree, you will plead not guilty. If you agree with the charges, you will plead guilty." The judge clears his throat and shakes his head. I wonder how many arraignments he's seen in his career that involve a child Madden's age. After a little research, I found that Rhode Island doesn't have a minimum age that a minor can be prosecuted in a family court. She could be charged as an adult if the court deems necessary. It seems unreal. Children like Madden need help, guidance, therapy, and maybe a different type of education, but I'm not sure what this outcome will be. From what I could find online, there are very few cases like this one. "I will also make sure you understand your rights throughout the process, and if you have any questions along the way, please be sure to let me know so I can clarify."

Madden seems to take in every word the judge is saying but I'm not sure she understands the graveness of what he's explaining. I can only hope Jared has done his due diligence beyond what I've been around for to make sure she understands what she might or might not agree to.

"Madden Smith, the charges against you are as follows: You *are* responsible for the crime of homicide. It is alleged that on June 9th, you brought your fifteen-month-old sister, Fallon Smith, down to the ocean-shore outside of your house's property. It is further alleged that you were alone with Fallon Smith when you left her unattended in the water despite knowing that, as a fifteen-month-old child, she could not swim. It is alleged that you did so with understanding that she would drown in that body of water," the judge states.

Silence fills the courtroom as the accusations linger like a thick fog over everyone's heads. I'm glad I can't see Madden's face because if she didn't understand the consequences to these actions before, she most certainly does now. She made it clear that whatever she's done is because of Lara. That must play a part in this.

Jared whispers something else into Madden's ear but I can't imagine it's much more than words of consolation.

"Madden Smith, do you fully understand why the charges are being brought against you today?"

Jared whispers once again into Madden's ear.

"Yes, Your Honor," she squeaks.

"Okay then. You have the right to legal representation, as you see," Judge Evans gestures to Jared. "It is important that you and your legal representative, Mr. Jared Keffner, have consulted on your impending plea."

"Yes, Your Honor," Jared says on behalf of Madden. "I have explained the options to Madden and we are both in agreement per her understanding of the question being asked."

"Madden, how do you plead to the charge of being an accomplice to the cause of your sister being missing? Guilty, not guilty, or no contest?"

Lara and Corbin both hold their hands in prayer over their chests. Their eyes are closed, and I can't help but wonder if they are unaware of what Madden is about to say.

Jared nods his head at Madden. "Not guilty, Your Honor," she says. Jared places his hand on her shoulder. "I'm not guilty because I didn't drown my sister. I was keeping her safe like I was told to do. She isn't dead!"

Like she was told to do...

A rumble of chatter waves through the courtroom and Jared's face of contentment changes to confusion and distress as he whispers more to her.

"Who told you to do this?" Lara shouts across the court-room. "Where is she, Madden? Where is your baby sister?"

"Order, order in the court!" Judge Evans shouts, tapping his gavel several times.

"Before we continue with the discussion of future proceed-ings, I'm going to call a brief recess to allow Madden to meet with her legal representative." Judge Evans checks his watch. "Ten minutes, please."

My jaw drops and I gasp among the commotion, covering my hand over my mouth. My palms clam up on the wooden bench I've been sitting on, so I rub my hands over my knees to dry them. *Lara and Corbin clearly already knew their daughter was missing before going out to a gala that night.*

A breeze of perfumes, colognes, and body odor washes over me as people spill out of the courtroom for their ten-minute break. I can't seem to unstick myself from this seat as shock holds me hostage.

A hand touches my shoulder and I jump out of my seat, the shock resettling into a state of panic. I clutch my chest and glance to my left. "I didn't mean to startle you," Jared says. "Could I borrow you for a moment?" What could he want from me at this point? Does he think I know something I wouldn't have already told him? Madden's confession is obviously a surprise to him even after spending whatever amount of time he's had to spend with Madden over the last day and a half.

I can feel Lara and Corbin's eyes burning against my back as I scurry out of the courtroom, finding Madden, Jared and the social worker sitting on a bench down the hallway. "The reason I asked you to be here this morning was in case we needed a testimony. It's rare that testimony is allowed during an arraignment and it's up to the judge's discretion if he will accept one, but will you be willing to confirm that neither Lara nor Corbin acted as if they were aware they had a missing child when they left you in their care for the evening?"

"Yes—yes, of course. I've already stated this when questioned, but—"

"That was about you. This is about Madden. It needs to be stated for the record on her case."

Madden is staring at me with what looks like so many questions floating through her eyes. "I'll tell them."

"Will Mommy and Daddy be taken away after?"

Jared waves his hands at Madden. "We can't ask any of those questions right now. Do you understand?"

"Yes, Your Honor," she says.

"Just Jared," he says, placing his hand on top of her head, offering a kind smile to help her through this.

Who would set up a child to go through this? It's clear how deranged Lara and Corbin are, but to put Madden through all of this is unthinkable.

"Let me know when you're ready to go back inside so I can approach the judge and request that he take testimony from Haley." Madden looks back and forth between Jared and me, seeming confused. I would be.

"Okay, I'm ready."

As we return to the courtroom, there is a ripple of growing volume from Lara and Corbin's side. I can only imagine their disdain to see me involved and up at the front table with Madden and Jared.

"Your Honor, may I approach the bench?" Jared asks.

"Yes," he replies.

"Haley," Madden whispers. "What about—"

"Shh, shh. Not now. We can't say anything more in the courtroom, okay?" I'm not sure what she was about to ask, but I'm aware that everything she says out loud can be held against her in some way, especially after all the legal jargon I've learned in the past week.

"Yes, I'll allow that," the judge says to Jared.

Silence returns without the need of the judge's drumming gavel. "Haley Vaughn, you may approach the bench to offer a testimony in reference to Madden's charge and plea," Judge Evans says. I remain standing as I reach the bench and face a court clerk who steps in front of me with a Bible. "Please raise your right hand. Do you swear the testimony you are about to give is the truth, the whole truth, and nothing but the truth, so help you God?"

"I do."

Jared approaches the bench and waits until I'm seated on the other side of a partition separating Judge Evans and me. "Haley, when you arrived to babysit for the Smith children on June 9th, was there any mention of Fallon, or Fallon going missing?" Jared asks.

"No. I have yet to even see a photograph of Fallon. Her name was never mentioned to me until the Smiths arrived home that night and blamed me for her disappearance."

"Objection. No relevance!" Lara and Corbin's attorney calls out.

"Admissible," the judge replies. "Please continue."

I avoid peering over in Lara and Corbin's direction, knowing they will make me trip over my words. My heart thunders in my chest as I try to take in a deep breath to finish my statement. "I was under the impression that I was hired to watch their set of twins, Blakely and Madden. There was no sign of Fallon anywhere in the house when they showed me around before leaving for their event."

"Thank you," Jared says. "And what would you say about Mr. and Mrs. Smith's moods when you arrived? Were they upset in any way?"

"Objection. Leading!" the other attorney objects again.

"I'll allow it," Judge Evan says.

"They seemed rushed and eager to get out of the house, but not upset in any way."

The judge removes his glasses and places them down on the podium. "Wait a minute, was the child already missing before Ms. Vaughn arrived to watch the children that night?"

No one answers. I'm not sure anyone knows who is supposed to answer his question. "There is no report on file of a missing child until eleven thirty p.m. on the night of June 9th.

Ms. Vaughn is stating she didn't know anything about the child and didn't meet her, and in the same breath saying Mr. and Mrs. Smith didn't seem upset before leaving home for their outing." The judge grumbles and drops his papers. "I am temporarily pausing this arraignment to allow further questioning of both Mr. and Mrs. Smith by their legal representation to provide further evidence for this case. We will reconvene once these matters have been addressed." Judge Evans stands from his seat and everyone in the courtroom follows his motion.

I step down from the bench as Lara and Corbin are being escorted out of the courtroom, away from Madden's direction. I approach the table where Madden is seated in time to hear Jared's plea to Madden: "Are you able to tell me who told you to keep Fallon safe? And how were you told to do so?"

Madden glances over at me with sad eyes. "The truth is always best," I say, trying to help persuade her to tell Jared what she knows.

Madden swallows what must be a lump in her throat. "I'll try," she says.

"Okay, let's go find somewhere private for us to talk," Jared says, waving over the psychologist and social worker.

"Haley, you're free to go. We're going to see if we can get Madden to focus on her answers with the psychologist at this time, but if we need anything more from you, I'll let you know. Again, I appreciate your cooperation with all of this," Jared says, reaching his hand to shake mine.

Like last time, I thought he might ask me to stay, but I will gladly leave and hope they don't need another testimony from me.

With my heart in my throat, I make my way out of the courtroom, rushing through the corridors, and exit the building, needing the silence and containment of my car. She's just a little girl. How could anyone convince her to do something like this? There must be a reason, another part of this no one knows about yet. Until Madden divulges the who and why of this story, the blind search for Fallon will continue, and accusations against everyone involved will just spread like wildfire.

If it's true that Lara and Corbin knew Fallon was missing before I arrived, they must know more than they are letting on.

I think—

My mouth runs dry, and the lobby of the courthouse narrows around me as I walk toward the front doors.

I think I was framed to be there that night...

FORTY-TWO
WEDNESDAY, JUNE 14TH 11:00 AM

My hand shakes as I turn the key in the ignition of my car. My lungs strain against each inhale I take. I'm still lightheaded which keeps me from backing out of my parking spot.

It's not fair. Every kid deserves a carefree childhood, one that comes without criminal manipulation. Lara and Corbin should be held responsible for whatever direction this case goes. They are the parents. They have a responsibility to protect Madden as well as Blakely and Fallon. Except, it seems they're only concerned about protecting themselves.

Maybe I'm wrong.

If a child hates their parent or parents, it's for a significant reason, whether a change in the parents' behavior toward them, or a life changing incident, or tearing the child away from their only form of comfort. In most life cases, children can be persuaded to forgive and forget. They naturally get over resentment and anger within minutes of the initial cause. When they don't move forward and on with their day or life, it's usually because the source of discontentment is constantly present.

The human mind isn't as complicated as most think. We survive off cause and effect.

The cause is the root.

I want to know I said enough to help Madden, but she could be lying. I'm sure that's what everyone who was in that court-room was thinking. Anyone would want to believe a young child over a couple of snooty uptight parents. But not anyone would put all their trust into a nine-year-old. Not everyone will believe her.

With erratic breaths still fogging my mind, I pull the gear into reverse and skid out of the parking lot.

Nothing can be ignored and forgotten. Everything must be dealt with to reach a true end that can be put to rest.

My foot is heavy on the gas, but I feel like I'm running out of time to act on my adrenaline-raged courage.

The minutes escape me as I drive down roads I've memo-rized. I don't need to press on my brake until I stop in front of the rickety old blue house with rotting shingles.

I slam my car door without concern for the warning they'll receive before I charge in through the front door.

The house doesn't smell like trash today and there aren't any bugs flying around.

Dad is resting on the sunken sofa, watching replays of a baseball game on the small TV resting on top of a short, single column bookshelf. "Where's Mom?" I ask.

"Where do you think she is?" Dad responds without breaking his stare from the TV. "Not even a hello for your dad before you come in here hootin' and hollerin' at us for some-thing else we've done wrong? I thought you were determined to get away from us again?"

"Mom?" I shout, figuring she's down the narrow hallway in her bedroom.

I hear her moving around but it takes a minute before she steps out of her room and closes the door behind her. "What is it now? Are you going to say more awful things and then run away again?" she asks, her voice calm and unaffected by my obvious anger.

"Why did you ruin my life?" I ask them as she sits down next to Dad on the sofa.

They twist to look at each other as if they can't believe the words coming out of my mouth. "Ruin your life?" Mom repeats.

"All you did was lie to me or keep things from me all while holding me up at home like I was your hostage. I tried to convince myself you were overprotective and there was such a thing as loving a child too much, but your behavior never made sense to me until I figured out what you both had been hiding from me. You made decisions that affected my life—that made me feel the need to break away from you."

Children are a mold of their parents' shadows and when they displace their issues onto innocent minds, corruption, confusion, and paranoia follows. This is what the Smiths have done to Madden and now she's facing a life altering consequence that she might forever be too afraid to tell the truth about.

"We chose to keep you safe. I hardly think that's a reason to hate us or feel the need to break away and shut us out of your life."

"What were you keeping me safe from?" I ask them, feeling the room wobble as I look back and forth between the two of them. "It was you. That's the answer. You didn't do right by me, keeping me locked up at home, silenced by the fear of what others might think of our family. I was forced to be a recluse to keep your secrets safe. But in reality, everyone in our town knew your truths before I did. Do you know what that was like for me?"

Dad exhales sharply and grabs his flimsy remote to shut off the TV. "Haley, we will always continue to remind you that not everything is as it seems, even your misconceptions of our reality. This is why you decided to go to school to study psychology, is it not?"

"Yes, so. I can repair the emotional damage you bestowed upon me?" I wrap my arms around my waist and clench my fists so tightly my knuckles strain.

"What damage did we cause you?" Mom asks, clutching the T-shirt fabric over her chest.

I grit my teeth, trying not to groan. "See, this is why I have stayed away and avoided contact," I tell them. "This conversation that we have repeatedly—it's painful. It makes me go home and cry until I pass out because I feel guilty for wishing I had parents with a different history, ones who let me experience life the way I should have been able to. The guilt is never ending. It gnaws at me constantly and even when I get a break from feeling so much resentment toward you, I quickly realize there is no such thing as a break because...well, here we are, right back where we left off two years ago."

Mom's lips part and she stares up at the ceiling. "But you are the one who keeps coming back to us," Mom says.

"I did not come back to you. I was dragged back to you by Dad."

"That's not true, Haley. You aren't making any sense, dear," Mom says.

These conversations with the two of them make the full circumference of my neck itchy like I'm having an allergic reaction. I scratch at my already sensitive and bruised skin. I shouldn't have come here just to remind them how detrimental their decisions were to my childhood. Just because I saw it all happening to another child today doesn't mean I can undo what they've done to me already. It's too late for me. It's not too late for Madden.

"I'm just going to say this to you...you cannot raise a child by making them believe the sky is orange when it's blue. You can't continuously say you are someone, when you are truly someone else, leading me to believe this until I was thirteen. Do you know what that felt like?" I shout. "Thirteen, Mom." My body feels like it's on fire with the rage running through me. "Thirteen, when I found out that you and Dad escaped from a long-term behavioral health facility, ran across the country, changed your names, and started a new life here where your past couldn't find you."

"Haley, lower your voice," Dad says. "I can't believe we're back to this again."

I sniffle, feeling the familiar pain creeping up my chest. "Why, are you afraid someone will hear me say you're ill and in denial about it? Or that you need serious help?"

"Haley," Dad snaps. "What you're accusing us of is not true. It has never been true and will never be true. There isn't much more we can do to convince you of something you refuse to believe."

"Avoidance doesn't make the problem go away," I shout back.

"We aren't avoiding anything," Mom says, dropping her shoulders with a look of defeat.

"All the kids in school found out about you, and that's how I came to learn how you two met, despite the stories of falling in love on a beach in Newport one summer. How easy it is for a kid to believe something so fictional."

"Of all people, I would think you'd be a bit more careful about labeling people, especially while going to school to study psychology."

"I'm not labeling you," I argue. "I would never do something like that. However, you and Mom are not well, and forgoing treatment for the sake of convincing yourself that you're in fact healthy, isn't going to help any of us."

"We are healthy, Haley," Dad says with a groan, dropping his head back to highlight his annoyance, continuing to fight back.

"Sure, that's what you've always wanted people to think. When you ignore a problem, it gets worse, not better. You didn't want to help yourselves, even for my sake. You were more concerned with everyone believing you were two people who didn't run away from forced confinement. Forced confinement means you were either a danger to yourselves and/or others. Of course you wouldn't want anyone to know that. That's why you had to be so kind to people, even those who weren't so kind to us, right? I even bet that's why you let people live rent-free, too."

"What—?" Dad grapples his hand around his forehead as if he's confused about something he knows quite well about. "What are you talking about?"

"The Hoyt family. They lived in our complex rent-free until the whole place suddenly burnt down one day."

"Haley, the Hoyt family? What do they have to do with this? And yes, they did pay their rent."

"And to which of your personalities was that rent paid to because I remember hearing you two argue about this matter. I remember it as if it was yesterday."

"I only have one personality," he says with a heavy huff from his nose. "And you must have overheard something incorrectly."

"Gary..." Mom says, holding her hands up for him to stop. "Let's leave the Hoyt family out of this discussion. Haley, what exactly do you want from us?" Mom asks, looking over at Dad as if she needs his support for asking me this question. "You came back here today for something, did you not?"

"She needed to remind of us how awful we were," Dad says.

"Gary, let her talk."

"No, I'm done. I can't take this anymore. I refuse to sit here while she tells us we're mentally ill because we escaped from some psychiatric facility, which apparently ruined her life. We didn't!"

"Gary, please stop. This is not helpful," Mom says, raising her voice.

Watching the two of them have this conversation stirs up memories I have tried so hard to forget during the years following the fire—the two of them blaming each other for everything that went wrong. "And this is why nothing I ever say to you will change anything between us. Until you come to terms with the issues you both have, your disorders, and obsession to keep everything you love locked up and safe, nothing will ever be resolved. I want parents, even at twenty-seven—I just want parents who I feel like I know. But we're still strangers. Maybe we always will be."

"We are your parents, and we love you very much, no matter what."

"You know, I thought if I went to school for a degree in psychology, I might be able to finally help you both. Even after you kept us, as a family, secluded from society so no one would know that you two tried to run away from incurable mental illnesses, I still loved you unconditionally enough to want to help. I've tried so many times, and you just wouldn't let me. I finally had to give up for my emotional wellbeing. Do you see now what your choices have caused?"

"We see as well as you see, sweetheart," Mom says.

"What is that supposed to mean?" I snap.

"Haley, come here. Give me a hug," she says. Her words force me to back up, almost stepping on the small bookshelf holding up the TV.

"No, no. I can't live like this. I can't be wrapped up in your denial any longer. I did that for too long."

Dad tilts his head and narrows his eyes at me. "Is that what you truly believe? That we're living in a state of denial"

"Yes, Dad. I do. My perception isn't the one you should be questioning."

My chest feels like it's caving in, and my ribs might all

collapse. It's like there's a knife slicing me into two—one part wanting to love my parents and sit in a state of denial with them, but I would only be hurting them by doing so. If I've learned anything throughout my studies, it's that: only people who want to be helped can be. This is why I plan to work with children. They are far less stuck in their ways.

I pull out my phone from my back pocket and type out a message to Liam.

Me: Are you busy? I'm having a hard day and could use some company.

"How are you going to fix all of your own problems now, Haley?" Dad asks.

"I don't have the same kind of problems that you do. I can take care of myself, Dad." It's painful to say that to my father, but it's the truth.

Liam: I am bored out of my mind, sitting on the beach under the sunless sky, and would love nothing more than to come keep you company. I can be over in a half hour.

Me: Aw, I'm sorry about the sun, but selfishly happy it's cloudy. See you soon!

"Where are you going now?" Dad asks as I take steps away from them. "This is it. You show up, make a mess, and leave. That's what you always do."

FORTY-THREE

WEDNESDAY, JUNE 14TH 1:00 PM

With Willa at work for the lunch shift, I'm reminded again that I still need to find a job. Of course, the second I think this situation with the Smiths is over, I get sucked right back in. If I had a job this past week, I would have had to call out so many times that I would have gotten fired already. Although if I hadn't chosen to work with the Smith family in the first place, none of this would be happening.

"I still can't believe the little girl said someone told her to hide the baby," Liam says.

"Madden," I remind him. "It's like she snapped under pressure. Not that I could blame her."

"But she didn't say who told her to do this?" Liam asks, scanning my notes as if he's trying to put the puzzle together too.

"No, after her confession, the judge stopped the arraignment so the attorneys could question the family."

"Are you surprised they didn't ask you to stay since they've asked you to be there during the previous questioning?"

This is the part that scares me, but I'd rather not admit so out loud and plant any ideas in Liam's head. They wouldn't ask me to stay for the questioning if they thought Madden might tell Jared that I was the one who told her to hide Fallon. Though that wouldn't make any sense since it's clear Fallon went missing before I arrived at their house.

"The new set of questions predates my arrival so I can see why they wouldn't ask me to be there."

Liam sighs and places my notepad down on the coffee table. "Well, I think that's a good thing for you."

"I hope so." But that's only one good thing. The situation with my parents this week isn't something I want to get into with Liam, especially on top of all the other activities. He emanates a force of light, and I, a restless moth, am desperate for an illusion of guidance.

A sign from above agrees with Liam as the clouds break apart outside, allowing the sun to fill the apartment. He stands up from the couch as if he's drawn toward the light and unlocks the balcony slider to step outside. "It's beautiful out here."

I follow him out onto the balcony, shielding my eyes from the late afternoon sun. He leans against the metal railing and takes in a deep breath. "Do you think I'd be here right now if you hadn't ended up in the middle of a criminal case?" His question is somewhat serious though a hint of a smile is present.

"Are you asking if I would have continued talking to you if my life hadn't gone haywire that first night I was on the job?" If I recall I sent him the first message and it took him a day to respond, and that was before this all went down.

"Maybe."

"Well, to be fair, before I messaged you, Willa scanned through your social media profiles and said you checked out pretty good, and I shouldn't miss the opportunity to—"

"To..." he pushes.

"You know, get back out there, or just get out there. Meet someone. Be social," I say with a snicker.

"You know, researching people's backgrounds online has

become so common that it's almost exciting when someone doesn't have a footprint on the web," he says with a smirk.

"I despise social media. That's why Willa did the dirty work for me. The amount of anxiety online context causes people just seems unavoidable to me. I know myself well and if I was scrolling through feeds mindlessly everyday looking at everyone's supposed abnormally perfect lives, it would make me question if I was on my own life path or following someone else's. I'm not sure if that makes sense because I might be babbling. Being influenced feels a little like the butterfly effect, swaying people away from the direction they were intended to travel, which could ultimately and unknowingly change their destination." It's been a while since I've brain dumped on anyone about my philosophical ideals but hearing it out loud highlights the fact that I was meant to be pulled into this case with the Smiths.

"Wow," Liam says, turning to face me while leaning his side against the railing. "Would you write that all down, because it's literally the most inspirational statement I've heard in forever."

I playfully shove his shoulder. "Don't tease."

"I'm not," he says, his eyebrows angling toward each other. "I'm very serious. In a day when we're all misguided and using recycled knowledge from the web to make everyday decisions, your words are beautiful."

They're only words, I want to tell him.

He sweeps a windblown strand of my hair away from my eyes and loops his arm around my back, pulling me in closer. "I didn't think you would speak to me again after the first-aid class," he says. "I thought meeting someone I had an instant connection with was too good to be true."

"Why is that?" It's because more often than not, something that seems beyond ideal is a mirage of the mind, designed to satisfy a person's current need or desire. I know this well.

"I just haven't had the best of luck when it comes to taking risks or stepping outside of my comfort zone. I usually come out on the other end with a million reasons why I should stop taking risks and stick to what I know."

"Maybe you just weren't taking the right risks," I say.

"All I know is, you are one worth taking."

My heart flutters for so many reasons in this one instance but I close my eyes and shut out the world around me to indulge in the waft of spiced coconut and warm, full lips against mine. He holds me tight like I'm something worth hanging on to and the feeling makes my stomach tighten as I loop my arms around the back of his neck, caving to the desire to eliminate all space between us.

The wind blows against us, and the water laps up against the row of docks. Seagulls sing in the distance, and I wish I could erase everything in between and outside of these lines. The sun beating down on the back of my neck adds to the heat rushing through me. Liam scoops me up and I wrap my legs around his waist, keeping my eyes closed as he walks us back into the apartment.

I focus on his touch, the effortless way he carries me without sacrificing the skilled way in which his lips devour mine. My bedroom door closes, us on the inside, the bed beneath me. This is the part I tend to overthink, debate, push away while wondering if it's my next best or worst decision. I'm not questioning any part of us, though. Not really...

Pizza in bed, a single silky sheet wrapped around us like a loose cocoon, the windows open to the seaside soundscape and breeze could be considered the best night of this summer, maybe even any summer I've ever had, and it's hardly just begun.

"I knew you were my type," he says with a pleasing sigh as he reaches for his glass of water on the nightstand.

"Your type is pizza in bed?" I ask, taking another bite of my crust.

"Uh, yes," he says, highlighting the obvious statement.

I've lost track of the time after hearing it would take thirty minutes for the pizza to be delivered but the front door to the apartment whooshes open, then closes with a thud. The cross breeze causes lots of commotion with doors around here. "Willa must be home from work."

My bedroom door flies open just as I'm finishing my sentence and my heart leaps into my throat. Willa, breathless, holding the doorknob within one grip and the threshold in the other. "They found the baby," she says. "It's all over the news."

"What? Fallon?" I ask, sitting bolt upright.

"Yes. The breaking news is still developing but she's apparently safe and alive."

"Holy crap," I say. Jared must be good at his job or maybe it was the psychologist, but my bets are on Jared.

"I wonder where they found her after all this time," Liam says, staring toward the wall beyond the foot of my bed. "I was sure there wasn't going to be a good ending to this search, especially with a child that—"

"I know," I cut off the sentence no one wants to have to finish.

"Uh, anyway, sorry to interrupt, but I tried calling and—"

"I left my phone in the living room," I say.

"No surprise there." Willa groans with a roll of her eyes. "Carry on with..." she says, flapping her arms at us, "your pizza date."

"Madden was telling the truth," I say.

"Do you think the parents set the little girl up to hide the baby?"

"If Lara saw an opportunity to take me down, she wouldn't think it through thoroughly, she'd just do whatever it took to see results."

"You don't think Lara moved past that fire by this point?"

I narrow my eyes as I try to stare through the wall between my bedroom and Willa's. "I wish I could think that would be the logical way to be, but she's never struck me as a logical type." If there's anything I know about Lara, Larissa Hoyt, it's that she always knows how to get what she wants.

FORTY-FIVE

THIRTEEN YEARS AGO

It wasn't too long ago that I refused to stay home alone at night. The creaks of the old wooden floor boards and the movements from other townhouses adjacent to ours made me think someone was trying to break in but I've come to realize those noises occur when Mom and Dad are home too, so I've compromised my fear by turning all the lights on in the house, locking myself in my bedroom and sitting on the floor against my bed while I focus on school work. Headphones and music help too, unless someone rings the doorbell. That, I can still hear.

I pull myself up by the edge of my bed and peek out of my bedroom window, able to see the stairwell out front but not the front door of our unit. As always, there are a bunch of kids, most of whom don't live here but all go to school with me, playing basketball in the dark at the sad rusty hoop cowering against the woods across from the complex.

Just as I remove my headphones, the doorbell rings again. My pulse races as I go through a short list of people who might need to come to our door at night. It could be any one of the residents who live here, having an issue they need Dad's help with.

I step into my parents' bedroom before heading for the kitchen door and grab Dad's heavy metal flashlight. It's something. I wish there was a more inconspicuous way to peek out the front door but when the curtain moves, it's obvious on the other side.

My eyes widen when I see Billy at my front door. Of all the people in the world, he's the last person I would have imagined. He's the one person I would dream about showing up here though. There are about forty pages in my diary devoted to him and his beautiful smile, but I'm pretty sure he doesn't know I exist. I was sure of it until now.

I unlock the deadbolt and open the door enough to see what he needs. "Hi," I squeak. "Do you need something?"

"Haley, right?" he asks, his voice deeper than some of the other boys in our grade. It seems like all the boys who play football look and sound a bit manlier than they did last year.

"Yeah," I answer.

"Do you have a minute?" he asks, looking over his shoulder toward the other kids playing basketball.

"What for?" I want to say of course. I have all the time in the world for you, but he wasn't even positive my name is Haley. Our town isn't big enough to act like you don't know someone.

"There's something I think you need to know."

He has my attention, but in a way that makes my stomach hurt and my throat tighten. I open the door more and push my way outside, forcing him to back up. I won't be inviting him in. I'm smarter than that.

He's taller, not by a lot but he's bigger in general, as if he was bred to play football. He's the only one on the team that doesn't have a shaggy haircut. He keeps his hair short and buzzed. He's also quieter than the rest of the bunch, like he'd rather take everything in around him than contribute, which makes this encounter even weirder.

I shove my hands into the front pocket of my sweatshirt and my bangs fall into my eyes as I stare down between us, waiting for him to say whatever it is he came here to say.

"So, uh—there have been a bunch of kids talking about you at school. I think a lot of them caught wind of the so-called-rumor going around. Or at least, they think it's a rumor, but according to my parents, it's not, so—"

"What? What, what rumor? What are you talking about?" I don't mean to sound so defensive, but I'm not known for my social status at school. I'm more of a loner with a couple of casual friends I only talk to at lunch.

"It's something about you—"

The rumors again. "Let me guess...my parents?"

Billy shifts his weight from foot to foot. "There was an escape from some psychiatric hospital. I thought you should know that others are talking about it because, well—I'm sorry if it's true. If there's anything I can do..."

My eyes strain with how hard I'm staring through Billy's head while trying to digest this ridiculous story. My cheeks burn and my heart thuds from embarrassment. Why did it have to be him who came here to tell me this? Of all the people. The little girl in me wants to burst into tears, but I take a deep breath and try to hold in my pain so he doesn't see how much this hurts. "Do you believe everything you hear?" I utter, gritting my teeth. I thought he was better than this, not someone who would sink this low for a boost in popularity. I realize now I had no reason to think this of him. I made him out to be a good person, but in my daydreams. I was wrong.

"Our parents know each other, Haley. I'm not the one who spread this information around, so I don't want you to think that, but I'm sure the information isn't something you want out there, either."

"It's not true," I say with a snap. "My family is no different than yours. Is this the best story someone could come up with?

It's pretty—it's pretty lame." I take a small breath, fighting the pains in my stomach.

Billy reaches into his pocket and pulls out a piece of newspaper. "So, this isn't true?"

I take the paper and unfold it, my hands shaking. I find an aged newspaper cutout with two crackled photos. My jaw drops as I read the caption beneath the image. I pick at the dry skin on my bottom lip while reading:

> *A successful escape from involuntary commitment calls for a late-night search.*
>
> *Following the escape from secured quarters, the property borders of Selina Behavior Health Facility were left unsecured. Authorities are searching the surrounding area to ensure their safety as well as the safety of everyone in the area. It's unknown how the escape was made possible, with security systems in place, but faculty and police are investigating. If you or anyone you know have any information about this case, please call Selina's Police Department.*

I gaze at the large black and white photo again and shake my head. "No," I say, swallowing the lump in my throat. "This is fake." My words do not sound confident or convincing, but I need him to believe me because these people look exactly like my parents, down to Mom's one crooked tooth and Dad's receding hairline. "These aren't even my parents' names." I point to where they're mentioned toward the bottom of the article.

Billy's lips stretch into an open-mouth grimace as he tilts his head to the side and lifts his shoulders into a shrug. He sucks in a mouthful of air through his tightly clenched teeth. "Geez. I don't know. I was just trying to help—"

"How's she taking it? Freak of freaks!!!" a kid shouts from the basketball court. "Is she confessing her love to you yet?"

"Shut it!" Billy responds, holding his arm over his mouth to hide the snicker I'm sure he's trying to suppress.

Faint high-pitched moans cry out, "Ohhh, Billy..." in mockery.

My nose tingles as hot tears burn the backs of my eyes. I need to keep it together. I can't let them think they're getting to me. "They all know what you're doing here?" I ask.

"It's not like that. I'll tell them you said it wasn't true. I just wanted you to know. You seem like a nice girl, and I felt bad listening to people talk badly about you." His voice sounds like a deflating balloon, losing the air needed to continue his lie.

I crumple the article in my hand and reach behind me for my front door, returning inside in one fluid motion before slamming the door in Billy's face. I replace the lock and spin around before sliding down the length of the door with the article pressed to my chest. Tears purge from my eyes as I unfold the crumpled paper, staring at the familiar tarnished portrait framed by vivid details about an escape from a behavioral facility. My parents must know this article has been floating around. Is this just supposed to be an event that we never talk about? Why would they keep this from me? They had to think that someone might eventually shove this very article into my face, leaving me dumbfounded?

By the time I make it to my bedroom, the squall of laughter from outside makes its way through the sealed cracks of my window, just loud enough for me to know he didn't tell them the rumors weren't true.

FORTY-SIX

THURSDAY, JUNE 15TH 9:00 AM

After going days without a good night's sleep, I'm taking a moment to relish the comfort of waking up in the morning rather than the middle of the night, and next to Liam who has clouded me with a distraction that has lingered for hours. He's been so understanding and supportive through all of this and for no good reason other than to impress a woman he just met. I guess life does work in miraculous ways while we're preoccupied. Or is it that we're too preoccupied to notice something that's not quite right?

My eyelids flutter open, searching for the source of warmth that has held me close all night, but the other side of the bed is vacant, the sheets strewn into a crumpled mess and the comforter piled up toward the end of the bed. I pull my sheet up to my neck and sit up, finding Liam sitting at my small desk between the closet and my nightstand. He's twisting around in the swivel chair in his board shorts and surf-brand logo T-shirt, one leg crossed over the other.

"For someone who hasn't been sleeping so well, you must have been making up for all those lost hours this morning, huh?" he asks, a smirk pinching one side of his face.

He fumbles with something in his hand, and I try to focus on what he's holding, but my eyes are still adjusting to the amount of light seeping in through the closed blinds. A familiar sound strikes a chord, a deep rusty scratch following a pop.

Liam has lit a match and has the stick pinched between his thumb and forefinger. "What are you doing?" I ask, rubbing my eye with the balls of my fist.

"I found the matches on your desk, but no candles," he says, staring at the flame as if he's entranced by the burning wood.

"Okay, well...blow it out before you burn yourself," I scold him.

"If only someone said the same thing to you that night..."

"Liam," I groan, "what are you—"

"How long did it take you to recognize me, Haley?"

"Recognize you from what?" I ask, my throat tightening.

He smiles and puffs a whisper of air onto the match, killing the flame. He places the blackened match down on my desk and proceeds to light another. "You know, I have wondered how easy it would be to recall someone from so many years ago when we were kids on the brink of puberty; scrawny little nothings who had yet to grow into the people we'd eventually become. Even with the facial scruff, the shaggy bleached out hair and some additional height and weight, it's still me, Haley, your favorite old neighbor."

I swallow hard and reach down to the floor to grab my hooded sweatshirt. I suddenly feel far more naked than I am with the flimsy silk top and shorts I'm wearing. "I think you're confusing me with someone else." I would like to convince myself of that too. It's obvious I'm flustered as I try to pull the sweatshirt over my head, struggling to poke my arms into the right holes. Once it's over my head, I move across the bed to put some additional space between us.

He laughs and I watch the flame on the match grow closer

to the tips of his fingers, wondering how long he'll tolerate the burn.

"Why did you do it, Haley?" he asks. His voice is different to how it's sounded the times we were together this past week. The look in his eyes is eerily dark and sinister and I don't know what changed in him between the hours we fell asleep and now.

With every muscle in my face tightening in response to his question, all I can reply with is, "I don't know what you're talking about," I cry out as my voice becomes hoarse. I'm obviously not very good at this guessing game he's playing.

"You must have thought you would get away with everything you've done," he continues.

I shake my head and squint at him. "Liam, you're freaking me out and I want you to leave." I realize I didn't grab my phone on my nightstand before scooting across to the other side of the bed to put some distance between us.

"You aren't going to get away with this again, you know that right?" he says. "I mean, my God, you even have a firefly necklace. It's like you're flaunting what you've done."

"What the hell are you talking about?" I shout, clasping the thin metal chain around my neck. I glance at the connecting wall between my room and Willa's, hoping I'm being loud enough that she will wake up and hear what I'm saying. "My parents gave me this necklace when I was a kid. Where is this all coming from?"

He blows out the match again, dropping it down onto the desk with the others before standing from the desk chair. His hair is a mess, and his eyes are practically bulging out of his skull as he steps in closer toward my bed.

"Where was the kid found, Haley?" he asks.

"The kid? Fallon? Did that family hire you to follow me? Because if so, you have wasted a lot of time. I've had nothing to do with what happened to Fallon." I gasp and slap one hand over my mouth, muttering, "Oh my God. Are—are you the one who—" I skate my hand down the length of my throat, touching my fingertips to my neck as I recall the night I was dragged off into an alley.

Liam laughs. "Hire me? That's almost funny." He laughs again, harder than necessary for the not-so-funny question. "Neither Lara nor Corbin would ever pay me a dime to help them, trust me."

"You-you kn-know them?" I ask, my words stuttering as my remaining bravery disintegrates into stomach pains. With subtle movements, I lean down to pick up the metal flashlight I keep next to my bed, unsure that I'd know how to use it as a weapon if I had to.

Liam rolls his eyes and tosses his head back with a grunt. "Give me a break, Haley. Of course I know them, and so do you. Well, Lara at least. You're just not as unfortunate as I am, having to be related to that money-hungry shrew."

"Great, so you're an estranged family member?" I ask, forcing my words to boom louder since I haven't heard any movement from Willa. I need her.

"Cute," he says with a huff of exasperation. "You know very well that I'm Lara's brother. You wouldn't just forget good old Billy Hoyt." He pins his hands to his hips and stares up at the ceiling, reminiscing. "I remember the last time we saw each other. Do you?"

"Billy?" I utter as disbelief washes through me. I shake my head and step back toward the corner of the room. "No. That's not possible."

He sighs. "Oh, drop the act. Billy, Liam—both nicknames for William. It isn't that confusing." I never thought twice about Billy's name being shortened from something. I don't really recall anyone calling him William other than his mom.

"The only act going is the one where you've been tricking me into thinking you were someone else. Why would you do that? I trusted you. I let you in, and I never do that so easily—"

A shuddered breath catches in my throat as I hold back a fear filled sob. My shoulder brushes against the wall between my room and Willa's. I can't move back any farther. My heart pounds as I struggle to think of a way out of this room safely, but he's in the path to the door. I slap my hand against the wall several times as hard as I can, silently pleading for Willa to wake up and storm in here.

"I can think of a few reasons why I would do this…" he says.

"Is this some kind of sick game? Why are you here? It's been thirteen years since I saw Billy Hoyt—you. We barely knew each other. I can't even remember what you looked like then."

Although that part isn't exactly true.

My bedroom is shrinking around me, making me feel like the walls are going to collapse in on us if I don't get past him and out of here. My heart is in my throat as I try to think straight with all these pieces scattered around in disarray. "Why would you hurt me like this? I really thought you were this great guy." I sniffle and gasp for more air than my lungs will take in. "You let this go on until you got what you wanted from me last night. Is that what this is about? Because that's—God that's really—sick."

Liam stumbles backward as if he's intoxicated and leans against the wall next to the door, letting his head fall back with a thud. "The sick part...is that I actually fell for you. I had a thing for you thirteen years ago too, but—"

"You couldn't let anyone know that then because I was just a freak to everyone else, right?" I cry out.

He wraps his hand around his forehead, pressing his fingers into the side of his temple. "I wanted to forget who the hell you are—who you were. I wish I hadn't known you before. Worse, I wish this wasn't going to end so badly for us both." I don't understand what he means and by the wild look in his eyes, I'm not sure he understands either.

I wrap my hands around my throat, feeling like someone is strangling me from the inside. "What was the point to all of this?"

"You wouldn't understa—" he says, his statement shortened by the sound of buzzing coming from the nightstand on the side of the bed he was asleep on.

He makes a beeline toward me, and I hop back on top of the bed and clamber over to the other side, switching positions with him. I should have grabbed his phone but then I'd be asking for a physical chase. I need my phone and the door.

But we both make it back to the door at the same time. He blocks my way out and answers the call that's still buzzing.

"Yeah," he says. I watch his eyes for a sign of what the phone call might be about. I doubt I'll catch a glimpse of the 'doe-eyed-look' that would brand any liar. "What are you talking about? That's not possible." Liam spins around, clutching at the back of his red neck. "No. No, Lara! Because I wasn't home last night. That's why. Why would I do that? What kind of monster do you think I am? Christ. This is low, even for you. Is this your get out of jail free card? I should have figured that would be your move. You've already taken everything else. You might as well steal my freedom too, right? Yeah, well screw you!" Liam throws his phone to the ground and the screen shatters, not enough to prevent him from using the phone again, but it'll be a pain.

I don't even know what to say after that phone call. I don't even know what happened, only that it was Lara on the other end. "Let me out of my room," I bark at him. "Willa, help me!" No one is in that deep of a sleep to not have heard this commotion by now.

"No, no," Liam says, breathing heavily as he pins the palm of his hand to the door. "I'm not going to hurt you. I didn't attack you either. It's her. She's out of her mind."

"Who? Lara?" I question, taking a hesitant step backward again, away from the door, where I need to be.

"You have no idea," he says with a choke as he grits his teeth. His cheeks inflame and he clenches his hands by his sides. "The police found Fallon at my apartment."

"Wait...what?" I gasp and press my hand to my chest. "You —you did this?"

"No. What? Why would I take my own niece?" he shouts at me like I'm the first to accuse him.

"I don't know! Why would you act like you're someone else and trap me like this? This is not the behavior of a sane person, so why wouldn't someone assume you had something to do with your missing niece?" Adrenaline is pulsating through my words, and I hope it's enough to get me away from him in one piece.

Liam grasps at chunks of his hair, ignoring me. "Shit. She's going to kill that poor baby."

"Who? Lara or Madden?"

"I don't even know," he says, his eyes bugging out and centered by a web of red veins.

"Tell me why you were at the first-aid course," I ask, demanding an answer. "That wasn't a coincidence."

"Family is family. My sister needed help, and I helped her. But I didn't see the rest coming," he says.

"The rest of what?"

"Becoming weak around you. I should have just let you be that night, but I didn't because—"

"Because what?" I demand.

Liam's expression changes and I swear it's the doe-eyed look I'm noticing. "It's human instinct to want what we should stay away from, right?"

Now I can forever question whether that too is a lie or not.

The internal question makes my blood boil. "Wait..." I snap at him. "You think you were supposed to stay away from me? Should I remind you of what your family did to mine? Taking everything from us for the sake of a lawsuit because the insurance wasn't enough. Money doesn't bring people back from the dead." I regret my words the second they slip out of my mouth. Despite everything, his sister, Libby, died in that fire and rumor had it that he took it the hardest. Now I'm wondering how hard...

He takes a minute, breathing sharply in and out of his nose. The veins on his temples pulsate, a sign of rising blood pressure. "Don't talk about my family. They're all gone except for Lara. I'm not defending any action here, but with all due respect, I was told to stay away from you because my dad is the one who found the newspaper article. We did feel sorry for you until that night. But before you go ahead and start making more assumptions, it wasn't me who spread that story around. It was Lara."

"Of course, it was Lara. Lara, who is swimming in riches thanks to the jackpot she inherited."

"The words keep flying out of your mouth, Haley, but have you stopped to think about the way I'm living in comparison to her?"

"I don't know how you're living. I don't know who you are, obviously. You've been conning me this whole time and now I'm supposed to feel sorry for you? I can't believe a word you've said."

"You never could believe anyone. That's half your problem." Liam opens the bedroom door and storms out. "Don't follow me. The cops are on the hunt and it's me they want, not you."

When the front door closes, I rush out there to twist the deadbolt and attach the chain link, not that the flimsy metal makes me feel any safer right now.

Willa's door was closed when I ran by, but I turn back to knock, wondering how she didn't hear what was happening in my bedroom.

She doesn't respond so I knock harder. "Willa, are you in there?"

Again, there's no response and my heart pounds, wondering where she is, knowing she was home last night. I try to open the door, but it's locked.

I pound harder, wishing I could just break the door down, but with how old everything in this apartment is, the doors must have been replaced just before we moved in because they are solid. "Answer me, Willa!" She isn't a deep sleeper. She has more trouble sleeping than I do.

I run back to my room in search of a paperclip so I can pop the lock on her door. My hands tremble as I yank open my desk drawer, finding my mess of sticky notes for my case study. These notes are likely irrelevant now. I push them to the side and grab a paperclip, then return to Willa's door, doing everything I can to steady my hand. After a few seconds of moving the paperclip around, the pop gives me relief. I grapple the knob and push, but the door doesn't budge. She has a chain on the inside of her bedroom door, one I didn't know existed, and definitely did not exist until this week. I can only see the side of her dresser and nothing more. "Willa?"

FORTY-EIGHT

My head pounds like a balloon expanding then releasing forced air, stretching past its elasticity. There's no one to rely on, not a trustworthy person within distance and it seems like the world has been charging toward me with pitchforks. I don't want to keep wondering what's next or who will poke their head out from around the corner.

All I know is, I'm stronger than this. I always have been.

"Willa, I know you're in there. Open the door!" I plead. "He's gone. It's just me. I need you. I'm freaking out right now. Please, Willa." I pound on her door with my fists over and over, wondering why she won't say anything or release the chain.

What if she's not okay? She wouldn't hurt herself, but I don't know if someone else is in there who might have.

I run back to my room, which now feels more like a crime scene, and search under my pillows and comforter for my phone, before recalling I left it on the bedside table. I snatch it up and stumble to unlock the display. *Come on.* I search through my contacts for Willa's number and call her as I press my ear up to the connecting wall. I hear a repeating buzz that continues until her voicemail picks up. "Willa!" I shout through the wall. "Answer me!"

I return to my list of contacts to find Jerry's number. I don't know if he's in there with her or at home, or what to say to him if he picks up, but I need to make sure Willa is okay. The phone rings, but I don't hear buzzing on the other side of the wall. The call goes to voicemail.

I end the call and stare at the screen on my phone, debating what to do. I can call the police.

I would have to tell them the man I've been spending time with has been at the forefront of a criminal setup, which they are already aware of. And my roommate's door is locked. Just locked. I don't know where she is because she won't answer my calls, neither will her boyfriend.

I might be beyond help from the police.

I could break down Willa's door. I clutch my phone in my hand and race back into the hallway. "I'm going to break the door down and we'll have to replace it. Just unlock the door, Willa. You're leaving me with no choice. Please."

I drop my forehead against the door and wait for a hint of sound but there's nothing. I take a couple of steps back and run into the door, using my shoulder to break the chain link. A searing pain is the only result. The door doesn't budge. I kick the door with the heel of my foot several times, trying to just break through the wood at this point, but nothing I do leaves anything beyond a mark.

"Willa?" I cry out again in between ragged breaths. I slide my back down against the length of the door and toss my head back as I reach the ground. "Why?"

I'm not sure how long I've been sitting against Willa's door, staring at the stucco wall across from me when I hear movement from within her room. I scoot away from the door and pull myself up along the wall.

"Haley?" My name sounds like it's been dragged over a cheese grater, but nonetheless, she's speaking from the other side of the door.

"Willa?"

The chain releases and her door creaks open. She's standing in the doorway, her eyes red and puffy. She's in an oversized T-shirt long enough to cover the shorts I assume she's wearing.

"Where were you? Are you okay?" If she is okay, she should be asking me if *I'm* okay.

"Hales, this is too much," she croaks, holding her fists up to her chest.

I glance around as if "this" is something I'll see around me. "What's too much? I don't understand. Why was your room chain-locked?"

Willa doesn't move from the spot she's standing on, and it feels like there is more than just a bedroom between us.

"The danger and trouble you've been in for the past two weeks...it's been too much" she says. She says this like I'm not the one directly impacted.

"Yes, I'm aware of what I've been through," I say, curtly.

"You aren't a risk-taker. You're a calculated decision-maker, but suddenly it's like you're ready to go bungee jumping off the Newport bridge." I would never do that.

"Why were you locked in your room?" I ask, trying to cautiously demand an answer.

She leans her shoulder against the doorframe. "With everything that was on the news last night... I'm kind of freaked out."

"They found the baby," I say, repeating her very own words from last night. Of course, I'm leaving out the part why Liam stormed out of the apartment. I'm still coming to terms with that portion of things.

"And then I heard everything going on in your bedroom this

morning," she continues. "This wasn't some random crime that you stumbled into." She heard everything and ignored my cry for help. She didn't even call for help. She left me.

"I did not ask for this. I didn't create this situation. Are you accusing me of instigating something?" The pain of being let down by my friend is replaced by anger as I question how long she would have stood by this morning if things had gotten any worse.

"You didn't know who Lara Smith was when you took the job?"

"No, Willa. How can you question me after—"

"After slowly coming to terms with how little I seem to know about you, it isn't hard. Look, I've been your friend, and by your side when you needed someone—to help you through—"

"What? Help me through what?"

Willa takes a step backward and shakes her head as if she'd like to redact what she just said.

"That's not what I meant."

"But it's what you said. You wanted to help me? That's why you live with me? What exactly do I need help with?" My cheeks and neck burn as I stare at her downcast gaze.

"Haley, stop. You're taking everything I say completely out of context."

"Am I? Why did you really stay here this summer rather than go home like you were planning?" She lives a few hours away, still within driving distance, but no one changes their mind that quickly about where they'll be living. She has Jerry as an excuse because no one likes a long-distance relationship. Instead, she claimed it was because she didn't want me to be alone while taking a new job.

"I didn't want you to be alone. I told you that."

"But why?"

Her brows furrow like she's confused. "Aren't we friends?"

We've been best friends for years, which is why I'm questioning every word she's saying right now.

"Yes, we're friends, Willa. And whatever freaked you out this morning, I'm sorry for making you feel like you had to lock yourself in your bedroom and not respond when I was shouting your name. Weren't you concerned Liam might have hurt me or something after everything you must have heard? Why didn't you at least call the police—do anything?" I'm trying hard to keep my outrage at bay but seriously, was any of this necessary? If anything, I needed a friend, and no one was there.

"Some things are too much, even for me sometimes, and this—"

"It's over."

"It's not over," she argues, "so what if they found the baby in Liam's apartment. Nothing is cut and dry. You should know that better than anyone after all this."

She really did hear everything this morning. "Do you think he's guilty?" I hate that we're talking about Liam. I hate that I fell for him and fell into a trap. I'm smarter than that.

"No, I think his sister, Lara, needs serious help. I could be convinced he was dragged into this just as unknowingly as you were—if it was in fact, unknowingly."

Her statement is a question, but an accusatory one.

"I did not know who the Smith family was when I took the job. I grew up next to a Larissa Hoyt who has apparently undergone every available cosmetic procedure known to man! Seriously."

Willa chuckles, a hint that she's lightening up. "I don't want to be scared to open the front door or walk into the apartment anymore. Jerry has already suggested I come stay with him, but I don't want to leave you here alone to deal with all of this."

"I don't want to be here either," I say. "I'm terrified of who will show up at our door next. I just—I don't know where to go or what to do."

She nods her head and scratches at the back of her neck. "Well, Jerry is on his way over. I'll tell him I want you to come with us to his place until we figure out what to do."

"I'm sure he knows you were just hiding from me," I say. I can only imagine what she told him after hearing everything between Liam and me. There's no way he'll want me to come back to his apartment with them.

"I'll explain everything when he gets here. He'll understand," Willa says, her eyes large and glossy.

No, he won't.

There are times when the world feels like it's turned its back on me. It doesn't matter how strong I've had to be throughout various struggles in my life, I still fall victim to the questions of why I am where I am and how I got to a particular point. I don't believe I make poor decisions, but every decision I've ever made has led me to this rock-bottom place. I'm living alone in my apartment, locked up in my bedroom out of fear of who might show up at my front door.

I lift my phone to check the display, finding nothing but my wallpaper design of a starry night behind a jar full of fireflies. I feel like one of those fireflies—trapped, a flickering light only visible for so long.

Still no response. Willa hasn't called or responded to me in the past week after Jerry denied Willa's plea to allow me to stay with them too. He said he had to protect Willa. She begged him to change his mind, but I told her to go. I told her I'd be okay. The last thing she said to me was, "I'll call you. Don't worry."

I'm not okay, but that's what friends do. They protect each other. She's very well protected now.

Me, not so much.

The only peace of mind I have is knowing Liam is behind bars without bail, waiting for his trial next week. While I feel a sense of relief, I'm also hurting because there was a part of him that seemed genuine and sincere. Of course, with Liam being the Billy Hoyt I knew thirteen years ago, I now know better than to assume there is anything genuine about him. He was responsible for my world falling apart that night he brought the newspaper article to me. All he wanted was to get a pat on the back from his friends.

All I wanted was to unsee those horrific truths written about my parents. I tried to leave the past behind me. I've tried to do that harder than I've tried to do anything else in my life, but my past just chases me. How can I ever move on?

I don't even know what the status of the Smiths is, but the news wasn't shy about snagging a clip of the family's "emotional and heart-warming" reunion with Fallon. Since then, there's been no public update. I haven't gotten any phone calls or messages, but quiet doesn't always mean the story is over. I'm just hoping for more answers after the trial takes place.

With a week of waiting ahead, it seems to be the most appropriate time to flesh out my final case study that might haunt me until the end of the summer.

With my laptop open on my lap, I pull up the document I've attempted to start several times, giving up with just my name and date. I begin to type the words that have been weighing on my shoulders the last few days, hoping more will come to me as I write.

Haley Vaughn | June 23, 2023

Course:

Advanced Level: Ethics and Decision Making within Social Work

PhD: Childhood Psychology

Case Study:

Through observation, determine long-term consequences of neglect in diagnosing children's psychotic behavior.

Background:

This case study involves a nine-year-old girl, twin A, who shows increasing psychopathic behavior, seemingly related to a new baby in the family.

Case Description:

~~Twin A, born in a pair of identical twins, began to comprehend abnormal behavioral traits among her mother after a third child was born into their family. The baby joined the family when the twins were eight years old. The occurrence altered the dynamic of the family's every-day life. The nature of the mother's experiences appears to grapple between overwhelming stress and the possible presence of postpartum depression, which resulted in verbalizing inappropriate statements overheard by Twin A.~~

No. That's not right. The statement needs to be more forceful and direct. I'm supposed to show the relationship between Twin A's environment and her psychological state, if there is one. There must be more to this than one awful comment made by Lara.

I close my eyes to conjure the next sentence, my fingertips hovering over my keyboard.

Twin A has been faced with a sudden shift in life while yielding to a new family dynamic. Firstborn children often experience a feeling of neglect while personal attention becomes unbalanced and shared with the newest member of the family. Children in this situation can often feel as if they've been replaced by something new and better, thus leading to unconventional methods for commanding attention.

A heavy bout of wind sweeps by the window, whistling along the water. A tugboat clatters against the nearby dock and the thud sends a shiver down my spine. I hope we aren't getting another storm.

I try to refocus my attention onto my screen, but another thud shatters any hope of regaining my concentration. The banging is coming from the front door this time.

My limbs turn to ice as I push my laptop off to the side and swing my legs off my bed. The door is locked. All my doors are locked. I could ignore the knocking. I should.

I unlatch the chain on my bedroom door, careful to ease the chain down rather than allowing it to fall against the wall. I don't want whoever is outside to know someone is in. While walking by the coat hooks on the wall, I reach into the pocket of my hanging sweatshirt and retrieve the can of pepper spray.

My heart pounds so hard I can feel it through every vein in my body. I press up on my toes to peek out the peephole, but there's no one in sight.

I ease down from my toes and step back, my heart still pounding. Maybe it was the boat hitting the dock. It sounded like it came from the front door, though.

I replace the pepper spray back in the pocket of my hanging sweatshirt, and a definitive knock on the door makes me jump. Again, I pad lightly toward the door and press up on my toes to look out the peephole.

I'm not sure which startles me more...what I don't see, or the additional knock that rattles through my bones. I stumble backward as thunder claps out in the back. Storm clouds cover the sky and rain begins to hammer down. I race to the balcony and close the wide curtain.

Static buzzes around the apartment and the cable box whines as it shuts down. The power's out.

FIFTY

The effects of prolonged stress can cause sleep deprivation and high blood pressure, which can then lead to cognitive impairment, and reduced coping abilities. That is my self-diagnosis for my current state. Psychology professionals should never self-diagnose, but it's hard to avoid while I'm living alone in this apartment that feels like it's getting smaller by the day.

Not only is the silence getting to me, but someone is getting a kick out of knocking on my door several times a day before running off. I can't see who they are, so I assume it's a child standing just below the peephole of my door. But why? I don't know any of the children in my apartment building, and there are a dozen other doors in this hallway to go knock on. Maybe they're knocking on everyone else's too.

The silence should have been a good landscape for working on my case study, but for every sentence I write, I delete two more. I just can't seem to center my mind. All I keep thinking about is the fact that there isn't one person left in my life who I can still trust. I could probably write a case study about what it might feel like to be the last living person on the planet.

I tap the screen of my phone again for the twentieth time in the past hour, finding it finally time to leave.

When a person has nothing left to lose, they are less concerned about consequences, which is my reason for leaving this apartment for the first time in the last few days. I pinch my purse beneath my arm and lower my sunglasses over my eyes as I scramble down the hall and out to the exterior stairs. The parking lot is mostly empty at this hour, and as an added bonus, I'd managed to snag a parking spot a few steps away from the stairwell landing after I made a quick trip to the grocery store on Monday.

The air conditioning blasts from the vents, giving me an instant shiver. Lately, if I'm not overly hot, I'm cold, and if I'm not shivering, I'm sweating. I'm wired as if I've had too much caffeine but I haven't had a coffee or soda in weeks. This hearing must be the end. There must be a verdict today.

I only wish a definitive verdict would resolve my sources of stress. If Liam isn't found guilty, he might come after me again. Lara and Corbin could come after me too.

The nervous tremble in my hands has become a side effect of living through this past month, but I still notice the unsteady grip as I go to unlatch my seatbelt then open my car door. It's the moment I silently pray no one is waiting outside for me, begging to play this game of cat and mouse that I keep losing.

"What are you doing here?"

The words make me scream and cup my hand over my mouth to quiet the unnecessary sound I've made. Her shadow covers the sun blinding me as I step out of my car. I grab the door to steady myself as my heart thrashes against the inside of my chest.

"I'm going to ask you the same question," I say, peering over my shoulder at Willa, whose keys are dangling from her finger. "I thought you fell off the face of the earth."

"I snuck down here because I knew you'd be here, and I wanted to be with you."

"You snuck down here? Who are you sneaking away from?"

Willa scoffs and mumbles: "Jerry begged me to give you some space until all this stuff blows over. I argued with him about it, but he got really upset and—"

"You don't have to explain," I say. I'd already assumed where I stood in her life now. I lock my car and cross the sidewalk across from the courthouse.

"Hales, wait. I'm coming with you."

"You shouldn't lie to Jerry about where you are. I didn't think you would care," I say, adding a question to my statement.

"Please, let me be with you," she says, whining as if I'm being too hard on her. She steps up beside me and tries to grab my hand, but I pull away. "Don't go into the courthouse alone," she says, stepping in closer.

"You've never pushed me away before," I tell her.

"I didn't push you away," she argues. She did. Maybe she's just outgrown our friendship. I suppose I can understand considering the circumstances this past month.

"The trial is open to the public," I reply.

Willa holds her pace beside me as we walk into the court-house and up to the metal detectors, waiting our turn to put our bags on the conveyor belt. "I don't understand why you suddenly care to be by my side," I whisper.

"Because you're my bestie," she coos. As much as I want to let out a groan, I sweep her comment off my shoulder. "You still like him, don't you?"

Her question makes me halt. I twist to face her. "What kind of sick question is that? That man is obviously deranged." It still pains me to say that about Liam and it shouldn't. It's been hard enough to come to terms with the fact that he was the same person I woke up next to that morning as the one I went to bed with the night before.

I want to believe Lara manipulated Liam to take part in this scheme and that he was too weak to turn away from his only living flesh-and-blood. Lara must have messed with his mind just like she did with Madden's, making them believe whatever they're doing is in everyone's best interest, when it might only be in Lara's. She's always been a selfish person; self-centered with an untouchable ego that's big enough to squash the world around her. Regardless of what she's capable of, Liam is still a man of his own mind and actions.

"Are you still thinking about him? Do you miss him, maybe?" Willa asks, keeping her voice quiet and her face filled with hesitation. She should have considered not asking what was on her mind.

"No, Willa," I utter. "I'm here to finish my case study. And you're here to what...just try and make things right after walking out on me like I'm no more than a one-night mistake you made?"

"Why would you say that?" She holds her hand up to her chest, a gesture of being offended.

I check my watch to see what time it is, worried about walking in after the trial has started and causing a scene. "After all the years you've known me, how ignorant do you think I am?" I continue walking forward, not waiting for a response that will likely come out in a stuttering array of words to avoid a direct answer.

I walk into the large, oak-clad courtroom and take a sharp right down the back row of seats, allowing my gaze to blur in the distance before I sit down. My heart flutters as I settle onto the stiff leather padding of the bench. Liam is on the opposite side of the room, sitting at one of the front counsel tables next to who I assume to be his attorney. On the other side are Lara and Corbin with their attorneys.

Behind them are the twins and a toddler sitting on a woman's lap. I wonder what they must be thinking watching their family fight each other like this. I also wonder if they were forced to be here—all of them. Madden I can understand, but Blakely and the baby I assume is Fallon shouldn't have to be subjected to this more than they already have been. My opinions don't mean much, but it's just another reason I believe psychological damage can be directly caused from poor parenting decisions.

"He doesn't look nervous," Willa whispers. "I wonder if that means he's innocent?"

FIFTY-ONE

THURSDAY, JUNE 30TH 10:30 AM

Liam has been at the bench for the last few minutes while the attorneys speak privately with the judge. I wonder if he's spotted me in the back. He tried calling me several times after he was released on bail, following his arraignment, but I didn't answer. There was something so evil brewing within him that last morning we were together. I had no inclination on that side of him. He had such a calm demeanor every time we were together, but it was all an act.

The attorneys return to their counsel tables, but Lara and Corbin's attorney remains standing.

The judge folds his hands together and focuses his attention on Liam. He lets his pause weigh heavily over everyone watching before speaking to him. "Liam, I want to discuss your history with your sister, Lara, following the passing of your late mother." Liam shifts around in his seat and straightens his tie. It's obvious he's uncomfortable. Anyone would be sitting in that seat. "According to your parents' will, Lara was named sole beneficiary to their inheritance. Is that correct?"

"Yes, that is correct," Liam says, leaning in toward the microphone.

"Are you aware that it's common to have multiple beneficiaries to a will, especially when it comes to siblings following the death of their parent/parents?"

"Yes, I am," Liam answers.

The attorney paces back and forth in front of the stand, his hands interlocked behind his waist.

"Your Honor, I have the letter that accompanied the will, which I would like to read to the Jury as a form of character reference."

Liam's attorney isn't even trying to stop this from happening.

"You may continue," the judge replies.

The attorney returns to his table to take the note into his hands.

Dear Larissa and William,

"Lara and Liam for short," the attorney adds.

William, Billy, Liam...they're all the same. Looks can change, but who we are inside—it's something he hid well... until he couldn't.

"William?" Willa whispers into my ear.

I shrug, refusing to discuss his name now.

I hope this letter finds you well. Though I'm saddened that you must read another one of these letters from your parents in such a short span of time. With a progressing illness, I have had time to carefully consider my final wishes for my Will and Testament, on the distribution of my estate. With this letter, you will find the legally prepared documentation which names Larissa the sole benefactor, with the request that William receive financial support when needed throughout the duration of his life or for as long as the assets are available. I entrust you with the care for your brother, William, and request that he receives proper treatment to withstand the duration of his illness with his diagnosed emotional disturbance.

Please know that my intention is to ensure you are both well cared for, which is my only final wish for the two of you.

Love,

Mom

Signed by *Anita L. Hoyt on 02/18/2017*

Willa is staring at me with her lips parted and I want to nudge her to stop looking over at me while I digest everything this entire courtroom just listened to about Liam's diagnosed *emotional disturbance...*

"Liam, did the contents of this letter come as a surprise to you following your mother's passing?" the attorney questions.

"Objection, lack of relevance, Your Honor," Liam's attorney chimes in.

"I don't mind answering," Liam says without giving the judge the opportunity to agree or disagree to the objection.

"Go on," the judge replies.

"My sister, Elizabeth, or Libby, as we called her, died in a house fire thirteen years ago. I was supposed to be inside with her as she was left to keep an eye on me. She was lost in a book, reading the night away in her bedroom like she often did. I smelled smoke when I was in the kitchen grabbing a soda, so I went to investigate where it was coming from. I went into Larissa and Libby's room, finding neither of them in there. I remembered Larissa said she would be back late, but Libby was home. She was in there somewhere. A pop of an explosion set off, making my ears ring and when I ran back out into the hallway, I saw my bedroom and my parents' bedroom engulfed in a thick wall of flames. Libby must have thought I was in my room when she smelled smoke. I could hear her screaming, but I couldn't get to her. I took the blame for her death, though I had nothing to do with the fire. I suffered a lot of grief, following her loss, and needed therapy to cope. I didn't get better in the time-frame my mother hoped I would and therefore she deemed me to be unstable when she became sick with cancer. I have since then recovered well with the help of therapy and though I still suffer with grief for the loss of my older sister, nothing hurts more than the neglect my surviving sister has shown me over the last five years. I have been nothing more than a nuisance to her and her husband, Corbin, while they live their lavish life as I—"

"Objection, lack of relevance," Lara and Corbin's attorney says.

"Sustained," the judge agrees.

His response is wholesome and believable. The jury is eating it up as some reach for tissues. His words have even pulled at my heart strings, but he's leaving out part of the story —the part I was there for.

FIFTY-TWO

THURSDAY, JUNE 30TH 12:30 PM

There have been two short recesses and the attorneys are once again in a discussion with the judge. Madden is sitting up on the stand next to the judge, barely tall enough to see over the short wall in front of her. She's fidgeting with her short hair, pulling the blonde ends toward her mouth.

When the silent meeting between the attorneys ends, Jared, Madden's public defense attorney, approaches the wall in front of Madden and rests his elbows on the sill. "Madden, can you tell the jury what you told me, about why you were playing—"

"Objection, leading..." Liam's attorney pipes up.

"Sustained," the judge says.

"Just go ahead and tell the jury what happened the day Fallon went missing," Jared says to Madden.

He tilts the microphone in closer toward her mouth.

"It's hard to remember everything," Madden begins, "but I'm the one who asked for help with Fallon, my baby sister." Madden looks up and stares over at Lara. "I heard Mommy say that Fallon was a mistake and making her life so hard that she wasn't sure if she could continue taking care of all three of us. I felt bad for Fallon, and I didn't know what to do."

Jared nods his head. "So, what did you end up doing?"

Madden stares down at her lap for a moment. "Well, my uncle stopped by that same day. He and Mommy were having an argument in the kitchen, so Blakely and I took Fallon outside to play. When Uncle Liam left the house, he saw us outside and came over to talk to us." The tips of Liam's ears are red enough that I can see the color from here. "He asked me what was wrong, and I took him to the side to talk to him alone because I didn't want Fallon or Blakely to hear what I had to tell him."

"And what did you say to your Uncle Liam?" Jared presses.

"I told him what Mommy said about Fallon, that she was a mistake, and she couldn't take care of her. Uncle Liam got mad and told me she should never have said anything like that to anyone. He also said she would feel much differently if Fallon disappeared someday and maybe she would start treating everyone a bit better if she learned a lesson."

A symphony of grumbles and groans waves through the courtroom.

"Objection, this is hearsay, Your Honor," Liam's attorney interrupts.

"Overruled, this testimony was given under oath and documented previously to the trial," the judge replies.

"You can continue," Jared tells Madden.

"So... Uncle Liam said we could help each other, and he would help me keep Fallon safe if I brought her into the storm cellar of our shed. He said we could call it a game of hide-and-seek so I wouldn't get into trouble. He told me he understood everything I was feeling, and he would make sure I never had to feel that way again, but I had to keep this plan a secret or it wouldn't work. I did what he said to do. He told me he would take care of the rest and not to worry."

"Why would you do that, William?" Lara shouts across the room.

"Order, order," the judge speaks out, tapping his gavel several times.

Jared clears his throat and straightens his tie before stepping back in toward Madden. "Madden, when your mom and dad realized Fallon was missing and asked you if you had seen her, what did you tell them?" Jared says.

Madden takes a deep breath and tears fill her eyes. "I told them that she was playing hide-and-seek with the mermaids because they were always the most fun to play with."

"But that wasn't the truth?" Jared asks her.

"No, I lied because Uncle Liam said I had to keep our plan a secret in order for it to work and keep Fallon safe."

Jared begins to pace in front of Madden. "And did you check on your sister after hiding her in the storm shelter under the shed?"

Madden nods her head. "Yes, I made sure she was okay, plus Uncle Liam said he was taking care of her. But then..." Madden stares out in a daze toward the crowded courtroom. "After a few days, she was gone. Fallon wasn't in the cellar of the shed anymore and I don't know where she went."

My hands are shaking as I try to digest these horrifying words from a nine-year-old. Willa puts her hand on top of mine and it's the first time I've appreciated her comfort today.

"Thank you, Madden. I know that was difficult for you to talk about."

"Does the defendant's attorney wish to question the witness?"

"Yes, thank you," Liam's attorney says.

He and Jared switch places and I worry about the way this attorney might speak to Madden, possibly forgetting she's only nine.

"Madden, you did a great job remembering all those facts. I only have one question for you now. Do you think your Uncle Liam was trying to protect Fallon from your mom and dad?"

"Objection," Lara and Corbin's attorney shouts. "Leading the witness."

"Sustained," the judge says.

"Okay, I will re-word my question. Madden, do you think your Uncle Liam was trying to protect Fallon?" the attorney asks.

"Of course," Madden says. "He loves us."

"Those are all the questions I have, Your Honor."

The judge straightens his posture, lifts a pile of papers and taps the edges against the lectern to even out the stack. "I'm going to allow for the closing statements now and then the jury will deliberate," the judge says.

Bile in my stomach is burning up through my esophagus and I might get sick right here, right now. I duck down and scurry out of the row toward the courtroom door to exit and make a beeline for the restroom.

I lock myself in one of the bathroom stalls and wait for my stomach to settle. I hold my head between my knees, rehashing all the questions of the family today. Most of the questions painted Lara and Corbin in the light of bad parenting, but not necessarily criminals. Although, I suspect there will be charges brought against them for waiting several days to report their missing daughter.

The one thing that became clear to me was that they needed to find someone to blame, someone who wasn't Madden.

My timing couldn't have been worse.

I had posted my availability on several local classified job websites and in sub-categories for parents who were looking for summer help to watch their children. One of the postings was even listed in the town weekly newsletter.

My name probably stuck out like a flashing neon light to them when they saw my ad looking for a nannying job. Who better to take the fall for their missing daughter than the person they'd already taken so much from. It's clear they always needed someone else to blame for the bad things that happened in their family.

"Haley?" Willa likely didn't have a hard time finding me. "Are you in here?"

"Yes, and I want you to leave," I utter.

"Hales, I was just making sure you're okay."

"That's all you're ever doing, right?" I realize there might be other people in the restroom but I'm not sure I care. "How long ago did you agree to this favor?"

"What favor?" she asks, her voice pitchy with an accent of confusion.

I tear open the stall door and brush by her to wash my hands and splash water onto my face. "Please leave."

"Haley, I'm honestly worried for you."

"For me?" I laugh. "Why? I'm here as a spectator, not as a person-of-interest anymore."

I shake my hands dry and leave the restroom without another second to think.

"I would be more concerned about yourself rather than me, Willa."

Two hours have come and gone. Willa left, and I've done nothing more than stare at the back of the seat in front of me, the oak wood with a black scratch that looks like a question mark.

The judge returned two minutes ago, which gives me hope that the jury has come to a decision.

Liam is aware I'm sitting back here. I'm not sure when he noticed me today, but he's peered back at me several times in the last twenty minutes. I maintain a straight line along my lips, making it seem like I didn't notice his glances. If only I knew what was going through his mind. He doesn't seem nervous. His attorney must have told him there's nothing to worry about. Kidnapping is kidnapping though, and they found Fallon in his apartment. Madden admitted that Liam made the plan with her. If anything, he needs psychological help. It would be the best thing for him at this point.

The front right-side door opens and the jury funnels back into their rows of seats, except for the bailiff who is last to step inside. The middle-aged woman with short coffee-brown hair steps up beside the judge and faces the jury. "Ladies and gentlemen of the jury, have you reached a verdict?" she asks.

One of the male jury members stands and responds, "Yes, Your Honor, we have come to a unanimous verdict."

"Thank you. Please hand the verdict form to the court clerk, sir," the judge says.

Another gentleman stands up from a seat near the front side door and takes the paper from the jury member's hand and reaches it over to the judge.

"Your Honor, I present the verdict of the jury," the bailiff says.

"Thank you, bailiff. Go ahead and read the verdict, please."

My heart thunders, my pulse raises, and sweat beads up along the backside of my neck as I bounce my knees in apprehension. I should be grateful I'm not the one sitting in his seat right now because that's where the Smith family clearly wanted me to be.

"In the Matter of the Abduction of Fallon Smith, the jury finds Lara Smith not guilty of kidnapping. The jury finds Lara Smith not guilty of conspiracy regarding the kidnapping. The jury finds Lara Smith guilty of emotional abuse and child neglect with a penalty of nine months of rehabilitation and psychiatric treatment as well as family counseling. The jury finds Corbin Smith not guilty of kidnapping. The jury finds Corbin Smith not guilty of conspiracy regarding the kidnapping. The jury finds Corbin Smith guilty of child neglect with a penalty of nine months of rehabilitation and psychiatric treatment as well as family counseling. The jury finds William Gellar Hoyt guilty of kidnapping. The jury finds William Gellar Hoyt guilty of Extortion. The jury finds William Gellar Hoyt guilty of Conspiracy."

"The defendant, William Gellar Hoyt is hereby remanded to custody, pending sentencing," the bailiff continues.

"Thank you, bailiff. Court is adjourned." The thuds of the

gavel hitting the wooden block sears through my head. I watch as Liam is placed in handcuffs and yet, all he can do is twist his head over his shoulder to stare back at me. There's so much I want to say to him right now.

All I know is, justice has finally been served.

FIFTY-FOUR

THURSDAY, JUNE 29TH 4:00 PM

While the information is fresh in my mind, I stop at a small park a few blocks away from the courthouse and take my laptop out from under the back seat. I have my eyes set on the shady spot under the tree. The words are practically bubbling out of me, ready to finish up this case study.

Case Prefix: Ethical dilemmas involved in tending to a vulnerable child.

Lack of direct or concise evidence of why a child is acting out can create a challenge in finding the correct solution in a timely manner. Avoidance or ignoring the child's behavior could provoke a turbulent outcome rather than the child setting their focus on an alternate plan to seek attention. Therefore, addressing the matter with the child is essential to behavioral correction.

The ethics of using varying approaches to address negative behavioral patterns in a vulnerable child are uncertain. Certain methods might be effective by utilizing fabrications to create a false sense of reality, while in other cases, frank honesty could be beneficial and well-received. This is when the path to proper treatment begins to differ between cases.

Case Objective Question:

Which is more detrimental, a child exposed to only truths or a battery of constant lies?

Case Comparison between SUBJECT A *known as* **"[EXPOSED SOLELY TO TRUTHS]" and SUBJECT B** *known as* **"[EXPOSED SOLELY TO LIES]":**

[SUBJECT A: EXPOSED SOLELY TO TRUTHS] spent the formative first few years of her life exposed only to the truth. She has faced some harsh realities and lost her innocence at a young age, left to navigate right from wrong based on fact rather than a systematic approach to problem solving.

[SUBJECT B: EXPOSED SOLELY TO LIES] spent the formative first few years of her life exposed only to untruths. Being lied to throughout every aspect of her life, she learned to trust only her own twisted instincts and unrealistic portrayals of perfection. This warped view of reality resulted in naivety and a false sense of who she is. This child cannot comprehend the difference between right and wrong.

Case Comparison between [SUBJECT A and SUBJECT B]:

[SUBJECT A: EXPOSED SOLELY TO TRUTHS]
can maneuver difficult situations when faced with adversities
and has the ability to trust others.

[SUBJECT B: EXPOSED SOLELY TO LIES]
believes and trusts no one and carves a path of deceit,
devising their own rules and guidelines, however twisted they
may be.

[SUBJECT A: EXPOSED SOLELY TO TRUTHS]
often takes the blame for acts not committed.

[SUBJECT B: EXPOSED SOLELY TO LIES] eludes
reality and most often escapes blame for committed acts.
SUBJECT B: gets away with everything...

The front door squeals and whines as I step back into the house that I've spent so long avoiding. Now it seems like I'm here far too often. The living room is empty, but the TV is on, playing a sports recap and the volume is turned up louder than Dad usually has it.

"Mom, Dad? Where are you?" I shout, walking past the TV.

The house smells again and the flies have returned.

A guttural groan tears through the air from the direction of their bedroom at the end of the hall and my heart skips a beat before lurching up into my throat. I sprint down the hallway, finding their door closed. I wrench my hand around the doorknob and shove it wide open. I gasp in horror taking in the scene. "Are you okay?" I cry.

The shades are still closed from last night, but there's enough light leaking through the blinds to highlight the horrific scene in front of me. They're in bed, bound to the bedposts, blindfolded, and gagged, both with shivering jaws. I run to Mom's side first, shaking as I reach for the zip tie tightened around her wrists. "What happened? Who did this to you?"

Dad mumbles, biting down on the handkerchief tied around the back of his head and lodged in his mouth.

I tug at the zip ties, feeling the sharp edge slice against my fingers. I need to cut these off. I crawl over Mom, in between the two of them, to pull down their gags and blindfolds.

"Haley," Mom cries out my name.

"Who did this?" I grit through my teeth as I hobble off the bed.

"It was dark. We were still asleep, and it all happened so fast. We couldn't see anything," Dad says. "I hope they didn't rob us."

I pull open Dad's top drawer, finding his pocketknife where he always keeps it at night and return to Mom's side first. "I don't know what they would have taken."

"I need to call the police." I stop fussing with the zip tie for a moment because it's going to take some work to remove this with how tight it is. "One second." I glance down at my phone, finding several missed calls from Willa. Maybe she's returning all the calls she ignored last week. I try to clear the screen to call 9-1-1 but mistakenly hit her name, which redials the number.

"Hey, girl, can we talk? Just us?" Willa says upon answering the call after one ring.

"Please just get us out of these ties, Haley," Mom cries.

"What's going on, Haley?" Willa asks.

"Sorry, I'm trying to call the police. I pressed your name by mistake. I can't talk right now. I'm at my parents' house. Someone broke in and tied them up. I'm trying to help them. I have no idea who did this..." My voice is shaking.

"Holy crap. Do you need help? I can be there in ten minutes. Never mind, I'm coming over. Don't worry. Everything will be okay. Oh my God. Okay—"

"Yeah, I have to go—I have—bye," I stutter while trying to end the call.

"Who was that?" Mom asks. "Is someone coming to help?"

"Yeah, I don-don't know," I say, fussing with my phone to get to the keypad.

"Just untie us first before you call the police, please," Mom begs.

I drop my phone and return to her wrists, studying the plastic tie to figure out how to cut this off without hurting her. "These ties are tight."

"How-how did you know to come here?" Dad asks. "We thought we'd be lying here forever until someone found us too late." I should feel bad, listening to his comment, but it's not my fault that I don't come around or have much of anything to do with them. It's their fault and I've spent so long taking the blame for their decisions. I can't do that anymore.

"I didn't—I just needed to get something for a research study I'm working on. Then I found you like this."

Minutes are passing as I try to use the tip of the knife to cut through the tie, but I can't slide the knife between her wrist and the plastic with the little room there is to work with. "I need to try a pair of scissors. I'm sorry. I'll be right back."

I run across the hallway and into my bedroom. I collapse to my knees by my bed so I can pull out some of my old shallow storage boxes from under the bed frame. It takes me a few minutes to rummage through all of them before finding the old red toolbox I snatched from the garage years ago. I unclasp the clips and pull out what I need.

I return to their bedroom just as the front storm door opens and closes, slapping shut because of the missing spring Dad hasn't fixed in at least five years.

"Who's here?" Dad asks, struggling against his restraints.

"Haley...wh-what in the world are you doing with that thing?" Mom cries out. "How did a gun get into our house?"

"It's the only thing that made me feel safe here while living with you two. What other explanation is there?"

"Haley?" Willa calls out from the living room. "Where are you? What can I do to help?"

"Last room on the left," I call out to her. "I need a pair of scissors."

"Willa's here?" Dad whispers. "Is that who called you?"

I hold the pistol up toward the open door, waiting for my former roommate and dearest friend to step into sight.

"Where can I find scissors..." Willa's eyes bulge when she turns the corner to find me, and the state Mom and Dad are still in. The doe-eyed-look is gone. No time left for lies now. "Whoa, whoa...what's going on? Why...why do you have that thing? Put it down, Hales."

I inhale sharply through my nose and hold my breath for a few, long seconds. "You know, I trusted you...like a sister, Willa, and you knew that. Yet, you could never bring yourself to tell me the truth about why we became so close in the first place. It wasn't just a natural friendship forming on its own, was it?"

"Haley," Willa moans, holding her hands up in the air as if she's innocent. "What are you talking about?"

"Put the damn pistol down, Haley," Dad growls.

"Tell me why my parents are giving you weekly payments," I say, keeping the pistol locked in my grip.

Willa's gaze floats toward my dad.

"What? No-no, they—they're not paying me..." Willa stutters.

I point the pistol in the direction of the kitchen. "Actually, there's a register of payments, clearly documented in their checkbook. I was flipping through the pages and through all my bewilderment noticed the checks stopped at the end of May. Well, until yesterday when a new one was written for a different, smaller amount than usual. Coincidental timing, seeing as you moved out, huh? Oh, and so glad you could make it to the trial today to sit with me. That's what friends do for each other, right?" I shake my head, still in a puddle of disbelief. "No wonder money was never an issue for you."

"It wasn't like that, Hales," Willa mutters.

"It wasn't like what? I wasn't born into this family yesterday. I've been under lock and key for as long as I can remember just to ensure that I wouldn't ever consider the option of divulging their true identities. I thought they were going to give up the battle of holding me hostage after I turned eighteen because I figured they might have been concerned I would end up as a ward of the state if they were taken back to a facility. But they only tightened their vise grip on me, and I couldn't figure out why. I chalked it up to their illness. I tried to be patient with their needs, but two years ago when I needed to devote my entire focus on my courses and research, I had to take a step away from them. I cut them out of my life." I let my statements sit with Willa for a moment as the rage continues to eat through every one of my organs. "Ironically, just after I cut them out of my life, you got a raise after a steady stream of payments you've been earning since we first met each other. I assume it cost extra to be the only one keeping tabs on me, right?" They must have found Willa and hired her before we casually met at a pre-first year orientation. I should have questioned the odds of finding the most perfect roommate so quickly.

"We have been protecting you from yourself, Haley," Dad grumbles. "You think we'd just leave you to your devices?"

"They were worried...that's all," Willa sighs, defending them.

They were worried. The two of them...who should be locked away for child abuse, among all the other crimes they committed when escaping a behavioral hospital before I was born. "Did I ever do anything to cause you concern?" I ask Willa.

"No, no, of course not," she says, peering out of the corner of her eye toward Dad.

Unreal. "You *should* have been worried," I tell Willa. "I bet they didn't tell you about their past—how Mom was incarcerated in a behavioral health facility, Dad was too, and helped her escape. They managed never to be caught under their new false identities."

Mom and Dad both groan. "Please can someone release us from these ties," Dad says.

"Is it true, Mr. and Mrs. Vaughn?" Willa asks, holding her stare steady at the barrel of the pistol.

"No. We told you everything and nothing but the truth," Mom tells Willa.

"Did you?" I question, cocking my head to the side.

"I left the checkbook out on the kitchen counter last night when I went to bed," Dad says. "It was locked away in a desk drawer before that."

"What are you saying, Gary?" Mom groans.

"Haley was the one who tied us up this morning before sunrise."

I clutch my free hand around my forehead, feeling a headache grow. "Why would I do that then come back to untie you? You probably did it to yourselves again. That's how deranged they are, Willa. This is who you were taking directions from—a couple who tie themselves up and cry victim."

"I don't understand what's going on," Willa utters. "Please, Hales, put the gun down. Whatever is going on, we can figure it out."

A fly buzzes in my ear and I swat at it. "God, the bugs in here are out of control."

"What bugs?" Mom asks.

"The flies, Mom. They're everywhere. Is there trash that needs to be taken out or something?"

"I—I don't think so. Gary, is the trash full?" Mom asks, twisting her head to look at him.

He shakes his head. "No, no, it shouldn't be."

"I'll take the trash out. To think you've convinced yourself that you've been taking care of me when clearly you two are the ones who need help...it's just unbelievable."

"We have taken care of you, sweetheart," Mom says, staring at me with a look of endearment that I'm supposed to buy into.

"By taking care of me, do you mean making sure no one ever finds out who you really are or what you've done? Did you think keeping me secluded with the exception of going to and from school would erase your past? Then, as if you couldn't do much worse, you let me think I had finally found a good true friend, one who has been a part of my life for seven years, only to find out you found her first and have been paying her to be your puppet."

"Haley, that's not—"

"What, did you just put a classified ad up, looking for a fellow college student to babysit me? What could you have told Willa to convince her I needed supervision? Did you even know anything about Willa before you hired her? Or did you just take her word for it that she would keep an eye on me, like a stalker, while you waved money in her face?"

"We told her you were sick and needed guidance some-times. She was in the psychology program too, and it worked out—"

"It worked out?" I repeat.

"Okay, we were wrong to do that behind your back," Mom says. They're just words. She doesn't mean it—she doesn't think she was wrong.

"Did Willa tell you I was attacked on the street while under her 'supervision,' or is that why you didn't pay for the entire month of June?"

"You weren't attacked," Dad says.

I laugh and point at the faint remaining bruise marks on my neck. "Oh, no? What do you call this?"

A growl forms in Dad's throat. "I tried to warn you. I tried to make you stop what you were doing, for getting deeper into the setup you were coerced into. None of my text messages made you stop and think? I had to get a phone with a number you didn't know just to get through to you."

"Those messages were from you?" I lower the pistol by my side. "You bought a burner phone and registered it under Willa's name?" That's why it was registered under her damn name.

"Why would you put it under my name?" Willa asks Dad. "She thought—"

"I thought you might listen to the warnings if you traced the number and thought it was her."

"That makes no sense," Willa says to Dad. "I would be honest with her. I was honest—"

"Honest?" I question with a laugh.

"I'm sorry, Willa. I didn't think things would end up—" Dad says.

"We can't do this anymore, Haley. We thought we were helping you by keeping an eye on you, but we were very wrong," Mom says. "You're beyond help."

"She's right," Dad says. "We've been trying to help you with your disorder, but it's growing bigger than what we can handle. We just wanted you to have a typical life." Dad pauses and a tear falls out of the corner of his eye. "You weren't attacked on the street. I grabbed you and pulled you away so I could talk to you. You did the rest to yourself," Dad says with a sob. "Do you know how awful it was watching you thrash your head against a brick wall and try to use my hands around your neck for the sake of bruises that would be larger than your hands. You are sick, sweetheart, and every time we watch you go through another episode like this, it destroys us inside."

My lungs fall flat, air is lodged in my windpipe and I'm trying to gasp but can't. I can't even look Dad in the eyes. He's still the same stranger he's always been to me, a man with too many personalities to keep up with. A liar, a manipulator, a criminal.

"There's only one difference between the two of us, Dad... your truth is type-written in black ink on a newspaper article. Some might agree that a person of your stature and suffering from your disability can make everyone around them look like the criminals and you the victim."

"Oh God, the article again," Mom laments. "Haley, who gave that to you?"

"Billy Hoyt. His father came across it and then their daughter told everyone in school about you two."

"That was the first time I had to cover up for our family. I was only thirteen and I had to come to terms with the fact that you had been lying to me about who you really were all my life. Even still, regardless of how hurt I was, I still wanted to protect you. I felt sorry for you. I felt sorry for myself. Then I felt scared of you, so scared I locked myself in my bedroom every night afraid one of you would show your true colors again."

"What article?" Willa asks.

"It's in the past, dear. It's nothing to concern yourself with, I assure you," Mom says, chuckling as if this moment could be confused as a laughing matter.

But I always have it on me. It's proof to remind me of the difference between a truth and a lie. I pull the article out of my pocket and hand it to her.

"Go ahead, see for yourself who you were really helping all this time."

Willa shakes her head as she reads the words and slowly glances up at me.

"Hales, this—I don't understand what—what do you mean you had to cover up for your family when Billy or, Liam, gave you this article?"

FIFTY-SIX

THIRTEEN YEARS AGO

I can't listen to the laughter outside. My windows are closed, and I can still hear their cackles. The newspaper clipping is vibrating in my tight grip as I read the lines over and over. How could they keep this from me? How could they do something like this?

The mirror on my closet door draws my attention and I step up close to stare at my reflection. How does someone know when their mind isn't working properly? Did Mom and Dad know they were mentally ill before being taken away? I wonder if someone can look into another person's eyes and just see that something isn't right. People might see me that way, especially when everyone finds out about this article—my family history.

I look down at the article again, searching for a date. All this time has gone by, and it's only now resurfacing. I wish I could believe this isn't real. I glance at my small desk in the back corner of my bedroom through the mirror. The glow from the computer monitor pulls me over as if I'm in a trance without control over my actions. I don't want to know the truth. I should already know the truth. This must be wrong.

With a few long strides, I'm sitting on the cushioned roller chair in front of my desk and swiveling my mouse around to open a new internet browser. I place the article on my desk to the left of my keyboard and type out the article headline and date into the search bar.

My heart aches as I watch the mouse pointer turn into a spinning circle, waiting on the slow internet connection to bring me the results.

Matching images to the article show up and there's a page full of articles with similar headlines but all from different news sources. It's real.

My head swells with pain as I push myself away from the desk and storm out of my bedroom. The green digits on the microwave tell me it's nine fifteen at night. Mom and Dad aren't usually out this late.

I walk out the door and search the dark grounds outside, finding the group of teen boys still huddled together beneath the basketball net.

My heart is in my throat, thumping aggressively as I approach their group.

"Guys, guys," one of them says.

"She's here."

"Yes, me, I'm here. You're standing beneath my bedroom window talking about my family I assume, right?" I say, feeling the rush of anger lace each of my words.

"It's not your fault or anything," one of the guys says. "We feel bad for you."

"No one needs to feel bad for me. The article you've all been passing around has nothing to do with me or my family. Whoever thought it would be fun to pass this gossip around is obviously blind, since those people look nothing like my parents. You'd have to be a real idiot to think they were the same." I sound unsure of myself, nervous, unprepared to say everything I'm saying.

"It was Billy's sister, Larissa, who showed everyone the article. She lives right next door to you," one of the guys says with a chuckle. "Why don't you go tell her that yourself?"

I step in closer to him. "Kyle, right?"

"Yes," he says, taking a step back. The wide gape of his eyes tells me he regrets entering this conversation. "Thanks for the advice."

"Su-sure, yeah no-no problem," he says.

I turn in Billy's direction next. "Billy, tell Larissa that she should have kept her big mouth shut." Billy has been quiet since I approached their little gang.

"I—uh...I, yeah I will," he says, his gaze flicking up toward the front window of his townhouse.

"Good," I correct him, noting the flickering TV glowing through their curtains. "Go now," I say. "Then after you tell her...then you two can figure out how to make this rumor disappear."

"H-how?" Billy asks, sounding strangled.

"Dude, just go talk to your sister," Kyle suggests, muttering under his breath.

Billy scuffles along the pavement and jogs back toward his townhouse to talk to his darling sister, Larissa.

"Don't worry too much, Billy. I'm sure this will all sort itself out because when someone lies, something bad always happens after. You know—karma...ever heard of it?" I say, calling after him.

He turns to look over his shoulder at me while continuing on his path home. "What? What is that supposed to mean," he questions.

I leave Billy's question unanswered and instead follow him to the townhouses. I have no desire to be out here alone with his crappy friends. By the time I reach the stairwell, he's closing himself up inside his unit. His deadbolt locks and echoes against the wooden paneling.

Jerks.

I make it back inside and throw my back up against the door, fighting the urge to fall into a puddle of misery and cry.

The tears never come. Instead, my blood boils through every inch of my body.

Everything I've ever thought to be true is in question. My parents—the two people who supposedly love me more than anything else in the world have been lying to me. My genetics and DNA obviously don't come from two healthy people.

What we don't know can't hurt us—that's what Mom has said to me many times over the years when my curiosity is beyond her liking. It didn't make sense to me until now.

What isn't a cold, hard tangible fact can't hurt me either. I need this article to be fake.

My heart is pounding so hard, I'm short of breath and a cold sweat is seeping down through my arms and legs until the air in my lungs becomes cold too. I'm dizzy as I make my way back into the house, circling around as if I'll find a fix for my problem.

When someone lies, something bad always happens.

On the kitchen table, Mom has a half-melted candle that smells like apples and cinnamon. I stare at it, knowing the scent of the melted wax has always given me comfort, made home feel like home. It's a scent. Just a scent. Mom and Dad should be making our house feel like a home.

I lift the candle from the table and take a whiff, then take the book of matches.

An echo of laughter seeps in through the cracks of my home. It isn't the boys outside this time. It's coming from next door. All I can hear is a female cackling.

I move to the side of the table and pull the blinds on our sliding glass door that leads to our small inset balcony. It's in the corner of the townhomes with a bit of privacy. It's nice to feel alone sometimes and listen to the frogs and crickets while staring up at the stars. Maybe the townhome will block the sound of laughter and give me a moment of peace to calm down.

The moment I open the door, I realize I'm out of luck, as their laughter carries on the wind. Still, I continue outside and sit down against the wooden railing, knocking into a tin canister of lighter fluid for our charcoal grill. It spills out onto the wooden deck, seeping through the cracks. I can hear the droplets hitting the deck below but only because the laughter has stopped for a moment.

Drip, drip, drip.

Laughter.

I can't listen. My chest hurts from my heart racing so hard. I stand back up and make my way toward the glass sliding door, the sound following me with every step I take.

Before closing the door behind me, I unclench the book of matches in my hand and tear one out to light. I stare at the flame dancing in the light breeze, watching as it burns the wooden stick. How can I be weaker than this small flame, unable to burn those who are unworthy of my presence? I toss the match onto the balcony and close the sliding door. I reach into my pocket, ensuring I have the article secured where it belongs, and return to my bedroom to collect a few belongings.

A pop from what sounds like a large, overfilled balloon alerts me before the smoke alarms do. When I step out of my bedroom, I see what I've done. What I will tell myself I never intended to do.

I watch the flames lick the wooden panels outside the sliding glass window. The sound of crackles drowns out the laughter. The fire is beautiful as it grows.

Bad things happen to those who lie.

It's the only way to stop the lies...

...teach them not to lie again.

All I see are three liars in front of me.

In a world full of lies, I will be the truth.

"The three of you don't deserve me in your life. I didn't ask for this...to be surrounded by deceit that has left me unable to trust the people I should love, so yes, I tied you up to make sure you didn't do anything stupid before or during the court trial today. You know, if you had just allowed me to keep the distance between us, we wouldn't be here like this right now."

"This doesn't make any sense, Haley," Mom says, tugging her wrists from the bedposts.

"Yeah, it does. Rather than teaching me how to manage my feelings and emotions or send me to therapy, you smothered me, spoiled me, showed me love and affection, but at the same time kept me at a distance from the rest of the world. You told me you could keep me safe and protect me from the cruel world. That's why you confined me to our home when I wasn't in school. Except, you didn't plan for what would happen when you weren't home, and someone came to the door to inform me my life was a lie." I try my best to push the memory out of my head so I can get through this, explaining again how they ended up here like this. "My parents weren't who they said they were. As I digested this tidbit, kids from my class stood around like an audience outside, laughing at me during the worst moment of my life. I had never felt more embarrassed, angry, upset, and tortured than I did at that moment. Not only did I find out you had been lying to me my entire life, but Billy, my stupid teenage crush, is the one who shattered my world, also breaking my heart in the very same moment. God, I was laughingstock of all those kids with thanks to his darling sister, Larissa, who got joy out of dragging our family's name through the mud. I didn't know what else to do but retaliate."

Willa clenches her fists by her side. Her complexion becomes pale and dewy as her lips part. She's debating what to say, but I already know what will come out of her mouth.

"You're the one who started the fire in your old home?" Willa asks, her voice trembling.

Mom and Dad both shake their heads at her, their eyes bulging with fear. Because they know the truth about lies and the lies about truths, what can happen when one is exposed after the other.

I shrug. "Yes," I answer.

She covers her mouth, her hands shaking as tears fill her eyes. "You didn't tell me," she mutters to Dad.

"You didn't ask. But now that you have, you know the truth," I say, waving the pistol around in the air.

Mom lets out a faint cry. "We thought we were doing right by you," she says.

"We knew you were different than other children after—" Dad continues.

"Gary," Mom hisses.

"After what?" Willa whispers.

Dad stares up at his restrained hands and shakes his head. "You stabbed your kindergarten teacher with a pair of scissors. You almost killed her."

"I tripped," I tell them. "I was running with a pair of scissors, and I tripped." The gruesome scene floods my mind. She was sitting in the large circle with the other kids and the blades went right into her left eye. I shiver from the chills trickling up my spine.

"You hated that woman, Haley. A day didn't go by where you didn't tell us so. Even on the day of the scissor incident. You reminded us several times that she deserved what happened."

"You told everyone we knew it was an accident and that I was traumatized from it. You did the same thing with the fire, right? Accidents happen, but the fire, that accident, at least it put a stop to the past coming back to haunt us. Not that you deserved my help after lying to me about who you were." I pinch my firefly necklace that I've had hanging around my neck since I was a kid. "Although I assume that's why you rewarded me with this necklace after the fire."

"You know who we are. We're your parents. We've always been your parents," Mom wails. "And nothing was an accident. We didn't give you that necklace. You said you found it outside of the children's rehabilitation center we had taken you to."

"I never said that," I argue.

"We went through so much to make sure you weren't taken away from us, especially after the incident with your kindergarten teacher. So, yes, we did cover for you so you didn't end up with a criminal record at thirteen for committing arson. It wasn't your father and I who you saw in that article, Haley. However, that article *was* the reason for your anger the night of the fire. We've been honest with you all along, but you chose not to believe us."

"How could I?" I still don't believe them now. I likely never will. "You didn't think I would benefit from some therapy with the hope of having a better future? No, you didn't. You don't believe in therapists because one would likely sniff out your truth and reveal who you two really are. When I realized this about you, I knew I had to do something to make sure I didn't end up like you."

"Haley... These questions are absurd. You're not like us. We prayed you'd become like us, but it hasn't happened," Dad says.

"You're right," I retaliate. "Unlike you, I tell the truth, only the truth. I told you exactly what I did after the fire, and just as you always had before, you lied about it to everyone. You claimed never to know how the fire began even though I was honest. Even when the Hoyts accused us of having something to do with the fire, you told them it was an unfortunate circum-stance that took the life of their daughter—the wrong daugh-ter." I thought Lara was home that night, not Libby, the nice sister. "That's why you didn't fight the lawsuit. You knew if you fought, the truth could come out, so instead you gave them everything they didn't deserve. They were the ones who tried to ruin our lives in the first place. They got what they deserved."

"Anyone can try to ruin your life, Haley, but only you can allow someone to do so. You were a victim to their cruel behav-ior, and they were wrong to do what they did, but what you did —" Dad grumbles.

"Can I please leave," Willa whimpers. "I'm sure you have a lot to talk out, but please—I'm sorry, Haley. I was trying to help..."

I lift the pistol and point it at Willa's head. "You're not going anywhere. Trying to help? You took money to watch over me like I was a child and pretended to be my friend. You're just another liar."

"Please, Haley. Please, can we just talk calmly. Put the gun down," she says, sniffling.

I grab a tissue from Mom's nightstand and reach it over to my former best friend. "You know, I might have gotten away with arson, but if anyone asked me if I started the fire, I wouldn't have lied. I'm not a liar like them, and anyone would

SHARI J. RYAN

know that if they had asked me if I started the fire. No one ever asked…until Kyle did."

Kyle stepped back into my life after his brief introduction the night of the fire. He was a part of Billy's entourage of laughing fools.

We ended up in some of the same liberal classes freshman year, and I did my best to act like he didn't exist. I had no desire to talk to him, but he was persistent in trying to catch my attention. He spent months attempting to convince me how regretful he was for the way he acted that night when we were thirteen. He told me how unfair it was for the Hoyts to blame my family for the loss of Billy's sister. He saw my side, my pain, and my embarrassment. It was easy to believe him since he and Billy stopped talking shortly after the fire.

What we had was nice, and easy. We were good together, until we weren't. Like every couple, we began having sporadic arguments over whose dorm we would stay at and which party we would go to—immature college kid things. The last of the fights was more serious, though. I refused to introduce him to my parents and didn't explain why. It wasn't something I wanted to talk about yet. We both got heated and said our fair share of unnecessary mean things to each other. I was on the brink of tears when he stormed out of my dorm room that night.

Just before he walked out, he said: "Do me a favor and calm down before you start setting things on fire again." It was either a deep dig at me or a hint at knowing the truth, despite pretending he thought I had nothing to do with the fire.

"Excuse me?" I called after him. "That's a low blow, Kyle. Why would you say something like that?"

He stopped just before letting my door close and turned to face me. "I would have never thought so until I saw how angry

THE PERFECT NANNY

you get over silly things. You aren't who I thought you were, Haley. You started the fire, didn't you?"

He walked out before I could answer.

The car accident that night was unfortunate. Of course, if anyone asked whether I had something to do with that accident, just like the fire, I would tell them yes, I did. I was the one with my high beams going the wrong way down a one-way road. I got out of Kyle's way in the nick of time. I didn't plant the tree that he crashed into, though.

Willa holds the tissue beneath her nose, her body convulsing as if she's standing naked in a snowstorm. "You were the cause of Kyle's death too?" she asks, her voice scratchy and whiny.

"It's just two people, or was—but who's counting?"

"Kyle," Mom says, matter-of-factly. "I never asked if you had anything to do with that."

"Because you didn't want the truth," I remind her. "You never believed in the truth."

"Willa, you should leave," Dad says, swallowing a lump in his throat while advising. "Don't call the police. Do you understand? Haley, let her go. Just let her go. You can keep us here for as long as you want, but don't hurt her."

Willa is so blindsided and baffled by the scene, all she can do is look back and forth between Mom and Dad, pleading with her eyes for more answers. "Don't bother, Dad," I say, hopping up to my feet to aim the pistol back at her face. "Willa's already proven she can't be trusted. I doubt she would tell anyone but Jerry, and Jerry is a loose end. I can't have that."

"I won't tell him anything. I promise. I swear to you, Hales. I-I-I won't," she utters.

I laugh because for once, I know she's telling the truth. "Oh, I know. It would be impossible to tell Jerry anything right now."

"What do you mean?" Willa cries out.

"Well, I didn't know how today would end up and I couldn't take any chances on a set of loose lips so, yeah—Jerry's gone." I pout and let out a heavy sigh. "I'm so sorry for your loss. I wonder how it happened. Did he seem okay when you saw him earlier? Anything out of the norm?"

Willa releases a loud, heavy sob. *She really did love him.* Liam would appreciate this Romeo and Juliet life lesson. You can't get rid of one without the other because if one knows something—they both know. That's what love dictates.

I release the safety on the pistol, glare straight into Willa's doe-eyed-stare and pull the trigger. Her body slumps to the floor with a thud.

"I didn't even flinch. Did you see that?" I ask Mom and Dad. "Actually, I don't feel anything at all." I take a deep breath and immediately feel a sense of relief. "Two less loose ends to worry about. Next time you bring one into our lives, give me a warning first, will you?"

I open my old dresser and grab a dingy T-shirt out of a drawer, wipe down the pistol and place it down on Dad's lap with the T-shirt still wrapped around the weapon. "Here you go. I assume since you failed at trying to kill me in a back alley of all places, you'd want a second chance."

"Stop," Mom says. "Don't take your anger out on your father."

"I needed to stop you—this—what's happening right now. You're our daughter...we love you and we didn't want your life to be like this. We tried to take care of you the best we could. We kept you safe for as long as possible, but your manifestations got too big for us to help with. We couldn't decide on what to do with you—set you free or have you locked up in some facility. The thought of putting you somewhere, stealing your life, it pained us so much. Love can make people do stupid things, and we did stupid things for the sake of loving you," Dad says. "We aren't the ones who are sick. It's always been you, lost in your thoughts and unable to determine what's true from what isn't. We didn't want this for you, sweetheart."

"Haley, we can't let you leave this time. You're a danger to society," Mom says, interrupting Dad's threat.

"What are you going to do with me?" I ask, curling my fringed hair that has fallen loose from my ponytail behind my ears. "You're still tied up, and I'm not."

"Haley, just stop. Where did you take that baby?" she asks.

"What baby?"

"The Smith baby. How many babies have you taken," Dad snaps.

"Haley, she's a baby. You kidnapped her and hid her here in our house for over a week. This is how far we've gone to protect you. We can't do this anymore. This isn't fair to us. You've taken advantage of our love for you and it's time we put ourselves first. We warned you what would happen if you didn't return the child to her parents. We gave you more time than we should have. Do you know what it's like to have to debate whether to protect your daughter or protect the community from her?"

"She's not here anymore, is she? I told you I was taking her somewhere safe when I left with her." Liam's apartment was safe, but not for him. "She was returned to her parents. No harm done. Relax."

"Someone could have caught us. They would have held us responsible. I took care of that little girl while you just left her here with nothing. Did you think any of that through or just fly off on another bout of retaliation? You could have come to talk to us first. We would have tried to help you through this."

"But you did help me through this. You were an accomplice, and by all legal means, in support of my actions. How would I think what I did was wrong when you let me walk out of here thinking it was right?"

I could never do anything wrong. If they'd ever made me

feel like there was something wrong with me, I would have known something was wrong and I would have been subjected to a life they didn't want for me. It makes me wonder what they would have done if I had some kind of disease. Would they have tried to cure me themselves and hope for the best? How is any of what they did a sign of love? They set me up for failure in life. I shouldn't have to feel bad for them now.

Dad glances over at the phone sitting on the writing desk behind his chair. I'm sure now that it's too late, he would like to call the police.

"You're right. We shouldn't have let things get this far with you," Mom says through sniffles. "We struggled with what to do but told ourselves we were doing the right thing by protecting you."

"Well, I guess there's a lesson in this for all of us: When it becomes hard to speak the truth, it just means you're still lying to yourself." I stare down at my pistol, truly wishing they hadn't put me in this situation.

FIFTY-EIGHT

THURSDAY, JUNE 29TH 9:00 PM

[Page 3] Haley Vaughn

Case Study: Ethics and Decision Making within Social Work: Long-term consequences of children under the influence of adult psychotherapy through observation.

Main Point:

A lie is an intentional false statement made by a person who is trying to conceal the truth. Ethics are a moral logic to support one truth—the only truth. Therefore, in favor of fortifying ethical psychological treatments, there can only be one side to every story.

*Per the case study subjects of **[SUBJECT A] vs. [SUBJECT B]**, one child was raised being fed only truths and the other with only lies.*

[SUBJECT A: EXPOSED SOLELY TO TRUTHS]
Raised to believe the truth deserves praise, even when there is
an undesired answer.

However, the constant use of the truth can cause eternal
emotional pain and cause psychological confusion.

[SUBJECT B: EXPOSED SOLELY TO LIES]:
Raised to believe the world is a perfect place. Constant lying
can cause problems like confusion and unrealistic views. This
form of parenting can result in psychological abuse.

Consistent honesty can encourage a world with less candor.
The truth can hold more weight and be used as a rebuttal for
self-defense. However, the truth requires proof and trust
following a history of being known for honesty.

In contrast, consistent truths can eliminate the idea of hope,
damaging a person's ability to create goals that may appear
unattainable.

Lies can create a bottomless well of possibilities, detracting a
subject from adapting to a common reality. Deception can be
used as a weapon, inviting a retaliation of the same nature.
Lies can create optimism and hope, making daunting goals
seem more easily achievable.

[SUBJECT A]: Study Scene 1:

[SUBJECT A: EXPOSED SOLELY TO TRUTHS]
parents were honest with subject even if it might have caused
emotional distress. **[SUBJECT A]** heard their mother
verbally regret having a third child, as it was taking her attention away from the other two children.

Observation Fact:

[SUBJECT A: EXPOSED SOLELY TO TRUTHS]
presented a solution for the mother. **[SUBJECT A]** told
their parents that they took the baby to the ocean for a swim
and the baby never returned. **[SUBJECT A]** was telling
their parents a lie, opposing the way they were raised.

SUBJECT B: Study Scene 1

[SUBJECT B: EXPOSED SOLELY TO LIES] grew
up being told lies by their parents to shield them from the
harsh realities of the world. As a result, they struggled to
accept negative outcomes.

[SUBJECT B: EXPOSED SOLELY TO LIES]
admitted to taking the baby out of revenge and causing their
parents to become accomplices in the kidnapping. Now, the
parents must decide whether to lie or teach their child about
honesty. **[SUBJECT B]** spoke the truth as punishment to
their parents when learning they were always fed lies.

FIFTY-NINE

SUNDAY, JUNE 11TH 8:30 PM

Three Weeks Earlier

While hiding up against the side of the shed outside the Smiths' residence, I'm left in silence as Corbin struggles to climb up the hill from the shore, seeking the noise he heard from me stepping on a pinecone while I was spying on him and Lara in their search for Fallon.

A whimper, one that could be confused with a wind chime or a heavy branch swaying, pulls my attention to the wall of the shed. The storm doors protruding from the dirt are unhinged and I quietly slither beneath one door panel and scurry down the steps beneath the shed. There's no light, not a speck, but as I reach a flat cement floor, I hear two sets of lungs breathing heavily. I take a matchbook out of my pocket, something I always carry on me in case my car breaks down and I have trouble lighting a flare. It's happened before. I strike a spark and illuminate a small space around me within the storm cellar.

After walking through a narrow corridor, two figures come into sight, up lit by a faint glow tracing the outlines of their bodies.

My heart stops, and my throat tightens. I reach for the wall for support and rub my eyes, thinking I might be seeing something that isn't here.

My flame burns out at the same moment, but their glow is still present. I stumble forward, needing to get a better look at what's in the corner.

When more of the glow spills to their side, I spot a child with short hair hunched forward with her side against the cement wall. Two small legs dangle over the side of her lap.

"Madden?" I whisper, making my way to the front of where she's sitting. A baby is in her lap, drinking from a bottle Madden's feeding her in the light of a small pocket flashlight.

Madden peers up at me, not seeming surprised to find me down here, or anyone for that matter. "Please don't tell anyone. You can't. You don't understand what it's like," Madden says. "They don't love Fallon. They call her a mistake and hide her in a room in the attic so they can't hear her cry at night. She has made Mom become a mean person, even meaner than she was before Fallon. I don't want Fallon around either. It would fix the problem and Mom might be nicer to me..."

"You don't mean that," I whisper.

"Yes, I do."

"Madden, let me help you," I offer, still unsure of what I can do to help aside from turning the little girl in and watching her take the fall for what she felt she had to do to reprieve herself of pain.

"I don't think that's a good idea," she says, looking back down at her sister while pushing the bottle into her mouth harder. "Drink it, stupid." Fallon begins to whimper, and Madden squeezes her hand around her wrist so tightly, I imagine it will leave a mark.

The bruises. She must be hurting herself and her sisters.

"Here. Why don't I feed Fallon and you take a break..." I

slide down against the wall next to Madden and take Fallon out of her arms, keeping the bottle situated in her mouth.

Madden drops her empty hands into her lap. "Mom and Dad blamed you for Fallon disappearing."

That wasn't a secret, and poorly executed. "But why?"

"They didn't want to blame me," she says, shrugging. "That news would embarrass her in front of the whole entire town."

"That's why your mom decided to call me?" I ask her, unsure of how accurate this information is. Madden nods. "No. That's not why. Mom and Dad didn't know what to do and they said they were running out of time, so they called my 'good-for-nothing' uncle for help."

"Your good-for-nothing-uncle?" I snap.

"Well, he's just my uncle, but they call him 'good-for-nothing' too," she says with a shrug.

"So, your uncle helped your parents..." My body overheats like a pot of water that just began to boil. Anger writhes through me.

"Yeah, they said he would do anything for a penny." Madden tilts her head to the side. "Which I don't understand because I find pennies on the ground all the time." She takes a deep breath. "But Uncle Liam came over a while later and told Mom he had come up with a plan, but he said it would cost her. I think that's where the pennies came in."

My pulse rings through my ears. *Uncle Liam. I should have known he was involved after I found out Lara was my good old neighbor, Larissa Hoyt. How could I be so stupid?*

"A lot of pennies, I think," Madden says. "Mom and Dad are rich because of the money Grandma and Grandpa left them, but they don't share their money. Not even with Uncle Liam, so I guess this made him happy."

They don't share unless their sacred reputation is at risk.

"So, this setup to blame *me* for Fallon being missing was your uncle Liam's idea?" The nipple of the bottle falls out of

Fallon's mouth. My hands become heavy as I stare across the opening into the darkness, imagining what I would do to Liam if he was standing here right now. Faint laughter grows from behind me, echoing like a taunt. "Shut up!"

"Me?" Madden asks. "I didn't say anything."

I shake my head and peer over my shoulder, coming face to face with the cement wall. "No, not you, sorry. I thought I heard something." *I hear it all the time. That teasing laughter directed at me.* Madden is staring at me with confusion, and I feel questions brewing. "Tell me what the idea was? What did your uncle Billy suggest?"

Madden tilts her head to the side. "You mean Uncle Liam? Mom and Dad only call him Billy when they're making fun of him."

"Yes, sorry, Uncle Liam," I correct myself. My lungs tighten and I might as well be breathing through a straw with how thick the air is down here.

Madden lets out a sigh. "I guess he saw your name in an ad you posted, saying you were looking for a nanny job for the summer. He said it must have been a sign because you were the perfect person to blame. Uncle Liam said that your family still owed them for what happened to their family. I don't really know what that means though."

It means Uncle Liam hasn't learned what happens when you pour gasoline on a flame. A roll of thunder booms overhead, vibrating through the floor. I look up at the shallow ceiling.

Liam must have thought I was a piece of low-hanging fruit that could be easily nailed for the crime. He thought the same thing thirteen years ago when he wanted to prove to his friends how tough and mean he could be to the girl everyone already picked on.

Some men never mature with age, and he must have thought I am as naïve today as I was thirteen years ago.

He didn't consider that I might figure out who he was...

He had me fooled. I didn't recognize him with the scruffy long hair, the man's body versus a scrawny teenager, and a head taller than he was. I haven't seen him in all this time because he and his family moved to another town after the fire. He must take me for an idiot, falling for his trap.

I close my eyes and try to take in a deep, calming breath. "Oh." I'm not sure what to say to Madden. On the one hand her parents were trying to spare her from what they seem sure she has done. On the other, Lara jumped at the chance to try and ruin my life again for her own gain.

"So, you brought Fallon down here, but told them she had drowned?" I ask.

Madden pulls at the ruffles lining the bottom of her night-gown. "Yes, I told them she was gone forever—just like Mommy wanted. And, I did try to drown her, but she screamed so loud that I got too scared to stay there so I took her to hide here instead, but they don't know that."

"That's when they blamed me," I say, feeling the need to reiterate this story as it sloshes through my mind like a riptide.

"I told them it was my fault that Fallon was gone, but they screamed at me and told me to be quiet. They told me never to tell anyone what I had done, or I would be punished for the rest of my life. That's why I didn't say anything when they blamed you."

"I wouldn't have either." It's one thing to do something spiteful to a mean person, but it's another to use them as bait for a crime. "I understand the way you feel," I tell her. "What's important is that we take care of ourselves, no matter what we do in life. No one will protect us like we protect us. Does that make sense?"

"Yes, I think so," she says.

"Madden, the police already know I have nothing to do with Fallon's disappearance. Your only option to save yourself from getting into trouble or caught, is to blame your uncle Liam.

I know it might sound confusing, but it will keep you safe from a lifetime of being in trouble."

Madden hesitates, taking a deep breath. "I can't do that to him. He's a good uncle. He's nicer than Mommy."

Of course he is, but he isn't as conniving as her. "Well, what if I told you your mommy and uncle were the real reason their sister died in that house fire before you were born. They were mean and bad things happen to mean people." Maybe they didn't light the match, but they certainly didn't expect a consequence for their actions. Ruining one person's life should be repaid with another life. It's only fair.

"I don't want something bad to happen to me," she says, her breath hitching in her throat.

"It won't if you do what I'm about to tell you. Okay?"

"Okay." Madden nods without hesitation. People like Madden and I say we love the people who are close to us, but I'm not sure we truly love in the same way as others. Love can force a person to put someone else before themselves, giving up their wellbeing for the sake of another. That isn't survival. Our minds run on survival mode and survival means keeping oneself safe at whatever cost. We can only ever depend on ourselves.

"All you have to say is: Your uncle told you to hide Fallon because your mom was being mean to her. It was the only way to keep her safe and you wanted to protect your sister from your mom. But then after you hid her, she was gone when you went back for her, and you don't know what happened. You were just following your uncle's instructions so maybe he's the one who is keeping her safe from your mom." Until then, I can play his game. In fact, I can play it better than he can.

Madden's eyes light up, knowing this is the solution to her problems. "If I do this, I won't get in trouble?"

"No, you won't," I tell her. "How about I take Fallon home with me until it's time for you to tell the truth about your uncle. Then I will take Fallon to his house so your story all lines up."

"You would do that for me? Because, the truth is, I'm glad Fallon didn't die, but I wish my mom did. I don't think she deserves to be alive. She's mean to everyone."

Madden reminds me of myself. "Yes, of course I will help you." Madden is suffering with symptoms of conduct disorder and Lara and Corbin think they are helping her by displacing her behavior onto others. They're right. They are helping her. She'll be stronger for this. Except their reason is to protect their image, fearful others might think their daughter isn't up to standard. They may never realize she's beyond any form of perfect.

People like us will always be the ones who survive at the end. It's a skill many don't have. Forms of psychosis aren't a disability, they're an ability to think in ways most can't imagine.

"Can we stay friends?" Madden asks me. "No one has ever been so nice to me before. I like you a lot."

"Of course, we can," I tell her. I hope if I have a daughter someday, she will be just as sweet. "But right now, your dad is outside looking for whoever made a sound. I'm going to distract him after I put Fallon in my car. When you hear him run after me, you need to get back into your house and get upstairs to your bedroom before anyone sees you aren't in bed, okay?"

"I can do that. I've done that a million times before." I don't doubt that.

I feel around the opaque air for Madden's arms and cup my hands beneath her elbows so I can take Fallon. "Don't forget. You must always protect yourself." Apparently lying is the only way to do that for her, but I'm confident she'll find ways around the lies as she gets older, just like I have.

"Thank you. You know, you really are the perfect nanny, just like your advertisement said. Mom hung the ad on the refrigerator a couple of days before you started." If Lara thought I was so perfect—perfect to take the blame for her missing child, she shouldn't have underestimated me again.

SIXTY

SUNDAY, JULY 30TH

.

Case Study: Page 4 | Haley Vaughn

Ethics and Decision Making within Social Work

Study Scene 1.2

Observation Fact:

The parents of **[SUBJECT A: EXPOSED SOLELY TO TRUTHS]** were unaware that their child had hidden the baby in a soundproof storm shelter because of feelings of neglect. **[SUBJECT A]** had their parents convinced of the lie that the baby had drowned.

[SUBJECT A: EXPOSED SOLELY TO TRUTHS] and **[SUBJECT B: EXPOSED SOLELY TO LIES]** cross paths and discuss the challenges of following ideals they were each raised with.

[SUBJECT B: EXPOSED SOLELY TO LIES] is much older and has experience in psychological manipulation, which may be used to protect both subjects regarding the case with a missing baby. **[SUBJECT B]** teaches **[SUBJECT A]** that sometimes a lie is the only solution to keep them safe. **[SUBJECT A]** understands and agrees that lying would be the correct answer.

Observation Fact:

[SUBJECT A: EXPOSED SOLELY TO TRUTHS] Lied in court, placing blame on a close relative who had a reputation for lying to everyone, including the people they loved. The "lying" relative was assumed to be dishonest when denying their role with the missing baby. The "lying" relative was then criminalized due to their lack of ability to convince anyone of the truth.

Observation Fact:

[SUBJECT A: EXPOSED SOLELY TO TRUTHS] got away with the act of kidnapping by utilizing the method of withholding important information.

Potential Cause:

The parents had ignored signs that **[SUBJECT A: EXPOSED SOLELY TO TRUTHS]** was suffering with symptoms of conduct disorder, disregarding the serious nature. The parents of **[SUBJECT A]** were more concerned with displacing blame from their child onto another subject in a form of protection. **[SUBJECT A]** witnessed the benefit of lying when used for the purpose of self-preservation.

The parents of **[SUBJECT A]** were unaware of their child's dangerous intentions toward the wellbeing of their family following the conclusion of the missing baby. The parents of **[SUBJECT A]** are still avoiding the symptoms of conduct disorder in their child, creating a volatile living environment for the entire family.

Differences between SUBJECT A and SUBJECT B:

[SUBJECT A: EXPOSED SOLELY TO TRUTHS] was not given proper therapy or consequences for side effects of symptomatic situations of conduct disorder. **[SUBJECT A]** has a history of showcasing violence and criminal acts to persuade the opinions of others to match their own. **[SUBJECT A]** observed their parents change ideals of sole exposure to truths, utilizing elaborate lies to convince others of what they want them to believe. In this case—that their child is not guilty of the committed acts. **[SUBJECT A]** has become aware of their power to control an outcome without the fear of consequence at a young age.

[SUBJECT B: EXPOSED SOLELY TO LIES] was lying when they stated their history of only being exposed to lies during formative years. **[SUBJECT B]** has lied about the method of their upbringing for the purpose of this case study to prove that the truth is no better than a lie when people only believe what they want to hear. **[SUBJECT B]** does not believe they are disabled with symptoms of psychosis but instead, enabled with the ability to protect themselves both mentally and physically in any presented situation. **[SUBJECT B]** is aware of their own truths and lies but does not believe the world is privy to the same information that is proprietary to each unique human mind.

Conclusion:

Treating children's symptoms of conduct disorder, better known as psychosis in an adult, may not have a conclusive solution as the symptoms can often only be masked rather than cured. The efforts in treating forms of psychosis do not depend on the ethical decisions by caretakers but by the patients themselves and whether they see their "psychological condition" as an abnormality in a world where normality is defined to be a common trait. Perhaps those deemed to have a psychological condition are the true voices of normality. Survival of the fittest has always been the outcome of psychological warfare.

If the world denormalized high standards of normalcy, the abnormal wouldn't be pushed out of our common society.

The flaming barrel of trash on my driveway is once again waiting for me to get rid of the last few reminders. It's been hard choosing what to keep and what to get rid of from the house I've spent the last few weeks organizing to make it feel like my home instead of theirs. I don't like making decisions. The last one was challenging enough.

Do I chop up the remains or do I bury them in the backyard and make a little cemetery for liars?

Burning is always the answer.

I guess I should let them know I'm leaving and that the fire will likely burn out in a couple of hours. I jog back into the house and unlatch the basement door. I flick on the buzzing light and head downstairs. "Sorry, I forgot the curtains."

"What's on fire?" Dad asks.

"You can smell that down here?" I glance at his wrists first because the glaring red abrasions from the zip ties are starting to bleed again. I should probably switch the ties over to ropes so I don't have to keep cleaning the wounds. "Is that still bugging you?" I lean toward his lap to get a better look at the oozing blood.

"You told us you wouldn't keep us tied up if we came down here," Dad mutters.

"I lied." I huff. That was before it took me three days to figure out how to get them down here without physically maneuvering them. The pistol might have been enough of a threat to get them to walk down here, but I couldn't take the chance. I had to get creative.

I made a little rope zipline, attached it to the oil tank outside of their bedroom window, then weaved it through their bedroom and down into the cellar where I secured the other side of the rope to the electrical box. I then gave them a new pair of zip ties that were attached to the zipline rope to help them stay on the right path while heading down the stairs. I was honest with them about how I secured the zipline. So, they knew if the rope was pulled the wrong way, the oil tank and/or the electrical box could break. Nobody wants an explosion, obviously.

"The fire, Haley, what is on fire?" Mom rasps.

"Willa," I say with a shrug. "I'm almost done."

Mom cries out. "Oh God. What have we done?"

"You're not burning in the fire, are you?"

"Haley, you can't keep us down here," Dad moans for the millionth time today.

"Dad, I'm protecting you and keeping you safe. It's for your own good. You'll thank me someday. Oh, keep an eye on the fire. I'll come back to check on it soon. I have an errand to run."

I walk past the burning barrel on the driveway and unlock my car door.

"Burning leaves over there?" our neighbor shouts from across the street.

"Yup, and some bodies too," I reply with a chuckle.

"What?" he replies. "I'm sorry, dear, I'm hard of hearing in my old age."

"Never mind," I shout a bit louder.

"Oh, okay. Well, make sure you put out the fire before you go to bed tonight. There are too many trees around here, ya know?"

"Will do!"

"Good. Tell your folks I said hi and hope they're doing well."

I slide into my car and spot the manila folder filled with papers on my passenger seat. I grab it and step back outside toward the flames. This stupid case study has been weighing heavily on my mind and taking up space in my desk drawer. After realizing how close I am to being on my own in this career path, I've decided against using this particular case study in my dissertation.

My research, my knowledge.

I must stand out in some way to make my mark in the world. With my unique findings, I will, no doubt, be able to direct other misguided people toward a proper pathway in life.

The only trustworthy place to house this information is in my head—a place where lies will never exist and there is no such thing as a mistake.

I toss the case study into the fire, watching the black ashes of paper flutter around the orange glow.

What we burn can never be brought back—truths and lies alike. That's what makes life so perfect.

EPILOGUE

Cigarette smoke laces the air as I walk through the front metal doors, my rubber soles squeaking against the damp floor. I shiver from the change in temperature between outside and in. The cement walls must keep out the heat. I wrap my arms around my chest, feeling as though the walls have eyes and every move I make is being watched with a magnifying glass. I don't know why anyone would want to live here.

This is the first time and hopefully the last time I'm stepping foot into a state prison but there are some things I need to take care of here.

"Good afternoon, ma'am. Are you here for visitation hours?" the desk clerk asks with a dead look in her eyes.

"Yes, I'm here to visit inmate William Hoyt."

"Okay, sure. I'm going to need to see your ID." The woman at the desk hasn't taken her eyes off me or blinked since we started talking.

I shuffle through my pocket and pull out my license, nervously sliding it through the small opening in the transparent divider between the clerk's office and the front entrance.

She rolls her seat back and stands up. "I just need to verify your information. While you're waiting, please go ahead and sign into the visitor's log."

The clerk returns within a short minute and hands me a badge rather than my ID. "We'll be holding your ID until you complete your visit. Please review the rules and regulations to abide by while you're here," she says, tapping her pen on the paper sign taped to the window between us.

"Okay, thank you." It seems odd they'd need to tell people not to bring weapons into a prison, but I shouldn't speculate.

"Your visitation time is thirty minutes. You can head through those doors for a security check, and they will point you in the direction of the visiting area."

I clear my throat and clench my fists by my side as I walk through the row of tables to reach the one Liam's sitting at. Even orange looks good on him. It's not my color.

"Haley?" Liam says. "I didn't think you'd show up."

He looks clean and maybe a bit more muscular than I last saw him. I wouldn't know he was an inmate if it weren't for the jumpsuit.

"Look, I wanted to apologize to you," he says. I can pull the wool over anyone's eyes, but this comment garners a look of shock. I wasn't expecting to hear this from him. I take a seat and wait for him to continue talking before I respond. "I dragged you back into a mess with my family. I should have let my sister handle her issues. I didn't owe her any help, not after what she's done to me over the years."

"I'd say she has her hands full at the moment." My eyebrow twitches.

"What do you mean? With Madden?"

I shrug. "Is that all you wanted to say to me?"

"No," he says glancing down at his cuffed wrists.

"I didn't expect things to go as far as they did between the two of us. There were many moments when I forgot why our paths had crossed again and I even tried to undo it all. Whenever I wasn't at work or with you, I was searching for Fallon. I thought if I could find her, you'd never find out that I'd originally spotted your name in the newsletter and saw you as an easy target."

Liam sighs heavily and glances around. "I don't know if you started the fire in our townhouse. Maybe it was just bad timing and a coincidence. Regardless, I wanted to blame the death of my sister on someone because it was easier than enduring the pain I was going through."

I want to ask why he thought I would be the best person to blame, but the events leading up to the fire don't help my case. "Why did you all choose me to constantly pick on before the fire? What had I done to you?"

Liam lowers his head in shame before continuing. "Everyone at school said you had psychological issues and weren't right in the head. I guess that made you an easy target too—kids are awful sometimes, okay?"

"They are," I agree.

"That's why we figured you had something to do with the fire too, especially after showing you the newspaper article that night." He lifts his head and stares into my eyes with what I think might be a hint of sincerity. "I shouldn't have done that to you. I'm sure you were humiliated. I'm ashamed of the way I acted when I was a kid, and deserve to be here, regardless of being blamed for a crime I didn't commit."

His words are heavy and my chest aches while trying to absorb them. "Everyone thought *I* had issues? I think you mean my parents?"

"Your parents?'" he questions. "The article was about you, wasn't it? You escaped from some children's rehabilitation facility and your parents had to take on the responsibility of making sure you didn't do anything to hurt yourself or anyone else again. I'm sure you had been through enough and I didn't need to add to it."

"Me? You think I escaped—" I choke out. "No. That article was about my parents escaping from a facility..."

Liam tilts his head to the side, squinting an eye. "But your name was in the headline. There was a picture of you."

"There was a picture of my parents..."

"Yes, one of the two of them holding each other in tears."

I swallow hard, wondering why he would call me here to visit just to tell me more painful lies. "You're an asshole," I whisper.

"Haley, I was apologizing. I never should have judged you. Look how you turned your life around after whatever you had gone through as a kid? It's incredible to overcome something like that, you know?"

I clamp my teeth together until my jaw muscles ache. "Incredible," I repeat. "Liam." I sniffle. "I did start that fire. I *was* responsible for Libby's death. And you can be sorry for setting me up to take the blame for Fallon's disappearance, but the only thing you should be sorry for...is bringing me back into your life. You broke my heart twice, and I let it happen." I scoff, disappointed in myself for falling for this ploy. "That one is on me."

"Wait, what-what does that even mean?"

"You broke my heart?" I repeat.

"No, I get that part..." He taps his cuffs on the table. "The part where you said you started the fire? And I should be sorry for bringing you back into my life... I know you now, and you wouldn't have done something like that."

I push my chair back and stand up. "I don't even know me, Liam. I never will. What I do know is...*someone* set you up to take the fall for Fallon." I'm that someone. The someone who is clearly better at cleaning up messes than you. "In any case, you can spend the next fifteen years figuring out who it was."

"Haley," he barks. "Wait."

Coming to terms with the truth is part of living with the truth. I have a lot to come to terms with still.

I retrieve my ID from the front desk and sign my name out on the log and turn to leave this place that I haven't managed to stay away from.

The sun is hot for a fall day and blinds me as I walk toward the parking lot. "What are you doing here?" a familiar voice calls out from ahead. The yellow blurry blob in the sky covers most of Lara's face. "Please don't tell me you were here visiting my pathetic brother."

"I was here visiting your pathetic brother," I reply.

"After he set you up to take the fall for what he did?" she questions.

I chuckle and sing out the last note of sarcasm. "Oh, Lara, Larissa, whatever your name is...Liam might have set me up, but—"

The sun slips behind a heavy cloud and thunder booms in the distance. I lose my train of thought and stare up at the sky.

"What are you looking at?" she asks.

"The thunderstorm rolling in," I reply, squinting toward the darkening cloud.

"Oh, okay," she says, laughing. "I think there would need to be at least one cloud in the sky for a storm to roll in. You had me going there for a minute." She tries to laugh again, but it comes out as a choke. "What were you saying about Liam setting you up?"

When Liam saw my name and ad in the Newport newsletter, looking for a summer job, he saw an opportunity to collect payment from his sister. People already speculated that I had something to do with the fire but there was no evidence to prove one way or another even though my so-called psychotic history made me look like the perfect suspect then, and again, now. If that's what he truly thought of me though, he should have been smart enough to realize what I'm capable of and what he's not...executing a criminal plan without a trace of evidence or remorse.

"What about Liam?" I ask, pausing to shake the thoughts out of my head. "Oh, right...nothing. Although—" I hold up my index finger. "If I may...just a silly unsolicited parenting tip from a regular old nanny...those teenage years can be a real bitch."

Madden won't pay a consequence for her attempt to murder Fallon, but that just means she'll be more careful the next time she wants to get rid of the person standing in her way. I know what happens when a daughter has no one left to blame but her mother.

"Watch your back, Lara. She's coming for you."

A LETTER FROM SHARI

Dear reader,

I'm beyond thrilled that you've chosen to read *The Perfect Nanny*. If you enjoyed the book and want to keep up to date with all my latest releases, just sign up at the following link. Your email address will never be shared, and you can unsubscribe at any time.

www.bookouture.com/shari-j-ryan

With so many books to choose from, I can't explain how honored I am that you've chosen to read mine. After months of working on this story, there's no greater feeling than finally being able to share it with readers like you.

I had so much fun spinning the plot and characters in this psychological thriller as well as toying with the twists to make it as fun for you as it was for me to write.

I truly hope you enjoyed reading *The Perfect Nanny*, and if so, I would be grateful if you could write a review. Feedback from readers like you help me grow as a writer, I love hearing your thoughts. Reviews also make a substantial difference when it comes to helping new readers discover one of my books for the first time.

There's nothing more rewarding to me than hearing from my readers – you can get in touch on my Facebook page, through Twitter, Goodreads, or my website.

KEEP IN TOUCH WITH SHARI

www.sharijryan.com

facebook.com/authorsharijryan

x.com/sharijryan

instagram.com/authorsharijryan

ACKNOWLEDGMENTS

Writing *The Perfect Nanny* was another wild ride in the world of psychological thrillers!

I'm so grateful to Bookouture for offering me more opportunities to write what makes me happy. The professionalism and top-notch skills within this publishing company have been invaluable to me throughout the past few years.

I would like to give a special thanks to Lucy, my editor, for spending so much time helping me work through the entire process of writing this book. From the very first few lines of the outline to the critical feedback on the last lines of the epilogue, your knowledge and ideas have been instrumental to me in so many ways.

Linda, your endless support and belief in me has brought me so much strength and courage over the years. I cannot express enough how much I adore our friendship.

Tracey, Gabby, and Elaine—my long-time first readers, thank you for your unwavering support, giggles, and friendship. I don't know what I would do without you!

To all the ARC readers, bloggers, influencers, and readers who are a part of this incredible community: thank you for your positive energy and influence.

Lori, the greatest little sister in the universe. Thank you for always being my #1 reader and my very best friend in the whole universe. Love you!

My family—Mom, Dad, Mark, and Ev, thanks for always

believing in me and supporting my wild dreams. You all mean the world to me.

Bryce and Brayden—my charming boys—thank you for always being proud of me and telling me what I tell you... "Hard work is always the best way." I love watching you both grow up, putting your hearts into everything you work on. I know you will find success in whatever you do in life. I love you more than you'll ever know.

Josh, my wonderful husband, to have your support is everything to me. Thank you for sticking by my side while I explore this scarier genre of writing. It's a relief to know you're never *too* concerned about me becoming one of the unhinged characters I create... I love you! I really do.

PUBLISHING TEAM

Turning a manuscript into a book requires the efforts of many people. The publishing team at Bookouture would like to acknowledge everyone who contributed to this publication.

Audio
Alba Proko
Sinead O'Connor
Melissa Tran

Commercial
Lauren Morrissette
Jil Thielen
Imogen Allport

Data and analysis
Mark Alder
Mohamed Bussuri

Cover design
Jo Thomson

Editorial
Lucy Frederick
Imogen Allport